MW00694694

Running Close *to the* Wind

ALSO BY ALEXANDRA ROWLAND

CHANTIVERSE NOVELS

The Mahisti Dynasty:

A Taste of Gold and Iron

Tadek and the Princess

Tales of the Chants:

A Choir of Lies

A Conspiracy of Truths

Over All the Earth

The Seven Gods:

Some by Virtue Fall

The Lights of Ystrac's Wood

NONFICTION

Finding Faeries

The Writer's Oracle

Running Close *to the* Wind

ALEXANDRA ROWLAND

TOR PUBLISHING GROUP
NEW YORK

This is a work of fiction. All of the characters, organizations, and events portrayed in this novel are either products of the author's imagination or are used fictitiously.

RUNNING CLOSE TO THE WIND

Interior illustrations by Christine Foltzer

A Tordotcom Book
Published by Tom Doherty Associates / Tor Publishing Group
120 Broadway
New York, NY 10271

www.torpublishinggroup.com

The Library of Congress Cataloging-in-Publication Data is available upon request.

ISBN 978-1-250-80253-8 (hardcover)
ISBN 978-1-250-80255-2 (ebook)

Our books may be purchased in bulk for promotional, educational, or business use. Please contact your local bookseller or the Macmillan Corporate and Premium Sales Department at 1-800-221-7945, extension 5442, or by email at MacmillanSpecialMarkets@macmillan.com.

First Edition: 2024

Printed in the United States of America

0 9 8 7 6 5 4 3 2 1

For the funniest and wisest and angriest of men,
who knew that as long as you can laugh,
there's still a part of you that's free.

GNU Terry Pratchett

PART ONE

1

> ***8. The Ship***
>
> Travel, ambition, victory, success, freedom. Adventure, opportunity, and promising new enterprises appear on the horizon. There is the possibility of great reward at the end of this journey, but there are risks to face along the way.
>
> (Reversed: Forcefulness, aggression, shipwreck. Be cautious. There may be a threat from outside. Attend to each small crisis as it comes up or you will expose yourself to increasing danger of catastrophe. May signify a becalmed period in the doldrums.)

As soon as he saw *that ship* come over the horizon, Avra Helvaçi said, "*Eeee,*" scurried to his tiny cabin so he would be safely out from underfoot, shut the door, sat on the bunk with his little rucksack clasped in his lap, and began to silently compose and rehearse the apology he would imminently need to present, if only to keep himself from being shoved overboard and left for dead. Again.

After a few moments of silence, he fumbled in his rucksack and pulled a single card from his deck of Heralds.

The Broken Quill: *Damaged lines of communication; frustration will ruin delicate things.*

Bit on the nose, really, and nothing he didn't already know.

He tucked it away, clasped his hands tight between his knees so he wouldn't vibrate out of his skin, and went back to visualizing minute variations of his apology. Teveri deserved only the best, of course.

Once *The Running Sun* overtook them, the rest was a quick affair. Avra prided himself on a single scanty fistful of common sense, and he was rather pleased to have correctly assessed the captain of this vessel as a man too sensible to put up much of a fight when boarded by pirates.

As the clamor and fuss on deck came to a resolution, Avra bounced his knee and hummed a nervous little tune to himself, one of his own compositions, and continued reflecting upon his predicament. Did he recollect what Teveri had been mad about last time? No. Tev was always mad about something. Who could possibly keep track of Avra's various wrongs?

He would apologize nicely for as many things as he could think of, then, and that would smooth any still-ruffled feathers. Definitely.

And if not, well . . . It was far preferable to die at Teveri az-Ḥaffār's hand than . . . the current most probable alternative. He tried not to think about that.

The noise quieted marginally, which meant that Captain Veris's crew had surrendered and that *The Running Sun*'s crew would now take inventory. They'd search the hold and each cabin, and eventually . . .

Someone—a big, brawny, sweaty someone with the sleeves ripped off his shirt and tattoos down his arms—shouldered Avra's door open.

"Ah! Oskar!" Avra said, slightly manic. He pasted a delighted smile across his face. "It's been too long!"

Oskar, Teveri's second mate, stared at him. "Aw, fuck," he groaned. "No, no, no."

Avra pouted. "Are you not pleased to see me? I missed *you* terribly."

"No no no no," Oskar said, backing out of the room. "*No, no, no.*"

"What's the matter?" said a familiar voice from behind Oskar.

"No," Oskar moaned again. "Fuck."

"You seem a bit concerned," Avra said. "Not to worry! I have a plan."

"Nooo," said Oskar.

"I," Avra announced grandly, "am going to say sorry! Then all will be well, and Tev will forgive me."

Another face poked around the doorway—a woman toward the end of middle age, with steel-grey hair cropped close to her scalp and dark skin weathered by sun and salt and wind.

"Markefa!" Avra beamed. The mild frown on Markefa's face melted into poleaxed astonishment. "What a nice surprise! You were talking so much about retirement last time, I was all prepared to find you'd gone ashore for good. How's the leg? All healed up? How's the family?"

"Ah, fuck," said Markefa.

"You know, I really think you're both overreacting just a little teensy bit, maybe," said Avra. "Listen, though, I can't decide—do you think Tev would like it if you delivered me to them hog-tied?"

"Hello, incandescent one," Avra said adoringly, lying hog-tied at Teveri's feet on the deck of their ship.

The Running Sun was a carrack of three masts, somewhere between *meh* and *decent* in quality: On the upside, she had been designed by the Shipbuilder's Guild of Araşt to its famously exacting standards, including quality-control inspection, certification, and her inaugural hull-painting, though that had long since worn off. On the downside, due to the circumstances around how Teveri az-Ḥaffār had become captain, all the other pirates sneered and said mean things about how the ship was cursed or haunted or what have you. This made the crew a bit collectively defensive, in Avra's opinion, and it was one of the many, *many* things Teveri was mad about.

Once, Avra had barely *mentioned* the rumors and stories of how Teveri had acquired the ship. Teveri had immediately dragged him by his hair out of both bed and the afterglow and had thrown him bodily out of the cabin, followed by his trousers and boots. He could not *prove* that they'd aimed for his head, but the suspicion was certainly there.

"Before we say anything else," he began in his politest tones, "I want to express my deepest and sincerest apologies. I see now that I have behaved in an ungentlemanly manner. I have been an outright blackguard. A cur. A cad. Not to mention disrespectful, impolite, and indeed both churlish and childish. Moreover, I have been that greatest of reprobates—a flibbertigibbet. Not a moment has passed that I have not regretted every aspect of our last parting. I have torn my hair over it. I have lost sleep over it. I ache with remorse. On my honor, such as it is, I shall be a good and sweet little Avra henceforth, particularly if you could maybe see your way to not putting me in a rowboat in the middle of the ocean and sailing off without even a wave of a handkerchief in farewell." *Again.* "I must say it's good to see you, though. You look ravishing in those boots. Are they new?"

Teveri kicked him sharply in the stomach. Frankly, it was an honor. "How are you alive?"

"Got lucky," he wheezed. "Tev, light of my life—"

Another sharp kick. It was somewhat less of an honor (though the boots were still ravishing).

"I won't do it again!" Avra squeaked. "I'm sorry! You're completely right to still be angry at me. I too would still be angry at me! I gave you a tip-off for what was probably a wild-goose chase, and then when you tracked me down to very correctly take vengeance upon me for wasting your time, I didn't even—"

"You think I bothered *following* your stupid little hunch, Avra?" Teveri snarled. "Stupid, incoherent, *written on the back of a napkin*—"

Avra wriggled valiantly and managed to tip himself upright with a little "*hrgkgh*" of effort, which he hoped came across as endearing, and pouted up at them. "You didn't go on my wild-goose chase? I really don't know what else you have to be mad at me about, then. Maybe you should apologize too—if I didn't do anything, then your response was maybe a little disproportionate—"

Teveri's black right eye flashed with fury, even brighter than the gold orb that replaced the left. "Your motherfucking *song*."

"The s—Ohhh, the *song*." Avra arranged his face into the most plaintive expression in his inventory. "You didn't like the song? I thought it was a good song. Complimentary, even." Some of his best work, really. He'd rhymed "strap-on" with "denouement" and had thought himself very clever. He'd added seventeen more verses to it in the time that it had taken to get a lucky rescue from that rowboat Tev had marooned him in.

The scarred side of the captain's mouth twisted up, baring their teeth. Gods, Tev was magnificent.

"Ah," he said. "Aha. Well . . ." Shit, he hadn't prepared for this one. "No accounting for taste," he said brightly. "Wait, fuck, no, that's wrong. Didn't mean that—" He flung himself aside with a high "*reeeee!*" of alarm, and Teveri's next kick just missed him. "It was supposed to be a nice song! I told everyone in that bar that your ship definitely isn't haunted or anything, and that you're great at both pirating and fucking! And that the only marginally spooky thing about you, since your ship is *incredibly* non-haunted, is that you've got a box full of terrifying spooky dildos!" He gave Teveri a limpid glance up through his eyelashes. "I thought you'd like it. I thought it would help your *reputation*. Should I have not mentioned your box of spooky dildos? Won't do it again. Honest, Tev."

"The sea will boil before a single honest word falls from your tongue," Teveri said, aiming another kick at him, which he rolled to dodge with another "*reee!!!*" that he thought gave him a rather pathetic air. Tev wouldn't kick a man who made undignified noises when threatened, would they? It would be beneath them.

Very few things were beneath Captain Teveri az-Ḥaffār, as it turned out. The next kick landed right on Avra's bum.

He groaned in defeat (and pain), rolled onto his back, and attempted to maximize the limpidness of his pleading gaze. "Tev—"

"Call me that again, I *fucking dare you*."

"Captain az-Ḥaffār," he amended. "Let's talk about this. I'm sorry about the song. Though you should know that lots of people told me it was surprisingly sexy! Well, technically they said 'unexpectedly sexual,' but the *tone* was ambiguous. Never mind that! If *you* don't like it, then every word of it is as ashes in my mouth! I can write you a new song. A new, different, better song. I've recently quit my day job to pursue my poetry, you see, so I have quite a lot of free time!"

Teveri put their hands on their hips and their head a bit on one side. "What do we have that's sticky? Just pitch for the hull, no?"

"What are you wanting sticky shit for, Tev?" Avra asked suspiciously.

"Tarring and feathering you."

"But I don't want to be tarred and feathered."

"Just pitch, Captain. We've got some extra from their stores," Markefa called from the rail where the crew was hauling the last of the contents of the other ship's hold into theirs on platforms hung from ropes and pulleys at the ends of the yardarms. The other crew had been released and was already scurrying to get their sails in order and run away before *The Running Sun* decided to take anything else from them. "Do you want to use some of this straw instead of tearing up one of those nice pillows we took from the captain's cabin?"

Teveri seethed. "We might as well." To no one in particular, they snapped, "*Why* do these people have a hold full of *fucking straw and nothing else*?"

"Fancy hats," said Avra promptly.

Teveri looked down at him with an expression of exasperation so profound it was nearly sorrow. "What?"

"It's for fancy hats," he chirped. "I asked too. Fashion for fancy hats in Map Sut this year, the captain told me. But to make them, they need this particular kind of braided straw, and the place that does the braiding isn't the same as the place where that specific variety of rye grows, so they have to import it. Hold full of cheap straw, take it to whatsits-place and pay to get it all braided, haul the spools of braid off to Map Sut, sell them for a fat profit. That's called a *good return on investment,* Tev. It is a solemn thing of great reverence where I come from, you know. Please respect my culture."

Teveri pinched the bridge of their nose again and breathed several times.

"Don't grind your teeth," Avra reminded them helpfully. "Remember what that dentist said? He was *far* more spooky than you, by the way. Remember he said you had to stop grinding or you'd crack one. Anyway, it's quite nice straw. Nicest straw I've ever seen, anyway, not that I know anything about . . . straw." He paused. "Maybe not what you were hoping to score, though. You seem grouchy about it. Are you having money problems again?" Teveri feinted another kick at him—Avra didn't see why that deserved a kick, but he obligingly made another pathetic, undignified sound.

The Running Sun was nearly always having money problems. Ships took a lot of upkeep, and crews needed a lot of food, and then there were things like the pension fund for any of the crew who got injured or killed . . . Money was never really *good* on a pirate ship, and *The Running Sun* had never managed a really big score—which only played into the rumors that the ship was cursed.

As soon as Avra moseyed past that thought, his brain pounced, supplying some lightning-fast calculations: It was awfully late in the season for *The Running Sun* to be out on the water—there was only a fortnight or so until the sea serpents rose from the abyssal depths for their breeding season, making the open ocean too dangerous for anyone sane to risk sailing into blue water for at least six weeks. (That is, unless they were an Araşti crew on an Araşti ship . . . and in possession of what was in the little rucksack Avra had been clutching for the past two days.) The ship they'd just captured was only a few days out from the port they planned to shelter in, but *The Running Sun* should have been *much* farther south—either already anchored safe in the Isles of Lost Souls or at least making her way there before the water frothed up into terrifying swarms of teeth and . . . well, mostly teeth. So many teeth. Teeth and horny rage.

There was no chance that the crew would be planning to anchor somewhere else—other captains might have contacts in secure ports that would allow them to shelter there if need be, but not Teveri az-Ḥaffār . . . And of all the pirates Avra was acquainted with, there was neither captain nor crew who would voluntarily spend the season of serpents *away* from the Isles of Lost Souls. It was a crucial and unmissable opportunity to be *seen* by the other crews, to brag and boast and bolster one's reputation in pirate society (such as it was), to make deals and alliances, to get even for past slights, to get yourself hired by a new ship if the old one no longer suited . . . And there was the fun and spectacle of all the festivities, of course. As far as Avra was concerned, the only people who would voluntarily miss the cake competition were the ones who didn't know about it.

In conclusion: *The Running Sun* must have money problems, and the crew, facing the prospect of a six-week enforced holiday they were too poor to enjoy, must have voted to try for one last score to fill their coffers before they flew back to the Isles, probably reaching port just as the sea was due to become . . . unpleasantly teethy.

Avra did not like the idea of being tarred and feathered—or tarred and strawed, for that matter—and summarily marooned again, especially when most of the other boats that could have coincidentally rescued him were already finding safe harbor and settling in for the serpent season.

He glanced down at his little rucksack, which held the entire reason that he quit his day job as a field agent of the Araşti Ministry of Intelligence in order to pursue his poetry career. Offering to share it would almost certainly absolve him of being tarred and feathered and left for dead, because selling the contents would solve *The Running Sun*'s money problems a hundred times over. A thousand. At that point, they might as well all retire and buy charming villas somewhere on the coast of Pezia.

He hadn't entirely decided whether he was going to sell it—it *would* be an unconscionable amount of money. The idea of sharing that amount of money with the crew was a much easier decision to make. He glanced up at the rigging, at the *mainsail* . . .

The literally *priceless* mainsail. It technically belonged to him. Technically. He'd won it off another captain in a card game, years and years ago. He probably could have quit his day job right then, but *selling* it hadn't even occurred to him. He'd given it to Tev without a second thought, because . . . well, because what was the point of having money if you didn't have friends? There was a difference between Tev being mad at him for something and Tev *literally never forgiving him*, after all, and selling that mainsail just to line his own pockets would have done it. It would have been disrespectful, bordering on sacrilegious, and there were things that even *Avra* had to take seriously. That mainsail, for one. Also the cake competition. And . . . what would happen if anyone from Araşt found out what Avra had taken.

He looked down at his little rucksack again. Sharing the wealth also meant sharing the danger. He'd been leaning away from the idea of selling it because thinking about the potential consequences made him want to throw up, and because he *did* pride himself on one single scanty fistful of common sense, which had suggested to him two days ago that the smart plan was to hightail it out of Araşt at top speed, cover his tracks, fake his own death, change his name, move to another country where no one knew him, find a cheap boardinghouse that would rent him a grubby room with a loose floorboard he could stuff his spoils under, live out the rest of his days eking out a living with his poetry and looking over his shoulder for assassins from the Ministry of Intelligence, and *never tell anyone about what he'd done.*

Well, that was the second smartest plan. The first was to immediately burn all the papers and keep his mouth shut, but every time he'd considered that, he'd thought, *But what if I* need *it one day, what if I need it to bribe someone not to kill me?*

He hadn't expected that *one day* to happen this soon.

Two of the crew rolled a barrel of tar over to Tev, and another person—a newcomer, as Avra didn't recognize them—guided the loading platform onto the deck and swung off one of the bales of straw. Avra wriggled fiercely, but Oskar and Markefa's knots were, as they had always been, impeccable.

Avra couldn't quite bear to play his trump card yet. Never mind the money or the potential consequences—the simple concept of *other people knowing about it* was still too huge and nauseating to contemplate. He compromised with himself and decided to try one more round of cajoling. "Listen, let's not do this!" he said loudly. "You'll probably get tar all over the deck, and I will be a *truly* pathetic sight during the whole process—you'll all be very embarrassed to know me!"

Teveri drew one of their knives and slashed the strings binding the bale together. Fragments of straw fell free, standing out against the worn, greyish deck in shards of a bright silver-gold that shone prettily in the sun and must have made for a very fine hat.

"You know, on balance, I don't think we should give him one of our rowboats this time," Teveri announced, viciously demolishing the tight bale into a loose, shining pile. "I think we should just toss him in."

"Reeee," Avra said piteously, but it made no difference. "But what if I suddenly prove *terribly useful*?"

"Oh, trust me, this whole situation is going to be *very* useful to me later tonight when I'm getting myself off to the thought of finally being rid of you. Markefa, open up that barrel."

"Aye, Captain," Markefa said complacently, and began to work it open with her big knife.

The black, hot scent of tar trickled into Avra's nose. "Tev, Tev, Tev. Teveri. Captain az-Ḥaffār. *Do not cover me in tar, please, we should probably talk first, I have a really neat thing to tell you about, I swear on my own dick that I've got something unbelievably nifty—*"

Markefa paused, the lid half pried off, and raised an eyebrow at the captain.

"*What?*" Teveri snapped.

"Swears on his own dick, Captain," she said, a little reproachful. "Oughta hear a man out when he swears on his own dick, no?"

Teveri glared. They were fairly well *covered* in straw—there were fragments of it clinging to their front and the stained threadbare sleeves of their shirt, pieces of it scattered through their hair, shards of it stuck to their golden-brown skin.

Ah, gods above and below, but they *were* splendid, even with their dark hair all ratty and mussed, most of it stringy and half-damp with sweat, the rest windblown, gritty, and dull from the buildup of salt spray.

So actually kind of disgusting, really, but . . . ah, just splendid, even so.

Teveri turned their glare onto him and snarled, "You have sixty seconds. *Only* because Markefa asked. Say thank you to Markefa."

"Thank you, Markefa," Avra said.

Teveri crossed their arms and stared down at him, impassive beyond a crisp air of expectation.

After a few moments, Avra said, "Oh, shit, did my time already start? You didn't say my time already started!"

"Oh boy," said Markefa.

"So it's kind of a long story," Avra babbled as fast as he could, "and really it'd land better if you were to hear the whole thing, because you'd probably think it was really funny—but, ah, right, to summarize it in an efficient, sixty-second sort of way—less than sixty seconds, really, because you didn't tell me my time started—anyway, the short version! So you remember ages ago when we went to Quassa sai Bendra and that thing happened, and everybody got huffy and called me a cheater 'cause I kept winning at card games, and then those other things happened and everybody got superstitious and called me a witch 'cause lucky shit kept happening to me, and I kept saying, 'What, that's stupid, I'm not a witch, my luck is normal'? Well, after the friendly misunderstanding wherein you marooned me at sea because of that *very bad and inappropriate* song I wrote—after that I sort of, well, ahaha, I sort of felt as though getting rescued from certain death by a ship conveniently bound for Araşt was the sort of *suspiciously* good fortune that was worth thinking about, and I said to myself, 'What if I tried poking my weirdly good luck a little bit, just to see what happens, maybe I'll just do a couple fun little experiments like a natural philosopher—'"

"Time's up," Teveri said flatly, and moved toward the barrel of pitch.

"I copied a bunch of secret papers from the headquarters of the Araşti Shipbuilder's Guild in Kasaba City and I have them with me right now!" Avra shrieked.

Teveri paused.

The entire deck went dead silent but for the sound of the water against the hull and the creak of the rigging in the wind.

"Good papers! Important papers! They were locked in a safe!" Avra panted, wriggling energetically away from the barrel of tar. "There was an incident where somebody tried to break into the Guild—let's not get into it, actually, not important—I just wanted to see how far my luck went! Answer: Pretty fucking far, actually! And at this juncture, I would like to tactfully point out that if I were to be shown some affection and generosity—for example, by not being dumped overboard—then I would absolutely feel inclined to reciprocate that affection and generosity by . . . by sharing? Sharing what I have? Equal shares! And maybe we can talk it through as a crew and someone more sensible than me can figure out how we can all be rich and, crucially, *not dead*?"

The entire deck was still utterly still and silent—he had *everyone's* attention. Maybe this was not sufficient to atone for his crimes. Maybe it was in fact all the more reason to dump him overboard. He flicked his eyes up, deliberate, to *The Running Sun*'s glittering cloth-of-silver mainsail.

That sail was a large part of why the crew had put up with him for so many years, and why he was pretty fucking confident they, with this little reminder, would intervene on his behalf if Tev kept refusing to be reasonable.

It had been his eerie luck working during that card game too, hadn't it? No one just swanned into the Isles of Lost Souls, anchored in Scuttle Cove, went for a drink at the Crowned Skull, challenged Captain Luchenko of the *Merry Maid* to a game of dice, won without losing even a single copper piece of any nation's currency, and walked away with one of the greatest prizes ever won in that dingy bar.

No one did that.

But Avra had done it.

Avra looked up at the silver sail, by far the biggest surviving relic of the legendary *Nightingale,* and listened to the crew fidget and shift on their feet as the reminder sank in. He added, just a little extra nudge, "I'm ever so inclined to be generous to friends—*family*—who have been so generous to me. Who's to say how much these papers could sell for? Lots of stuff you can buy with an unimaginable mountain of money. Probably still have some left over. You could spread it out on a bed and roll around naked on it. Could do all sorts of things with that much money." He paused again. "What's-his-name, Captain Ueleari—doesn't he have a standing offer to sell the *Nightingale* relics he's got? What was it—the mizzen royal and the flag for the bargain price of one million Araşti altınlar? Imagine. Imagine having the mizzen royal, the mainsail, and the flag of the *Nightingale,* and *still* having enough money left over that you're sleeping and swiving on gold and picking silver and copper out of your asscrack."

The crew stirred again. Avra glanced at Tev, who was grinding their teeth with no regard for the advice of spooky dentists, and then at Markefa, who was giving the captain significant looks.

"It'd do a great deal to ease the sting of this bullshit," Markefa murmured with an almost invisible nod to the straw. "Go a long way to making everybody feel better about the two last month as well."

"What were the two last month?" Avra asked.

"Boxes of fucking *rank* swamp muck from Kaskinen, bound for Heyrland. Didn't see the point of taking anything from them but their food and supplies."

"Wow," said Avra. "Bad luck. So fancy straw's kind of a step up at the moment, huh? Well, fancy straw and your favorite poet in the whole wide world and a bunch of papers constituting what is very possibly the most expensive secret in recorded history. Well, half of it," he lied quickly as the thought occurred to him that "your favorite poet in the whole wide world" was the sort of cargo that could and arguably should get thrown overboard. "The other half is in my head. So you've got to keep me alive if you want it to be worth anything at all." A classic gambit, but it was a classic for a reason.

Tev grimaced. "Put the tar away, and throw this motherfucker in the rope locker. *Don't* untie him. I haven't fucking decided what I want to do with him. And *don't,*" they added in a snarl, loud enough for the whole crew to hear, "*do not* speak to me about him, do not mention him to me, and I *fucking dare you* to hum even one bar of that song." They glared fiercely—fierce enough that several of the crew in the immediate vicinity muttered about not being that horny for a fight.

"The rope locker!" Avra said meanwhile. "My old friend the rope locker! Cozy! Oskar, carry me gently, all right? You were so rough a minute ago, and I bruise so easily. I'm delicate, Oskar, you *know* I'm delicate—"

Captain's Log

Day 3 of the 6th month, 199th yr Mahisti Dyn.

23 days out from last port. ~410 nautical miles SE of Makloi.

Overtook the Roitelet *(Cpt Veris; Ancoux, Vinte). Restocked supplies (food, raw materials).*

Other takings:

3 feather pillows

1 pair good boots

4 hammocks

unspeakable # bales "fancy straw"

1 stupid motherfucker (WHO CAN GET FUCKED IN THE EYE WITH A PIG DICK)

Course uncertain; hold now quite full. Considering Birrabar to offload takings; cannot possibly show face in Scuttle Cove like this.

Nagasani calculates approx. 10 days safe sailing left. FUCK.

2

28. The Thrown Dice

Pure random chance. There are no greater powers at stake here. No fate or destiny, just chance and happenstance. "It could have happened to anyone." (This card is identical both upright and reversed.)

After a few hours, Ellat—the youngest member of the crew and Markefa's nephew—came to bring Avra a cup of water.

After another few hours, he brought another cup and a lump of ship's biscuit, and Avra screeched at the top of his lungs until the boy scampered off to find an adult to give him permission to untie Avra's ankles so that he could be taken to the side of the ship for a desperately needed pee.

Ellat tied him back up when Avra was done. Avra allowed this with his best performance of gracious patience, only to find that the boy's knots had become as good as his aunt's. He considered crying and wailing like a cat stuck in a crate, but he *had* promised to be a good and sweet little Avra, and he was rather curious what might happen if he showed willing for more than six hours at a stretch.

He curled up for a fitful nap with his head pillowed on his little rucksack.

He didn't quite sink properly down into true sleep—there was no way to get comfortable enough, being hog-tied with nothing but the surprisingly hard nests of rope to cushion him—but the light dozing made the time pass quicker. In the Araşti intelligence ministry, they'd been taught to sleep when they could, since active field agents never knew when the next safe rest would be.

Not that Avra had been a very *good* field agent. He'd long since adopted a personal philosophy of taking a rather lackadaisical approach to his day job, which meant no promotions and less and less interesting assignments—he hadn't had anything but courier errands for a couple years now—but it left him ever so much more time for his poetry.

The light had entirely gone when the door of the rope locker slammed open. Avra startled awake, saw Oskar in the doorway with a raised lantern, and grinned. Oskar looked around suspiciously, bent to check Avra's ties, and huffed.

"Hallo," said Avra, wriggling his fingers in a little wave. "What brings you to this fine rope locker? Do I get anything else to drink? Or maybe another pee break?"

Oskar huffed again and set the lantern down and began untying the ropes from Avra's wrists and ankles. "Captain wants to see you."

Tev *wanting* to see him sounded unlikely, but he'd take it. "Does my hair look all right? I probably have creases on my face from napping on my rucksack, don't I? No, don't tell me, it will spoil my confidence." As soon as his hands were free, he stuffed his deck of Heralds into his rucksack and hugged it close.

Oskar wordlessly dragged him to his feet—ooh, he was stiff and sore!—and escorted him to Teveri's cabin as if Avra didn't know the way to the other end of the ship.

"Probably pointless to ask," Oskar said, in tones of vast resignation, "but could you try not to piss them off?"

"Don't have the foggiest idea what you mean," said Avra.

Oskar sighed and knocked on Teveri's door, opened it, and shoved him in.

"Ah! You've redecorated," Avra said immediately, staring around the room with interest. There was a different carpet on the floor—the old one had been nicer. The fancy gold-embroidered silk coverlet on the hanging bed had been replaced with a quilt that Avra recognized from the old days, early in their acquaintance. Definitely money problems, then. Bad ones. No wonder they were so touchy.

Teveri was writing in their logbook at the same old desk as always, though, and they still had that glorious old chair that had always been on the ship—intricately carved ebony with heavy, thick legs and arms. Probably worth a lot of money, but they'd only ever tried to sell it in Scuttle Cove, where no one would buy it.

"Too spooky" was the general consensus. Several of the stories about the night Teveri had acquired the ship cited this chair in particular. Avra's favorite of them was that Teveri had found the old captain's corpse still sitting in this chair and they'd had to pry his death grip off the arms with a letter opener. Another was that the old captain's soul had been bound to the chair by dreadful enchantments while his body rotted into a shambling, undead ghoul, and that sooner or later everyone would see the same happening to Captain az-Ḥaffār too, surely any day now, just you wait and see.

It *was* a spooky-looking chair, Avra wouldn't deny that, but he'd been fucked in it or on it or over the arm enough times and without suffering any curse-like effects thereafter that he couldn't bring himself to put any stock in such rumors. Well, maybe just a little, for the sexy thrill of doing something taboo. *Ooh, the Forbidden Chair, oooh, are you sure it's safe, Captain?*

He helped himself to a perch on the battered old sea chest next to a decent wardrobe that he recognized from the previous ship. "This is nice," he said, nodding to the wardrobe. "Suits you."

This at least got Teveri to look up from their logbook and glare at him. In the light of the lamp hanging over their desk, their eyes flashed—the natural one as black and sharp as an obsidian knife, the golden false one shimmering eerily. "You're not here to compliment the furnishings."

"Oh. More apologies, then?" He made an attempt to lounge enticingly and said, "I can apologize all night long if you want me to, Tev, you know that."

Teveri slammed the logbook closed. "What *exactly* did you take from the Shipbuilder's Guild?"

Avra gave a nervous little laugh. "Ah. That thing. You want to hear about that thing. See, I've been thinking it over, and maybe you don't want to hear about that thing at all."

Teveri narrowed their eyes at him and very slowly tapped their fingernails, one by one, against the cover of the logbook.

"It's for your own good?" Avra offered. "On account of maybe you would be better off not knowing about things that will bring, um, basically all of Araşt down on your head if you are suspected of knowing about them. Or . . . or selling them. I think it would probably be very bad to sell them. Very, very, very bad. Imagine the maximum amount of bad, and then set it on fire. That bad."

"Sounds lucrative. Tell me what it is so I can sell it."

"What if I don't want to tell you? What if I have *so much love in my heart* for all of my friends on this ship, and I don't want to see the maximum amount of Araşti badness happen to them? Have you thought about that, Tev? Have you even considered my feelings?"

"No," said Teveri flatly.

"I need you to rescue me. That is the main thrust of my feelings in this matter. I need to be just so far away. I need you to shove me in a crate"—Teveri made an interested noise and quirked one eyebrow inquisitively—"*with* air holes, Tev, I need to be shoved in a crate and labeled with something innocuous and smuggled into the Ammat Archipelago, because it is as far away from Araşt as it is possible to get and they do not have trade agreements with anyone but Heyrland. Though extradition agreements might be different than trade agreements. I left in too much of a rush to check." He giggled nervously and hugged his little rucksack to his chest. "My main goal here is to *not die, please,* and I need you to be incredibly heroic and rescue the shit out of me."

Teveri blinked at him, slow and bored. "What do you have?"

"Promise."

"No."

"*Teveri,*" he wailed. "I have had a very hard and scary time lately! I am looking for comfort and security! You are being so hurtful to me, kicking me all over the deck and throwing me in rope lockers and not accepting my apologies and then callously demanding—*demanding!!!*—my cargo manifest with no regard to how I have been fearing for my *life.*"

"Answer the fucking question."

"I shan't," Avra cried. "You can't treat me like a silly little slut, Tev, I'm a person! A person who has been through *so much*—"

"You're certainly a silly little slut as well."

"A silly little slut who has been through *so much,*" Avra amended, because at least *he* knew how to compromise, unlike some people, specifically some Teveris. "In the last two days, I have been through more than any silly little slut should ever have to go through!"

"You probably brought it on yourself."

"I did not! These troubles have befallen me through no fault of my own! It was an *accident.*"

Teveri blinked at him again, unimpressed. "You stole from the Shipbuilder's Guild by *accident.*"

"Yes!" Avra said vehemently. "Would a silly little slut be able to do it on purpose? This is why I am begging abjectly for you to rescue the shit out of me! And then I am going to fake my death and you'll probably never hear from me again—"

"Avra, *what do you have from the Shipbuilder's Guild?*"

"You just want to know how much it's worth," he quavered. "You aren't even interested in how the accident happened. I ask for so little, you know! I throw myself at your feet and own up to all my mistakes, I make all kinds of oaths about being a good and sweet little Avra from this day forward, I go out of my way to make you sound magnificent every time I talk about you, and then when I beg *abjectly* for rescue and tremulously hold out my little bowl of orphan gruel—"

"What."

Avra cupped his hands in front of him in illustration. "I am an orphan, and the only possession I have to my name is a little bowl! I ask for barely anything but a spoonful of gruel so I don't starve to death in the freezing cold winter!"

"We're barely north of *the tropics*."

"It's a *metaphor*, Teveri! Even in the tropics, you're miserly with my orphan gruel!"

Teveri closed their eyes for a moment as if praying for strength. "This one isn't as funny as the one about the possums."

"Oh? You liked that one better?"

"*Liked* is a very strong word. I found the mental image of you living in a dingy crate in an alleyway and being mobbed by possums for every scrap of stale bread I kick toward you with my boot to be a more plausible image."

"I felt orphan gruel was more sympathetic, though."

"You're a thirty-five-year-old man with, apparently, a very expensive Guild secret in his bag. Orphan gruel is a *big* stretch."

"I ask for so little," Avra said. "Yet when you deign to kick a stale, *moldy* heel of bread to me, you simply walk away and leave me to fight off all the alley possums before I can eat even one crumb of a nibble. You don't even *care* that I have developed mange. You don't even *care* that the possums are exploiting me! You could just *hand me* the moldy crust of bread instead of wrapping it around a rock and kicking it at me—"

"You do see how this is superior to the orphan gruel one, don't you?"

"Here are the things I need right now, as a silly little slut, damp and bedraggled in an alley, scrabbling in the dirt with the possums," he said with an injured little sniffle. "I need you to be interested in the terrible accident that befell me, and I need you to vaguely consider the idea of *rescuing the shit out of me* so that the maximum amount of Araşti badness does not happen to me. Think of the possums, think of how traumatized they will be. I will be arrested right in front of them, and tortured, and killed, and dismembered, and fed to tigers, and—"

"If you don't tell me what you stole from the Shipbuilder's Guild, I will solve all my problems at once and dump you overboard." Teveri steepled their fingers.

"Except the money problem," Avra said quickly.

"That's the rope you're currently dangling from, yes. Over water infested with sharks and sea serpents and—"

"Possums. Aquatic vampire possums."

"Sure," Teveri said, far more dryly than necessary. "Aquatic vampire possums."

Avra gathered up his nerves in both hands. "I will tell you what I have stolen from the Shipbuilder's Guild," he said with another little sniffle. "But I have to start before the actual stealing, for the necessary context. Otherwise when I say, 'So there I was, wandering down the street because that truthwitch gave me the idea of committing a crime,' you'll say, 'Wait, what truthwitch?' And then I'll have to go backward and explain anyway." He paused. "Do you know about truthwitches, Tev? They're sort of like that spooky dentist who could tell just by looking at your teeth that you were grinding them all the time, but with lies instead of your mouth."

Teveri ground their teeth, because they didn't listen to spooky dentists any more than they listened to Avra. "Is this the only way you will answer the question?"

"Most assuredly, yes," Avra said solemnly. Teveri ground their teeth again, but didn't kick any moldy bread at him, which was almost the same thing as expressing appreciation for his pluckiness and general moxie.

He told it from the beginning.

There had been a break-in at the Shipbuilder's Guild, and presumably someone had been told to investigate it, but Avra didn't know who, because that morning he'd been nursing a hangover and leaving for a courier errand up to Kafia. By the time he'd gotten back to Araşt, the situation had unraveled into some kind of kerfuffle involving peril to the entire royal family and very real concerns that there might be traitors in the civil service, which meant that *everyone* had to be interrogated.

Avra hadn't known that part until later. In his view of things, he'd been accosted just inside the front door and told that he was going to be questioned by a truthwitch to see if he was a traitor. He'd burst into tears immediately. As he'd desperately tried to remember if he'd committed any actual treason lately, his superior officers of the Ministry of Intelligence had hurled him into an empty room with a foreign lady, who had asked him questions about whether he intended any harm to the royal family, whether he'd ever been involved in any conspiracies, and whether he'd ever been tempted to be involved in one.

He had denied all three questions. On the last one, she'd said he was lying, so he'd been forced to confess to his little fantasy about a conspiracy to commit sexy crimes.

"What sort of sexy crimes?" the truthwitch had said.

Avra had answered, "I don't know, the fantasy doesn't really get that far, usually I am done jerking off *well* before we get around to committing any crimes," and proceeded to babble about all the various pretexts the sexy conspirators might have for why they all needed to get naked and prove with their bodies that everyone was *really committed* to the crime they were so sexily conspiring to commit.

The truthwitch had interrupted eventually and asked whether he'd ever thought of any other crimes against the royal family, and Avra had answered with the first thing that popped into his head, to wit: "Haha, nah, I dunno what I'd even do. Wow, what?"

The truthwitch had gone to the door and reported to the supervising officer that Avra was cleared for service, and also that it was her professional opinion that he was too birdbrained for them to *ever* bother suspecting him of a crime in the future if it came up again.

"This man's skull is empty like a new bucket," she had said, pointing right at him. "Write this down: He does not have a single thought in that pretty little head. There is *nothing* going on in there."

Avra's feelings had been rather hurt, and the whole experience had *very much* rattled him, so he'd gone to calm his nerves with a walk and a drink and a cuddle at one of the pleasure-houses down by the docks.

"But by then I had the *idea* in my head," he declared to Teveri, who had dropped their forehead into their hand. "The idea . . . of crime. Wasn't there before, but then it was. The truthwitch put it there with all her questions about my private sexual fantasies."

"So you broke into the Shipbuilder's Guild."

"By accident," Avra said, nodding. "The important thing to remember is that I broke into the Shipbuilder's Guild by accident."

He had been a bit tipsy after the drink and the cuddle, and he'd gone for an aimless mosey down by the harbor. He had not been able to stop wondering to himself, *Hm, if I were hypothetically going to do a crime, what crime would it be?*

His mosey had brought him right past the Shipbuilder's Guild, and that wondering had crashed into a second, different wondering that he had not been able to stop for ages, which was about the so-called *witchy luck* that Teveri and the crew had spent years very meanly punishing him for, and whether that had had anything to do with conveniently getting rescued from being marooned in a rowboat at sea, and what kind of experiment might prove once and for all whether it was real or not.

Standing there in the shadow of the Shipbuilder's Guild that night, the last conscious thought he'd had ("Because, as you know, Tev, I am a silly little slut and my brain is empty like a new bucket") was *Hey, didn't somebody just break in here a couple months ago? I wonder if . . .*

He had duly moseyed laps around the Shipbuilder's Guild three or four times, and then he had stepped on—

He paused and looked up expectantly at Tev until they grunted, "What was it?"

"Ring of keys."

Teveri sighed and pinched the bridge of their nose. "A ring of keys."

"A ring of keys, yes."

"You found a ring of keys—"

"Fancy keys they were, too."

"—lying on the ground in the middle of the shipyard. Where anyone could find them. And you *just so happened* to be that person."

"Yep," said Avra cheerfully.

He had picked them up, moseyed up to the doors of the Guild, stuck keys into the lock at random, got it open on the second or third try, and let himself in. He was not surprised to find that security had been increased since the break-in and that there were guards patrolling the halls, but he had felt it would skew the results of his luck experiment if he were to sneak, skulk, or otherwise contribute any particular effort into not being caught.

So rather than sneaking or skulking . . . he had *traipsed.*

He'd gotten himself quite thoroughly lost. He had traipsed up and down the halls, into a water closet for a pee break, and up to the doors of the Guildmaster's offices, where he discovered that he'd forgotten the keys in the water closet.

So he traipsed back to fetch them, then traipsed again to the Guildmaster's offices. He traipsed *indefatigably.*

During the whole process, he'd seen half a dozen guards. One of them had been leaning down to fix something with his boot as Avra traipsed right past not two feet away from him and, without looking up, had addressed Avra as Lazari and asked him to go check the south end.

Avra had said, "Sure," and continued traipsing.

He had spent several minutes at the door to the Guildmaster's office, testing the keys in the lock and making no effort to keep the jangling quiet, and as soon as he'd gotten it open, he traipsed inside and spent a moment admiring a statue of Asanbughaa, the ancient founder of Araşt.

"Then I opened up the safe in the pedestal—"

"How did you know there was a safe in the pedestal?"

"Tripped on the rug, banged my knee on the corner of it, accidentally triggered the mechanism to open the hidden panel." He clasped his hands together. "You know. A lucky break."

"Right," Teveri said tightly. "Of course."

"So I opened up the safe, found all those papers, took them over to the desk, lit the lamp, and started flicking through them."

Teveri leaned forward, their elbows on their knees.

Avra gave them his most limpid glance. "Are you *sure* you want to know what was in there? Even if it puts your life in *mortal peril*?"

"Yes," Teveri said immediately.

"There were a lot of schematics and blueprints, and research reports about fluid dynamics, hull technology, sail technology, experimental designs . . . and . . . !"

"And," Teveri said. Their expression was intent. A bit terrifying, to be honest, but the sort of terrifying that made Avra's insides all squirmy and warm, made him want to roll onto his back and bare his throat and stomach to be eviscerated.

"And toward the middle of the stack, there was a recipe. For . . . !"

"Get the fuck on with it."

"Right, sorry, I forgot you don't like edging," Avra said. "It was a recipe for the stuff that lets the Araşti ships get past the sea serpents' breeding swarms without being hassled."

Teveri sat back with a sharp exhale.

"Yes. You see now why I am fleeing the country and faking my own death. *That* secret. The big one," Avra said.

"Undeniably a *very* big one," Teveri breathed.

"I don't know if you've ever seen it done? They just dump it in the water and call it 'offerings to the sea.' Then they sail wherever they want—even right past a hungry serpent or through the middle of a breeding swarm—and nothing happens except a few bumps from below that might be accidental."

Teveri was breathing carefully, their hands clenched on the arms of their throne. "I've heard the Araşti give offerings. I've heard . . . rumors."

"Yeah, everybody's got a hunch about what it is. One time, *long* time ago, I was sent to make nice with a scholar and suggest to her that it might be a kind of poison."

"Which means it's not a poison."

Avra gave a huge theatrical shrug. "Don't know. The recipe was in fancy scholar language."

"So any potential buyer will need a scholar to make it for them. Hm."

"Probably, but that's not a huge obstacle. There's scholars all over the place. Mostly drunk in public houses, in my experience."

Teveri's eyes narrowed at nothing—Avra could almost see the calculations running through their mind, the lists of black-market fences in Scuttle Cove who might handle the transaction without backstabbing them all.

They turned their gaze back on Avra. "So you were in the Guild, copying out papers. When did your fool head realize you'd just committed treason and decide to flee the country?"

"I finished copying out the papers, cleaned the ink off the Guild-master's pen—"

"You were using *his pen*?"

"It was right there on the desk, Tev, who else's pen was I supposed to use? I cleaned up after myself and left the keys on the floor outside the Guildmaster's office as if he'd dropped them. Then I ambled out."

Teveri raised one eyebrow and waited.

"I ambled out past all the guards, left by the front door, noticed with interest that nobody was raising an alarm, continued walking for a while, and, ah . . . stopped dead in my tracks when I realized that nobody was *going* to come after me because there was no evidence to suggest I'd ever been there. And then I thought about how I had the most valuable secret in the world giving me paper cuts on my nipples because I'd shoved it down my shirt. I considered selling it for two whole seconds. *Ooh,* I thought to myself, *I could quit my day job and pursue my poetry career.*" He gave a solemn nod. "Then I broke out into cold sweats and threw up in someone's flowerpots."

"In the middle of the street with paper cuts on your nipples."

"Tragically, yes. That was two days ago and they're still a little tender, do you want to inspect them?" Avra put his hands to the collar of his kaftan as if he were about to yank it open and send the buttons flying all over the place.

"No," Tev said witheringly. "And did this so-called *experiment* with your luck prove anything to you?"

"Yes. I have revised my perspective. I am no longer a luck atheist. I am now luck agnostic."

"After *all that*?" Teveri demanded. "After all that, you're *agnostic* about whether or not you were blessed by the Bendran goddess of luck for winning a card game against one of her priests? Fuck off. Here, let me guess what happened next. You went to the harbor and *luckily* found a ship that was about to leave—"

"Nope! Next thing I did was to go back to the palace barracks, spend a couple hours throwing up in the latrines, tell everyone I'd picked up some exotic Kafian disease while I was there so they wouldn't come anywhere near me, and submit my paperwork for partial retirement." Avra clasped his hands tightly in his lap. "Now, I'm sure you are wondering: 'Avra, why would you do something so unnecessarily sexy?' Partial retirement is a perk available to Intelligence agents who have served at least fifteen years, which is an anniversary that I hit during my errand to Kafia. It is just like regular retirement in that they stop giving you a salary. However, if you keep an eye out and write reports every now and then about things that might be relevant to the Ministry, they sometimes send you a bonus if any turn out useful. Also for special occasions like the sultan's birthday. Also you still get your medical costs reimbursed if you send in your receipts from the physician." He nodded serenely and added with a little laugh, nervous bordering on manic,

"Say what you will about Araşt and the certainty that if they find out what I did, they will track me down and make my gruesome death look like an absurd accident or almost-incompetent suicide, but at least the civil service does come with excellent benefits. They take care of their people, until you give the impression that you are not interested in being their people, at which point maybe you are not even considered *people* anymore, just a particularly troublesome type of meat. Meat that moves around by itself and causes problems. Spooky, haunted meat. Honestly, who *wouldn't* hack that into bits with a sword in a dark alley?"

"That's governments for you," Teveri said flatly. "Ask anyone on this ship about the infamously thin line between *people* and *meat*."

"I have been realizing this on a visceral level lately, and occasionally throwing up about it," Avra said, nodding serenely again. "For the love of fuck, please rescue the shit out of me, Tev. You can just drop me off somewhere that doesn't have extradition treaties with Araşt and I will change my name and vanish and hide all the papers under a floorboard, and you can tell everyone you finally got around to pushing me over the side and leaving me for dead. But in a way that stuck this time."

"You won't be hiding the papers under a floorboard, Avra, I'm going to sell them." Teveri extended their hand. "Give them to me."

"Tev!" Avra shrieked, clutching his rucksack close. "Was there no big takeaway from the *spooky haunted meat* part of this conversation?"

"I've been considered spooky meat since I was born. I'm used to it," Teveri said sharply. "*Give me the papers.*"

There were certain gambits in their squabbling that Avra had learned from long experience were a clear signal for *Now is REALLY not the time to be fucking around.* For example: any mention of Teveri's childhood.

"I will give you the papers," Avra quavered piteously, just to camouflage the fact that he recognized the signpost and was cooperating. "But only if you promise to remember that there's a bit in my head that only I know about and that the secret will be worthless if you throw me overboard. If you decide to throw me overboard anyway, I would prefer if you do so in one of the sea serpent breeding swarms, so that you can tell people I died in a massive fuckpile like I have always dreamed of. Promise?"

Teveri closed their eyes, clenched their jaw for a moment, and said, "I promise you are safe until we sell the papers. After we sell them, I would imagine that I'll be in such a good mood that I'll have at least a week's worth of patience for you."

"A whole week," Avra said, marveling. "Imagine the bullshit I could get up to with a whole week of patience to spend."

"I would prefer not to. *The papers, Avra.*"

Avra rummaged in his little rucksack, got up from the sea chest to hand Teveri the papers, had some difficulty in *letting go of them,* and felt rather queasy when Teveri yanked them out of his grip.

"I'm gonna go throw up real quick, I'll be right back," he announced, though Tev was already hunched over the papers and squinting at Avra's wobbly diagrams.

"Bring Julian," Teveri said absently.

"I don't know what that is," said Avra as he went out the door in a manner that could be considered the exact opposite of *traipsing.* He leaned over the railing for a minute, trying not to think about spooky haunted meat, and when that didn't entirely work, he valiantly attempted to develop a sexual fetish about it. It had worked that time a ghost in the Turtle Shallows had tried to chat him up.

"All right there, Avra?" Markefa called from the helm.

"I'm adjusting to my circumstances," he called back. "It's very difficult and I would appreciate it if everyone could feel sorry for me."

"Aww," chorused several of the nearby pirates in a strange harmony of either sarcasm, playing along with the joke, or both.

"Thank you," Avra said, and leaned over the side again. Unfortunately the sea spray and the cool wind were very refreshing, and he was left only queasy without any of the physical relief of having done something about it. He levered himself up. "Does anyone know who or what a *Julian* is? Teveri asked me to bring one to them."

3

20. The Crow

In the wake of disaster, some will find a way to benefit, like crows feasting on the corpses in a battlefield. The cycle of death and renewal. Having intelligence enough to turn a bad situation to your advantage.

(Reversed: You're too clever for your own good. Exploitation. Stagnation, a situation with no winners.)

"Julian," said Markefa, "is our newest and most decorative member of the crew."

Avra narrowed his eyes. "What kind of decorative?"

"Six foot four, blond, shoulders like you've never seen."

"Hm," said Avra. "Suspicious. Why do you have . . . that?"

"Found him on one of those Heyrlandtsche ships filled with swamp muck a couple months back. He begged us to let him join the crew, and . . . well, he's *very* good-looking and there's not a lot of that on the crew. Captain took one look at him and said yes and invited him for drinks in their cabin."

"*WHAT?*" Avra shrieked, pierced to the very heart. "They're *replacing me*?"

"Don't know that I'd call it replacing," Markefa said philosophically. "Seeing as how you are not in the same hemisphere of handsome as our new friend Julian. You're, what, five foot four? Scrawny like a starved rat? Pointy little rat face? Always look a bit grubby and bedraggled even when no one's pushed you in the gutter?"

"I have a *sparkling personality,*" Avra said. "I have *bags of charisma.*"

"Bags of it," Markefa said, because she was arguably Avra's best friend on the whole crew. "Bags and bags of charisma you scrounged out of a rubbish heap and carry around with you in damp burlap bags."

"Julian does not have so many damp burlap bags of garbage charisma, I wager," Avra said loudly. "How could he? I have all of them. I have *cornered the market on them,* according to the teachings of my culture."

"Mm," said Markefa, which could have been agreement. "He's very enticing. Whole crew's been trying to seduce him and no one's succeeded. Well, maybe the captain, but if so they're being *discreet* about it. Oh, also he's a Vintish cleric."

"So he's hot *and* smart," Avra said, choked up. "He is hot and smart and Tev's new boytoy, and I've been *abandoned* in the alley with the possums and my empty orphan gruel bowl and my damp burlap bags."

"Yep."

"*Why* did he beg to join the crew?"

"Said he had a treasure map," Markefa said, a little mistily, which was *appalling.* She didn't even get misty about her own nephew Ellat, and *he* was a gangly seventeen-year-old infant. "If we hadn't been so won over by his handsome face and good figure, we would have been *charmed to bits* about the sweetness and innocence of claiming to have a treasure map. It was heartwarming. We cooed over him like he was a box of newborn kittens."

Avra drew himself up, indignant. "This is *unfair.* This is *persecution.* After all the times that *I* claimed to have a treasure map! None of you were charmed to bits then! It's just because he's *cute,* isn't it! *Isn't it!*"

"Goes a long way, cuteness, absolutely."

Avra made a sound that didn't have any vowels in it to express how appalled he was and slammed back into Teveri's cabin. "Well, well, well! Now who's the traitor!" he screeched.

Teveri did not look up from the papers. "I've been a traitor since I was fourteen, Avra," they said absently. "Everyone on this crew is also a traitor except Ellat, whose only crimes so far are adolescent moodiness and wanting to be just like his auntie when he grows up. It is you who is the newcomer to treason. Where's Julian?"

"I don't trust him," Avra declared. "I won't bring him into your presence. He lied to you about having a treasure map. You should put him in a rowboat and leave him for dead."

"No, he's too decorative. Vastly improves the scenery on deck." Tev lowered the papers and scowled. "I require him to improve the scenery in here as well. *Go fetch him.*"

A thought occurred to Avra: Vintish cleric. Hot *and* smart. "A *scholar,*" Avra gasped. "You have a *pet scholar.* You're going to show him the papers! Teveri! Teveri, no! What if he is a spy and he betrays all of us! What if he steals the papers and absconds in the night!"

"Then I will kill him and have him taxidermied so that he can continue improving the scenery."

"You can't trust him!" Avra shrieked. "You have known him for . . . not long enough to trust him!"

"He needs a new puzzle," Teveri said coldly. "He was very disappointed when his treasure map led to Eel-face Yusin's bar."

Avra clutched at his heart. "You're *giving him enrichment activities*?"

"I am getting my pet scholar to translate all this impenetrable science that I can't read," Teveri snapped, flapping the papers at him.

"Hah! A likely story! You know how to read, I've seen you read! You just want *Julian* to read it to you in a sexy voice with his tits out, don't you!"

"I can't read *scientific notations*! I can't even read them in *my* language, let alone your barbaric tongue-flapping—"

"Oh, cultural insults? A new low!"

Teveri slapped the papers down on the desk and leaned across it to spit, "I'm allowed to make cultural insults about Araşt all I *fucking* want as long as they keep forcing all the captains in Scuttle Cove to choose between signing the *fucking Pact* or watching all their friends die of starvation in the season of serpents."

Avra shut his mouth with a snap and gave them his most injured and piteous glare. "Not really fair play to bring a ballista to a knife fight, you know."

"Get out of my cabin. *Oskar!* Oskar!" Teveri bellowed. "Come here and drag Avra out by his hair!"

Avra stood calmly and busied himself with buttoning up his little rucksack as he edged slightly away from Teveri's desk.

Just as the doorknob turned, he hurled himself toward Tev's giant stupid wardrobe, scrambled up into the cramped space between the top of it and the support beams of the deck above, and crammed himself into the corner, making himself as small as possible and wriggling mightily until he had a good view of the room. He brandished the tiny knife he'd palmed from the rucksack, just in case Tev was already hot on his heels and trying to murder him.

Tev was still standing at their desk, looking up at him with incredulous outrage. Oskar stood in the doorway with a figure of unspeakable and *suspicious* good looks just behind him, which could only be Avra's new archnemesis, *Julian*. Oskar seemed as though he might imminently weep, but Brother Julian looked like he was trying not to laugh. This would normally have caused Avra to categorize him as a potential ally or protector. He was too appallingly gorgeous for that. He had to be up to something. People that pretty were never not up to nefarious schemes.

Julian was indeed huge and blond and projecting the general air that he'd just stopped cradling a newborn lamb a moment ago in his strong yet gentle arms and might go back to it if he wasn't otherwise required for anything. He was dressed in the long grey linen robes of a Vintish cleric, though it had been smocked up and belted at knee length, and his sleeves were rolled up past his forearms and pinned—presumably so everything would be out of his way for activities related to sailing a pirate ship. His hair was ash-blond, tied back into a hip-length queue wrapped in grey fabric. He had a few fish scales stuck to his hands and a smudge of flour on his cheek, as if he'd been *cooking*, because of *course* he had.

He had to be haunted. He was the spookiest thing Avra had seen since that dentist or Tev's box of spooky dildos.

"Now Tev, let's be calm and reasonable," Avra said reasonably, or in a rough approximation thereof. "As you can see, I am armed."

"Oskar," said Tev.

"Aye, Captain." Oskar tromped over to the wardrobe. "Witch, get down."

"No."

"You're a grown man. Have some dignity, son."

"Absolutely not. I am going to stay and guard Teveri's virtue from the depredations of this very haunted and suspicious man, thank you."

Oskar climbed onto the same sea chest and reached for him; there was a brief struggle.

"Brother Julian," said Teveri, as if Avra were not smacking, kicking, and half-heartedly stabbing at Oskar's hands. "Please, do sit down. May I offer you a glass of rum?"

"Get off, you little piece of shit—ow!"

"Don't grab at me and I won't have to stab you!"

"I would love a glass of rum, thank you," said Brother Julian absently, evidently much absorbed with the commotion on top of the wardrobe. "That is a marvelously small knife, sir," he said.

"It's for my nails," said Avra, resettling himself while Oskar sucked at his bloodied fingers. "But I killed a man with it once."

"He seems like a very determined sort of person," Julian commented to Teveri. "One of your associates?"

"No," said Teveri, and shoved the glass of rum across the table to him. Julian caught it, swirled the rich dark liquor in the glass, and sipped.

Oskar launched another, more energetic attempt to get Avra

down from the wardrobe and managed to latch on to an ankle. Avra screeched, flailed, and slashed for all he was worth; Oskar lost the round and stumbled off the sea chest and to the floor after a solid kick took him in the jaw.

"Captain!" Oskar cried, frustrated nearly to tears. "If he won't come down by himself, there's no getting him down for love nor money!"

"They're *my* secret papers that *I* committed treason to accidentally steal from the Shipbuilder's Guild, and if Teveri is going to show them off to some *untrustworthy newcomer* then I have a right to chaperone these proceedings so that nobody gets fucked! Nor fucked over!"

Teveri gave Oskar a tight smile. "Thanks for trying."

"I want combat pay!" Oskar said, pointing to a slash on his forearm, which was bleeding sluggishly from a swipe with Avra's tiny knife.

Tev swore under their breath, stomped to the liquor cabinet, and poured a third glass of rum, which they shoved at Oskar. "There's your combat pay. Dismissed, Oskar, *thank you.*"

Oskar cast a dark look at Avra and stomped out with his rum.

Avra glared at Julian. Suspicious. Too suspicious. He didn't look like he ought to be on a pirate ship, except as a hostage. Or Teveri's concubine, maybe, but that was *Avra's* job. Julian *certainly* didn't look like a pirate either. For one thing, he had both his eyes, ears, and hands—including all ten fingers—*and* both of his real feet. *Suspicious.* Probably a spy. Avra had been a spy until very recently, and he too still had both eyes, ears, hands, and feet, and all ten fingers. *For now.*

"You remember when you tried to tell us that you had a treasure map that you'd decoded all by yourself?" Teveri said, swirling their rum. They stretched out their long legs and crossed their ankles. Avra narrowed his eyes. "I've recently come into the possession of some *actual* treasure, and I need you to decode it."

"Oh!" said Julian, as if pleasantly surprised. "Of course. I'd be happy to."

"And you won't steal it and abscond in the night, will you," Teveri said with a tight smile.

"We're heading back to Scuttle Cove, aren't we? And then we'll be ashore for six weeks." Julian smiled, looking amused and perplexed. "Where would I abscond *to*?"

"Once you figure out what all the science says? Anywhere you want, and damn the serpents," Avra muttered, wriggling around on the wardrobe so he could arrange himself more alluringly. Sometimes the enemy had to be seduced to get information out of them. Or so Avra had heard.

"Besides valuing my life, I really have no interest in cheating you and your crew. You have something very valuable, and you have a ship to look after, and crew to feed—and presumably at least a few of them have families who need the money." He gave Teveri a heart-wrenchingly beautiful and sad half smile. "I don't believe in stealing bread out of the mouths of children, Captain, especially not the children of people who have been so kind and hospitable to me."

"They've been *kind and hospitable to you*?" Avra demanded. "Tev, I don't trust this man. He's too pretty and he's too nice. He's saying he doesn't care about money, Tev! I'm the only person who doesn't care about money, and that's because I've had a steady job for fifteen years and the only thing I spend money on is alcohol and gambling and visiting the Street of Flowers and fleeing the country!"

Teveri had narrowed their eyes. "Julian, explain something to me. You had a treasure map—you were *very* eager to tell us all about it, and as I recall you spent the better part of an hour describing the years and years you have spent making sense of it. You were *very* distraught when you found out that your treasure map led to Eel-face Yusin's bar in Scuttle Cove. And now you expect me to believe that you do not care about treasure." They swirled the rum in their glass. "Surely you don't think we'll think less of you for being mercenary."

Julian's smile grew more sad. "You didn't ask me what the treasure was."

"What was the treasure, anyway, I'm dying to know, I've been dying to know for ages," Avra babbled loudly.

"Ignore him," said Teveri sharply.

Something in the way Julian was talking twinged a long-ignored instinct in the back of Avra's mind, whatever it had been that had made the Araşti intelligence ministry say, *Sure, we'll give him a shot, let's see if he can avoid fucking it up.*

He set his knife down, easily in reach if Teveri decided to lunge for him, and rummaged in his little rucksack for his cards.

He drew number twelve, The Alchemist: *The secrets of the world, discovery, new understanding, changing lead to gold; pursuing immortality through great deeds, art, or scholarship. Potentially represents a scholarly person, or one who seeks knowledge.*

"Years of decoding the map, yes," Avra said, eyeing Julian over the edge of the card. "Being a cleric, and all. And a Vint. Vintish cleric. Personal research project, was it?"

"Absolutely ignore him," said Teveri sharply. "But what was the treasure you were looking for?"

Julian kept his eyes fixed steadily on Teveri and cleared his throat. "The teachings of my faith primarily concern the pursuit of knowledge. I was on something of a religious quest or a pilgrimage, and calling my research materials a treasure map was . . . a shorthand. The teachings of the church say that our founding prophet, Herannuen, journeyed into the Uttermost West and meditated in a cave until she achieved a moment of total illumination—that is, transcendent Understanding of the entirety of the Celestial Emperor's creation, an enlightenment so vast and comprehensive that the doors of Felicity opened for her and she ascended—and that the disciples entombed her mortal vessel in the very cave where the miracle had occurred and bore the news of it back to Vinte. Through my research and translations of the diary of one of her disciples, I suspected she was murdered." He shrugged one shoulder. "That was the treasure I sought. Just the truth, and . . . perspective on questions that had been troubling me for some time. Perhaps a moment of my own transcendent Understanding." Another wry, sad, heart-stopping smile. "Hence the state in which you and your crew found me when I returned to the ship."

"Weeping beautifully on the prow and looking off into the middle distance?" Avra asked suspiciously.

"Laughing so hard we thought he'd snapped from staring at the horizon too long," Teveri said flatly. "We were taking bets about whether he'd start claiming that the ghost of Xing Fe Hua appeared to him and kissed him full on the mouth, or if he'd kill us all in our sleep."

Avra whipped out another card from his deck of Heralds, grimaced at it, and pulled another, hummed, and pulled a third. "I would have wagered that he was utterly sane and just going through a personal crisis."

"What did you get?" Tev asked suspiciously.

"The Proclamation, for important news and outward announcements after inward reflection. And The Knight, reversed, for oathbreaking." Julian flinched a little at that one. "*Aha!*" said Avra, pointing at him and scrambling for his tiny knife, which fell to the floor with a clatter. "Tev! Did you see! Did you see that! I said *oathbreaking* and he made a suspicious face!"

"You made a suspicious face when you drew the first card," Teveri said. "And you drew *three.*"

"You don't need to know what the first one was, it's not relevant. Don't change the subject! He's definitely guilty of *something*—"

"Thought the first card is usually the most relevant one."

"The deck was being bitchy! It was a fun little joke!"

"What was the card, Avra," Teveri snapped.

"You don't need to know!"

"Avra, *what was the card?*"

"The Bower. Don't yell at me, it's not my fault! I didn't stack the deck this time—and it's not always about sex! Sometimes it's about happy secrets and joyful futures!"

Teveri made a scathing noise and turned back to Julian.

"Wait!" Avra peeked over the edge of the wardrobe to his tiny knife lying on the floor. "Can someone hand that back to me, please?"

Teveri ignored him and smiled tightly at Julian. "Sorry about your prophet. Probably a good thing there weren't relics in there, because I would have taken them off of you and sold them. The littlest fingerbone of somebody's prophet could sell for a respectable amount if you found the right buyer."

Julian smiled and shook his head as if this was a very funny little inside joke that he and Teveri already had. Avra seethed. "They were probably swept out and dumped in some rubbish heap hundreds of years ago. I appreciate the compassion, though."

"Maybe he's a fake monk," Avra declared. "I think it is *highly suspect* that he is not more bothered by the idea of a bar being set up in his religion's holy site, even if Eel-face Yusin *does* have the best yellow curry in town."

"I'm not a fake monk," Julian said gently. "Although I admit that the yellow curry was fine enough to be a balm to my spirits when I wandered inside in shock and trying to make sense of . . . the understanding that I had pursued and achieved."

"I don't believe that," said Avra immediately. "Tev. Don't believe him. Don't show him the papers."

"So I have these papers to show you," said Teveri, kicking their heels up onto the corner of their desk and pushing the papers across to Julian with two fingers.

"This is a disaster," Avra announced as Julian picked them up and studied them. "He will betray us all. He will decode the science into small words that you and I can understand, Tev, and then he will do something shocking with it. We cannot predict what someone that pretty is going to do. We don't know how the minds of pretty people work, Tev. He could decide to do anything and we would never see it coming."

Julian was frowning at the pages, flicking through them. "I don't think schematics for hull design will be very useful," he said, discarding several of the pages on the desk again. "Araşt does sell their ships to foreign countries." And occasionally lose them to pirates named Teveri az-Ḥaffār through a sequence of unfortunate and *extraordinarily* spooky tragedies, but Avra was not about to bring that up in Tev's hearing. "Whoever wished to reverse-engineer their construction techniques could do so easily."

"There's a bit in the middle," said Avra, attempting to find a more alluring position to lounge on top of the wardrobe than Teveri's boots-on-the-desk thing. "The recipe. The one I labeled 'Serpent Juice,' do you see it? That is also not important. Don't look at it. You can just hand it back to me, and I'll tear it into bits and throw it overboard for you. Haha."

"That's the one I'd like you to work on," Teveri said, taking a slow, sexy sip of their rum.

Julian flicked through and found it, sitting up straighter as he skimmed through.

"I'm sure a man as clever and learned as yourself will have no problems with it, will you?"

"It's in alchemical notation," Julian said absently. "But the quantities are unusually large. It makes a batch of twenty or thirty barrels." He set it down, shaking his head. "I'm not sure how much use this will be. There aren't any instructions about how or when to use it."

"Avra has already provided that information," Teveri said. "They dump it into the ocean and call it 'offerings to the sea.'"

"That's something," Julian said, raising his eyebrows. "Am I still ignoring him, or may I ask him a direct question?"

"I shan't answer," Avra said. "I've been trained by the Araşti Ministry of Intelligence about how to withstand interrogation."

"What question?" Teveri asked.

Julian shrugged. "Anything else he knows about the circumstances surrounding its use, any rumors he's heard about it, anything he's personally witnessed . . . Considering how effectively Araşt has been able to suppress this technology in the last two hundred years, it has to be a complicated process, so *any* further information beyond this recipe could be the difference between triumph and disaster."

"Told you there were bits in my head that only I know, Tev," Avra said. "Told you it would be worthless if you threw me overboard."

"Please don't throw him overboard, Captain," Julian said seriously. "He's important research material for my work."

"Oh, well, that changes things," Avra said as Teveri made disappointed faces and muttered grouchily into their glass. "If he's wanting to do *sexy experiments on my body,* then I consent."

"He doesn't," Teveri snapped. "Shut up." Then, to Julian, "Interrogate the twit at your leisure, and get me something coherent I can sell on the black market. You'll be needing a quiet space to work, won't you? And a desk. Can't have you working belowdecks in the common room, or someone's liable to spill something on it. You'll work in here."

"Thank you, that would be very helpful." Julian hesitated, then clasped his hands in his lap and looked frankly at Teveri. "I will do my sincere best with this project, Captain, but I have a question. If my work is not to your satisfaction, is my life in danger?"

"We'll cross that bridge when we come to it," Teveri said firmly. They smiled and lowered their voice to just this side of a purr. "Not to worry, Julian, we're not about to throw a strong, hardworking man overboard for the sea serpents."

"Certainly not one who is suggesting that he do sexy experiments on my body," Avra said quickly, rearranging himself into his alluring lounge and sticking one leg out in the hopes of increasing his allure.

"Certainly not," Teveri agreed, their smile widening. "It would be a waste of a handsome face."

Julian's green eyes flicked between them. "Ah . . . I thank you both for the compliments," he said delicately. "Apropos of nothing in particular," he added, clearing his throat, "and since we're all still getting to know each other, an interesting fact about me is that I took a vow of celibacy when I joined my order." There was a long, ringing silence.

"Ah," said Teveri. "Well. That is an interesting fact to know about you." They sat back.

Avra stubbornly kept his leg stuck out in his posture of aggressively alluring lounging, and met Tev's glance smugly when they glanced up at him.

"Well!" Teveri said brightly, whipping back to Julian and rising from the desk. "I hope you'll keep us all apprised of your relationship with your faith! I myself left the cult of Qarat'ash when I was fourteen, so I know very well how these things can develop over time. Are you finished with your rum? Very good—go get a good night's sleep, and you can start work first thing tomorrow morning."

"You left the cult of Qarat'ash?" Julian said in astonished tones as Teveri hustled him to the door and opened it.

"I did." They met Julian's eyes firmly, which Avra recognized from long familiarity as a small rebellious gesture. In their once-homeland, making eye contact was considered exceedingly rude—indeed, so was the display (or scrutiny) of any part of the body beyond the hands and wrists. "Hard to tell these days, isn't it? Perhaps we could have drinks tomorrow night and talk religion then. So interested to hear more about that fake treasure map you thought you had." They pushed him out, slammed the door closed, and turned to Avra with a baleful look.

Avra kept his leg sultrily stuck out.

"Put that away," Tev snapped.

"I don't have to. It's my leg, I can do whatever I want with it."

"Come down from there."

Avra studied them suspiciously. "Am I in trouble? If so, is it the sexy kind of trouble or the fighting over stale bread with the possums kind of trouble?"

Teveri shut their eyes for a moment. "You are not currently in trouble, but if you don't *obey orders from the captain of this vessel* that could change astonishingly quickly."

"Well, you could say please," Avra said, wriggling to the end of the wardrobe and lowering himself slowly until he was hanging off the side and flailing around with his foot. "Where's the sea chest? *Tev, where's the sea chest, did you move it, where is it*—"

"Literally two inches under your foot!"

"Oh. Ah, there it is."

As Avra got himself down and pulled his little rucksack after him, Tev flung themself back onto their throne, ground their teeth for a long moment, and burst out, "I want you to find out about him."

"Coming to your senses about whether it's smart to let the hot newcomer mess with the spoils of my treason, eh?"

Teveri's mouth twisted in a silent snarl for a moment. "He hasn't told us about his past. Nor his motivations, except for just now."

"What, and you want *me* to do it? Is this some kind of cruel initiation ritual I have to endure to be counted amongst the ranks of all you experienced, professional traitors now that I've begun my treasonous apprenticeship?"

"No, I want you to do it because it's rude and you're an appalling twit."

"Rude how?" Avra's jaw dropped. "Wait, is it *rude* to ask people how they became pirates? I've been asking people that for ages! How else am I supposed to make conversation with new friends?"

"Oh, I don't know," Teveri snapped. "Maybe by politely giving them privacy about what is always a *sensitive fucking subject*?"

"It's not sensitive for Ellat! He's just an auntie's boy!"

"Go be rude to Julian and find out why he's kicking around on a pirate crew instead of begging us to drop him off somewhere he can catch the first ship back to Vinte."

"Maybe he just has a yearning for adventure and the glamorous piratical life," Avra said. "Probably he is having a crisis of faith and imminently about to give up his oath of celibacy."

Teveri gave him a suspicious look, but only raised their eyebrow.

"See, I know about Vintish monks, Tev, and he already told us a *lot*. Like that I have a very real chance of finding out what his dick looks like. Vintish monks take vows. Do you know what they take vows *for*, Tev?"

"As you may recall," Teveri said in a lower, sharper voice, the one that meant *actual* danger, "I have a somewhat contentious history with religion. So *no,* Helvaçi, I cannot say that I have ever cared to take much notice of the finer details of their theology."

Gods, Tev was outright tetchy today. "Fine, that's fine. Here is what I know," Avra said, holding up a finger to punctuate his dramatic pause. "Not every Vintish monk takes vows of celibacy."

"And how do you know that?"

"Fucked a couple of 'em once."

"Of course you did."

"One of 'em refused to get drunk with me, and she said it was because of her vows. The other wore a blindfold whenever she went out among common folks, because she said that seeing beautiful clothes *distracted her mind from the contemplation of holiness.*" Avra nodded triumphantly. "So you see. They don't all take vows to give up the same things. They each give up the thing that takes up the most space in their head so that they can better pursue holy understanding or whatever. Which therefore means—"

"Aha," said Teveri.

"—that Julian must *really fucking love sex.* I'm going to swallow his dick like a python."

"You will do nothing of the sort."

"I'm going to do unspeakable things to him with my tonsils."

Teveri gave him a mean little smile. "Not if I get to him first."

Avra scoffed. "*You* didn't even keep showing him your legs. *You* gave up. *You* were being respectful of his piety. Meanwhile, I was paying attention and I just kept being alluring—"

"Oh, is that what you were doing? I thought you were trying to do grotesque contortionist tricks."

"I bet he's into that. If he swore a vow of celibacy because he was too horny, I bet he's *gagging* to see some grotesque contortionist tricks in a sexual context."

"Get out of my cabin."

"I have questions," Avra said loudly, bracing himself against the doorframe as Teveri tried to shove him out. "I have exactly two questions and then I'll leave you be!"

"*What?*"

"Do you want to keep the papers in your desk, or are they going to be safer if they're on my person at all times, where they will theoretically be protected by the luck that I am still agnostic about?"

Teveri snarled, stomped to the desk, snatched up the papers, stomped back to the door, and shoved them into Avra's chest. He rolled them up neatly and stuck them into his little rucksack, and did not take the opportunity to pout about this very terrible treatment he was so nobly enduring.

"I guess we're going back to Scuttle Cove, then? Finding a buyer for this sweet precious baby that could get us all extravagantly killed?" He patted his little rucksack meaningfully.

Teveri exhaled slowly through their nose and clenched their jaw for a moment. "Yes," they said, tonelessly. "Some of the fences have contacts with deep enough pockets to be worth inviting to an auction. Black Garda, the Mainmast, Sareen mes Rakan, Papa Kavo . . ."

"Black Garda might still be mad at me from that time I sneezed in the punch bowl at her wedding. What about Barno the Barnacle?"

"Grimy little drunk."

"Yeah, but he knows people out in Heyrland and they're big shippy sorts of people. They've got *trading companies* out that way." Avra squealed in dismay and clung to the doorframe as Teveri once again tried to lever him out. "One more thing!"

"You said you only had two questions!" Teveri snapped, shoving their shoulder into his stomach and heaving him right off his feet. "That was two!"

"Just a little extra question! And then maybe a couple comments!"

"I've had enough comments from you." They took him three strides out onto the deck and dropped him, but he caught them around the neck and shoulders and clung with both arms. "*Let go.*"

"Is Ambassador Asena still appointed to Scuttle Cove?"

"No," Teveri said tightly, wrestling themself free. "She retired."

"Ah. Good for her. Very good. Do you know who . . . the

replacement is?" Avra laughed nervously and clutched the rucksack close, scuttling after Tev as they strode back to their cabin. "It's just that they might recognize me," he said, his voice getting higher and more plaintive. "And it would be great if they didn't hear about us trying to sell the precious baby right under their noses, so maybe we should just *not sell it,* Tev, have you considered that? Not sell it and be poor but alive?"

"I will take it under advisement," Teveri said, and slammed the door in his face.

Captain's Log

---

cont'd—Day 3, 6th month, 199th yr Mahisti Dyn.

Course determined; turning south. Cargo of 1 stupid motherfucker turned out to have something fucking good. Markefa est'd sale profits, said a # that genuinely almost made me come.

Cutting it close to make it to IOLS before serpents come up; Nagasani est'd 9d to the turtles if wind stays w/ us, less than 10d til serpents are due. Would be more nervous abt situation if we didn't have motherfucking Avra on board w/ his motherfucking luck. Keeps insisting on being useful right when I'm on my v last nerve.

Julian unfort discovered to have vow of celibacy. Crew will be heartbroken when they find out. Debating which I prize more: beating the stupid twit at own game & fucking J. first, OR not being a colossal dick & respecting J.'s holy vows.

A. clearly w/o ethical qualms abt this. Trollop.

4

25. *The Logician*

Cold hard facts; steady, thorough, methodical work; pure theory. Look at what's in front of you, and only what is in front of you. Merely knowing the facts is more important than seeking practical applications right now. Remain calm, collected, and analytical.

(Reversed: Falling into illusion, unhealthy thought cycles, a distorted or unrealistic perspective. Someone may be deliberately manipulating or misrepresenting the truth. Be careful of assumptions. You don't know what you don't know.)

Avra found Markefa down in the cabin that served as pantry for the common rations of the ship, where she was instructing Julian on taking inventory of the provisions they'd stolen from the other ship. The rest, if there was any, would be down in the lower hold with the golden straw and whatever else they were planning on selling or bartering once they reached port.

Avra clung piteously to the doorframe. "Markefa."

She held up one finger, not taking her eyes off of whatever Julian was scribbling in chalk on the slate that Markefa usually used for her calculations. Avra obediently shushed. A moment later, Julian finished and tilted the slate toward her. "Not only a man of letters, but numbers too," she said approvingly, clapping him on the shoulder. "With arithmetic like that and the better part of a year to get your sea legs, you could take a respectable shot at getting yourself named bosun or quartermaster. 'Specially if I retire like I keep threatening."

"I also know arithmetic," Avra said.

"Yes, my boy, but if you've ever met a sense of responsibility, you insulted it in a bar and ran off into the night with the cutest courtesan available," Markefa returned easily. "But unfortunately responsibility is a quality that the crew wants in someone elected to be in charge of the ship's purse and provisions."

Avra pouted at her. "You could just say, 'Yes, Avra, you're very clever too,' in a condescending voice."

Markefa laughed aloud, so raucously she had to bend over with her hand on her thighs and wheeze. Julian bit his lip on a smile as he studied the slate, glancing up only once to meet Avra's eyes. "I believe you mentioned before that your wheelhouse is more in the line of poetry than numbers?"

"Oh, it certainly is." Avra perched himself on one of the barrels and kicked his heels in what he hoped was a fetching sort of way. "I should be *so happy* to share some of my poetry with you sometime, if you would like. No one on this crew appreciates it. Or me, for that matter."

Markefa, still gurgling with mirth, clapped him on the shoulder. "Sure we do, lad! Just like a sad, mangy pet."

"If I were a pet, I would certainly have mange, yes." Avra grinned winsomely at her.

Julian smiled at his slate as he said, "Master Avra—"

"No," said Avra and Markefa in unison.

"Don't give him honorifics," Markefa said, scrunching up her nose.

"I neither deserve them nor want them," Avra said, mimicking the scrunched face. "I prefer it when people feel sorry for me. Some may ask if it is better to be loved or feared, and I say: Neither. It is better to be pitied. Then people don't expect anything of you."

"What an interesting philosophy," said Julian. "Master Oskar gave me the impression that you win every game of chance you partake in, is that true?"

"Yes," said Markefa. "Do not under any circumstances play cards with him. *Definitely* do not play dice games with him. Do not lay bets on the flip of a coin if he's betting against you. He will take all your money, and you will spend several years trying to figure out how he's cheating and taking your money off him again by force, and then you will have to accept that he is a witch, because there is no other explanation but sheer idiot luck."

"Oskar told me all this," Julian said mildly. "And he said no feats of physical strength or dexterity as well."

"Probably true," Avra agreed.

"If there is any element of chance involved, do not play it against him," Markefa said. "Oskar is very bad at assessing this. I recall an incident wherein Avra wandered up and offered to keep Oskar company on watch one night, immediately got bored, and suggested a contest for who could stand on one foot the longest."

"It is not my fault we got hit with that rogue wave out of nowhere and Oskar almost went overboard," Avra said, faintly injured.

"There was another incident where Oskar was lured into a 'let's see who can swim out to that rock fastest' game and a passing seagull—may they all burn in the hellish fires of the mountain—"

"Fuckers," Avra agreed.

"—a passing seagull thought his tattoos were fish and attacked him."

"There was also the 'ooh, Oskar, I'm so bored, are you bored? Let's go for a walk on the beach and throw knives at crabs' game," said Avra.

"Which was how Oskar nearly lost another toe," Markefa finished. "Chess is generally safe as long as you're inside or the wind isn't blowing too strong."

"Or if you secure the board to the table and put a bit of sticky candy on the bottom of each piece so they don't get knocked off the board by some unrelated incident. Fortunately, I am happy-go-lucky by nature, so it is not so difficult to endure this terrible burden." He turned to Markefa and clasped his hands under his chin. "Speaking of which, Markefa, if you'd like to help me continue to be happy-go-lucky—"

"Generally preferable to the tantrums. Or the piteous wailing." She looked up from her slate, squinting thoughtfully at the bulkhead. "Like a cat when you've shut it out of your cabin. The meowing and the crying and the carrying on."

"Can't deny that," Avra said. "Let's avoid having me in that kind of mood—do you know the name of the new Araşti ambassador at Scuttle Cove?"

Markefa snorted and scoffed under her breath, "Ambassador."

"What do you prefer? Supervisor? Nursemaid?"

"City watch?" she said archly. "That's who I feel like I'm being monitored by when I see the Araşti flag flapping in the harbor. That's what I'm *supposed* to feel, I'd wager."

Avra gave a nervous little giggle. "Aha. Ha. Yes. I have recently acquired a new perspective on the world and I understand your point. Yes. Very intimidating. And—well, they're Ministry of Diplomacy, you know how I have always felt about Diplomacy—"

"Smug fuckers." Markefa nodded. "Smirking and pretending not to notice that we're all grubby brigands and smugglers."

"More annoying than ten of me," Avra said. "Probably that's why I can get away with being Araşti in Scuttle Cove, eh? Most of the other Araşti that you people have met are Diplomacy eggheads, so probably I seem really fun and easy to get along with by comparison."

"And no one's ever been able to discover whether you have a scrap of personal dignity."

"I don't. And I'm not good at being polite. Tev has just informed me that it is impolite to make friendly conversation by asking people why they became pirates, for example. Innate politeness and manners is probably something they look for when they're selecting for Diplomacy."

"There's polite," Julian murmured, "and then there's holier-than-thou."

Markefa snapped her fingers and waved one toward him. "There it is. He knows."

"If one holds oneself apart from others, or lives within a community without participating in the mundane troubles of ordinary life, resentment can easily take root in the hearts of those who do."

"Wow," Avra purred, batting his eyelashes—Julian wasn't looking at him. "So wise. You're *so* right." Markefa, who *had* glanced at him, rolled her eyes and went back to counting whatever it was she was counting. "Couldn't have said it better myself. Not every day you come across somebody so wise and so shoulders."

"Oh god," said Markefa.

"I mean so good-looking. And having shoulders. Not everybody has shoulders, it's not weird to respectfully admire somebody who does. I mean, look at me, I basically go right from neck to arm."

"Scrawny little rat-faced man," Markefa muttered. Then, louder, "Right, I'm done with my section." She hung her slate on one of the hooks by the door and dusted the chalk off her hands.

Avra caught her arm at the door. "The new ambassador-supervisor-nursemaid–city watch?"

"Oh, right. Name's Baltakan, I think. Why? You know 'em?"

Avra made a troubled little noise and let go of her sleeve. "Hard to say. I could think of a dozen Baltakans in the civil service—you don't know the first name?"

"Nah."

"Gender? Age? What they look like?"

"Seems to be a man." She shrugged. "Haven't seen him up close, so I can't speak to anything else. Doesn't carry himself like he's all that young, nor all that old. That's all I've got."

Avra made another little noise. "If I don't know him, I probably know at least one of his relations. Very patriotic family, the Baltakans. Seems like they send most of their kids to the service at some point."

Markefa shrugged again and went out into the passageway, saying over her shoulder as she went, "I'll be on deck later if you want a game of chess."

"Most joyfully I would, madam!" Avra called after her. He

turned his attention and his grin back on Julian. "Soooo," he said, slathering his voice with allure. "What's a, uh, tall drink of water like you doing on a, erm, b . . . oat?"

Julian glanced up from his slate. There was a long moment of ringing silence. "I beg your pardon?"

"Like this," Avra said. "A boat like this."

"Ah. Just one moment," Julian murmured, scratching something on his slate.

"So fascinating to meet a Vintish monk. I just love talking to Vintish monks, learning everything about you all, hearing your life stories, maybe sharing a couple drinks and then taking a little tour of the spooky dentist's old cabin if nobody's using it . . ."

Julian finished whatever he was writing, hung the slate carefully on the hook, and turned to Avra with a slow smile and a look from under his eyelashes that could only be described as sultry.

Avra put his head a little on one side, intrigued. Usually his charms and flirtations didn't work *quite* so fast, but then he supposed that with a vow of celibacy, a man like Julian would be ready and waiting to crumble into temptation at the slightest nudge.

It was probably the alluring lounging on top of the wardrobe that had done it. If that was enough to get *sultry looks* and *smiles,* then another dollop or two of further allure would no doubt have this poor man panting. This poor, horny man. How many years had he endured this terrible oath? Perhaps it had been long enough that he'd have that shy, virginal air about him that came from sheer amazement at the privilege of getting to touch another person's body. That was the thing about inexperienced people—they didn't take anything for granted.

Avra beamed at Julian and opened his mouth to say something like *Or we could skip the drinks,* but before he could speak, Julian stepped into his personal space, set his hands on the barrel on either side of Avra's hips, leaned in, and very deliberately looked at Avra's mouth.

Avra's stomach swooped in shocked delight, and he thought, *Ah, he is even hornier than anticipated, excellent.*

"Hey," Avra squeaked. Perhaps Julian was a spy. That was fine. Lots of people were spies. The vast majority of Avra's former coworkers were spies. Avra could definitely forgive him if he was going to look at Avra's mouth like that.

"May I . . ."

"Yes, yep, you certainly may."

"—ask you a question?"

"Oh. Sure, of course, what is it?"

Julian's voice was low, rich, *rumbly.* More of a purr than Tev had ever managed, Avra thought deliriously, and then Avra didn't think anything at all, because Julian's tongue—he'd licked his lips and raised his eyes to meet Avra's again. "Seems like you've known the crew a while."

"Ages," Avra said breathlessly.

"And you really want to get the captain's attention."

"How did you know that?"

"Just a lucky guess."

"Oh. I'm lucky too, you know. I'm lucky about a lot of things. Nonstop luck every day. Are you going to kiss me?"

"Maybe," said Julian, smiling. "How would you like to make the captain very, very happy?" His voice dropped to a whisper, and he leaned in a little closer, so that he was almost whispering in Avra's ear, almost brushing their cheeks together.

Avra squirmed and giggled feverishly. "Is this a trick question? Do you want to have a threesome? They won't do it, they'll just snatch you from me and slam the door in my face." Julian's hand came up to tuck a lock of hair behind Avra's ear. "You don't want me shut out in the dark in the rain to starve, do you?"

"I would hate to see you shut out in the rain to starve," Julian agreed. "I bet it would make the captain very happy if you told me things that were helpful for figuring out how to use that alchemical formula you found."

"Serpent juice," Avra said automatically. "It's serpent juice, it's juice for the sea serpents. See some serpents in the sea, give them serpent juice. No more serpents. Easy as . . . juice. Sea juice."

"Wow, that's amazing. You're so clever for knowing about that," Julian purred. Avra could feel Julian's breath against his neck. "Tell me more."

"No," Avra squeaked. "You're a spy and you're manipulating me. This is so suspicious of you. This is the most suspicious thing that has ever happened to—" Julian's warm hand had slid to cup the side of Avra's neck, and Avra spluttered to a stop.

"Maybe I've just been paying attention to all your hints, and this seemed like the quickest way to have a useful conversation with you."

"Mgnrhk," said Avra. "Four barrels of serpent juice. Poured off the prow into the water when the lookouts call for it. Everyone hides belowdecks. Because of all the teeth. So many teeth. Too many teeth. An unseemly number of teeth. Embarrassing for them."

"How many people know about this, do you think?"

"Shipbuilder's Guildmaster knows about the serpent juice."

"You're right, he does," Julian said encouragingly. "So smart, Avra. Could there be any other part of the puzzle, do you think? Or is it just the serpent juice?"

"Dunno," Avra said, breathless. His hands reached for Julian's belt, but Julian caught them and placed them so firmly on either side of Avra's hips that Avra could not bear to move them again, even when Julian returned to gently cupping his neck. "What if I wanted to interrogate you? I could. I know all about interrogating. I was a spy. Why have you decided to become a pirate? See, I did it. I did an interrogation. Answer the question."

"I'm a monk."

"You are a monk who seems quite happy to be on a pirate ship," Avra said deliriously. "Comfortable. Cozy. Having a nice time."

"Of course. I'm talking to you, and that's very nice."

Avra squeaked under his breath. Julian's hand was *very* warm on the back of his neck, heavy and firm. "How is your crisis of faith going?"

"It's all right," Julian said smoothly. "I'm thinking about things."

"Like how horny you are, probably."

"Definitely. So clever of you, Avra."

"Hgmrhn. Why are you, a monk, comfortable on a pirate ship?"

"I used to be a revolutionary. They're my kind of people."

"Lying. Liar. That's so fucking hot but you're lying. I used to be an Araşti spy, I know all about lying. That's a lie. Monks aren't revolutionaries."

"Not for a long time, no. My turn now. Do you know anything else about the technique? Anything at all?"

"Maybe. Maybe. You should, eeee, torture it out of me. In a sexy way. Like spies do."

That was the sort of thing that would get Teveri to scathe and make disgusted faces and throw Avra out of rooms and sometimes overboard, but Julian just said, "Oh, okay," slid his hand up the back of Avra's head, leisurely clenched his fist on Avra's hair, and pulled—almost gently, but steady and inexorable and irresistible. Avra's jaw dropped on a gasp and he went limp.

"Tell me everything you know about the serpent juice or the technique of using it," Julian breathed in his ear.

Avra chattered at maximum speed: "The technique for passing safely through the breeding swarms was invented by three siblings of the Mahisti family—Tarhan, Sabûr, Gülpaşa, a brother and twin sisters—in the thirty-eighth year of the Shahre Dynasty, four years before Tarhan's son Karaman was born. Old merchant family. Wanted to corner the market and make lots of money when nobody else could travel at all. Maximizing profits. Worked *very* well. They figured it out and made so much money that Karaman overthrew the Shahre Dynasty with zero bloodshed, just by hiring all their kahyalar and civil servants out from under them. Also by offering better perks and benefits, like paying for their educations and medical expenses. Merchants, am I right? Just throw money at the problem until it goes away, even if it's a government. Want a country? Sure, says Karaman Mahisti, I'm richer than fuck, I'll just *buy it*. Funded with the proceeds of being the only merchant family around who didn't have to stop sailing. This is everything I know about it, I—hgrhgkh." Avra shuddered all over and tugged against

Julian's grip just to feel the sting. "What are you going to buy when Tev sells the serpent juice recipe? Probably not enough to buy a whole country. I'm going to buy an island and a lot of crossbows, and a squad of alley possums to be bodyguards, and enough rations that I can live out my days there and make sure that Araşt never finds me. I will write poetry and read it to the possums."

"That sounds lonely."

"It's not ideal," Avra said feverishly. "Ideal would be a villa where I could lie around drinking wine with people who want to fuck me, and also snuggle with me afterward, and all of them will like my poetry. Too dangerous. Conspicuous. Easy to find me that way. Then I will be so dead. The real kind of dead. Not the sexy kind of dead where people clasp my corpse to their bosom and weep on it and then have a tearful funeral orgy while sobbing 'It's what he would have wanted.'"

Julian's breath had stuttered to a halt somewhere in there, which Avra only noticed because Julian was so close to Avra's ear when he started breathing again. "Thank you for telling me that," Julian said. "Good boy, Avra."

He released Avra's hair and pulled away. Avra slumped back against the wall, panting for breath. "Oh . . . Was I?" he heard himself say in a small kittenish voice he usually only pulled out to make people think he was a pathetic little creature and they should feel sorry for him. It was very difficult to look away from Julian's handsome face. He shook his head and clawed his way back to coherency. "I think I should have a reward. I think you should let me suck your dick."

"Alas," Julian said apologetically. "I've taken a vow of celibacy."

Avra blinked at him. "But. You were taken in by my wiles, though?"

Julian visibly fought back some kind of wave of amusement that lit up his face. "My apologies."

Avra called up the sad-pathetic-kitten-creature voice. "This was interrogation tactics? You would pull my hair and call me a good boy and pump me for information and now you won't even let me suck your dick?"

"Yes," said Julian, unrepentant.

"That's so sexy of you."

"Thank you."

"We could go visit the spooky dentist cabin together. The cabin where our spooky dentist once lived. It's haunted. People use it for sex now. We could stand on opposite sides of the room and jerk off and not touch at all."

"Regretfully, I must decline."

"*But you pulled my hair,*" Avra wailed. "On purpose! With malice aforethought! You knew that you weren't going to follow through and fuck my mouth!"

Julian was still clearly struggling to keep a straight face. "Well, I have taken a vow of celibacy."

"Why are we only talking about your vows? What if I have vows? What then?"

"Do you have vows?" Julian asked, all polite interest.

"Very solemn ones," said Avra, still slumped back against the wall. He probably looked all louche and disarrayed. Many people found that enticing. Probably Julian found it enticing if he was the sort to go around seductively breathing on people's necks and pulling their hair and saying "good boy, Avra" like that. "I've taken a vow to swallow your dick like a python."

"Ah," said Julian, and Avra could have sworn—he could have *sworn*—that Julian's eyes flicked down to his mouth. "My condolences. We seem to be at an impasse."

While Avra was still collecting his jaw from the floor, Julian had the gall to calmly walk out and just barely brush his fingers against Avra's wrist as he passed.

Avra skittered up to Teveri's door and, as his luck would have it, stopped a split second before they opened it.

Tev swore colorfully and called him several rude words. "Have you just been standing there the whole time?" they demanded. "I gave you orders."

"Yes," said Avra. "I mean no. I mean, no, I wasn't here, yes, you gave me orders, and yes yes yesyesyesyes I went and took care of them and, hhhhh, *Tev,* I know things, oh Tev, the things that I know, the things I have discovered and now know and have the knowing of, because they are in my brain and I know them—"

"Pillars of the fucking sky, what the hell is wrong with you?" They leaned close and sniffed his breath. "Are you on drugs?"

"I'm high on knowledge, Tev," Avra said breathlessly.

"You're manic."

"Tev, he's a secret monk. I mean, not a secret monk. A monk who is something else, secretly. He says he used to be a revolutionary. A fake monk. That's what I meant, Tev, that's what he is. I have discovered this cunningly through the use of my wiles. He tried to *seduce* me, Teveri. He tried to do unspeakable things to my virtue."

They raised an eyebrow. "Tried?"

"Succeeded. Had me in the palm of his hand. Metaphorically. Also literally. Not my dick. He pulled my hair. Tev, he is *monstrous.* I'm in love with him. He refused to let me suck his dick."

Tev's expression was tilting increasingly toward the incredulous and exasperated. "He pulled your hair and refused to let you suck his dick, and therefore he's a fake monk?"

"Yessss," Avra said with great relish. "Yesssssss. Yes, Tev, you understand, you are following me with such precision, you are fully and comprehensively absorbing all of this intelligence, you are—"

"Shut up, Avra."

"—achieving the ultimate Understanding just like Julian's prophet what's-her-name."

"Markefa," Tev shouted. "Throw Avra in the rope locker until I'm finished on deck."

5

> *80. The Penitent*
>
> Regrets, a wish to reform and change one's ways, a sincere apology. To seek resolution, take responsibility for your actions. With good grace and an open heart, all wounds may be healed. True honor lies not in the avoidance of all mistakes, but in owning up to one's errors with dignity and self-respect.
>
> (Reversed: Emotional manipulation, guilt-tripping, false apologies. Remember: Words are cheap. Wait until there is evidence of real change before moving on.)

Avra was let out of the rope locker after an hour or so and immediately forced to wash his hands in a bucket of salt water because, as Markefa told him crisply, he had been "awfully quiet" in there.

He played two games of chess with her, at which she trounced him soundly, and then he was cheerfully sent right back into the rope locker for the night so that he wouldn't get into any further mischief.

At the crack of dawn, he awoke again from fitful sleep to Oskar ringing the ship's bell in the pattern that meant, as Avra liked to think of it, "all hands on deck for a family meeting."

Teveri stood before the helm on the poop deck with their arms crossed, wearing one of their swoopy coats. This one was a rather fine example of Bendran tailoring, made in a deep purple wool with yellow-white embroidery around the bottom hem. It had once had fancy silver buttons, but—well, piracy wasn't always a reliable way to make a living, and in scanty years, the quartermaster's budget had to be met somehow. That was probably where the nice rug and embroidered coverlet in Teveri's cabin had gone too.

Tev had owned a hat once. Avra didn't know what had happened to it. It had been a marvelous thing made of stiff black felt—the Bramandonian style, wide-brimmed but jauntily pinned up on one side, accented with a long spike of tiger-striped pheasant feather. When had they stopped wearing it? It must have been years since Avra had seen it.

Avra was not, of course, let out of the rope locker for the family meeting, but the cracks between the boards were wide enough that he could peer through and hear just as well.

The sky was pinky golden and hazy blue when the mass of sailors finished assembling on deck.

Teveri put their hands on their hips and gazed stonily down at the crew. "Well, no point in trying to be cagey about it, is there? You all heard Helvaçi's wibbling on deck yesterday. Let's make sure that we're all on the same page. The twit is shut in the rope locker. Markefa and Oskar have been guarding him while I come up with a plan. Yes, he stole valuable papers from the Araşti Shipbuilder's Guild in Kasaba City. No, we cannot simply take them off him and throw him overboard."

There was a ripple of laughter through the crowd.

Tev smiled faintly and waited it out. "It may not have quite sunk in for you yet, so let me be clear. What he has is *the* single most valuable thing *in the world.*" There was only the sound of the water and the wind in the lines. "Some of you are enterprising by nature. You may be considering what life would look like were you to acquire the information Master Helvaçi carries and sell it yourselves to the highest bidder. I find this thought entirely reasonable. However, I will remind you that every person on the crew is likely having the same thought as you are at this moment." Teveri tucked their hands behind their back and turned to pace along the rail of the poop deck, back and forth before the silent crew, their coat swinging around their legs when they turned to walk back across the width of the ship. "Here is what you need to know: Yes, Master Helvaçi has turned coat on Araşt."

Avra felt rather queasy. People and spooky, troublesome meat—would he be able to tell which one he was, or did he have to wait to be stabbed about it?

"Our new friend Julian will shortly be sitting down to study the papers and do what he can to simplify them. The plan that I propose to you is that upon reaching Scuttle Cove, we contact three or four of the best and most reputable fences—the ones with the very best and highest connections—and organize the sale of the papers through their contacts. I also propose that upon receiving the profits, we earmark one million altınlar to buy Captain Ueleari's *Nightingale* relics: the mizzen royal and the flag itself." Tev turned back to the crew, eyes blazing. "You think a million altınlar sounds like a lot of money. You doubt how much will be left over for yourselves, either to send to your families or to start a new life somewhere very far away from Scuttle Cove."

"A million is nothing," Oskar boomed at the crew.

The crew, nearly as one, turned their glances on Markefa, who was leaning against the starboard rail with her arms crossed. "Bosun?" someone quavered.

Markefa's smile didn't waver. "At a certain level of wealth, it all starts blurring together, 'specially if you've been used to living without much. You won't notice a difference between two hundred thousand or three for your share. Trust me, friends, you won't miss a million from a pot like this. All going well," she added pointedly.

"Of whatever is left over," Teveri continued, "one tenth will go to the ship's share for her upkeep. The rest will, naturally, be split evenly amongst all of us."

"And what if we'd rather have an extra hundred thousand

instead of the *Nightingale* relics?" shouted someone from the back of the crowd.

"That was Bald Baric," Avra shouted helpfully. "Captain, that was Bald Baric that said that!"

Groans ran through the crowd.

"Shut up, Avra!" Teveri howled at him. "I'd almost managed to fucking forget about you!"

"You were just talking about me, though!"

Teveri visibly seethed, even all the way at the other end of the boat, and collected themself. "Baric, you are also welcome to shut the fuck up. If we get a ridiculous pile of gold, we're buying Ueleari's *Nightingale* relics, and that's not up for negotiation."

Baric scoffed. "I feel like it ought to be! A million altınlar? Begging your *pardon,* Captain." Really a bad attitude on that man, there always had been. Sarcastic. Poor sense of humor. Selfish. The kind of build that meant he could have crushed Avra between finger and thumb if he'd felt like it—so basically he was exactly Avra's type, inasmuch as Avra had a type beyond "just so incredibly mean to him all the time." "Begging your *incandescent* pardon," Baric said, and this was dripping with mockery (which just went to show that Avra really had no taste at all), "but I don't give two wet shits about those fucking relics. I'd rather have the money." There were a few scattered murmurs of agreement, but only a very few—the rest were *thinking* about it.

"Did you not hear a single word Markefa just said?" Avra demanded. "*Gods,* Baric, you're so *stupid.*"

"Which brings me to my next point," Teveri said loudly as Baric turned and took one furious step toward the rope locker, "and back to the issue of enterprising minds. Some of you will be fantasizing about taking the prize off of Avra and pitching him overboard. I cannot blame you for this in the slightest. I would be very happy to partake in such fantasizing. In fact, I have already partaken in such fantasizing. I spent several hours last night thinking about how we could shackle him to some very large rocks and hurl him overboard the next time we're sailing across the Amariyani Pit. I thought about how once we have mastered the technique that the Shipbuilder's Guild has kept so jealously to themselves, we too will be able to sail wherever we want, whenever we want, and pay no heed to the season of serpents, and so we could sail right into the middle of a breeding swarm and dump him into it. I thought about—"

"Captain." Oskar coughed.

Teveri paused and cleared their throat. "Thank you, Oskar. Unfortunately, we cannot kill Avra, because Julian says he might need to ask him questions." The dubious murmurings immediately shifted. Several people said variations on *Oh! Well, in that case* in tones of understanding, cooperation, and a general willingness to accommodate Julian as long as he kept being hot in front of people. Avra began plotting his revenge. "For those of you who are still on the fence, I will remind you that he has part of the secret in that no-good, miserable little wretch of a skull. If we take what he has on him and toss him overboard now, we don't get any of the money. More to the point, if any of *you* become particularly enterprising and decide to kill him, steal the secret, and attempt to sell it yourselves once we get to Scuttle Cove, *it will be worthless.*

"That said, you are pirates, and I do not believe that any of you are particularly averse to a challenge. Some of you may be thinking that you could simply torture the missing part out of him. I sympathize with this impulse as well, and in any other circumstances I would insist on being informed of and invited to all Avra-torturing parties happening on board the ship. However . . ." They paused to sigh. "I do not want to risk endangering the value of the secret, and if we hurt him he will only find some way to fuck it up for us, either on purpose or by the witchiness of his luck."

"It's true," Avra yelled. "I'll definitely fuck it up."

"Therefore I will point out, to my great regret, that it is more prudent to wait on the matter of beating him up and leaving him for dead until we have a contract for the sale in hand. At which point, we can maybe just butcher him and sell the meat to Eel-face

Yusin as some weird kind of fish. Until then, I would present this idea to you all for your consideration: You do not know what anyone else on this crew is thinking. Look at the person next to you—they could be planning to *steal* your rightful share of the proceeds of this sale. They could be thinking that they are more deserving of it than you are, more entitled to it than you are. They could be, even now, scoffing to themselves in their head and planning to betray *you personally* for their own profit."

Avra's breath caught and he bit his lip on a little croon of glee. So *clever,* Teveri! Any other captain would have attempted to win control by keeping their information secret until the last possible moment in a vain attempt to avoid the loss of their prize.

But that wasn't Tev's style, and it wasn't Markefa's style either, brilliant chess player that she was. (It was, unfortunately, often very much Oskar's style. Oskar just wasn't a very creative man.) Easier to spread the work around and make protecting the secret *everybody's* problem.

Teveri looked out over the crew, the breeze tugging at the salt-and-sweat-grimed, stringy locks of their hair. "There are one hundred and sixteen people on this crew. There is one of you. Do you want to bet those odds? Do you want to bet that *you* can get to Avra, drag out of him what parts of the prize he carries in his head, and profit from it before any of the other hundred and fifteen people you're up against does the same?" They raised their eyebrow. "Do you want to make that gamble when you're up against *Avra Helvaçi's luck*?" The crew shifted and muttered variations on *fuck no.* "We put Helvaçi on a rowboat, with no water or food, and marooned him in the middle of the fucking ocean. Yet here he is, bright-eyed and bushy-tailed—do you really think you could get information out of him by force before his witch-luck ensured that you were *conveniently discovered in the act*?" They let that hang in the air for a moment and turned to Oskar. "What do we do with thieves, Oskar?"

"Cut off their hands and throw 'em overboard for the sharks and serpents, Captain!" Oskar barked.

"For the sharks and serpents indeed." Teveri looked back at the crew. "I suggest that it would be *much* better odds to gamble on ensuring that you and the rest of the crew all get your *fair* share." They smiled. "But I leave it to your conscience and your willingness to gamble against Avra Helvaçi. I'm sure that the rest of the crew will be *delighted* to discover a traitor or two and pitch them overboard. It will enrich all of us that little bit more."

"Not that we'll notice that increase either," Markefa drawled. "We'll all be rich as—well, as rich as the sultan of Araşt, eh?" A wave of laughter ran through the crew.

"Which brings me to the last point I wanted to make," Teveri said. "If we sell the most valuable thing in the world and Araşt finds out it was us specifically, they will probably go out of their way to make sure we all end up dead. I thought I'd bring that up in case anyone thought it was a serious problem."

The mutterings of the crew shifted toward distinctly baffled.

"Well," said Anxhela, a redheaded and wildly freckled woman with quite a few missing teeth and three missing fingers. "Probably more of a problem if they say we broke the Pact and decide to take revenge—no more Araşti food shipments to Scuttle Cove during the season doesn't make us look that good to the others . . ."

"The secret regards the technique of sailing past the serpents," Teveri said. "If we're able to make our own supply runs, then there's no danger of starving, no reason to rely on Araşt to feed us—"

"Oh!" said Anxhela. "Oh, fuck! Oh shit, Teveri! Well, fuck the Pact, then! Fuck it five times over—"

"I have a stupid question," Ellat called from directly above Avra, presumably perched on the edge of the fo'c'sle. "Don't laugh at me for asking, though."

"Depends on how stupid it is," Markefa called back. "More specifically, depends on how much you ought to know better already."

"Don't laugh at him," Avra wailed. "Promise. He's an infant, he is a tiny baby, he is trying to *learn*."

"Shut up, Avra," said Tev. "Ellat, speak."

"If we say fuck the Pact," Ellat said, in the tones of someone working through a suspiciously simple math problem for the fifth time and still second-guessing the answer they'd come to, "and Araşt stops sending food to Scuttle Cove during the serpent season, then . . . we'd be allowed to go after their ships, right? Like in the old days?"

The entire crew inhaled sharply and with an air of dawning, horny wonder. Teveri wobbled a little on their feet as if they had not fully considered this possibility.

"Ellat," Markefa said seriously. "Auntie Markefa is so proud of you. Captain is also extremely proud of you."

"Yes, Ellat—" Teveri's voice cracked a little. They cleared their throat. "Yes, Ellat, if there is no longer a Pact, then there is no longer any legal reason why we can't be pirates on or near Araşti vessels."

"So the only actual *risk* here is that we *might* die in a blood-soaked blaze of glory and they'd sing songs about us in Scuttle Cove for the next thousand years?" Anxhela said. "That's the only catch?"

"Not that big of a catch when you balance it against everything else," said Nonso, whose rich buttery voice was unmistakable. He was the only one on the crew besides Julian who was making significant contributions to the improvement of the scenery: A tall, slender man with obsidian-black skin and long braids, the lower half of which he'd dyed green sometime since Avra had been marooned in a rowboat and left for dead. He'd once been a professional dancer in the court of the king of N'gaka, Avra had found out, because *obviously* he'd made conversation with the crew's token hot one by asking how Nonso had come to a life of piracy. "A score that fucking big, and then we die like heroes? So long as we get the chance to *spend* some of it first, that sounds pretty good to me. We've all had Death come knocking at the door at least once already. Except Ellat Goodquestion."

"Do *not* name me that," Ellat snapped.

"Sounds like we don't need to take a vote on anything," Teveri said. "Thank you for your attention, you're dismissed!"

"Do I get to come out now?" Avra yelled.

"No," Teveri yelled back. "Shut up."

"Tev! Teveri!" he wailed in his best sad-little-creature voice. "Captain!"

If there was one strength Avra had besides his hypothetical luck, it was that he never got tired of himself.

He did not want to be shut in the rope locker anymore, and besides that, he still had to take vengeance for the crew being willing to accommodate Julian's unreasonable requests just because he was gorgeous, when with Avra they only stood back and watched Teveri kick moldy bread at him.

He therefore spent the next half hour screeching, "Captain," at intervals of several seconds. Occasionally he varied this with the occasional "Captain, please!"

Oskar, as usual, was the first to crack. "Captain, I'm about to throw him overboard, and *to hell with the prize money.*"

"What if," said Ellat, clearly attempting to continue his streak of having good ideas, "we put him in a rowboat again, but we tie a long line to it and sort of tow him behind us."

"No," said Teveri through gritted teeth. "Then he'd be upwind and we'd still be able to hear him."

"Oh," said Ellat. "And if his luck made the rope snap, that wouldn't be good."

"No, it would not, Master Ellat."

"Captain," Avra screeched, and continued screeching it until Oskar had a full-scale mental break, burst into tears, charged toward the rope locker like a raging bull, and had to be wrestled onto the deck before he killed Avra. Avra regarded the pile of Oskar and crew through the slats in the bulkhead with mild perturbation, then screeched, "Captain!"

"Oskar! Get ahold of yourself, man!" said Nonso. "Think of the money!"

"Captain," Avra screeched. Oskar roared and nearly thrashed off everyone pinning him down.

"Captain," said Nonso, shouting over his shoulder at Teveri. "Do you propose to keep Helvaçi locked up and caterwauling all the way to Scuttle Cove?"

"He'll lose his voice eventually," Teveri snapped.

"Captain," Avra screeched, extra annoyingly.

"This is an unsustainable situation," said Nonso, as two more people came to help pin down Oskar. "Ought we take this to a vote?"

"It's *my ship*," Teveri said tightly. "Mine by *right*—"

"And *this*," Nonso said, gesturing to the wriggling, weeping Oskar, "is *your* first mate, who is begging for any solution more tolerable than the current one!"

"Captain," Avra screeched, helpfully right on cue.

"We could gag him," offered one of the others—that new one, the one Avra hadn't met.

"He'd chew through it," someone else replied.

"Or," said Nonso, "we just let him go free and put him to work."

"You remember the last time he got up in the rigging and decided to have a tantrum?" That was Beng Choon, sitting on Oskar's left leg. "How many hours did we spend trying to get him down?"

"He did the same thing on the captain's wardrobe yesterday," Oskar grunted. Beng Choon gave an exasperated there-you-have-it gesture.

"Captain," Avra screeched.

"Plenty of jobs on deck," Nonso said. "Plenty of eyes to watch him and keep him from sticking his fingers into any mischief. And—"

"Captain," Avra screeched.

"—even chatter has to be better than this racket."

"Captain!!" Avra screeched.

"I'm not going to reward this behavior," Teveri said incredulously. "He'll just be worse next time! He promised to be, and I quote, 'a good and sweet little Avra'!"

"In his defense, he hadn't *done* anything yet to warrant getting locked up. As far as I know," said Beng Choon. Avra vaguely recalled that he'd been some kind of apprentice lawyer as a teenager in Map Sut, before he'd thrown it all away to rob his patron blind and stow away on a pirate ship. "Annoying the captain doesn't count. He could do that just by breathing."

"Cap—" Avra screeched, but he was interrupted by a bloodcurdling scream from Oskar. The pirates holding him down froze and looked down at him, but after that one sharp scream, he fell silent again and didn't seem hurt. There were a few seconds of emptiness, just the wind and rigging and the ever-present sound of the sea.

Avra drew breath. "Captai—"

Oskar screamed again.

"This is even less of a sustainable situation," said Nonso.

"Cap—"

Oskar screamed over him.

Avra waited until he fell silent, then quickly screeched, "Captain!"

Oskar screamed, a tenth of a second too late.

"Love this so much," said Beng Choon.

"See, your problem is that he has a short attention span," said Anxhela, tossing the long ends of her kerchief over her shoulder and climbing off Oskar, who was now lying stony silent and still except for the occasional sobbing breath. "He only responds to short-term reward." She crossed over to the rope locker and peered through the slats at Avra. "If you shut up, I'll let you look at my tits later."

Avra considered this. "Later" could have so many different meanings, for one thing. For another, Anxhela's tits were nice enough, but Avra had seen a lot of tits in his life on all sorts of people and had sometimes even been allowed to touch them or nuzzle his face in between them. The prospect of merely *seeing* them wasn't particularly enticing.

"Captain!" Avra screeched. (Oskar screamed.) "Anxhela is sexually harassing me!"

"Anxhela, leave him alone," Teveri said peevishly.

She turned around with her hands on her hips. "Well, what if we say we'll let him pick the next couple work songs?"

"Ooh," said Avra. Anxhela grinned at him over her shoulder.

Teveri glowered.

"Four songs and you let me out," Avra said. "That is the price to buy my silence."

"That sounds so incredibly reasonable to me," said Anxhela. "Captain?"

"Captain," Avra screeched, and this time he tried to harmonize when Oskar screamed.

Teveri swore and slammed their hand against the helm. "Fuck! Fine! Fucking pillars of the fucking sky, fuck, fine!"

Avra composed his face into innocence as Anxhela unlatched the door and swung it open for him. "Thanks, ma'am. Sorry for tattling to Captain." He batted his eyes at her. "Can I let you know next time I'm in the mood to be sexually harassed?"

She snorted and let him out on deck. "You can if you like, but it won't do you any good past flirting. Got somebody these days."

"Fair, fair." Avra edged around Oskar, who was taking several deep breaths and muttering that he'd be fine now, and moseyed down the length of the ship toward the helm. He froze at one warning finger from Teveri. "Captain?" he said, all innocence.

(Oskar, behind him, made an uncharacteristically high-pitched noise of dismay. "Peace," Nonso said firmly. "Oskar. *Peace.*")

"You're not permitted aft of the mainmast. Nonso!"

"Aye?"

"Since you're so concerned with a *sustainable situation*, you can supervise Avra."

Avra turned over his shoulder and gave Nonso his very best, most ravishing smile.

Nonso, who was now scowling, did a small double take and seemed puzzled. "Ah . . . Are you all right?"

"Splendid," Avra chirped. "I'll be exquisitely well-behaved. Has anyone ever told you that you have amazing bone structure?"

"Captain, I believe Avra Helvaçi is sexually harassing m—"

"If anyone says the word captain *again in the next hour, I'm going to have you hung by your ankles from the yardarm."*

Oskar, who had just collected himself, burst into tears again and attempted to lead the crew in a rousing round of cheers. Avra participated enthusiastically, but he was the only one.

When they were done, Tev leaned their elbow on the wheel and pinched the bridge of their nose.

"Tev," Avra wheedled. "Remember what the spooky dentist said."

Teveri raised their head and looked up into the rigging with an odd expression.

Avra peered up as well. He didn't see anything of note beyond those members of the crew working the rigging. "Whatcha looking for?"

"Their patience, probably," Nonso muttered.

Teveri took a deep breath. "Nonso, go down into the hold and fetch a couple bales of that—that *fancy straw.*"

"Aye, sure," said Nonso warily. "What for, can I ask?"

"I want it all braided so we can sell it to the people making fancy hats out of it."

"Why? We've got those papers to sell."

"Do you want to put all your eggs into a basket carried by Avra Helvaçi? It's a *backup plan*. More importantly, it will keep his horrible little hands busy."

Avra gasped. "Tev! Aw, Tev! That sounds great, I would love to braid so much straw for you! I can do fancy braids, you know, they teach you that sort of thing when you go to school at the Araşti civil service academy! I know *all kinds* of braids."

"Ah, Cap—Teveri," Nonso said, clearing his throat pointedly. "*I* don't have to braid straw, do I?"

"I should make you braid straw for coming out onto my deck with all your fucking bullshit about *sustainable situations,*" Teveri snapped. "But unfortunately you're capable of *useful, competent* things."

Avra looked suspiciously back and forth between Teveri and . . . the unspeakable handsomeness of Nonso's bone structure. He hurriedly arranged himself alluringly against the railing and gave a casual toss of his hair. "Wow, huge compliment. Enormous," he said, batting his eyes. "Maybe you're thinking Teveri's compliments are the biggest you've ever seen. I can guarantee you that mine are bigger—"

"*Avra, shut up. Nonso, the straw.*" Teveri gripped the wheel with both hands until their brown knuckles went pale. They were definitely grinding their teeth now, because they said through a clenched grimace, "*And we're all going to try to get through this with our so-called friendships and sanity intact until we can fuck Araşt over and die in a blaze of glory.*"

Captain's Log

Day 4, 6th month, 199th yr Mahisti Dyn.

Continuing course back to Scuttle Cove; wind very good, weather fair. Slept like shit.

Crew appropriately threatened w/ prisoner's dilemma. Avra fortunately (regrettably???) not killed in the night. Forced to let him out of the rope locker, forced moreover to let him sing the next few shanties, gods have mercy on our souls. Barely keeping all this shit together as it is. Considering the benefits of being eaten by sea serpents.

Julian calmly getting work done. Incredibly attractive quality. Nice change from A. who insists on being just the worst creature alive.

6

10. The Midwife

Possibility of a pregnancy, often metaphorical. May signify someone calm and experienced, an old hand at the current difficult task. Harbinger of a great reward to come. Potentially a sign that things may need to be helped along before there is progress.

(Reversed: Sometimes signifies small personal tragedies; a new and joyful prospect unfortunately comes to nothing. Alternatively, an opportunity to take control of fate and make informed choices about the future.)

The fancy straw had to be soaked in water to make it pliable enough to braid, and Avra quickly made the interesting discovery that using regular seawater caused the bright golden color to leach out and leave the straw a rather pretty shade of silver.

It made Teveri scowl ferociously, call for Markefa, and engage in an intense debate with her about whether they could spare a single bucket of the drinking water for this project.

Avra was tucked cozily into a corner by the railing with his bucket, sheltered from the wind as much as possible but still surrounded by loose golden straw gradually spreading all over the deck. He beamed up at Tev and Markefa as they came across to inspect what disasters he was wreaking with the straw. He had chosen to sit *exactly* on the line of the mainmast. When he folded his legs, tailor style, the edge of one knee just barely poked over the invisible boundary of where he wasn't allowed to go. Teveri had not noticed yet.

Avra proudly held up his garlands of braid—toward the beginning, it was clumsily done, spiky with broken fragments of brittle golden straw. Then, as the straw soaked longer, the braid became a great deal neater. Following the line through the couple hours of work, the color shift became gradually more evident—first, the gold became paler and paler, until it was an almost pearly white. The section Avra was working now had reached the color of fresh-polished silver, nearly the same color as the glittering sail of *Nightingale* on their mainmast.

"Do you think *that's* going to sell?" Teveri said to Markefa, who examined it dubiously.

"I can do a fancier braid, maybe," Avra offered.

Markefa looked dubious. "Do we know what color the fancy hats are supposed to be?"

"Nope," Avra said cheerfully.

"Feels like we'd better find out that information before we go and do stuff to our raw materials that might make it all useless, Captain."

Tev turned their gaze on Avra. "Right. Leave off, then."

Avra pouted. "But it looks nice! I'd buy a hat made of this!"

"Good for you, I don't give a shit! I don't want you spoiling any more of it!"

"I'll just excuse myself, then," Markefa said, edging away.

Avra shook his garlands more vigorously. "It's pretty!"

"I don't care how pretty it is!"

"We have a whole hold full of straw! You can't think I'll get through enough of it all by myself to make a difference!"

"Perhaps not, but"—Teveri gestured furiously around the deck at the slowly spreading pool of scattered straw—"I think we can count on half of it blowing overboard!"

Avra clutched his bucket of salt water close to his body and frantically scrabbled to gather fistfuls of straw from the deck and stuff it in. Teveri cursed and tried to wrestle the bucket away from him. "No! No! No, Tev! I'm doing it! I'm making fancy braid for you!" They were indisputably stronger than him and wrenched the bucket out of his grasp and dumped it over the side. "No!" he shrieked, clinging to their leg.

"Let go!"

Avra did so, but only because he still had all his garlands of straw—he stuffed them hurriedly down the front of his kaftan, and wrapping his arms around it, glared at Teveri. "This is mine, then! I made it!"

"You look pregnant."

Avra simpered up at them. "Good thing Araşt has matrilineal inheritance laws, hm? It's doubly mine, and I don't have to share claim on it with anybody. Are you hoping that I'll name you the father? I don't even know who the father is."

Teveri rolled their eyes hugely, kicked Avra's knee, and snarled, "No coming aft of the mainmast, I said." They turned on their heel and stalked off. "Ellat! Get a broom and sweep all this mess up!"

Avra rubbed his knee and scooted one inch forward of the mast, glaring mulishly at Teveri's back as they were intercepted at the steps up to the quarterdeck by the navigator, Nagasani.

Avra noticed that the garlands of straw braids stuffed down his front were, firstly, terribly itchy and, secondly, still quite damp, and began to extricate himself. If Teveri had been watching—they were *decidedly* not—he could have at least contrived to get himself hopelessly and pathetically entangled. There wasn't much point in it if they weren't paying attention to him, was there?

They hadn't been paying much attention to him at all since he'd come aboard. They hadn't even seemed to *notice* that nice little touch of him being hog-tied when he'd been thrown at their feet.

Hardly *anyone* was paying attention to him. They all liked Julian better, even though he was a fake monk, and had no good explanation for being on a pirate ship, and went around pulling hair and *purring* at people.

After a moment of listening to Nagasani's terrifying star-math, Teveri shouted an adjustment to their course and strode up to take the helm. Oskar went to the mainmast and once again clanged the ship's bell. "All hands!" he bellowed. "All hands to the braces! Tacking leeward!"

All at once there was a flurry of action—Avra more hastily pulled the itchy straw braids out of his kaftan and, as soon as he was free, flung himself toward the capstan and scrambled atop it. "I get to pick the songs!" he shouted over the noise of boots and the clamor of preparations.

He crouched on top of the capstan and grinned toward the helm. His promise to be a good and sweet little Avra henceforth floated across his mind, but that did not outweigh the fact that Tev had kicked his knee and taken away all his straw, and had not laughed at *any* of his jokes so far, and slammed doors in his face, and thought Julian was prettier than he was—which was objectively true, but was Julian as *exciting* as Avra was?

Avra mentally cracked his knuckles and wriggled in anticipation.

Markefa strode up and flung her arm around his shoulder. "Hello, friend."

"I get to sing the song," Avra said, his grin widening. He kept his eyes fixed on Teveri.

"I *heard* about that," Markefa said. "You definitely do get to sing the song. That was the deal for not screaming and carrying on, right? Nobody would dare to go back on that deal."

"I," he said with great relish, "am going to annoy Teveri."

"Hm! You know, I had a feeling you were going to say something like that. Saw you grinning like a shark and thought I'd come over here—"

"Mosey."

"Yep, that I'd mosey right on over here and see what my very best friend Avra was up to, looking like a feral little sea wretch with straw in his hair and a weird expression. Annoying Teveri, just as I thought."

"It's supposed to be a five-minute job," Avra said, finally taking his eyes off Teveri and smiling beatifically at Markefa beside him. "I'm going to make this take at least half an hour."

She nodded, smiling back. "You know, this was the thing I moseyed over to talk about."

"I am going to cause problems," he said, smiling and nodding back. "Then Teveri will pay attention to me."

"Well, probably they'll yell at you."

"That's what I said. They'll pay attention to me, with yelling."

"I was wondering something earlier," Markefa said, giving him a companionable little squeeze. "Sort of a thought experiment. Would you rather have one large cake or, say, one hundred small cakes?"

Avra paused. He thought deeply about this.

"Because when you look at it one way," Markefa continued, "you could get paid one big cake's worth of yelling attention from Teveri—"

"I love cake."

"*Or, or* . . . You could do a really fantastic job with the shanties, and maybe scuttle around to drape yourself and your luck on whatever seems most useful. And then," she said, lowering her voice conspiratorially, "everyone on the whole crew would be a little bit happy with you. Some of 'em might clap you on the back, or say, 'Hey, good job, Avra,' or invite you to sit with them at meals. A hundred small cakes' worth of attention, doled out over days and days and *days* . . ."

"Yes, but here's the problem, you see, Markefa—if I do that, then Teveri will ignore me. When I am good, they ignore me and kick my knee and throw bread at me even when I'm getting bullied by the possums in the alley." He nodded. "Causing problems works a lot better, you see."

Markefa seized Ellat's arm as he was rushing by and yanked him over. "What about the opportunity to be a role model for kids?" Avra regarded Ellat thoughtfully; Ellat tried to wriggle free; Markefa tightened her grip. "Look at this baby boy. Look at this little infant child."

"He's extremely small," Avra agreed.

"I'm *seventeen,*" Ellat snapped.

"Teeny baby, still wet," Avra said.

"He wants to be a poet when he grows up," Markefa said.

"Um, no, I don't," said Ellat.

"Hear that? He thinks that everybody yells at poets," Markefa said, looking intensely into Avra's eyes. "He's about to give up on his dreams."

"Oh no," said Avra.

"Don't you want to show him the sort of marvelous admiration a poet can command from a happy audience?"

"You're cajoling me," Avra said, holding eye contact with her. "I am being *managed.*"

"Am I?"

"You want me to not cause problems. But you see, Markefa, I have decided to cause problems."

She released Ellat and leaned in close again. "What if you could have one hundred small cakes *and* one big angry cake from Teveri?"

Avra considered this. "Hmm."

"Isn't it true that sometimes Teveri is mad at you for doing a *good* job?"

"Hm. Yes."

"Because those are the times when they're expecting you to cause problems, right? And then they're ever so annoyed that you surprised them again."

"I did a good job with the straw," Avra said, pointing to the straw by the railing, which someone had kicked aside into a pile.

"Yes, and they were so irritated about it, weren't they?"

"Yes."

"So now they're expecting you to cause problems."

Avra mulled on this.

"Think of how irritated they would be if you did such a good job that *everyone* was really nice to you. They'd *hate* that, no?"

"They *would* hate that," Avra agreed, still transfixed in her gaze. "Yes. Yes. I will cause . . . *different* problems."

Markefa tapped the side of her nose and winked at him. "Just like a chess game. Causing problems *strategically.*"

"Yes. Strategically. Thank you, Markefa."

"Thank *you,* Avra. This was a good game."

"Hm?" he said absently, but she'd already gone off to the team at one of the whatsits that went up to the thingy. Ropes—or lines, rather. These ones went up to the yardarms—or, as Avra sometimes liked to think of them, the sticky-outy bits.

He didn't really need to know the names of anything to know the beat of the shanties the crew liked to sing at each step of executing a maneuver with the ship.

Markefa *had* been managing him, of course, this was a fact he was readily aware of. She didn't want to spend half an hour on tacking; she probably didn't want to deal with Teveri in a worse mood than they already were, either.

It was a little game they played, much like their chess games. Markefa was smarter than him and generally seemed entertained about the prospect of emotionally manipulating him for the benefit of the crew. She got the satisfaction of playing against an opponent who was just good enough to be a challenge, but not good enough to ever beat her, and he got the fun of squirming about until she argued him out of whatever he was going to do, whereupon he got to figure out how to change the rules of the game and win in his own way.

Then they both won, and that was nice.

He had reflected from time to time that Markefa was, arguably, his very best friend.

He had a few minutes to prepare while the crew got themselves sorted out and ready to pull the thingies to rotate the whatsits, et cetera, so he used the tune of a shanty everyone knew, "Twelve Days to Amariyan," and started mentally composing the story of a sad little cat half-drowned in the rain.

The crew eyed him suspiciously. Oskar heaved a huge sigh and said, "Ready, Helvaçi?"

"Yep," said Avra. "I have a new one. It's called 'The Wettest Pussy in the World.'"

A titter ran through the crew. Ellat, because he was seventeen, was struck by a fit of helpless giggles and had to sit down.

Oskar squinted at Avra suspiciously. Avra smiled back at him. "Right," said Oskar, and raised his voice to call the first instructions.

It was a long-haul shanty, and thus structured as a call-and-response. The call, which Avra sang, was about the titular sad little cat in the rain and the various unfortunate adventures that befell her as she grew increasingly moist. The response, which the crew was supposed to join in on, was "Meow MEOW meow *meow* meow MEOW."

The whole affair took perhaps fifteen minutes longer than it should have. Avra sang cheerily of the travails befalling the wettest pussy in the world, and the crew gradually fractured into hysterics at each iteration of the chorus.

By the time they'd finished, nearly everyone had either turned a funny color or had tears streaming down their face. Ellat was flat on the deck, possibly dying. When Oskar finally cried, "Avast hauling!" the bracers were tied off with shaky hands while several people dissolved into laughter so violent they had to be sick over the side.

Avra kicked his heels and beamed around at the crew.

Oskar, after a moment of contemplative silence, said, "Oh. It's about woman parts."

This did not help the state of the crew's composure.

Teveri, when Avra dared one smug glance up at the helm, was banging their head gently against the wheel.

7

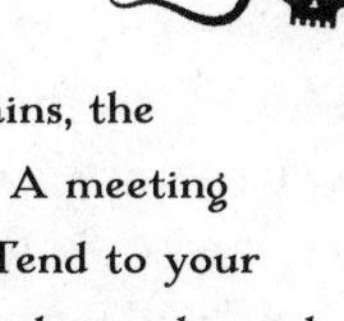

54. The Marketplace

Business dealings, striking bargains, the exchange of information or gossip. A meeting of many people and many minds. Tend to your relationships with acquaintances and casual social connections; the more people you know, the better off you'll be.

(Reversed: Beware those who would seek to profit from your ignorance. A crowd of one hundred possesses at least one hundred and one opinions.)

By the time they reached the final approach to the Isles of Lost Souls, Avra and Teveri had come to something of a strained detente.

This was necessary: Julian spent a portion of each day deciphering the alchemical notation in the captain's cabin, which meant Teveri and Avra both had to be there to supervise Julian with the papers and each other. Julian had eventually politely explained that it was difficult for him to focus on the work he had been ordered to do if the two of them were squabbling.

The first day or two, Teveri had ground their teeth and gripped the arms of their throne and glared, and Avra had entertained himself by playing staring contests with them that they didn't know about. When he got bored of that, he'd made faces at them to see how darkly they would scowl. When he got bored of *that,* he'd lounged on the sea chest, batted his eyes, and sucked lavishly on his own fingers until Teveri's eye twitched. He was almost certain that Julian had noticed this in his peripheral vision, but Julian had done nothing more than smile mildly to himself and continue working, the scratching of his pen or scrape of chalk on slate the only sound besides the occasional slurp from Avra.

Teveri, in a low-down dirty move that offended Avra to the depths of his soul, eventually withdrew their attention entirely, *even the glaring*, and sat there writing in their log, consulting maps to review Nagasani's navigation, or, most insultingly of all, *reading a book*. Yes, it was *The Running Sun*'s *Book of Wrecks*, in preparation for the Turtle Shallows and the ghosts they would encounter there, but books were books.

Avra had had no choice but to lower himself to the same dishonorable petty tactics. He got out his deck of Heralds and pretended to play solitaire while having silent gossip sessions with the cards about Teveri, Julian, or other members of the crew.

He kept drawing The Bower, and he was starting to get both suspicious and vaguely horny about it.

He was just pursing his lips at the seventh time he'd drawn The Bower in the last forty-five minutes, *even though* he'd shuffled the shit out of the deck, when a knock came at the door and Nagasani stuck her head in. "Captain, you asked me to let you know when we're about an hour off from the Turtle Shallows."

"Thanks," Teveri said, closing the *Book of Wrecks* with a snap. "Call the all-hands, please. You're ready?"

"Aye, and the others."

Avra had frozen in place, staring at The Bower. He cleared his throat and said nervously, "Um, hm, ma'am, what's that sex thingy you have?"

"Sextant," Nagasani said instantly.

Avra shut his eyes and took a deep breath. "I'm going to be very brave and consent to have it used upon my person."

"A sextant is a fancy ruler, Avra," she said without batting an eye. "Before you ask: No, not for spanking. For stars."

Avra cracked open one eye and looked down at The Bower. "Are you sure?"

"It's a precision instrument. Using it for spanking would not be advisable if I wanted it to continue being precise, which I do. Also, it's made of a couple pounds of solid brass."

"Oh," said Avra, relaxing. "It's that thingy with the spyglass on top?"

"That's the one."

Avra risked a glance at Teveri, who had laced their fingers together on their knee and was looking at him with an absolutely blank expression of transcendent patience. Julian was still working, but he was smiling in that way that meant he thought Avra was being funny on purpose.

Avra glanced down at The Bower. "Hm."

"Might not be about me, you know!" Nagasani said cheerfully, and shut the door.

"Why don't you know what a sextant is?" Teveri asked, in a terrifyingly normal voice that immediately set Avra on edge.

"I don't know everything about everything," he said, scrambling his cards into a pile. "Leave me alone."

Teveri, *terrifyingly,* did so. They turned to Julian and said, "You can pack up for the day. All-hands includes yours. Someone explained to you, I hope?"

"About the approach?" Julian sat back and wiped ink from the nib of the pen with a spare scrap of paper. "I was told, and I quote, 'There are these spirits or ghosts or whatever you want to call 'em,'" he said, in a delightfully good imitation of Oskar's accent, "'but it's mostly boring, just make sure you've got your smalls on backward today.' End quote."

"If you wear smalls," Avra said. "I don't."

"That's Oskar's own superstition," Teveri said, still alarmingly calm. "He seems to believe that ghosts wish to steal or curse people's genitals. You may follow this belief or not, as you wish. I don't know where he picked it up."

"Probably from when I told him about that time that one of

the ghosts tried to feel me up," Avra said. "The first time I went through, remember? When I gibbered on you about it afterward? And made you roleplay a ghost so it'd be a sexy memory and I wouldn't have nightmares?"

Teveri's eye twitched slightly, but that was the only reaction. "Ah."

Avra turned on Julian. "If a ghost shows up saying 'Hey gorgeous, I haven't seen you around, first time here?' just say no. She's into virgins and she's got weird bony fingers." He paused. "Someone should make sure Ellat's got his smalls on backward."

"Ellat confided in me a few days ago that he fooled around with someone in one of the last ports," Julian said, shutting the lid of the inkpot.

"WHAT?" Avra shrieked, fumbling his Heralds. The deck hit the deck, scattering cards everywhere.

"Ah. Markefa's going to kick his ass," Teveri said, terrifyingly, *terrifyingly* even.

"He's a tiny wet baby, what's he doing *fooling around* with people! *Who?*"

"I don't know and I didn't ask," said Julian.

"How did this come up?" said Teveri.

"He approached me when I was on watch the other night and said, 'Monks keep secrets really well, yeah? I'm going to tell you a secret,' and then he told me." Julian packed away the writing supplies in the drawer of the desk and added innocently, "He neither asked me directly to keep it a secret nor gave me a chance to agree as to whether or not monks do keep secrets well, nor to explain that in fact my order is technically founded on the philosophy that the sharing of information freely is an act of piety. He merely told me his secret, seemed very proud when I offered my congratulations, and left."

"Very good," Teveri said. "Thank you for this information."

Julian gave them both a smile of saintly benevolence as he stood. "I hope you make good use of it."

Avra scrabbled the papers together as Julian departed, rolled them up into a scroll, and stuck them into a leather tube that one of the crew had made to keep them safe. He eyed Teveri suspiciously. They watched him with no expression whatsoever.

He scrabbled his cards together as well, fumbled them, saw The Bower for the eighth time as it fell out of his hands again, and scrabbled it back into his deck. "I'll just leave now."

"A moment," Teveri said. They folded their hands and placed them on the desk, looking at Avra with that terrifying, *spooky* nothing expression.

"Yeees?" said Avra, slightly turned on.

"What are your plans for the final approach?"

"Ah. Well. Uh. Thought I'd. Help out. As usual. I'm a very helpful sort of person, Tev. You should know this about me by now."

"Hm," said Teveri, with a series of small, slow, thoughtful nods that seemed to go on rather longer than was seemly.

When Teveri said nothing else, Avra giggled nervously. "Yep . . . Just. On deck. Helping. Chatting with ghosts. Uh. That sort of. Whatsits. Thing. That sort of thing."

"I see."

"Unless I get bored," he said, slightly high-pitched. "Then I might just go below and have a nap."

"Like all the other times," Teveri said, *terrifyingly terrifyingly terrifyingly* calm. "Like every other time we've crossed the turtles and you got bored in the middle and wandered off for a nap."

"Well, you know," Avra said, clutching his little rucksack close. "I get sleepy when we have to drop anchor and stop for low tide."

"Hm," said Teveri again, with another unsettling series of slow, small nods.

"Are you all right?" Avra asked in a squeak.

"Do I seem not all right?"

"Ah—just weird and calm. Are you possessed? Did the haunted throne finally get the better of you?"

"No," said Teveri calmly. "I have simply reached a decision and made my peace with it."

"Well, it's terrifying," Avra said. "And also it's turning me on. Those are unrelated."

"No, they're not," said Teveri calmly.

"No, they're not," Avra said, panicking.

"It is not ideal when you nap," said Teveri calmly. "We get a much more tedious array of ghosts when you nap."

"Well, I've never met any of them."

"Yes. Because you are napping." Another series of slow nods. "Some of them comment specifically on the fact that they wouldn't have shown up if you were awake."

Avra hummed a high-pitched little note of alarm in his throat. "Yes, well, I get sleepy, so . . ."

"Yes, you do get sleepy," said Teveri calmly. "Which is why I have decided that if you do a decent job and don't nap through the second half, I will fuck you when we get to Scuttle Cove."

Avra choked on his own spit and spent several moments hacking his lungs up. Teveri watched him impassively. When Avra was able to compose himself, he cleared his throat and attempted to lounge in a way that was beguiling but not too invested. "That's all I have to do?" Avra hiccuped. "Just be helpful and refrain from napping?"

Slow, calm nods. Teveri added tonelessly, "I expect the quality of the sex will depend on how good of a job you do."

"Of course," Avra said, and hiccuped again. "Wouldn't—*hic*—expect anything less. Ha. Haha. *Hic.* Sorry. Ah, um, you're just going to back out of it, though, right? You're just going to decide I didn't do a good job, or—or something. Or you'll tell me I hallucinated this whole exchange."

"You are not hallucinating this."

"Oh fuc—*hic*—uck." He laughed nervously. "Really? Really really?"

"Really really."

Avra panicked. "What are you going to swear it on?"

Teveri gave him a slow, calm blink. "Need I swear it on anything?"

"Yes! Yes, absolutely! *Hic!* Witnesses! Swear it in front of—um—Julian. He's a monk, monks are good at swearing things. *Hic.* I'm not making an Ellat mistake, you know. Julian swore his own thing about not fucking anyone, so he'll definitely be down to be a witness for your thing about how you'll definitely for sure fuck me and all I have to do is not nap!"

"And do a decent job."

Avra hiccuped and said deliriously, "The quality of my work impacts the quality of the sex, not the existence of the sex! That's what you said! *Hic!* This is why I need a witness!"

Teveri shrugged one shoulder, terrifyingly calm. "Fine. Call Brother Julian back in."

"I—*hic*—will! I will!" Avra said, scrambling for the door.

Captain's Log

Day 13, 6th month, 199th yr Mahisti Dyn.

Reached final approach to IOLS. Thankfully (regrettably??) not eaten by sea serpents.

Going to have to sleep with Avra again. Keeps sitting there silently—infuriating of him, knows I like that. Has tricked me into viewing him as fuckable by intentionally *being tolerable for more than ten minutes.* Intentionally. *I resent this. He knows what he's doing.*

Avra hiccuped, staring wide-eyed out beyond the prow. The night was very, very dark, dark enough that it seemed to swallow up the lamplight only a foot beyond the railing, despite the fact that they'd lit enough lanterns all over the ship that the stars were dimmed out, which Nagasani always sighed about—but it was necessary. They needed to be *seen*.

There was no other light—the moons had waned, and there was

only a sliver of Beyaz visible, the brighter of the two, low on the horizon.

Avra hiccuped.

"Why can't we go through during the day?" whispered Ellat, who was squeezed up next to him at the prow, ostensibly to keep watch from the fo'c'sle.

"Ghosts," said Avra, slightly manic. He was going to do a good job. He was going to do such a good job. "Turtles. Reefs. Uh, whatcha—*hic*—callit. Will-o'-the-wisps."

Footsteps on the steps up to the fo'c'sle, and Julian murmured, "Coffee?"

"Yes," Avra said, reaching back without tearing his eyes away from the featureless dark. "Yes, give. Give me all the coffee. No naps. I'm doing a good job."

"I suspected as much," said Julian, pressing a warm mug into his hands. Avra slurped it without blinking. "Have you crossed the Turtle Shallows many times, Avra?"

"Wonder if that's a rude question," Avra said. "Like asking how someone became a pirate. Or maybe a spy question. I don't have time for your espionage, Julian, I'm *busy*."

"Second time for me," said Ellat.

"Have you seen any of the turtles before?" Julian said. "I was told they were very large, and I've kept a sharp eye out, but I haven't been so lucky yet."

"You've never seen a turtle before?" asked Ellat with snotty adolescent skepticism. "*Ever?*"

"No, I have. Normal ones, though, not the large ones here."

"These ones are normal."

"Kid was born in Scuttle Cove," said Avra. "Has no concept of a normal turtle. Thinks the natural size for a turtle to be is *really fucking big*. Island-sized."

"*Beg pardon?*" said Julian.

"Turtles," said Avra insistently, staring harder into the dark. "Huge fuckoff turtles. Sometimes, turtles on top of turtles. Why?

Who knows. Presumably they fuck. Old shipwrecks and ghosts on top, then reefs, and then turtles all the way down."

There was a pause. "I think I have fundamentally misunderstood the scale of the turtles," said Julian. "On the voyage out, Ellat, all those reefs and islands we saw at low tide were the turtles?"

"Yeah, obviously? Or the stuff on top of their shells, technically."

"Ah," said Julian. "When I was told about large turtles, I was envisioning them to be the size of rowboats."

"Oh," said Ellat blankly. "You mean babies?"

Avra hiccuped. "*Shush.*"

౿

A long, near-silent hour later, Avra saw the first eerie ghost-light flicker above the lapping waves. "Light ho!" he screeched.

"Mark!" Teveri shouted, and there was a flurry of noise on the deck behind Avra. He didn't have to look behind him to see what was happening: Nagasani would be flipping one of her hourglasses and reading the time off the stars, scrambling through her spooky math while Markefa stood by with the *Book of Wrecks* ready to flip through and find which one the light signaled—

"They walk in a circle, you know," Avra said absently to whoever was still standing nearby.

"The . . . turtles?" said Julian.

"Like planets, Nagasani says. Orbiting the Isles." He twirled a finger in the air. "Like a wheel. Big wheel of haunted turtles."

"Why?"

Avra considered this deeply. "Why do turtles do things? You have struck upon one of life's conundrums, Julian. Very sexy of you."

Nagasani must have been making progress, because Markefa shouted, "Avra, what color?"

Avra squinted at the light. "Sort of greenish?" he called back. "Pale greenish? Might be the water, though."

"Is it the *Gallant*?"

"Julian. If you would reach into my little rucksack—it's at my feet—and get out my Heralds." He held out his hand, and a moment later, Julian pressed the deck into his hands. Avra shuffled without looking away from the light or blinking, drew a card, holding it up to Julian. "Direction?"

Julian tugged his wrist so the card was angled more toward the nearest lamp. "Upside down."

"Not the *Gallant*," Avra yelled.

"Fuck," Markefa yelled back. A moment later: "There's eight others it could be. You got anything else?"

"I think I'll just guess," Avra murmured to Julian.

"Captain," Ellat shouted urgently from the steps of the fo'c'sle. "He said the thing!"

"Avra!"

"Kid's lying, I said I *didn't need* to guess," Avra screeched. "It's definitely the *Frog*."

"He's guessing," Julian called.

Avra whipped to face him, jaw dropped. Julian shrugged ruefully.

"Make him draw a card!" Teveri yelled.

Avra drew a card and looked at it himself, since he'd already taken his eyes off the ghost-light. "Ah . . ." he said. "The Ship, reversed."

Julian burst out laughing. "It's not the *Frog*, Captain!" Avra grumbled and shuffled the card back into the deck. As Markefa and Nagasani attended to whatever other math needed to be done about it, Julian said, "You know, I did not understand what the crew was doing last time."

"Or the time before that?" Ellat said sarcastically.

"I was confined belowdecks for my first crossing and told to stay out of the way."

"Know the ship, know the ghosts on it," Avra said. "Know the ship, also know the turtle it's on. Know the turtle, know where we are in the, ah . . ." Avra waved his hand. "Turtle astrology. You know astrology? It's like that. But regarding turtles. Right? You get it."

"It is beginning to dawn on me, yes," Julian said. His voice was laced with warm amusement, and Avra could *almost* forgive him for the betrayal.

Avra sniffed and returned his attention to that distant twinkle of ghost-light out in the darkness. "Don't distract me. This is a matter of life and death."

"And specifically your sex life."

"That's what I said. Shush! Hush! I will tell you all you could possibly wish to know about turtle astrology when we run aground and I start getting bored."

"Shouldn't be too bad of a crossing," said Avra, moseying down the deck a little while later, after they had ascertained where they were in the turtle astrology. "We'll go aground for low tide at the usual place? That rock with the support columns?"

"That's the plan," said Nagasani. "And if we can't quite make it there, we'll anchor in its lee. Should be safe enough there when the turtles breathe, or if any of them get peckish."

Avra perched himself on the edge of her desk and kicked his feet. "What's next?"

Nagasani checked her charts. "Should be *Pandera's Sorrow* any minute. We've got enough lanterns that the *Queen Bavia* ghosts should have spotted us by now—Markefa, could you check the book on that one?"

Markefa flipped through the *Book of Wrecks*. "*Queen Bavia,* wrecked in the fifty-second year of the Mahisti Dynasty, or 5145 by the Arjuni calendar . . . Blah blah blah, rituals and requirements, names of the dead . . . Ah, yep, there it is. Female turtle, and Captain Hakurai claims his crew witnessed a mating twelve years ago. Probably paused to lay her eggs, hence the gap."

"Congratulations, mama," Nagasani murmured, making a note on her charts. "Interesting to know Hakurai wasn't lying about that after all. And a nice bit of information for us to announce in port, with any luck." She eyed Avra doubtfully.

Avra was about to reply that his luck was not even a provable thing, let alone something he could *invoke at will,* when a ghost appeared on the deck, greenish-glowing and water-rotted.

"Ahoy the *Pandera's Sorrow* and her crew!" called Markefa, flipping quickly through the book while the others joined the chorus. "Ah, a song and a sexy dance! That's for the fiddlers and Nonso!"

"And me! I'm so helpful!" said Avra, scrambling off of Nagasani's desk and snatching up a concertina from the box of jumbled instruments that had been brought up on deck. "Let's sing 'The Wettest Pussy in the World,'" said Avra loudly. "A sad song for a boat with a sad name!"

"I can't do a sexy dance to *that,*" said Nonso.

"Sure you can, sure you c—"

"A TRAITOR," screamed the ghost, who had been standing very still in one place. "'WARE, MY FRIENDS, 'WARE THE TRAITOR."

There was a beat of ringing silence; the ghost trembled, its tattered clothing whipped by an ethereal wind. Its eyes were white and wide, its hands as bony and scrawny as claws.

"Hmm," said Markefa and several other people.

"Thank you, honored dead," Teveri said solemnly. "Would you be interested in a merry song and a sexy dance to send you on your way?"

"A TRAITOR. A TRAITOR STANDS UPON THIS DECK."

"Oh, this is *very* good to know about," said Nagasani, gesturing for Markefa to hand her the *Book of Wrecks.* As she scribbled in it, she muttered, "Wants a song and a sexy dance unless there is a, quote-unquote, 'traitor' aboard the ship, in which case that information takes precedence . . ."

"Can you tell us what you would like us to do with the traitor?" Markefa asked the ghost, which was weeping into its hands.

"Reveal him," the ghost sobbed. "Reveal him, and save yourselves from the depredations of his lies . . . Save yourselves from our fate!"

"Ah," said Nagasani gently. "You died because of a traitor? Your whole ship?"

The ghost wailed again, louder—loud enough that every bracer under tension *thrummed.* The silver *Nightingale* sail glimmered with an eerie spectral light above them, and the ghost's wail turned sharp and strange enough to make all the hairs on Avra's entire body stand on end.

"Oskar, take the helm," Teveri said calmly.

"Oh shit, Captain's up," someone whispered as Captain az-Ḥaffār descended to the main deck. "Fuck yeah."

Tev had done this once before. It had not surprised the crew to witness it, nor Avra to hear about it later. After the way Teveri had acquired *The Running Sun* in the first place, everyone knew that Captain az-Ḥaffār wasn't afraid of the dead.

Teveri said something in Tashaz, their native tongue, and then: "Be at peace, lost one. It is too late for you, but you have passed on the message while there was still time for us."

The ghost lowered its hands—the edges of it flickered like a candle flame, whirling like dust blown off a shelf or steam rising into the air. "Captain?" it murmured, reaching out.

"Not yours," Teveri said.

"This ship's?"

"Yes."

The ghost seemed to sigh. "A ship of the dead."

"Once upon a time, yes. Now a ship of the living." They pointed upward. "And we carry the mainsail of the *Nightingale.*"

The ghost looked up sharply. "Oh." A shudder ran through it, and its wind-whipped edges fell still like sails in the doldrums. In a clearer voice than it had yet spoken in, it said, "I think I would like that song now, if it's still on offer."

No one spoke for a moment, unwilling to break the solemnity of the moment.

Avra cleared his throat.

"Buddy, no," someone muttered.

"I've written a new song," he said to the ghost. Teveri pinched the bridge of their nose. "It's called 'The Wettest Pussy in the World.' Would you like to hear it?"

"Perhaps," Nonso said through gritted teeth, "a song more appropriate to the mood would be more suitable."

"Perhaps," Avra replied haughtily, "we follow the directions in the book about what kind of songs and dances the *Pandera's Sorrow* ghosts like."

"Perhaps—"

Avra honked the concertina and launched directly into the chorus. "MEOW MEOW MEOW MEOW—"

8

23. The Charger

Bravery in confrontation, determination, forward momentum, an unstoppable force. Choose action over passivity. Fight for a noble cause. Chase your goals passionately, regardless of what obstacles may arise. To achieve victory, unleash your full power and strength of desire—hold nothing back.

(Reversed: Leaving things in the dust, fighting against the bridle, undirected energy, being swept away, forcefulness and coercion. Beware that your desire and passion do not turn to bitterness and anger. A too-fiery personality may easily burn others—even if you yourself do not feel scalded.)

The glow of the ghost-light and the strange luminescence of the creatures of the reefs was already drowned out by the first blush of color in the eastern sky. *The Running Sun* had dropped anchor and furled sails atop a broad rocky outcropping to wait out low tide. It was the summer solstice, and the double new moons brought the dramatic sweeps of the king-tides when the water surged to its highest point at high tide and plummeted to its lowest point at low tide, revealing reefs, rocks, and shipwrecks that would normally be several meters below the surface.

The wind had died down just as they'd dropped anchor, and the water was utterly calm, still, smooth as glass in that particular way that only happened just before dawn, when there was a sense that the water *had* to be still, that it was *right* for it to be still. Already there were wrecks visible above the surface, breaking the mirrorlike vista, to port and starboard, fore and aft, from where the ship was now moored and all the way to the north horizon and the distant swell of Three Tits Island to the south. As the tide fell farther, the receding waters would reveal a jumble of jagged remnants and hulking piles of driftwood, held together only by the reefs, barnacles, and seaweed meadows that had grown over them and through them, and the areas of safe passage in between the wrecks and reefs would shrink into an impossible labyrinth that only the smallest fishing vessels would be agile enough to traverse.

The bustle of activity on deck died down as the tasks to secure the ship were completed and tools were stowed away. "Right then," bellowed Oskar. "Before we all knock off for breakfast and a nap, we've got some *business* to sort out."

Teveri stood at the rail of the quarterdeck, gripping with both hands, their golden eye flashing. "Yes," they said through gritted teeth. "I think we need to talk about *that fucking ghost.*"

"Damn right we do," said Nonso, jumping down the last few feet from the rope ladders to the deck. "Which of you *motherfuckers* is thinking of treachery, eh?"

"It's Julian!" Avra screeched, pointing to him. "Julian is the traitor! I told you all along! I told you not to trust him!"

"It's not Julian," several people shouted across the ship.

"You're only saying that because you all want to fuck him!" Avra bawled. "Who else could it possibly be?"

"You, for one," Teveri snapped. "And also *technically* everyone else aboard this ship—"

"Hey now," Nonso said, raising his hands. "All *I* did was kill one of the king's death consultants."

"His what?" said Ellat, horrified.

"A kind of priest; it's normal in N'gaka—"

"If we're being *technical,* Captain," added Markefa, "*my* arrest warrant was only for embezzlement, because they hadn't yet figured out that the amount I stole crossed the legal limit that qualified me for treason as well—"

"I feel like you're still a traitor, though, even if you aren't formally accused of it," said Beng Choon. "Arguably Nonso as well. Legally speaking, treason is the crime of betraying your country, and in N'gaka the death priests *are* government officials, no? Was it assassination or murder, Nonso?"

Nagasani whistled, loud and piercing, and the babble of voices faltered. "We've encountered *Pandera's Sorrow* before," she said, putting her hands on her hips. "And we *definitely* did the song and the sexy dance that time, rather than getting a ghost crying about traitors. A lot of the crew with us now were also with us then—not everyone, but a lot."

"Maybe it's not about who's *done* a little treason, but how recently," someone offered.

"So it's Avra," chorused several people.

"When was your treason, Avra, twelve days ago?" Nagasani said.

"Why would it matter how recently the treason has been done!" Avra shrieked. "The ghost was *warning* us, as in a traitor who has not betrayed us yet!"

"Seems like *one of you,*" snarled Teveri, "isn't sufficiently imaginative to visualize what the rest of us will do to you if you fuck up the sale of Avra's papers for all of us."

The crew descended into shouting and squabbling with all the ferocious determination of a flock of seagulls at the cake competition—accusations were volunteered, allegations of motive were flung around, feelings were hurt. Teveri stood above it all, grinding their teeth and clearly wound up almost to the breaking point.

"It is Julian! It is utterly Julian!" Avra screeched above the noise.

"Who would I betray you *to*?" Julian asked, baffled.

Avra flailed wildly. "I don't know! Vinte! You're Vintish!"

"Yes, I presumed it would be someone in Vinte, but *whom*?"

"The king! Your church! People! Lots of people in Vinte you

could betray us to!" The squabbling of the crew petered off into palpable strain and discomfort.

Julian visibly fought back a laugh and bit his lip. "Before I explain why that's absurd, may I ask what evidence leads you to believe I am here to betray you?"

"It is very simple! You're too good-looking to be a pirate!"

Julian lost the battle against his laugh and muffled it in his hand.

The crew shifted from foot to foot, or in many cases from foot to peg leg. "He *is* suspiciously hot," Anxhela muttered. "Avra's got maybe *part* of a point."

"Thank you!" Avra said loudly. "Look at him, he is still wearing his monk robes. And, and! He has all of his appendages!"

"You have all of your appendages too," said Markefa.

Avra raised one finger. "Yes, *but* . . . my toes are weird from that time I dropped one of the capstan thingies on my foot. Handles? Are they handles?"

Several of the crew supplied the word *bars*, which Avra immediately chose to forget; a few people murmured agreements that permanently weird toes probably did count as being piratically maimed in the line of duty; and Oskar scoffed that Avra's toes had been weird before that.

Avra ignored him. "If Julian is so suspiciously hot, why is he here? I asked him the other day and he told me weird lies about how he used to be a revolutionary and how he just likes it here because you're 'his type of people' or something. Nonsense, I say! Codswallop! You know why? During that conversation, he also pulled my hair and whispered into my ear in a sexy way! Very advanced interrogation techniques, this man has! I would have babbled everything I knew!"

Julian cleared his throat and composed himself. "I am not going to betray you to the church of Vinte, because there wouldn't be a point. The central core of our faith is that the pursuit of knowledge is the only path toward holiness—we teach that when the Emperor of Heaven created the world, he filled it with mysteries, and that he wishes for us to understand not only his great works, but the workings behind the works: Why the sky is blue, why a dropped pebble falls to the earth, why a ship floats in water but a coin sinks, what makes the stars shine . . . If I were to approach the council of abbots with the secret papers stolen from the Shipbuilder's Guild, they would say, 'Interesting, thank you,' and spend the next five to ten years researching it and arguing over it. I would absolutely *not* be paid or compensated for my trouble. In fact, the very suggestion that the idea of payment would even *occur* to them is screamingly funny. The church takes materials of learning as *tithes,* not as trade goods.

"I would not betray you to the king of Vinte either, because I *was* a revolutionary, and I still have a price on my head. The warrant for my arrest was suspended due to the fact that I begged for sanctuary in the monastery from an abbot who happened to be exceptionally good-hearted and believed that the foolishness of youth need not be the foolishness of maturity, as long as one devotes oneself piously to the holy pursuit of understanding. If that suspension were to be revoked, I would be arrested and hanged, just like all my compatriots were. In short, I do not have a relationship with the crown that inclines me to be cooperative."

"There are other kinds of benefit you might be rewarded with," Teveri said, stalking slowly back and forth along the edge of the quarterdeck like a golden-eyed panther. "Promotions within the hierarchy of your church. A nicer set of rooms in your monastery. Praise and glory, and your name remembered unto the twilight of the world."

Julian smiled—appallingly gorgeous and holy and soft—and shook his head. "As for praise and glory, I could expect perhaps a footnote in someone's research essays or an interview with a historian or archivist. As for the rest, those are nice things, but they do not occupy my thoughts, and they are not what I pursue."

"What about a royal pardon?"

Julian's gentle smile didn't waver. "I would tear it up and hurl it in the messenger's face."

"What? Why?" demanded several people.

"Because I am a revolutionary!" Julian said, spreading his hands. "I don't know what to tell you! I don't believe in monarchies! Why would I accept a pardon from a man that my companions and I once sincerely considered assassinating? Why would I accept a pardon from a man who had those companions executed?"

"Words are cheap!" declared Avra. "He is very beautiful to look at, so he can say anything he wants and we'll all try our hardest to believe him! He can't prove that he was a revolutionary! Anyone can sound like a revolutionary if they want to, can't they! It's about *action*." He punctuated this with a sharp clap. "It's about traipsing into government buildings you're not supposed to be in! Accidentally committing crimes just to see what happens! And having too much curiosity and moxie for your own good!"

"Another weirdly good point from Avra." Nonso gave Julian a hard up-and-down look. "Do we even have proof that he's a monk?"

"I have nothing to prove myself but my knowledge and my word," Julian said quietly. "And I assure you I have no interest in betraying you."

"Words! Cheap words!" Avra said. "Buying a drab grey robe is also very cheap! Fake monk is a very affordable disguise!"

Julian spread his hands. "You may test my knowledge if you wish."

"I'll vouch for his knowledge," Nagasani said. "He has more than a layperson's understanding of astronomy; he asked me to teach him a little about dead reckoning and seemed to be following my explanations easily; and he is capable of having intelligent conversations about meteorology and navigation. He knew the term *portolan chart*. And he doesn't giggle like a twelve-year-old at the word *sextant*." Avra was not the only one to giggle like a twelve-year-old; Nagasani rolled her eyes magnificently.

"Sounds like no one can come up with a good reason to push Julian overboard—" Teveri started.

"Me!" Avra said, scrambling for his little rucksack. "Me, I can! I will pull a card that says he is the traitor, and we'll push him overboard and Nonso can be the pretty one again!" Amongst the ensuing swell of bickering about whether Nonso still held that illustrious title simply by dint of either not being a fake monk who would betray everyone, or not being a real monk with an oath of celibacy, Avra fumbled through shuffling his Heralds and pulled one card so violently that a second fell free with it. "Hah!" he said, holding it up in Julian's face.

"The Innocent," Julian said.

Avra looked at the card in outrage. It was The Innocent. He looked down at the card that had fallen. The Bower. *Again.* "The deck is biased," he announced loudly. "The deck has also been beguiled by Julian's forearms and jawline, we can't consider this a reliable source of information—"

"Anyone wondering why Helvaçi is so dead set on this?" growled Oskar, crossing his arms. "*He's* the Araşti here. *He's* the one that works for the Ministry of Intelligence. This could be some kind of a sting operation—someone might've sent him in with fake documents as bait to see whether we're still complying with the Pact. It'd be an awfully good excuse to stop the supply ships from coming in."

A cold chill ran over the deck.

"It's not a sting operation!" Avra protested. "I really did all that treason! Accidentally, yes, but my life is in danger as much as yours!"

"*As much as ours?*" Bald Baric jabbed a finger toward Three Tits Island, off on the horizon. "You know how many fucking tourists are in there for the festival? You know how *fast* we would starve without the supply ships?"

Before the Pact (as Avra had heard), Scuttle Cove had been barely more than a grubby, run-down outpost where the pirates gathered to fence their stolen goods to people with connections and to take shelter during the sea serpents' breeding season. The corresponding festival had arisen to give all those bored people things to do so they wouldn't get drunk and spend six weeks murdering each other out of stress and hunger, especially if the takings had been slim and food started running out before the season of serpents did. Some of the oldest residents of Scuttle Cove still remembered years when there had been stewed boot leather on the menu during week six—or, gods forbid, week seven, if the serpents came up from the depths a bit later than expected, or stayed up longer than they should have, or if a storm blew across and prevented sailing, or if there had just been a freak accident with a stray serpent in the offseason and people were cagey of going out. There was at least one ancient, decrepit crackpot of a captain who claimed that a little bit of cannibalism between friends in tough times was completely normal, and that the actual taboo was eating your *own* leg.

After the Pact with Araşt, the hungry season became a thing of memory. Security in survival had bred pride and community, and the festival had grown bigger and more ostentatious, and then *outsiders* had started trickling in to be there for it, and they'd spent money on room and board and courtesans and gambling . . . Within a few years, they were spending money at the actual *businesses* that had started appearing to accommodate them—hotels, shops, restaurants, gambling houses, and the Street of Flowers. What was a town of perhaps three or four thousand people during the offseason became a bustling city of two or three times that size during the season of serpents.

Ten thousand people, fed for six weeks courtesy of Araşt, whose only requirement for such generosity was that the pirates harass everyone else's ships *except theirs*. Avra's teachers in the civil service academy had happily labeled this a "good investment" and praised the Pact to the skies as a triumph of diplomacy and mutual benefit between allies.

It *was* a good investment for Araşt.

Depending on who you asked in Scuttle Cove, it was a hostage situation, an extortion racket, or a terrible idea that had ruined the ambiance of a perfectly good murder village. ("Roofs!" scoffed those people. "Shutters! Back in my day, you were lucky to have half a roof, and shutters were only for keeping the seagulls out!" Or: "I went out for a walk the other night and *no one* threatened me with a knife! This place is going *soft*.")

Teveri must have been running through the same kind of math, because they cleared their throat pointedly. "Setting aside the two main suspects—Avra for being Araşti in public, and Julian for being suspiciously good-looking—is there anyone *else* on this ship who is planning to betray your *whole fucking family*? And would anyone care to snitch about it?"

The crew burst into furious squabbling, pointing at each other and shouting to the captain that so-and-so had an unpaid bar tab, and so-and-so got a lady in Scuttle Cove pregnant and could probably use the money, and so-and-so *always* gambled away their coin immediately—

"That was a test!" Teveri screamed. "Shut the fuck up!"

The crew dropped off into confused silence.

"Markefa and Julian are the only ones who passed," Teveri snapped. Markefa had put her forehead into her hand. Julian had tucked his hands into his sleeves in the most monkish possible pose and was looking guileless. Neither had pointed and shouted.

Avra sulkily stopped pointing at Julian, since *apparently* not-pointing earned a good grade from Teveri.

"Maybe that ghost meant treason that's already occurred recently. Maybe it was just starting to rot away in the seawater and saying whatever weird shit was in its head when it died, and seeing the *Nightingale* sail bought it a little more time. But maybe it was right, and someone is considering betraying us," Teveri said, leaning forward on the rail with both hands and baring their teeth. "You're thinking of all the money you could make by stealing the secret and selling it yourself. Or *maybe* . . ." Their voice lowered into the range that made a chill of genuine wariness run up Avra's spine. "Maybe you're thinking there might be reward money just for fucking *traipsing* up to the ambassador's house and reporting us. Not as much money as selling it, of course, but a whole lot easier to do on your own. And, crucially, puts you in Araşt's good books. Wouldn't *that* be nice?" This last remark was so low and ferocious that the entire crew—every last one of them a pirate and a criminal, except for Ellat, who was seventeen—shifted back half a step. "If you steal the secret and abscond in the night, we'll still chase you down and give you a slow and painful death, but at least I'll respect you enough to ensure your mangled corpse gets a decent burial. But if you sell out to fucking *Araşt . . . I will desecrate your grave.*"

Captain Undertaker, whispered people in Scuttle Cove, because everyone there remembered how Teveri az-Ḥaffār had gotten their ship fifteen years ago, had *watched* what they'd done to claim it, and hadn't dared to speak up in protest afterward. Avra had heard every possible threat from Teveri against his and other people's life, limb, and personal contentment. He had *never* heard this one.

"Keep the real enemy in mind," Teveri said, still low and furious. "And think fucking carefully about whose side you want to be on. A *country* cannot be your friend, especially not the richest country in the world, whose singular goal is to preserve their own wealth and power. Think *fucking carefully,* because six weeks is a long time, and Scuttle Cove is a *very* small town. Step one godsdamned toe out of line, I *dare* you. Breathe one ill-advised word when you're drunk in a bar. Gossip to the Flowers. I dare you to do it, and watch what will happen to you. This is not the time to be *fucking around* and letting your shitty little egos get in the way of what we're trying to achieve." A ray of dawn broke over the horizon and their eyes flashed with fire—the natural eye dark and hot, the false eye golden and blazing. Avra resisted the urge to fall over and squeal, *Oh, Teveri! Incandescent one!!*

Silence. At last, Beng Choon tentatively raised his hook-hand. "Am I allowed to ask Julian one more question about his alleged revolutionary tendencies?"

Teveri raised their eyes to the heavens in exasperation, which at least was better than the low, furious growl. "Fine."

"What was the actual crime you and your friends were accused of?"

"Conspiracy to assassinate the king," Julian said evenly. "Though *conspiracy* is a rather strong word for what we were doing. We were toying with the idea of theoretically making a plan to assassinate the king."

There was a long pause. "What, that's it?" said Nonso.

"As a youth, I attended university and became involved with

a society of my peers. We thought ourselves intellectuals. Rebellious in thought—we questioned the teachings of the church. We took pleasure in our own stupidity." His mouth twisted in something almost akin to amusement. "We thought ourselves fashionable ignorants. When we tired of that—for it was tiresome in the extreme—we questioned the state instead. When our discussions eventually turned to how we could make our point by killing a member of the government—preferably the king—someone betrayed us. Many of my comrades were arrested. None of them avoided a sentence of execution. I fled to a monastery outside the capital, and I petitioned the abbot for sanctuary. The abbot said that he would not lie on my behalf, but that if I took the cloth in truth, then he would tell them truly that I had done so, for then they could not arrest me without his permission. I decided I preferred to live. So I agreed."

"But did you manage to kill *anyone*?" Nonso pressed.

"No. No one. We were raided before any of our plans could be put in motion." Julian lifted his chin. "I have lived with the shame nearly half my life."

Nonso burst out laughing, as did half the crew, dissipating the last of the uncomfortable tension on the deck. Even Teveri crossed their arms, a wry half smile twisting the scarred corner of their mouth. "The shame!" Nonso crowed. "The shame of his crimes, he means!"

"No," said Julian evenly. "The shame of running away instead of sticking with my convictions and taking at least one of the bastards down with me."

Nonso laughed even louder and staggered forward to clap Julian firmly on the shoulder. "Too pretty to be a pirate after all!" he gurgled, and stopped to wipe a tear from his eye. "Y'know—hah—most of *us* succeeded at our assassination plots."

"Hey, now," said Markefa through her wheezes of mirth. "Some of us were only in it for the money."

"Some of us," Avra said mulishly, "were in it because we were bored and unattended and were struck with a *whimsical impulse*."

"Of course, yes," said Nonso. "I should have said 'succeeded at their *crimes.*' That's more inclusive phrasing."

"Other than being born, I never committed any crimes," said Teveri, touching their lips with their fingertips to hide their smile. "Not until I got to sea, anyway."

"Running away from the cult of Qarat'ash isn't considered a crime where you come from?" said Avra.

Teveri inclined their head, allowing the point. "Except that one."

Captain's Log

Day 14, 6th month, 199th yr Mah. Dyn.

Anchored in Scuttle Cove. Final inventory of stores below.

All good spots already taken, ugh. Way out at the end where the fucking Araşti supply ships anchor. Will be tedious long row back+forth or a very long walk around the cove to town; most everyone preferring not to bunk on the ship, instead camping on beach or staying w/ friends. Personally undecided. Avra undoubtedly planning to come by a stack of money and snuggle his way through whole Street of Flowers. Am wondering what is wrong with me that I am going to fuck him. Will attempt to convince myself out of it; prospect grim.

Ghosts persist in overdramatics.

PART TWO

9

35. The Knight

Loyalty, swearing oaths, protection. The promises you make now are serious and will bind you possibly for life. Make sure that you mean it. Possibly: An upstanding, trustworthy, honorable person.

(Reversed: Oathbreaking, betrayal. An oath you made has become toxic and burdensome, have a care that it does not embitter you. Alternatively, be wary of those who claim to be loyal to you; their true loyalties may lie elsewhere.)

"I was helpful," Avra said as soon as the anchor had struck the bright turquoise water of the cove. "Tev, I was so helpful."

"Shut up," Tev muttered through gritted teeth. "We can discuss how helpful you were later."

Avra made a soft noise of woe, just for his own amusement, and went off to harass Oskar, reflecting that there had been a time when he would have hung off of Teveri's sleeve and batted his eyes for twenty minutes before leaving them be.

"Oskar," he said, sauntering up to where the first mate was getting the dinghies into the water to ferry the crew ashore. "Oskar, I really feel as though I've grown as a person lately."

Oskar gave him an incredulous look.

Avra was dry when they left the ship, and he was dripping wet when they made it to shore, on account of Oskar losing his temper—usually so patient and calm! He had clearly not grown as a person lately—and shoving him out of the dinghy. Julian helpfully scooped him back in, and even picked up Avra's rucksack so it wouldn't get drenched when Avra tumbled wetly into the boat with a piteous noise.

"I will consider forgiving you for your crimes," Avra said as he wrung his clothes out. "For the crimes of being suspiciously good-looking and pulling my hair." And taking up Teveri's attention. "I was just telling Oskar earlier that I think all my recent suffering has improved me."

Julian did not give him any incredulous looks, just smiled at Avra with a laugh twinkling in his eyes, which was all that Avra was ever looking for in response to his outrageous remarks. So many people did not understand this about him. As positive reinforcement, he entertained himself and Julian for the rest of the trip to shore by pointing out a few of the ships that he could recognize by sight. There were a dozen different types: the tall ships of Araşt, Vinte, and Quassa sai Bendra; the junks of Map Sut, Keroo, and Imakami—even a strange two-hulled boat with a deck very low to the water, the likes of which Avra only vaguely recalled from sketches in geography textbooks.

When they reached the shore, most of the crew pitched tents on the beach, which was as crowded as the aquamarine waters of the harbor, or dissipated into the streets to the homes of friends or family. A few of them trooped up to one of the hotels to take rooms—Teveri, Oskar, and Markefa, as the officers, were almost *required* to spend their coin, however scanty, on a bit of comfort and luxury. The social cost of being seen camping on the beach would have been devastating, and Teveri's status in the community of other captains was and always had been precarious.

Avra went with them, because he'd been helpful and at some point Teveri was going to deign to fuck him. Julian also went with them, because apparently Julian still had spending money.

Their usual place, the High Tide Hotel, was a bit ramshackle around the shutters and shingles—but then nearly every building in Scuttle Cove had that very *lived-in* air. Not worn, necessarily, and certainly never *lifeless*, but well broken in and well mended, like a pair of shoes whose holes had been patched half a dozen times by cobblers of wildly varying skill.

Avra was just about to step across the threshold of the hotel when, out of the blue, it occurred to him that it would be very pleasant to take a walk.

He regarded this thought with some suspicion.

"Avra?" said Markefa, looking back.

"Mmm," he said.

He was certain that a walk would be pleasant. He had never before had the thought that a walk would be pleasant. Perhaps this was a symptom of all the personal growth he'd been doing lately, because he didn't *go for walks*, not intentionally. The only other time he could recall recreationally walking was . . . the night he'd accidentally committed treason, when he'd gone for a walk to calm his rattled nerves.

"Julian," said Avra, still squinting suspiciously at the doorstep. His feet itched. Did that happen to people? Perhaps he was coming down with a flesh-eating fungus. "Julian, have you ever considered writing a memoir?"

"Hadn't considered it, why?"

"Very monkish sort of thing to do. Since you're still claiming that you're not a fake monk. If you were to write a memoir, do you think it would be very exciting in your memoir if I went for a walk?"

Julian turned back to look at him and tilted his head with that amused smile. "Should I say yes? What does this walk involve?"

"I *don't know.*" Avra's eye twitched. "How are you going to write about me in your memoir?"

"Avra Helvaçi was over six feet tall and of a strong and statuesque build," Julian said without missing a beat or batting an eye, "a man as ravishingly handsome as you could imagine, with dark hair and sparkling eyes and a clever, generous mouth and a wit as quick as a swallow on the wing. He was the perfect antithesis to the crew—his clothing was fashionable and well pressed, his bearing dignified yet entirely personable and approachable. He was the soul of charm and charisma, and the word *dashing* was far too mild to describe him. One would need to reach as far as *debonair*, and even further beyond that! He was always in control of both the situation and himself. No expression came across his face but the one that he intended to show—he was a man of many masks and many mysteries. The name he gave me was a false one, I believe, but I saw immediately that he was a man of great influence and keen insight—and indeed, a most righteous spirit."

"*Markefa*," Avra wailed. "Julian's calling me *dashing and debonair*!"

"Fighting words," Markefa called from the desk where Teveri was arguing with the owner about taking rooms. "I ought to draw steel and duel for my boy's honor."

"As we girded our loins to attempt the crossing of the Turtle Shallows, Avra Helvaçi stood at the prow, a windswept vision of noble grace, though his clothing was rather rakishly done up, revealing a great swath of powerfully masculine chest hair and musculature," Julian continued. "His eyes glittered eerily in the lamplight as he sought in the dark, calm and sober and serious—he had told me earlier that day, with a solemnity that struck me to my foundations, that making this crossing safely was a matter of life and death."

"I'll have you know," Avra said haughtily, "I only have one chest hair and it's six inches long. I think we have determined that you *should* write a memoir, but have we determined if it will be exciting for me to walk?"

"Why don't you draw a card?" Julian asked, crossing his arms and leaning on the doorjamb.

Avra still had not crossed the threshold. Fortunately—a word that nearly made Avra break out in hives; was this his luck trying to run his life in a strange way again?—there was no one behind him to complain that he was blocking the door. "I am not speaking to my cards at the moment," he said. "Not until they calm down and stop giving me The Bower all the time. Horny bastards. *Are walks exciting in memoirs?*"

Julian hummed and thought for a moment. "Avra Helvaçi, ever a man of mystery and enigmatic motives, vanished as soon as we got to the hotel, confiding to me with a dazzling wink that he had some private business of his own to attend to, by which I understood that he was heading out to make love, in senses both archaic and modern, to all the professionals of intimacy in the vibrant capital of the pirate republic where we had dropped anchor."

"Alright, but do *not* say they would surely all offer to do it for free on account of Avra Helvaçi being just that gorgeous and irresistible," Avra said, pointing a stern finger in Julian's face. He had to reach quite far. "The only part of my reputation that I care about is that I pay my tabs immediately and tip as generously as I can afford. I won't have you besmirching that by saying otherwise."

Julian smiled faintly. "Trust me, I would not dream of claiming otherwise."

"Because in your memoir, you are ensorcelled by my smoldering sexual presence?"

"No comment."

"That means yes. But also because you believe that people should be paid fairly for their labor, expertise, and artistry, right?"

Julian looked surprised and then very pleased. "Oh. Yes, actually."

"Good. Good. I trust you to continue with our semi-fictional memoirs. In the meantime, I will go for a walk. I will endeavor to walk as excitingly as possible. Maybe I'll start a riot or something."

"I won't fuck you if you start any riots," called Teveri from the desk, having won their argument and snatched the key from the owner.

"I will not start any riots," Avra said immediately. "I will start zero riots. If I see a riot, maybe I'll make it stop, actually. I won't even nod politely on the street to the riots."

He turned on his heel and gave all of his attention to his feet, which were squishing and squelching and squorching rather magnificently in his wet boots.

Avra walked almost at random, and then he found a Genzhun penny on the ground, which he took to flipping at every intersection, following its directions along the sandy road and winding his way through the town.

The houses were mostly brick and driftwood, because that's what was around to build with, and they were brightly and beautifully colored. Rather garish, Avra had thought the first time he'd ever visited, but garish in a way he'd *liked*, and which had grown on him more with every subsequent visit. They were mostly two-story houses with roofed balconies along the fronts, painted bright pink or purple or celestial blue or mint green using gorgeous alchemical admixtures from Amariyan, Ephucca, and Lapaladi. The only trees of note were palms—coconut palms, date palms, and oil-nut palms thick with red and orange fruit—but as bougainvilleas took quite well to the thin, sandy soil, people trained them up the sides of buildings and around the railings of the balconies above, until their shiny, deep green leaves and riotous blooms of fuchsia or royal purple bracts cradling tiny white flowers were as much a dominant color of the house as its paint job.

At this time of year, Scuttle Cove was *alive*. The sizzle and scent of frying festival food wafted out of the doorways of taverns and restaurants and gaming houses; there was music and noise and laughter on every street; there were *people*. There would be more people as the heat of the afternoon passed and the denizens of the city and festival tourists emerged from the cool shade, fully recovered from their hangovers from the night before and ready to acquire new ones for the next morning.

Avra, purely content, let his feet and the toss of the coin lead him where they would.

The only thing marring his contentment was the whitewashed stone building up on the slope of the northernmost of the eponymous Three Tits, easily visible above the roofs of the houses: the villa of the Araşti ambassador to Scuttle Cove.

Avra kept glancing up at it. He couldn't make himself stop—every time he looked away, his Ministry of Intelligence instincts told him that as soon as he glanced up again, he'd see someone up there peering directly at him with a spyglass and knowing he was guilty as fuck. It felt . . . strange, the sight of that villa. It felt like a weight hanging over him, a threat, a *reminder.*

He had been coming and going from Scuttle Cove for fifteen years; the ambassador's villa had never set his teeth on edge like this before. It had always been a neutral, ignorable part of the landscape.

Avra was squinting up at it and wondering whether it qualified to be called a palace in Julian's memoir when someone spoke behind him: "Helvaçi?"

Avra froze. *Do not run,* his Intelligence instincts told him firmly. *Do not scream. Do not burst into tears. Do not panic. SHE DOESN'T KNOW ANYTHING.*

He turned slowly, his smile affixed to his face. "Ah, Lieutenant Viyan. Hello. Wasn't expecting to see you here. I thought you would have left with the old ambassador."

"No, I asked to stay on! I thought it would be nice to help Ambassador Baltakan get settled in." Lieutenant Viyan was a kahya, a member of the Araşti royal guard—the fringe guard, to be precise, who were assigned as bodyguards and attendants to ministers and government officials like the ambassador, just as the core guard were assigned to the royal family themselves. Her uniform was an immaculately laundered, knee-length kaftan of sky blue, which she wore neatly buttoned and belted over trousers and boots according to regimental guidelines, with her hair tied back simply—again according to regimental guidelines. She had a very wholesome and practical demeanor and, like most of the kahyalar that Avra had ever met, she was almost uncomfortably patriotic. "Good to see you—and such a surprise! Weren't you assigned to a new route after we got the semaphore system in place?"

"I was!" he said, forcing his voice bright and casual. "The semaphore system! So clever. So much more convenient than crossing the Turtle Shallows just for letters and messages, isn't it!"

"Yes, but it does mean we see fewer faces from home these days, unfortunately," she said ruefully.

Unfortunately for *her,* she meant. Very fortunate for people who might have accidentally committed treason. Avra resisted the impulse to burst into nervous giggling. "I am not here on work, to be clear," he said quickly. "I caught a terrible illness in Kafia, and I have taken partial retirement."

"Oh dear, are you all right?"

"Ha, well enough. Alive." He forced his smile wider. "All we really have is our health, you know," he recited, because that seemed to be a thing that people said.

"So true. But you chose to come *here* to recover?"

"The physicians recommended that I take the sea air," he said. "And this is where most of my contacts are." He tried to exude the same kind of wholesome patriotism that she did. "I'd like to continue being helpful to the Ministry however I can, you know?"

"Good for you!" Viyan said energetically, clapping him on the shoulder. She even looked a little choked up at that, because kahyalar *always* got choked up about people doing their duty. Avra had never been sure whether this was the result of secret brainwashing that the teachers did to certain classes in the civil service academy or whether it was just a common trait among the students selected for the guard track. He wondered how they tested for that sort of thing. "I saw you looking up at the house—were you on your way to say hello to Ambassador Baltakan? I don't think he has any appointments, so he should be free."

"Ah. Great. Yes. Definitely. Definitely heading right up there," said Avra. He looked down at the Genzhun penny in his hand and hurled it down an alley. What kind of luck was it that led him right into a situation where he'd have to spend hours making small talk with an egghead from the Ministry of Diplomacy? Even on previous occasions, he'd needed several days to resign himself to the idea, and today he would have liked the opportunity to bolster his nerves. His Heralds never would have done this to him.

Viyan took his arm companionably and led him down the street. "He'll be delighted to meet you. He's still adjusting to life here—you do have to admit that it's different from back home!"

"Yes," said Avra. "So incredibly true. Uh. What is he adjusting to specifically?"

"Mostly how lax everyone is with schedules around here. Not used to the heat either. Also, he was under the impression that the house came with a library, but all those books belonged to the previous ambassador, and she took them with her when she left. Oh, what else . . . I gather he really enjoyed going to art galleries and the opera . . . You know, just all the little things that they don't really have here."

Viyan kept chattering away, interrupting herself only long enough to say, "Let's go this way. It's a shortcut," and turn them onto the Street of Flowers, where all the best and nicest pleasure-houses were.

Avra had *always* had fantastic luck on the Street of Flowers, even before that weird incident in Quassa sai Bendra when he'd started winning all his card games. There was always a collection of beauties lolling around on the balconies above, calling out to the passersby or talking across the street to each other about the gossip of the town—and watching absolutely everything that happened and everyone who passed by. Whenever Avra had been sent to Scuttle Cove, all he'd had to do to get bucketloads of material for his reports was walk down the street, flirt with a few of the courtesans, and use some of his travel stipend to buy an evening of unfailingly pleasant company. Was the information generally useless to his superiors? Yes, but that wasn't his problem. The important part was that it always sounded like he'd worked very hard to collect it.

The moment they turned onto the street, one of the beauties on the balconies cried out, "Ooh, as I live and breathe, that's never Avra Helvaçi!"

This immediately drew the attention of everyone else on all the other balconies, and at least thirty of them cried out, "Hi, Avra!"

"Hi!" he sang back. "I don't owe any of you money, right? Paid all my tabs?"

There was a general chorus of assent until one of the beauties, a young man with henna-scarlet hair and arguably the sweetest mouth on the island, shouted down, "I think you left an open tab with us, but it was only a bottle of wine."

"Sorry, hang on, sorry," Avra said to Viyan, stopping in his tracks and digging in his little rucksack. "Terribly sorry, Cat!" he called up to the beauty with the red hair. "Work's kept me away—I should have mailed the money or something."

Cat waved his hand idly. "I had a feeling it was an accident of circumstances, rather than intent. We've got ledgers going back a dozen years that say you've always been good for it."

"I damn well am," Avra said. "An Araşti always pays his bills, don't you know!" This was met with a vague titter of laughter, and everyone else returned their attention to the rest of the passersby. "Ah," he said, reaching the bottom of his little rucksack. "Cat, beauteous one, I'm currently out of pocket. Hang on one moment!" He turned to Viyan with a tragic expression. "I'm so sorry, perhaps I could meet the ambassador another time? I simply *cannot* delay my obligation to this house any longer, and I'm incredibly embarrassed to discover myself in this situation. I need to rectify it immediately—so sorry, Viyan, so very sorry, goodness, and I was so looking forward to meeting the new ambassador—*Cat!* Beautiful Cat, are there any house chores you all would like done? Not to pay for the wine itself, of course, but just as apology and to cover the accrued interest?"

"Sorry, dear, we hire extra help during festival season to do the tidying and laundry and dishwashing."

Avra grimaced. His hypothetical luck would probably get him a lot further if *other people's decisions* weren't as much of a factor. "Are you sure? Does anyone need a foot rub or anything?"

"That'd go onto your tab too," called one of Cat's colleagues, and several people laughed.

"Any errands?" Avra said relentlessly. "Anything that needs to be done right now immediately?"

"I could stand to be done right now immediately," another person called from the house opposite Cat's. "But then you'd have an open tab with us too." Another wave of laughter.

Avra resisted the urge to throw himself into the dust and roll around in exasperation. He looked up piteously at Cat and attempted to telepathically convey that he needed a convenient excuse to escape from Viyan and that he would be happy to have such a service added to his existing tab. "Calm down, dear, there's no rush," said Cat, draping himself over the railing and blowing a kiss to one of the other passersby before turning his grin back at Avra. "Everyone knows Avra Helvaçi isn't out of pocket for more than an hour or two at a time."

Dammit. He'd known Cat for too long, that was the problem. This was what happened when people trusted you. This was what happened when you had *good credit*. "You're a jewel, Cat, thank you. And I am most *exquisitely* sorry, and I shall be more than happy for you to charge me interest on the bill in whatever form you like, since I can't wash dishes to make up for it."

"That won't be necessary, but you can bring me some sweets if it makes you feel better. Will you be visiting me properly later, when you're in pocket again?" Cat said, with a smile that Avra was rather flattered to see seemed rather genuine rather than purely sultry.

"Ah, thank you for the offer, but I have a previous engagement tonight."

"Goodness," said the woman next to Cat, slinging her arm around his waist. "Who's the enterprising soul who snapped you up so quick? You've only been ashore for an hour or so, no? I saw *The Running Sun* come in."

Avra beamed. "I did a great job and was ever so helpful with the turtles, so Captain az-Ḥaffār is deigning to fuck me."

Everyone on the balcony of Cat's house and the one across the way groaned. "Really, Avra? Again?"

"You wouldn't understand."

"Oh, no, we definitely would," Cat said. "And we are judging you for it. And we will all be here to console you and your dick when you and your captain break up again."

"*Again* again," muttered Cat's friend, whose name Avra couldn't remember. She had changed it a couple of times, and might well have changed it again since the last time Avra had been in town.

"I had them once," called someone across the way. "Captain az-Ḥaffār, I mean. They're not even that good in bed."

"Well, that's subjective," Cat replied. "They're evidently very good for Avra."

"True, true. A man of broad tastes, our Avra."

"And we are all very fond of him for it," said Cat. "Gods bless you and keep you, Avra Helvaçi, and best of luck with your captain."

Avra swept him a florid bow in the Bendran style. "I will certainly stop by once I have any money whatsoever and buy at least a round of drinks for you beauties." Viyan, behind him, cleared her throat. He jumped. "Ah, I must be off. Good to see all of you, I missed you terribly!"

The beauties waved him off, and he set off down the street again. "You're popular," Viyan commented. "I hadn't realized, somehow."

"I pay my bills on time and I tip generously," Avra said seriously. "And I'm a very easy customer. Sometimes I just ask for a cuddle and have my hair petted. Sometimes I read them my poetry. Sometimes I get a hand job and then cry."

Viyan blinked at him politely and Avra remembered suddenly that they were not in fact part of the crew, not even a pirate, but a *normal respectable member of society* and therefore would very possibly not understand any of his nonsense. He scrambled mentally for a moment, disoriented, and then forced out a raucous laugh. "A joke!" he said, sounding as jolly as he could even as his nerves set back in and he became aware of the weight of the ambassador's villa hanging above his head like a future landslide. "Ah, your face!"

"Oh," said Viyan, and relaxed with a laugh too. "You're very convincing at sounding sincere—but I suppose that's why they assigned you to the Ministry of Intelligence."

"Just so, just so," said Avra, and changed the subject.

ൟ

Ambassador Baltakan had a short salt-and-pepper beard, as many Araşti men of his age did—perhaps mid-forties or thereabouts, or a well-preserved mid-fifties—and he wore a kaftan of spring green, and although he was seated at a desk and Avra could not see his waist, he knew that it would be belted with a cobalt and white sash denoting his office and the fact that he spoke as a representative of the sultan. Avra felt distinctly queasy just thinking about that sash.

Baltakan glanced up as Viyan led Avra in and made the introductions, and he gestured Avra to a chair after they exchanged pleasantries. "Have you messages for me, Helvaçi, or are you merely passing through?"

"No messages, alas! I've taken partial retirement, and I thought it would only be polite to say hello and offer my service to my fellow countryman and semi-colleague."

One of the greatest skills that Avra had ever learned from the Ministry of Intelligence was how to carry on a coherent conversation while utterly *gibbering* with terror on the inside. He did not want to be here. He did not want to be in this house, with Viyan and her sword and a man wearing the colors of the sultan of Araşt herself around his waist.

"Don't offer too much of your service to us!" Viyan said. "He is recovering from an illness, Ambassador."

"Very kind of you to offer, Helvaçi." Baltakan smiled. "If your illness was serious enough to take partial retirement, you must guard your health. It's all we really have, you know."

"So true," said Avra, in exactly the tone Viyan had used when he'd said the same to her.

"May I ask what rank you reached with Intelligence?"

"Oh, bottom rank," Avra said promptly. "Mostly courier duties."

"Ah, I see—in my youth, I was a courier with Intelligence for a very brief time, but I proved myself quickly and, well . . . here we find me."

"How are you enjoying it so far?" Avra asked politely.

Baltakan opened his hands. "I would not have chosen this appointment for myself, but I serve Her Majesty joyfully."

"Of course," said Avra, and let himself simper a little. "And one does strive to face with equanimity the trials that the Lord of Judgment sends us."

"Indeed. Equanimity and a readiness to take up the challenge." Baltakan tapped his fingers on the desk. "I'm attempting to find a delicate way to ask you about something, and it is eluding me."

"I have just come from the capital recently," said Avra. "If there is any news you are lacking, I would happily answer questions."

"No, no, it's not that . . . I suppose it's the sort of thing that would be all over the service, and particularly all through the Ministry of Intelligence. Did you hear about any, ah . . ." He paused, clearly searching for a noncommittal way of phrasing things that would bring up the topic neatly if Avra knew what he was speaking of, and which would not give Avra any more information than he already had if he didn't. "Did you hear about trouble at one of the guilds, earlier in the spring?"

"Oh, the break-in at the Shipbuilder's Guild, yes. That is indeed well-known throughout the service. Please do not feel like you must hold back anything—the issue has been resolved, as far as I know, and the perpetrators apprehended. Nothing of note was found to be missing."

Baltakan relaxed. "Good. That is very good to hear. The last message we had from the capital was that the investigation was ongoing."

"Oh?" Avra said, thinking a terrified *reeeeeee* as loudly as he could. "When was that?"

"Just over three weeks ago."

Avra nearly fell out of the chair with relief. "Oh! Well, my news is fresher than that—it's not quite two weeks since I was in Kasaba City, and they'd just apprehended the perpetrators," Avra said. "You can relax."

"Relax? Certainly not. Just because nothing was *found* missing doesn't mean that nothing was taken." Baltakan shook his head. "No, now more than ever, it is the time for vigilance."

"Such a good point," said Avra, returning to gibbering panic in the back of his mind. "Yes. Who knows if something was stolen? So true."

"Where else would it be taken but here?" Baltakan spread his hands. "To the den of thieves itself, the city where all pirates and smugglers come to fence their prizes?" Baltakan rose from his desk and stepped to the window, his hands clasped behind his back. He looked down at the city, nestled into the great encircling cove. "It is a sad misfortune that such a thing would happen now."

Misfortune, Avra's brain snagged on. Misfortune for Baltakan, in other words, which might well mean *fortune* for Avra. "Ah, when you are new to the post, you mean?"

He sighed. "My predecessor had twenty years here. I had thought—hoped, rather—that I would inherit some of those connections, that I would be able to call on favors that people owed her."

"Ah," said Avra. "No. No, that's not how they work here."

"It is unfortunate timing that in the moment when I most *need* those connections and networks of influence, I have not yet had time to build them."

"So unfortunate," Avra babbled, feeling like he was about to fly apart into pieces from sheer nerves.

Unfortunate for *Baltakan*. Fortunate for Avra. It was moments like this that really got to him, when he started trying to work out ways to prove whether or not his luck existed. Had it been *his* luck that caused the previous ambassador to retire, and for Baltakan to be installed in her place without enough time to consolidate his informants and establish a foothold in the economy of favors?

That was the thing about luck. There was no way of proving anything.

Baltakan turned back from the window. "But you do have those connections, don't you?"

"Ah," said Avra, still quietly having an existential crisis. "Well. Ahaha."

"He knows everybody," Viyan said. "*Everybody.* Everyone on the Street of Flowers greeted him by name and seemed happy to see him."

Baltakan chuckled. "Well, courtesans are all well and good, but I meant people of influence."

"Mm," said Avra vaguely, and reflected to himself that Cat and his colleagues were the first people he would have started sweet-talking if he'd been new to the city and had an agenda such as Baltakan's. Hell, those *had* been the first connections he'd made in Scuttle Cove when he'd wandered in as a fresh baby courier, all of twenty-two or so and still wet behind the ears, wide-eyed at all the exciting pirates—criminals!—with their exciting criminal lifestyles going about their normal business and normal lives in the city, buying newspapers, eating curry in Eel-face Yusin's bar, wiping mustard off their coats and muttering curses under their breath.

Granted, Avra hadn't made a pet of himself to all the courtesans on *purpose,* but then that was possibly why it had worked so well. He'd just gone in with the earnest intent of exchanging money for goods and services, and he'd been polite and paid his bills and thanked those nice people for their time and for sucking his dick, and somehow that was enough that everyone on the Street of Flowers smiled when they saw him and seemed happy to make small talk with him and had never once thrown him out. That was really all it took: Being a pleasant customer. People remembered pleasant customers. People *liked* pleasant customers.

Being a pleasant customer got you all kinds of perks, such as real conversations, hints whispered into his ear about something going on. He hadn't even *tried* to get those things. He hadn't been angling for them; it hadn't even occurred to him at the time that he *could* use social connections like that, not really. Presumably they trained you about those things when you graduated from the couriers into being a proper field agent, but Avra never had. He'd invented it all himself, just by going into the pleasure-houses with the general air of being friendly and easy to get along with, and he'd said *please* and *thank you,* and *I really liked meeting you* or *it was so nice to see you again,* and he'd looked them in the eyes instead of the tits.

He'd tried it out on purpose elsewhere with other people. It kept working, was the bitch of the thing. Not just with courtesans—it worked on shopkeepers, publicans, coffeehouse staff, servants at fancy parties, guards and the city watch . . . Anybody whose job primarily involved dealing with other people, really.

Baltakan had been saying something—examples of what he meant by "people of influence," for Viyan's benefit. Captains (but only the respectable sort), fences (but not the ones who dealt in smuggling immoral goods, which was clearly much more wrong to do than smuggling moral goods, whatever those were), one or two of the tavern owners, and exactly one of the owners of the "houses of leisure" as Baltakan put it (and this only because that particular lady had formerly been a priestess of the Bendran goddess of love and pleasure, and therefore more respectable than ordinary small business owners, apparently).

"You said you were a courier in Intelligence? How long exactly?" asked Avra before he could think better of it.

"Oh, very briefly, as I said. Only one or two courier missions, and then I was transferred to the Ministry of Diplomacy. But, ha, you know what they say about the two."

Avra knew quite well, and suppressed an eye roll on behalf of all his former colleagues. *Diplomacy* always happily claimed that they and Intelligence were alike as two twins; Intelligence privately and staunchly disagreed.

Diplomacy worked within the higher levels of society—spoke to kings and queens and great lords, negotiated treaties and attended banquets and tended to the garden of Araşt's allies, and were always on hand to offer helpful loans at very friendly interest rates to whichever nation was in need of a little extra pocket money. They didn't know about wriggling up a tree two days before a great feast and camping there like a bird just to overhear a piece of gossip. They didn't know about grubbing around in mucky alleys on rainy nights to find a message in a dead drop behind a loose brick.

They weren't at all the same, really, and anyone who was in Intelligence for more than one or two courier missions knew it.

"So," Baltakan said, turning his attention from Viyan back to Avra again. "You'll be a great help with that."

"Eh?" said Avra, twitching back to alertness and gibbering panic. "Sorry, we crossed the turtles last night. I didn't get much sleep."

"Introductions to the luminaries of the city, such as they are."

"Oh, sure, sure," said Avra. "Sure, yes, I can definitely do that. Absolutely. Would love to, really."

"Excellent. And you'll keep your ear to the ground during this . . ." He waved his hand vaguely toward the window. "*Festival.*"

"Can't go sailing," Avra said, a little delirious. He did need sleep. All this gibbering panic was getting to him. "On account of the fuckswarms. Gotta stay here where it is safe, yes. Have a big party about it, why not? And a cake competition. Very important event, the cake competition. Height of the whole festival."

Baltakan seemed thrown for a moment, then laughed awkwardly. "You must have had a late crossing indeed, Helvaçi. You're beginning to sound incoherent."

"I'm fine. Ear to the ground, yes. Make sure nobody's trying to sell something they shouldn't have. Yes." He rallied himself back into his jovial, personable face. "Ambassador, I am truly exhausted—we ran into one of those ghosts that screams 'Captain!' every few moments when we were anchored on the big rock for low tide, haha. Before I excuse myself, I shall say I am so glad you are here to take care of these very important matters, and I have such admiration for your vigilance and watchfulness and, ah, looking-out-for-problems-before-they-happen skills. Truly the man for the job."

Baltakan nodded modestly. "One does one's best in pursuit of one's duty."

"One certainly does," Avra said enthusiastically. "I can tell you're a kindred spirit, sir, and I look forward to furthering our acquaintance. We should have dinner sometime! Ha ha!" Avra immediately hated himself for suggesting that. Why had Teveri not thrown him overboard days ago? Hopefully Baltakan was the *really* snobby kind of Diplomacy egghead. "If you don't mind associating with a bottom-rank courier, that is."

Baltakan laughed and stepped forward to clap Avra on the shoulder, leading him to the door. "We are all equal in Her Majesty's service, as they say."

"They do say that!" Avra said brightly. "They do consistently say that."

"And really, Helvaçi, you're the expert around here. Lieutenant Viyan is something of a homebody when she's at leisure, I have gathered."

"Yes, sir," she said with an apologetic smile. "Early to bed, early to rise, and not that interested in the local pastimes, I'm afraid."

"Drinking, gambling, fucking," Avra said. "The cake competition. Life-risking wagers. Stabbing. Wholesale seagull murder."

"I enjoy walks out to the cliffs on my days off," Viyan said. "I often take a book and a picnic and go out to the point—there's a good view of the cliffs at the cove entrance and that madman's, ah, artistic project."

"Goodness, I have been wondering about that," said Baltakan. "Did no one think to stop him?"

"Why would they stop him?" Avra asked. He was getting legitimately fuzzy-brained from gibbering and lack of sleep. "It's a giant fuck-off skull carved in the side of a cliff. Or it will be one day. He's been working on it for twenty years. Name's Skully. He showed me the plans once. Amazing stuff. Incredible ambiance. Tourists hate it."

"I can see why," Baltakan said. "If there were a city council or a planning committee of some kind, they wouldn't have let him begin."

Avra pulled up the corners of his mouth into something approximating an agreeable smile and shrugged. "Well, everybody has a passion project of one kind or another, eh? Whether it's strange sculptural projects or serving the sultan of Araşt with our, ah, fervent devotion."

Baltakan laughed aloud and clapped him on the shoulder again. "What a generous man you are, Helvaçi! No wonder you get along so well with all sorts. But enough small talk—get some rest, and perhaps you could join me for tea tomorrow afternoon, if you have no other plans?"

"Oh, sure, sure. Tea tomorrow afternoon, that sounds great, yes."

"Do you have accommodation in town?" Viyan asked suddenly. "I wondered earlier, but then you mentioned Captain az-Ḥaffār to that person on the Street of Flowers . . ."

"A captain?" Baltakan said, raising an eyebrow. "One of the pirate captains, I take it?"

"One of my contacts," Avra said. "Yes, I'm staying in their hotel with a few of their crew. Ah, used to be appointed to their ship, you know, the previous ambassador hired them to ferry me around on a few courier missions. Unofficially," he added quickly, because Baltakan's next question would have been to see Teveri's paperwork. "Just one of those delicate matters that the higher-ups don't want on the books. I can't talk about it."

"Have they made port in Araşt recently?"

"No," said Avra, who *would have known about it* if they had. "Not for at least a year."

Baltakan nodded. "So even if there were illicit materials taken from the Shipbuilder's Guild, it wouldn't be likely that they would have them," he said, sounding incredibly satisfied for a man who was dead wrong.

"Oh goodness me, Captain az-Ḥaffār? Noooo, no, definitely absolutely not. You're certainly right and I agree with everything you are saying right now." It was really rather shocking how often Avra could get away with saying things like that. "I'll take my leave, sir, I'm dead on my feet. Marvelous to make your acquaintance—I seem nice."

"You do seem nice!" Baltakan said with another companionable pat on Avra's shoulder.

Easy. *Easy*. It shouldn't work. It should be a strange thing to say, that little manipulation of telling someone how to feel about him. But they never did notice, and they almost always agreed that he seemed nice.

Avra had a great deal of practice in quitting while he was ahead, and therefore got himself the hell out of there with all speed.

"Tev, Tev, Tev, Tev, Tev," Avra said, banging on Tev's door at the hotel. "I have to tell you something."

There was a slosh of water and a grumble. "Come in."

Avra slammed into the room, froze, and gibbered. "Ah, you're naked, that's very nice. Hello, naked Tev. One of my favorite kinds of Tev. All Tevs are my favorite Tev but naked Tev is a special treat to encounter. Hello. Hello very much." Tev was in a very large bath up to their nose, the water steaming and milky with soaps and what have you. "That smells nice," Avra said, holding himself up with the doorframe. "Sort of incense-y. Sexy. Hm."

"Fuck's sake. Close the door."

Avra closed the door and held himself up by the knob.

"You had something to tell me," Tev said.

"Your hair looks nice like that. Wet."

"Avra."

"Mhm," he said, rather high-pitched. "I went to see the new ambassador. Baltakan. Very competent person. Very handsome if you like older men, but not too old. Sort of a paternal age."

"You're thirty-five, Avra. A paternal age for you is upward of—"

"Fifty if he started young, and that's not the point, Tev."

Tev lifted one wet, golden-brown arm from the water and reached for a glass of wine on a little table. They sipped it and squinted at him. "Are you developing a *daddy thing* about the ambassador?"

"Are you jealous?" Avra babbled. "I could have a daddy thing about you if you gave me half an hour to work myself up to it."

"Ew. No thank you. You visited the ambassador, and . . . ?"

"And definitely did not develop a daddy thing for him, because it is not an area I am interested in, ha ha," said Avra, who had suddenly remembered that Teveri had *promised* to fuck him if he was helpful. "Also because I was maybe busy panicking a little bit because he said that he got a letter from home a few weeks ago about the break-in at the Shipbuilder's Guild—not mine, I mean, the first one—and now he's being very, um. . . ." Avra blinked, swallowed several times, and said, "Could you put your arm back in the water, please? It makes it hard to think of words."

Tev rolled their eyes and set aside their wine. They even scootched back down until their shoulders were only vague shapes under the water. Like turtles, maybe. "He's being very . . . ?" Tev prompted.

"Hm?" said Avra urgently. "Oh. Baltakan. Yes. On the lookout for people selling illicit materials they might have stolen from the Shipbuilder's Guild. Vigilant. Watchful. Invited me to tea tomorrow afternoon. You should come. I am inviting you on a date, to be clear. Very fun date activity, going into the ambassador's house and eating his food and drinking his wine and maybe making out in his broom closet while we have all the illicit materials physically on our persons."

Teveri had closed their eyes and dropped their head back against the side of the bath with a sigh of annoyance. "Your *fucking* luck, Avra."

"I don't know if it's my luck. We can't know for sure that it's my luck."

Teveri opened one accusing eye at him.

"Not everything happens because of my luck," Avra said. "Some things are normal. Most things are normal, I would say. Normal things just happen the way they do. People retire as ambassador of Scuttle Cove after thirty years, and that's normal. Other people get appointed to replace them, and that's also normal. People make smart conclusions about events and—and happenings in their lives, things like 'Hm, maybe we should be careful for a while just in case anything did get stolen from the Shipbuilder's Guild! Nothing wrong with double-checking the things it's my literal job to keep an eye on,' and that's normal. People maybe meet a colleague who has taken partial retirement, and they update each other about *work stuff*, a very normal kind of activity to partake in!"

Tev had raised their eyebrow at him. Avra froze in the middle of wild gesticulations, cleared his throat, and nodded firmly.

"A series of very normal and completely unremarkable events," Teveri said. Avra couldn't parse the tone, due to the fact that they'd shifted a little and he could just see the very point of their knee breaking the surface.

"Yes, naked Tev, exactly so. Normal as hell."

"And now we have the good fortune of being forewarned."

"Getting a little lucky sometimes is also normal, Tev. You can't *prove* whether it's normal events, or normal luck, or witchy luck. Could be anything."

"Very important to prove these things," Tev said. Avra's thoughts, such as they were, skidded to a halt. Tev sounded almost warm. Almost approving. Like Avra had done a useful thing and made their life a little more convenient and the general annoyance of his demeanor was not currently outweighing his contributions.

"Mhm," Avra said, very high-pitched, and held himself up with the doorknob again. "So important. Did you still feel like, um, charitably donating some sex to my fund which I will be using to maybe one day move out of the alley where I am being mobbed by possums on a daily basis and digging in the rubbish pile for scraps of edible shoe leather? You don't have to, haha. You did promise, but I'm not going to hold you to that if you've decided that I haven't earned it. Or if you want to, um, have your bath all by yourself without. Without me keeping you company. Or guarding the door from swarms of bloodthirsty aquatic vampire possums. Or polishing your boots."

They looked him over slowly and reached for their wineglass again. "You don't look too mucky, I suppose."

"Oskar pushed me out of the dinghy earlier when we were coming ashore. I was very wet and pathetic. Markefa said I looked like a sad rat. No muck at all. Just, um, salty." Avra held himself very, very still, just in case he moved one muscle in a way Teveri took exception to and they decided to throw him out instead of . . . He mentally screeched. Instead of presumably being about to invite him into the bath.

"Hm," said Teveri. They took a long sip of wine. "That'll do, I suppose. In you get. *No,* Avra, clothes *off* first—gods and fishes."

Somewhere in there—he could not remember the precise order of events of the last second and a half—he had scrambled for the bath, scrambled away from the bath in reflexive terror, scrambled to take his boots off while he was still standing in them, and fallen over. Presumably they had happened in roughly that order, but he could not be sure. The perspective of the room was rather different, so it appeared that falling over had been the most recent event, and he was mightily struggling with his boots and belt at the same time.

"Do I regret this already?" Teveri said to their wineglass.

"I can assure you that you absolutely do not regret this, incandescent one," Avra said. "I am entirely positive that you do not already regret this and in fact that you are delighted with my entire personage."

"Is that what this emotion is called," Tev said, dry as—dry as—well, dry as something very dry, which was a thing that Avra was imminently about to not be, as soon as he could figure out how to untie his belt.

Captain's Log

Day 14 (addendum)

SIGH. *Circumstances beyond my control have once again forced me to sleep with Avra. Had the absolute gall to be typically falling-all-over-himself ready to please, which he knows I like—incredibly annoying. Refuses to do me the basic courtesy of being outright shit in bed; insists on intentionally, maliciously continuing behavior that gets me hot, like "helpfulness" and "saying please" and "following directions." UGHHHHHH.*

10

> *1. The Innocent*
>
> New ventures, fresh starts. If you aspire to greatness, there is a journey to embark upon, a quest to accept, or a task to complete. May indicate a child or an amateur.
>
> (Reversed: Foolishness, impulsiveness, starting too many endeavors with no follow-through. Alternatively: You may be hesitating at the threshold. The first step across is the most difficult.)

The next morning, Teveri had their brawniest crew members guard the door of one of the hotel's private parlors. The parlor was decorated in the typical style for Scuttle Cove—plain plaster walls draped with lengths of cloth, shabby scuffed floors, a mishmash of unmatched furniture from a multitude of different countries and fashions. Everything in the room—everything in nearly every room in town—had been stolen at some point. That was the only route by which luxuries were imported.

A great many luxuries, however, passed *through* Scuttle Cove on the pirate ships. The vast majority of this business was handled by the fences—the most powerful, influential, wealthy, and well-connected people in the city, several of whom had just walked into this meeting. Teveri offered them coffee and rum, which they really could not afford, but appearances had to be maintained, and at least this counted as a business expense that could be paid from the ship's purse rather than Tev's personal funds. Tev had implied that there might be more sex in Avra's future if he were quiet and well-behaved in the meeting, but there was really only so much boredom he could take before he got fidgety.

He lasted about a minute and a half or fifteen eternities before sidling over to Julian. "Did you write about my exciting walk yesterday?" he whispered. "I think you should write in your memoir that I had a terrifying run-in with our archnemesis, the ambassador. A man with eyes as cold and black as iron, ruthless. Bloodthirsty. He dropped a few clues about his terrible plan to me—so terrible that you cannot bear to write it down. I decided to turn coat on my homeland and throw my lot in with the pirates, so I tricked him into telling me the rest of what he was up to and escaped by the skin of my teeth, and I came back to the hotel and flung myself tearfully into your arms."

Julian had at least seven different expressions going across his face in rotation, but amusement seemed to be winning out. "That's quite good. Thank you."

"You're so welcome." He wriggled a little closer and lowered his voice further. "I will tell you about the fences now. For your memoir. I don't even need to make any shit up—you can just write down their actual lives verbatim and it'll fit just fine, tonally speaking."

Julian arranged his face into an attentive expression, which took Avra a bewildered moment to identify, because *no one* used that expression at him. It was unsettling.

He shook it off. "Starting at Tev's left, we've got Madam mes Rakan." She was a short, elderly woman. Her leathery brown skin was so wrinkly and her mouth pursed so small that she looked like a drawstring pouch, and she had both hands resting atop an elaborately carved ivory cane topped with a giant green stone full of crackling inclusions that sparkled like bottled lightning. "Everybody says that she was a great beauty in her youth. She used to be one of the concubines of the king of Mangar-Khagra—bore him a son and a daughter. She also killed his head vizier and claimed that he was trying to usurp the throne. They say that the king had to convict her of murder because there wasn't hard evidence of any planned coup, but he had suspected that the vizier was up to *something*, so in thanks for saving his life, he gave Madam mes Rakan a pile of money and exiled her instead of having her killed, which was how she came to Scuttle Cove. The daughter she bore is chief vizier to the queen, her half sister. So: Very good connections there, could definitely let some very rich people know that we have goods to sell.

"Next to her, the pimply teenager with the infuriatingly bored expression is Jassen Kavo, and beside him his father, Harek Kavo. People call him Papa Kavo because he's got about twenty-two kids. And counting." Jassen was scowling and slouched down in his chair with his arms crossed. He was somewhere in the vicinity of fifteen, and his face was more pimple than skin at the moment. Except in bearing and temperament, he looked a great deal like his father, a man in his fifties with steel-grey hair and startlingly bright greenish-gold eyes. "Young Jassen is widely regarded as a generally useless heir to his father's legacy, but he's the only legitimate child and the Kavo family has *views* about that. Old, old, *old* family in Scuttle Cove. They've been here since there was a here to be.

"Then next to him is . . ." Avra squinted at the man sitting beside Papa Kavo. He was in his late twenties or early thirties, with pale, freckled skin and a shock of ginger hair—true red, not Cat's henna-dyed ruby. He was wearing scarlet boots, a russet tunic, and a mild, interested expression. "Dunno who that is. Never seen him before in my life. Maybe a new fence. I'm sure we'll be introduced at some point, and then we'll find out what's exciting about him. Next to *him*—uh. I don't know who that is either."

"They're Tashaz, aren't they?" murmured Julian. "Like the captain."

The person sitting beside the ginger man was indeed wearing Tashaz dress: They were covered from head to toe in loose, flowing robes of a muted plum and a headscarf that entirely covered their face, and every hem was intricately embroidered in many shades of purple. Though even their eyes were blocked by the veil, the sleeves of their robes reached only to their mid-forearm, leaving their wrists and hands bare, folded in their lap on what looked like . . . some kind of doll.

As Avra watched, the ginger man leaned over and whispered something; the Tashaz tilted their head toward him to listen, and nodded at whatever it was a moment later.

"Yeah, no idea who that is," Avra said. "*Next*—that's the infamous Black Garda. Proper pirate queen back in her day, you know. You could make up any wild shit for your memoir and probably all of it would have been true. They don't make 'em like Black Garda anymore, mostly because she killed a lot of the competition back in the good old days. Retired ten years ago to get married to a lady she consensually kidnapped off one of the ships she raided. I accidentally sneezed in the punch bowl at her wedding and she's probably going to have me killed. Great baker, her wife. One of the town's finest. We will see her work at the cake competition in a couple days."

"I keep hearing about this cake competition," Julian murmured.

"Can't have a festival without a cake competition. Barely a festival at all, I'm sure you'll agree. Anyway, next to Black Garda are her hounds." Avra regarded the pack. "I don't remember their names, I'm not really a dog person. What happens is that people find a fancy dog on a ship they're raiding and say, 'Hey, y'know what, I'd love to get on Black Garda's good side! Let's take this dog back to Scuttle Cove as a present for her.' So they do, and she's always fucking happy. Takes better care of 'em than their original owners did, probably. Goes *striding* around the town with them, and all up and down the hills. Very vigorous and energetic walkies regimen."

Black Garda glanced over at them; Avra squeaked and straightened immediately and bowed very politely to her. She narrowed her eyes at him and returned her attention to the table. She was a great tall woman, roughly Julian's height and Oskar's build—broad shoulders and strong arms, tree-trunk thighs, a barrel chest—all healthy fat covering powerful muscle. She had black hair, just long enough to be tied back in a stubby ponytail, medium-brown skin, and aggressively practical attire. The five or six dogs ranged around her were all different sizes, from very large to a pocket-sized lapdog, but all of them very clearly of *impeccable* breeding and immaculate training.

When Avra was sure that Black Garda wasn't about to turn and shoot him another death glare, he continued: "And lastly, the Mainmast, so called because he is very tall."

Julian looked at him expectantly, then raised his eyebrows more expectantly, then made a continue-please gesture that was almost painfully expectant.

"What is it?" said Avra, startling out of his reverie.

"You had things to say about all the others."

"Oh. I was reflecting on whether it was rather dull to call him the Mainmast just because he's tall. It would be funnier if he were short, right? Actually it'd be even funnier if he were perfectly average height. Some people just aren't very creative. Anyway, he's from Genzhu—oh, and this is something you should put in your memoir: *No one knows his real name.*"

"Very dramatic."

"I never sneezed into the punch bowl at his wedding. I think he has a daughter. That's all I've got."

∞

"Look, I don't see a reason why we can't be realistic about this," said Black Garda, one hand resting on the head of the enormous wolfhound sitting beside her, another gently scratching the small brown-and-white lapdog, which Julian had whispered to Avra was a very famous Vintish breed called a butterfly dog, due to the lovely shape of its ears. "Why are we assuming we just sell this thing once? There's nobody in the world that can afford to buy exclusive rights to it."

"Except Araşt themselves," said Papa Kavo with a shrug. "And if they find out we have it, then they send their entire navy, call in every loan they've got to every country that's in their pocket, and either buy enough fireworks to blast the Tits into gravel or assemble a blockade of ships and let us starve. Money will *not* be an object when it comes to maintaining mercantile hegemony."

"Exactly," said Garda, snapping her fingers at him. All of her dogs looked up at her instantly, ears pricked forward. "So why not sell it to a dozen people? Why not sell it to *whoever wants to buy it*?"

"Perhaps there are unrelated benefits that *some of us* would prefer draw upon," said Sareen mes Rakan primly. "Political influence, shall we say, rather than . . . vulgar amounts of money."

"Friends, colleagues," said the Mainmast. "I respect your thirst for profit, but we have not yet addressed the main problem."

"A good and valid point," said Black Garda, sitting back in her chair. Her dogs relaxed, looking away or putting their heads back down on their paws. The little lapdog rolled over onto its back; Black Garda transitioned seamlessly into rubbing its belly. "I respect your prudence, Mainmast, as much as you respect my thirst for *vulgar profit*." This last was said with a pointed look to Madam mes Rakan.

"What is the problem, may I ask?" Teveri said tightly.

The Mainmast shrugged one shoulder. "You are a well-known captain of middling reputation—"

"Ouch," whispered Avra.

"—and yet I cannot help but notice that you have not brought us much of value this season." He looked around the table at his colleagues. "Unless any of you have had private dealings with the captain that I have not heard of?"

"You can also write in your memoirs that his eyebrows are *amazing*," Avra whispered to Julian, who nodded in agreement.

The fences all shook their heads. "Thin season for *The Running Sun* by all accounts," said Papa Kavo.

"One cannot help but wonder—and no insult is intended, Captain az-Ḥaffār—but one cannot help but wonder what lengths you would go to in order to fund your ship's maintenance, outfit her for the next voyage, and pay your crew something for their efforts."

Teveri was silent.

"They're grinding their teeth again," Avra whispered to Julian. "The spooky dentist told them to stop doing that, you know."

"I," said Teveri in ringing tones, "am a captain of far more than *middling reputation.*" They stared down the Mainmast; the Mainmast held their gaze as he leaned back in his chair and puffed at a long gilt pipe, the smoke thick and incense-heavy. "My ship bears the mainsail of the *Nightingale*! Do you accuse me, sir, of *pissing* on that honor?"

"I accuse you of being a captain," the Mainmast replied wryly.

Papa Kavo snorted; his son Jassen scowled harder and slouched more aggressively in his chair; Black Garda laughed aloud and raised her glass of whiskey. "Having once been a captain myself, can't argue with that." The Mainmast exchanged a pointed look of amusement with her, and she added, "Ships gotta be fixed. Sails gotta be mended. That shit is never-ending. Crew's gotta be fed and paid, else you've got a mutiny—well, not for *you,* Teveri. Who would dare mutiny against Captain Undertaker?"

Teveri's eyes flashed.

"Now there's a story," said the redheaded, red-booted man, who had introduced himself as, to Avra's squinty-eyed suspicion, *Red.* He and his Tashaz companion had otherwise not spoken much. "Captain Undertaker?"

"Must have been a bit more than fifteen years ago. Little whip of a thing, Teveri was in those days," said Black Garda, sipping her whiskey. "Nineteen or twenty, weren't you? I was still queen of the pirates, and Teveri was bouncing from crew to crew—couldn't keep their temper for shit. Had big ideas that they could do it better."

"And then one day it's festival time, just like now," said the Mainmast, trickling smoke from his nose like a salamander. "And a plague ship drifts into the harbor on the very day of the cake competition. Araşti flag hanging from its mast, sails flapping loose. Who knows how long it had been drifting. You could smell the death all the way on shore."

Avra watched Tev carefully—they'd gone tense, their back as straight as an iron bar, their black eye flashing, their gold eye blazing.

"Is this the story you promised to tell me at some point?" Julian whispered. Avra checked to make sure none of the people at the table were watching before he nodded.

"The whole town was arguing about what to do about it," said Papa Kavo. "Every worthy captain refused to go anywhere near it, let alone touch it. Haunted by the souls of the dead, some said—the angry, vengeful dead, nothing like the ghosts who have a good clean death wrecked in the Shallows and spend a few centuries with the turtles. Other folks said that going aboard a plague ship was a death sentence even without any vengeful spirits—said the foul miasma or the ship's rats would spread the disease. But Teveri, for some reason, decided they didn't give a fuck."

"The *reason* was that they wanted a ship of their own real bad," said Black Garda. "Real, real bad."

Teveri said nothing. Their hands were clenched in fists on their knees.

"So they stole a dinghy and rowed out to the plague ship alone," Madam mes Rakan croaked. "And everyone at the cake competition watched from the shore as Teveri dropped corpses over the side into the dinghy, one by one, until it was low in the water. Then they rowed it out of the harbor past the cliffs, dumped them in blue water, and came back for more. How many trips did it take, child? Remind an old lady."

"Thirteen," said Tev through gritted teeth.

"Thirteen," said the Mainmast. "Came back to shore with blood pouring from their eye, because on the thirteenth trip, just after they dumped the last corpse out where the currents would carry it away and suck it down to the bottom for the turtles to eat, the oarlock cracked in half and the end of the oar got 'em." He smiled, the curl of his mouth echoing the curl of smoke around him. "Lost the eye, of course, as you can see. But everyone said that was a cheap price for a ship of the damned."

"Stupid move," Madam mes Rakan muttered. "Someone else would have taken care of it eventually. Let other people lose their eyes, that's my advice."

"And from that day," said Black Garda, "folks called them Captain

Undertaker." She tipped her head to the side, considering. "At least for a few months, and then Teveri took them to task rather violently. Now they only say that behind their back." She sighed and finished off her whiskey. "Never could figure out what made you be that fucking stupid."

"You were one of the captains who refused to touch the plague ship, though," said the Mainmast.

"Well, it's true that I wouldn't touch a plague corpse for all the gold in Araşt. But recall that I had prior commitments that day, such as guarding Granny Layla's cake at the competition. Couldn't just go running off and leave it—there were a lot of seagulls that year. We needed all hands on deck."

"If I may consult with my colleague for a moment," said Red, and turned to whisper something to them. The figure in the enveloping purple robes listened intently, then leaned close to whisper in Red's ear. Red sat back with a nod. "Were your family gravediggers, Captain?"

Teveri fixed him with a look that would have made Avra fall to his knees in terror and horniness. "I fail to see how such a question can be construed as anything but *egregious* presumption, sir."

He held up his hands. "My apologies, I meant no offense. It is the nature of my profession to ask presumptuous questions."

"Since when do fences ask questions?" Markefa snorted. She was leaning against the wall between two windows just behind Teveri.

"I am not a fence," said Red pleasantly. "I am a guest of Black Garda, and she thought this an interesting meeting for me to witness."

"And I already told you out in the hall that I'll vouch for these two," said Black Garda. "Stake my honor and reputation on it. What's this about gravediggers, though?"

Red cast a look to Teveri. "I truly meant no offense—is it a private matter?"

Teveri stared him down for a long moment and then snarled, "No."

"Perhaps I should say nothing," Red said, glancing at his companion, who gave a tiny shrug of one shoulder.

"Why stop now, when you have already told them half of what you have to say?" said Teveri. Their voice was an ice-cold dare. "You might as well finish."

"Ah . . ." Red shifted slightly. Avra peered at him—he did appear a little embarrassed, but strangely not at all nervous. "Well. My companion is from Tash, and I myself speak a little of their language. Your surname is Tashaz in origin, is it not? And indicative of your family's occupation?"

"Your point?" said Teveri coldly.

"Just that I would not be surprised that someone with that background would have some expertise or at least knowledge of the handling of bodies, as well as less . . . squeamishness about it in comparison to a layperson. Perhaps some knowledge of medicine, as well. Perhaps some of the magic . . . My companion says you have the accent of those regions that bear a magical resistance against sickness?"

"How fascinating that a man who provided no surname of his own—and did not introduce his companion whatsoever—would presume to comment on my history."

Red shrugged and spread his hands. "It was presumptuous of me, and I apologize."

Teveri stared at him for a moment, then pointedly shifted their gaze to Red's companion and stared even harder at them. Finally, they turned their attention back to the Mainmast. "You were accusing me of being a captain, sir, and hinting that because I have had, as you call it, a *thin season,* that I might be tempted to lie to the four most well-connected fences in the city and their two breathtakingly rude guests. Do I have the right of it?"

"More or less," said the Mainmast affably.

Avra leaned over to Julian. "I've remembered something else about him you should put in your memoirs. He breeds fancy miniature turtles. He had Skully build them a model of the Isles in a big enclosure, and he glues little bits of coral and miniature shipwrecks onto them."

"The details we have provided thus far on the provenance of these research papers are not worth anything to you, I take it," Teveri said. "You would pass this up because you don't think it's real. Because you're—" Teveri stopped speaking abruptly and shut their mouth tight.

"A bunch of cowards?" said the Mainmast. "Please, finish your sentence."

"I don't need to."

"It's just an issue of doing good science, isn't it," said Black Garda. Papa Kavo hummed in agreement, nodding slowly. "If you've got the thing that tells you how to dodge the serpents, then we've gotten quite lucky, haven't we?" Teveri's eye twitched at the word *lucky,* Avra noticed. They didn't look at him, but he could feel a telepathic glare directed toward him. "Your timing is splendid—all you have to do to prove what you've got is to take it on a trial run. A jaunt, if you will."

"This seems entirely reasonable to me," said Papa Kavo. "How will we prove that they've done it?"

"Perhaps we'll have them fetch something back," said the Mainmast. "Something unique."

Black Garda smacked the table with her palm; her hounds jumped and looked up at her as one again. "Oh, you'll all laugh at me, but *could* I make a request? There's an island about a day's sail away. Damn wretch of a place, no one ever stops there. But on that island, there's a particular kind of dog—" Papa Kavo and the Mainmast burst out laughing. Red clapped his hand over his mouth as his shoulders shook with mirth, and his companion snorted, the first sound that they had made. Even Madam mes Rakan smirked over the great green jewel at the top of her cane. Young Jassen, of course, rolled his eyes. "Yes, yes, I know," said Black Garda with an indulgent smile. "I'm getting soft in my middle age. It's that wife of mine, you know, she feeds me too well."

Papa Kavo shook his head, still laughing into his beard, and gestured for her to continue. "The special dogs on this island, Garda, go on. What's so special about them?"

"They're blue."

"Oh! Like that fucking mongrel you were dragging around back in the day!"

"Yes. Claw, his name was. Best dog I ever had." She glanced down at her hounds. "Sorry, gang, but it's true."

"That thing bit a chunk out of Eel-face Yusin's cake at the competition one year, do you remember?" said Papa Kavo. "Also out of several people's legs."

"Twelve people's legs," Black Garda said with a wistful sigh. "Miss that boy every day. So!" She slapped her hand on the table again. "Go off to Blue Dog Island, and get me another one of those blue dogs. A good one, for preference. Then we'll assume you either have what you say you have, or that you really are as batshit as we all thought you were when you were hauling corpses out to sea just because you wanted their ship."

"Hm," said Papa Kavo. "I'm not happy with those odds."

"Nor I," said Madam mes Rakan and the Mainmast in unison.

"Just send someone along," muttered Jassen with another magnificent eye roll. "It's not hard."

"You volunteering?" said Papa Kavo sharply. "Volunteering to go out on the sea into a salty fuckpile of serpents? Those things have teeth that'll bite an oar in half. You volunteering to go out in that, my son?"

"Ugh," said Jassen, clearly more about his father's tone than the idea of the serpents. "*No.*"

"You'd have to be batshit to go out in that," said Papa Kavo.

"Or an exceptionally good sailor," said Red slowly, turning to exchange a look (presumably) with his companion.

His companion raised the doll from their lap. Avra saw that it was, in fact, a puppet. "And sailing a boat with an exceptionally shallow draft," said the puppet.

"Or all three for preference," said Papa Kavo. "Do you have someone in—Oh. The new arrivals?"

"I get the impression that they're up for anything," said Red with a shrug. "They crossed the Unending Ocean."

"What, in *that*?" said the Mainmast, jerking his head in the general direction of the harbor. "That strange contraption with two hulls?"

"And in perhaps a third of the time it would have taken any of the other ships out there," said Red pointedly. "Their ship might look strange to your eyes, but they sure know how to handle it."

"They think it's funny that everybody's holing up here for the breeding season," said the puppet. It was *extraordinarily strange*—Avra knew that it was the person in the purple robes who was speaking. But somehow whenever the puppet spoke, it really did seem like the *puppet* speaking. He could have sworn that it was breathing.

Avra leaned over to Julian. "I think that's not a real puppet," he whispered. "And even if it is a real puppet, you can't say that in your memoir. Say that it was cursed by a necromancer or something. Or they've got an enchantment on them that means they can only speak through the puppet. Or there's not a person under the robes, just a pile of bones, because their spirit has been trapped in the puppet until they can find a princess to kiss."

Julian gave him a pained look and bit his lip on a laugh.

Madam mes Rakan narrowed her beady little eyes at the man calling himself Red. "How are you speaking to them? Nobody in town has been able to speak to them without an extended game of charades."

"Part of the job," he replied vaguely. "But would you accept them as an escort or witness, if they'd be willing to go?"

"Are they likely to ask what it's for?"

"Probably not," said the puppet.

"But," added Red firmly. "I think it only fair that they be offered compensation for their services, particularly since this is a job that they are uniquely suited to, both in expertise and personal disposition. And even with the right ship, there is still a risk."

"I'll foot the bill for that," said Black Garda easily. "But I want two blue dogs. A breeding pair."

11

56. The Forest

Being lost, unseen danger, vast interconnections and dependencies of which you can only see a small part. Uncertainty, a creeping sense of dread. You are in the wilderness, where the only goal is survival. Tread with care; secure your position.

(Reversed: Take advantage of every small resource, whether it is a brook of clean water or a handful of berries. Remember that you too are capable of being dangerous.)

Avra was in the middle of bothering Tev over their breakfast the next day—mostly by threatening to put coconut jam on his nipples—when Red and his companion knocked on the door.

"Ah," said Red apologetically when Teveri yanked the door open. "We're interrupting."

Avra was laid out nearly naked across the breakfast table with a fistful of silk scarves in his hands, which he had been shaking insistently at Teveri. He sighed. "Well, yes, a bit, but you weren't to know."

"What do you want?" Teveri demanded, holding the door open with one hand and their coffee cup with the other.

"We just came by with an update. We asked the crew from the Ammat Archipelago if they would be willing to escort you on your . . . excursion."

"And?"

"They're not."

"They said it sounds boring," said the puppet. It was quite a small puppet, just big enough to cover the person's forearm, with a pair of sticks attached to the puppet's hands. The puppet was dressed almost identically to Red.

"That's so creepy," said Avra conversationally. "What's the puppet about? Is it a cursed puppet? Is it a magical puppet of any kind? I need to know this, it's very important. Is Red the actual puppet and you're controlling him with the small puppet?"

"It's not a cursed or magical puppet," said Red. "It's just a puppet. No, it does not control my actions."

"That's just what someone controlled by a puppet would say," Teveri said flatly, and Avra cackled with glee.

Red glanced back and forth between them. "Ah . . . I do agree that it's probably a bit creepy if you're not used to it."

"I don't think it's creepy," said the puppet.

"*If you're not used to it,*" said Red.

"It's because people look at the puppet when I talk instead of at me," said the puppet, which was very confusing.

"That's very confusing," said Avra, vaguely recalling a *long ago,* offhand remark from Teveri about eye contact being considered rude in Tash. "Does the puppet have a name?"

"No," said the puppet. "It's just a puppet."

"Do *you* have a name?"

"You can call me the Puppeteer if you need my attention specifically," said the puppet.

"Could we focus?" Teveri snapped. "I'm in the middle of something, as you can see." They gestured sharply to Avra. "Why do they think that it sounds boring?"

"They said your ship is too slow. I explained about the dogs, and they said they'd be happy to go get Black Garda a couple dogs if she wants them, but they think it sounds boring to watch you do it."

"Did you tell them it was to win a bet?" Teveri snarled.

"More or less," said Red.

"Go back and tell them that they can fuck my mouth," said Avra. "Tell them I'll swallow their dicks like a python. Tell them I eat pussy like I'm dying of dehydration in the desert."

"How . . . compelling," said the puppet delicately.

"Tell them I don't care what they've got going on down there, I'll put my mouth on it."

"Tell them," said Teveri, grinding their teeth just like the spooky dentist told them not to, "that there's a lot of money on the line and I'll cut them in, equal shares with the rest of my crew, in addition to the money Black Garda is paying them."

Red glanced back and forth between them and Avra again. "And, ah, is the oral sex a serious part of that offer, or . . . ?"

"Well, that makes it sound transactional," said Avra. "And while I have nothing but fondness and respect for the profession, I feel like in this situation I'm coming more from a place of expressing my genuine respect and gratitude for their assistance. I am offering my mouth as a gesture of friendship and affection." Teveri raised their eyes to the ceiling with a hearty sigh. "Lovemaking is about all kinds of different beautiful connections that two or more people can share," Avra went on. Teveri sighed again. "You can tell them that I am so willing to explore the beautiful connections we might discover between us. Specifically between my mouth and their nethers."

"All right," said Red, openly dubious.

"It's fine, you can say it," said Teveri with their bitchiest smile. "He's kind of creepy and strange. Unlike the puppet, however, you cannot expect to get used to it."

Tev slammed the door in their faces and turned around with thunder on their face.

Avra wriggled enticingly and held out both the coconut jam and the silk scarves. "What if we explored our beautiful connection, Tev?"

Unfortunately, it seemed that Tev did not want to explore their beautiful connection, and summarily threw him out.

Avra, filled with regret and terror, decided to do the sensible thing and keep his tea appointment with the ambassador that afternoon.

He was met at the door by Viyan. "Oh, Helvaçi, come in. Ambassador Baltakan will be very pleased to have you. He's a bit grouchy about the festival."

"More than a bit grouchy, Lieutenant!" Baltakan said, sweeping into the room. "Helvaçi! Good to see you, good to see you. Do come in. Lieutenant, if you'd tell the cook to send the tea out onto the west salon? Thank you, my dear." Baltakan gestured Avra through the entryway into the central courtyard.

It was a *very* Araşti building. It had taken years of visits before Avra had begun to notice just how painfully Araşti it was. In the early days, it had just looked like a normal big house, nothing unusual about it at all. He had not been as well traveled in his youth as he was now.

There were all the classically Araşti architectural features: Two stories built in a square ring around a lush courtyard garden, with elaborate archways ornamenting the cloisters both above and below. The garden was rather more fine than anything else Avra had seen on the island, excepting the Mainmast's personal garden with his model of the Isles and fancy miniature turtles. The previous ambassador had specially imported the soil from Araşt, because the rocky, sandy ground of the island—especially this high above the water—was too poor for any of the things she wanted to grow. Besides the profusion of ornamental grasses and flowers, there were also a couple of dwarf orange trees, a rose-apple tree, a number of spiky fountains of pineapple, and a sprawling plant with leaves the size of serving trays, pierced with holes. It grew a kind of fruit that looked quite like a dick covered in lizard scales. Avra had carefully never mentioned this observation to the previous ambassador, though it had been touch-and-go there a couple of times.

"Such pretty . . . plants," he said, which was what he'd always said to the previous ambassador. "So many of them. So green."

"I was very pleased to see the garden when I first arrived, yes. My predecessor did a remarkable job getting at least this house to a civilized state." Baltakan looked around wistfully. "A little piece of home away from home."

"That's nice," said Avra. He felt rather suffocated in the courtyard, which the ambassador of course insisted on walking through while they made small talk.

Somehow, Avra managed to give the ambassador the impression that he was a reserved and prudent sort of person. Somehow, he managed to last through all the small talk and the first course of afternoon tea—which seemed to be rather more like a full dinner. They ate at a low table in a sunny west-facing room with a wide arched door overlooking the outer slope of the North Tit and the sparkling sea beyond. It was a *very* low tide, which was difficult to notice from inside the cove—especially when the sea gates were closed during the worst days of the king-tides to keep at least *some* of the water in the harbor. An expanse of wrecks and reefs rose from the sea, and even the shells and heads of a few of the largest turtles.

When the third course of "tea" (late luncheon? Early dinner? It was a strange time for such a large meal) had been brought to the table, Baltakan said, "This has been very pleasant, Helvaçi. If it is not too rude of me to say, I'm very surprised that a man of your wisdom and experience has never been promoted past the lowest rank of field agents."

"Ah, well, you know how it goes," Avra said vaguely, sipping the tea that Baltakan had insisted he try. Apparently it was expensive. Avra thought it tasted like tea, and wished that there was sugar for it. "You make a youthful mistake and embarrass yourself in front of one of your superiors and then there just doesn't seem to be a way to work past that."

"Ahh, one of those situations," Baltakan said sympathetically. "It happens all over the world, you know. When I was a young man, I was sent on diplomatic envoys to Inacha, Vinte, Cascavey, Pezia . . . In all those places, I met talented people who had been kept from advancement by the pettiness of others. It is a terrible shame."

"Yes," said Avra. "Though, ah, I believe the person in question is considering retirement, so perhaps when there is someone else in charge, and if my health has recovered to return to service, I will have some opportunity to advance." This was entirely fiction, of course, but he knew the sort of things that people said. Sensible people, that is. Good members of society. "I probably wouldn't make it anywhere close to your achievements, Ambassador, but one can hope for one or two promotions before I retire again to, um, raise sheep in the countryside."

"You should consider teaching!" Baltakan said with terrifying enthusiasm. "I'm sure that would be easier on your health than field duty!"

Avra pasted a modest look onto his face. "Oh, do you think so? I'm not sure . . ."

"You'd be a marvelous teacher for the Ministry of Intelligence's new recruits! With all your years of experience in the field? Now, granted, I know a bottom-rank field agent doesn't get the most exciting missions beyond courier duty . . . But you know, all too often teachers do not remember what it is like to be learning the basics for the first time—a teacher good at imparting the core fundamentals to their students is surely one of the thousand blessings of Sannesi, don't you agree?"

"It would be incredibly stupid of me to disagree with you."

"I have an idea," Baltakan announced. "At the end of the season of serpents and if your health has recovered, I'll write you a letter of recommendation to show to—not your superiors, not if the person you had problems with is still around . . . One of the chairs of the cadet academy, that's a better plan. We'll see if that helps you at all—unless you want to stay on courier duty for a few more years?"

"Noooo," said Avra. "No, I'm ready to, uh. Move on from that."

"Of course you are! But first we'll see to the dreadful business here, because of course I need to see your talents in action in order to represent you effectively in the letter."

"Ah, what dreadful business?"

Baltakan occupied himself with refilling their cups and chewing a few bites of lavash dipped in the savory juices of the main course. "One of my scanty few sources in the city informed me that several of the most influential fences in the city met up in secret in a hotel—the High Tide Hotel?"

"Oh," said Avra, widening his eyes as far as they'd go. "But that's where I'm staying! I didn't see them at all! But I suppose I wasn't watching for them particularly . . . I've heard they meet up all the time. They all know each other socially, of course."

"Hmm . . ." Baltakan frowned into his tea. "So I hear. But it seems fishy in conjunction with the news about the Shipbuilder's Guild, don't you think?"

"Maybe," said Avra, gently panicking. "In my line of work, we're supposed to be awfully careful of coincidences. So easy to, um, see connections between things when you want one to be there, when really it's just a collection of random happenings. No reason to run around screaming like the house is on fire. And, and, and sometimes there's a much simpler explanation than whatever you concoct in your head. 'If you hear hoofbeats, don't look for zebras,' as they tell us in little field agent school. Unless you're in Kholekhole, Tayemba, or the Zobui grasslands. Where they have zebras as a native species to their climate. But on the other hand, they also have, um, giraffes. I think giraffes have hooves. Do giraffes have hooves? Musk oxen have hooves. Water buffalo have hooves. Um, gnus have hooves. Antelopes. Gazelles. Uh, uh, warthogs. Lots of behoofed things in Kholekhole and Tayemba and Zobuo, no reason to look specifically for zebras."

"Well. No reason not to be thorough either."

"So true, definitely agree about that. Thoroughness is the best." Avra set his elbow on the table and attempted to deploy a casual lean while he sipped his unremarkable tea. "So what are you planning on doing about it? Do you have plans?"

"A few. One of the courier ships passed by last week. I was already concerned about the break-in, so I signaled a few requests to them. We should have the resources we need in another day or two, I should say."

"Mm," said Avra. "Yes. Yes. Well. I will be around to help in whatever way I can—uh. Except for the next two days."

Baltakan raised his eyebrow. "You have other appointments that outweigh this work?"

"I will be going out of town. For a bit. On Captain az-Ḥaffār's ship."

"In the middle of the serpent season?" Baltakan asked, bewildered—and then, for just a flash of a second, deeply suspicious.

Avra forced a raucous laugh. "What a daredevil move that would be! Out on the open ocean, in the middle of the salty fuck-pile, in a ship other than one of ours? Ahahaha, oh Baltakan, you old jokester, even I'm not that stupid. No, no, no, no no no no, no, it's just that Captain az-Ḥaffār has, uh, been challenged to a . . . a wager. Of sorts."

"A wager?"

"A dare! Very daring and boastful people, these pirates. Always trying to one-up each other about how, how, how brave they are and what sort of wild shit they're willing to do just to prove that they've got bigger balls and better cakes than anyone else. So my captain—I don't know if you've heard of them? I do forget if we discussed them last time. Captain Undertaker, they call them, because they once found a plague ship and single-handedly cleared all the corpses out of it—that's *The Running Sun,* same ship they sail now—and they have a spooky haunted throne that they sit on and it gives them, uh, unsettling powers."

"What unsettling powers?"

Avra increased the casualness of his lean and just barely saved his elbow from landing in the dish of hummus. "Oh, you know, mostly just the air of unsettlingness. Anyway, somebody was talking shit about them, so here we are. Proving that we're not chickenshit by making a run to some other island and, um, bringing back some of the local wildlife as proof."

"I see," Baltakan said slowly. "That does sound like it's in character for these sorts of people, but—why do *you* need to be on board that ship?"

Avra panicked for a moment, then winked and tapped the side of his nose. "Classified information, unfortunately. I'm sure you understand how it is. All I can say is that I was asked to keep an eye on them as a special favor when I submitted my paperwork for partial retirement. I have to give precedence to the orders I've received from on high. It wouldn't do to skive off, I'm sure a hard-working and devotedly loyal servant of the crown such as yourself would understand."

Baltakan was giving him an odd look. "But you do not give a care for the serpents?"

"The giant turtles eat the serpents, you know," Avra lied. "Most of them. Of course it is a risk, but one has to pursue the goal of one's mission, come high tide or low. Isn't that right?"

Baltakan's odd expression had eased—he was entirely sober now, almost sorrowful. "Yes," he said. "Yes, one does have to accept the orders one is given." He shook his head. "I can't imagine that I would ever have the courage to do such a thing, but then I suppose that's part of why they reassigned me from Intelligence to Diplomacy."

"A little day trip, barely getting out into blue water, and then back," Avra said, waving dismissively. "A risk, but not the most terrifying thing I've ever been asked to do. And besides," he added with another wink. "I have a knack for being in the right place at the right time."

Sextidi, Brumaire 6th (Heliotrope Day), An XVII

To my dearest family—greetings.

I love you. Before all else, please know that I love you, that I have always loved all of you, that I have only ever wanted to remain a part of our family, that I would have done anything to remain your Julian.

Tomorrow, I am choosing to take an enormous risk and put myself in a situation that might become very dangerous. I do so with my eyes open, and because the pursuit of knowledge and Holy

Understanding isn't always easy. Sometimes it is hard; sometimes it is frightening. But sometimes you know that what you're pursuing could change the world, *and so what other choice is there but to chase it with your whole heart, fearlessly?*

I am confident that I will not lose my life. I am! I have done my utmost, and I have faith and trust in my work, and in the rest of the crew. I WILL survive this—but just in case I don't, this letter will be on its way to you soon. If you do not hear anything after this, at least you'll know my fate. At least you won't wonder whether I have forgotten all of you.

I have met a number of new people, and all of them have given me valuable things to consider. I have befriended a mysterious spy going by the alias Avra Helvaçi (six foot tall, fashionably dressed, the most dashing, debonair, charismatic man you could imagine, immaculately manicured and groomed at all times, with a roguish glint in his eye as bright as his emerald earring, a poet of great unsung talent) who has suggested I write my memoirs about the adventures I have faced, and the more I ponder it, the more I like the idea.

There are also a pair of new acquaintances who are historians, scholars, and travelers—seekers after wisdom, just as the Emperor of Felicity bids us to be, though they do not follow our faith. Yesterday and today we had very deep and philosophical conversations that have made me rethink . . . so many things. My new acquaintances, known only as Red and the Puppeteer, have come to Scuttle Cove to seek knowledge, because they believe that the stories and histories of the people who live here are valuable and important and worthy of being remembered. They are passionate about this—Red especially. He is fiery *with his passion. I remember feeling like that. I miss it, oh Felicity, how I miss it! The passion to live according to your values, the passion to take action based on what you* know *in your heart is right instead of what other people have told you is right, the passion to meet the world with open arms—*

And they are not even the only two whose zest and passion have struck me so powerfully. It seems like every other person I have met since coming aboard The Running Sun *has said or done something that stirred a part of my soul which had been deeply asleep, and now it is blearily opening its eyes and lifting its rumpled head from the pillow, and I keep remembering who I used to be and how* alive *I used to feel.*

Can one return to the crossroads of choice? Was the turning I took the right one? Can a choice be remade?

Some choices do not need to be remade. The choice to love you and to fight hard to be a living and present part of our family even when I am thousands of miles away from you—those are choices I would make a thousand times over.

*Captain az-Ḥaffār wishes to sell a great treasure—*needs *to sell it, because everyone in the world needs money. But, oh, my darlings, it wrenches my heart to think of it, and I cannot bear to write down the hesitation I feel, or what I would do if the choice was mine alone.*

That is the ember of passion that still flickers bright, and which might be enough to set the whole of me aflame once more. But I have enough control now, with age and wisdom, to temper myself until I spend time at those crossroads and make the choices that feel right. *When I write to you again (for as long as there is one more letter after this one, I promise there will be more eventually that come after that one) I will tell you about what I have chosen. I know you will understand. When I write to you again, after the next letter to tell you that I got back safely, you will be reading the words of a Julian who has committed himself to the path he knows is right and true and* his own.

And that Julian will still love you so much, *just as I do. Adieu, my dears, I hope this letter finds you well.*

With all my heart,
Your Julian

12

15. The Loom

Finding a pattern in things that at first seem disconnected and meaningless. Putting chaos in order, settling into a rhythm. It is only when the cloth is already woven that you may look back and see the results of your choices.

(Reversed: What seemed orderly is falling into chaos. The threads are tangled, the pattern is skewed or spoiled. Your errors are recorded and will remain visible; it will be all but impossible to undo them.)

"But I don't want to be on that boat," Avra said plaintively.

"Get in, Avra," Teveri growled.

"But I want to be on that other boat. With all those nice people who have agreed to escort us. Have you seen their biceps? Where do they get biceps like that?"

"Presumably the same place that Oskar, Nonso, et al., get theirs," said Julian. *He* was already sitting in the dinghy with the last batch of crew, ready to go out to the ship. "There seems to be a lot of bicep work involved in sailing."

"It's different."

"No, it's not," Teveri said. "Get in the boat."

"It *is* different."

"It's different because those biceps are on a group of people who have never met you before," they snapped. "And thus they have no natural defenses against your *fucking bullshit.*"

"But they smile at me," said Avra. "I like them."

"Julian will smile at you."

Avra glanced at Julian, who smiled. "But he's taken an oath of celibacy, Tev. I don't think Kapono and Heirani have. Haukea *certainly* has not. By the way, Kapono is my new best friend."

"Markefa is your best friend."

"Close as he's likely to get, anyway," said Markefa. "Avra, get in."

"Kapono!" Avra sang over to the other crew, whose entire *ship* was dragged up on the beach, because it had no keel and barely any draft at all. Marvelous thing. The Ammatu sailors seemed to be doing all the usual things that one did with a boat in preparation to set sail—messing about with the lines and stowing away food and water and suchlike—and a few of them were talking to Red and the Puppeteer on the sand.

Kapono looked over, grinned like the sun itself, and waved before returning to his work. He was arguably the nicest person that Avra had ever met, outside of the beauties on the Street of Flowers. This was possibly because he only spoke about twenty words of Arasük and therefore could not tell when Avra was saying something outrageous.

"See?" said Avra. "We're best friends. Red introduced us and I liked him instantly. I want to go on that boat, with my best friend Kapono and Captain Heirani. I have packed up my little rucksack, Tev. You can't stop me. I don't see why I need to go on *your* boat. On *your* boat, I will be neglected and bullied and made to eat worms."

"Couple maggots in the hardtack never hurt anybody," Markefa said.

"I cannot thrive on your ship, Tev," Avra said loftily. "I have experienced the warmth of true friendship—"

"You haven't even spoken to him."

"*The warmth of true friendship,*" Avra insisted. "And now I have been irretrievably spoiled."

"You were already irretrievably spoiled. Get in the boat."

"I'm going to get on that other boat. And then I'm going to get on Kapono's boat. Yes, that was a dick joke."

Teveri had closed their eyes in pain. "Do you need to explain it every time?"

"I'm practicing clear communication by telling you when I've made a dick joke," Avra said, injured. "This is just what I was talking about, Tev. This is why I can't thrive on your ship. I am going on this other ship, where I will be happier. Where I will be valued and cherished. I keep drawing The Bower lately, you know, and that is all about 'soon you will be valued and cherished as a whole and imperfect person.' I think that day has arrived."

"It's rude to invite yourself," Julian said. "One should wait to be invited."

"I've invited you to let me swallow your dick like a python, though, and that hasn't made a difference," Avra said crisply. "Feeling very rejected and unsexy lately. Who have I become if I can't even tempt a man to give up his oath of celibacy? Hm? I've resolved to be more proactive."

"Avra," said Teveri in a very different tone to what they had been using. "Please get in the boat."

Avra gasped and clapped a hand to his heart in genuine horror. "*Tev,* you can't do that."

"Please, Avra, I would really like it if you got in the boat."

Avra looked to the crew for support; they met his eyes expressionlessly, except for Julian, who had sucked both lips into his mouth to bite back a smile. Avra turned back to Teveri and spluttered for a moment. "These tactics are beneath you, Teveri."

"If you don't get in the boat, I'm going to cry," said Teveri seriously.

Avra screeched in protest. "This is emotional manipulation! This is persecuting me personally! Fine! I'll get in the boat! But I'm going to go tell Kapono that I can't go with him and that I'm very sorry!"

Avra stomped across the sand and looked beseechingly up at Kapono, standing on the deck of the Ammatu catamaran. "I'm very sorry. Captain Teveri has made a heartless decision to forbid me from having friends and unfortunately I think it's very hot when they're ruthless like that, so I have to go make the voyage with them instead. I will be thinking of you."

Kapono listened intently, frowning presumably at Avra's mournful demeanor, and turned to call over his shoulder, "Kantu?"

Red and the Puppeteer both looked up, and Kapono beckoned. The Puppeteer murmured something to Red and then trotted across the sand; Red turned back to his conversation with one of the other Ammatu sailors. Kapono said something very fast to the Puppeteer—or rather to the puppet—and then the Puppeteer and their puppet turned to Avra. "Would you mind repeating what you said to him? I will translate."

"No, no," Avra sighed. "It wasn't very important. I was only saying farewell."

The puppet relayed this to Kapono, who howled with laughter and said something else.

"He thinks you're funny," the puppet translated. "He thinks it's extraordinarily funny to say goodbye like you're dying when the island is a day away and they're escorting you to it. He says this is the funniest thing he has ever heard in his life. He told me to tell you this specifically."

"That makes me feel better, thank you," Avra said to the puppet. "Tell him that if his biceps happen to get more salty than he prefers them to be, I will lick them for him."

"All right," said the puppet without missing a beat, and did so. By the time Avra had staggered through the disorienting wave of confusion at the overall lack of reaction, Kapono and the puppet had had an entire exchange involving Kapono repeating what had just been said, the puppet nodding, Kapono pointing to his biceps in perplexed inquiry, the puppet nodding again, Kapono saying something that was probably "And you really meant *lick*? You meant that word? Like *licking*, right?" because he mimed *licking* with an incredulous expression while the puppet kept nodding.

Kapono put his hands on his hips and said something that sounded unmistakably like a serious question.

The puppet turned to Avra; the Puppeteer was nearly motionless, which was just very spooky, except that he could see the fabric of their veil move slightly as they spoke, whenever he managed to tear his eyes away from making polite eye contact with the puppet. "He is concerned that bicep-licking is a cultural or religious practice of yours, and we don't wish to offend you by replying inappropriately."

"It's fine," Avra said with a mournful little sniff. "Nobody understands me anyway."

"Kantu," said Kapono, and the Puppeteer and the puppet looked up at him again. He seemed concerned, and gestured vaguely as if he were trying to find the words.

"What's Kantu mean?" said Avra. "I thought we were supposed to call you the Puppeteer."

"It's a title," said the puppet.

"Oh. What's it mean in his language?"

"Nothing, it's just the closest phonetic approximation of the word."

Kapono sighed and made a gesture that was fairly universally recognizable as *Ah, never mind, I can't think of what to say.*

"It's all right," said Avra. "Tell him it's all right and that I still cherish his friendship. I have to go get on that boat now, which by the way is a terrible boat and I will be so, so, so sad the entire time that I'm on it."

The puppet duly translated this. Kapono looked perplexed to the foundations of his soul and said, "Aisea?"

"He asks why."

"Yes, I got that," Avra said. "You can kind of tell when someone is asking you why in any language, in my experience. It's because no one understands me, The Puppeteer."

Avra went to sulk in the rope locker so that he would be out of the way of the crew, but he found Julian already in there and none of the ropes in sight—they had all been replaced with large barrels. There was a sharp tang in the air.

"Why have you filled up my rope locker? Where am I supposed to sit by myself and think about what I've done?" said Avra peevishly.

"It's the ingredients for the, ah, concoction," said Julian.

"Serpent juice," Avra said.

Two of the barrels had planks laid across them as a workbench, where Julian had set a box of mysteries and a large stone mortar, in which he was pounding up . . . things. He also had a beeswax-soaked cloth tied across his nose and mouth, and when Avra climbed onto one of the barrels to perch morosely, he handed another waxed cloth to him. "Wear this if you're going to be in here."

"Why?"

"The dust of this substance is highly corrosive. Coughing up blood and chunks of lung will probably not help you get laid."

"I bet I could make it work," Avra said, but Julian gave him a puppy-eyed look and he tied on the cloth. It smelled of honey and stuck strangely to his skin. "I'd frame it like this: Hello, I'm a tragic consumptive. The physicians say I only have a week to live and then I'm going to perish peacefully in my sleep with a single picturesque drop of blood dabbed at the corner of my mouth. Are there any really embarrassing kinks you've never been able to tell anyone about, and do you want to try any of them out? Because I'll be dead soon, so I won't have time to tell anyone about them. This is a great opportunity for you and I think you should take advantage of it."

Julian snorted but didn't stop grinding his spooky alchemical compound into a fine and lethal-looking white powder.

Avra lounged alluringly across the barrels, propping his head up on one hand. "Y'know, I love a man who knows his way around a big rock shaped like a dick."

"A pestle."

"Do you want to do that to me? I'd let you do that to me."

"What, pound you into dust?" Julian asked innocently, and Avra's head slipped off his hand and banged soundly against the barrel. "Are you all right?"

"That's not *allowed,* Julian!" Avra screeched, rubbing his head.

"How dare you respond to flirtation with extremely hot sex jokes! Yes, that is what I meant! I did mean I would let you pound me into dust! Do you think you can beat me at this game, Julian! You cannot! You are a monk!" Avra rolled off the barrels and flung open the door. "Tev! Tev!!! Julian's bullying me!"

"Good for him. I'm promoting him to Deputy Avra-Bullier," Tev shouted back from the helm. "Shut the fuck up."

"I'm going to run away and join a Faiss acting troupe," Avra said, slamming the door and clambering back onto the barrels. "What's in all these?"

"Extremely bad vinegar," Julian said.

"And stuff that'll burn your lungs out? What else?"

"Oil of vitriol. A few other things. If I attempt to explain, you will whine that I am using words that are too big and hard for you, and then we'll have to swing through another round of dick jokes to get past it."

Avra sat with this for a moment. "I'm feeling very loved and understood right now. Thank you. Kapono seemed somewhat put off by my offer to lick his biceps if they got saltier than he wanted them to be."

Julian carefully scraped the white dust out onto a scrap of fabric. "Oh no, that's terrible."

"Thank you for the attempt at a sympathetic tone." Avra sniffed. "It sounded almost genuine."

"It almost was genuine."

"Fucking gods," Avra screeched. "Why are you so funny all the time?"

"Am I not allowed to be funny?" Julian gathered up the corners of the fabric scrap, produced a length of twine from his box of things, and wrapped it up snug.

"I think it's just a little inconsiderate of you to be funny in front of me and then turn around and smile your butter-wouldn't-melt monk's smile like 'Oooh, sorry, Avra, didn't mean to get you all riled up! I can't do anything to help you about it, though. You know, because of my *oath*.'"

"And here I was feeling like that was the funniest part."

"Bullying Avra is funny, is it? You're in good company if you think so. Everyone else does too. I don't know why."

"Well, you make it very easy." Julian smiled at the mortar as he added in another measure of some white chunks of stuff and red grains of some other, different stuff from glass vials in his box of mysteries, then greyish flakes of something else.

"What are you making? Is that for the serpent juice?"

"This? No, no, I made the serpent juice yesterday. This is just a backup plan."

"What is it?"

"Do you want the big hard words explanation or the teeny little words explanation?"

"Teeny little ones. I don't like having too many things in my brain. I like it to be really tidy in there, like a nearly empty white room."

"Just in case I made any errors with the formula of the serpent juice, as we seem to be calling it, we are not entirely undefended." Julian unhooked a bucket from the wall and tipped it toward Avra; it had a number of the little fabric-and-*stuff* balls in it, each one about the size of a large walnut. "If we get attacked by sea serpents, we throw these in the water. In technical terms, powder get wet, water go boom, serpents say *No thanks, I'm leaving.* Theoretically."

"Perfect," said Avra, satisfied. "Perfect amount of explanation."

"I thought you would appreciate that."

"I never need to know anything more than which things go boom and what I need to do to them to achieve that."

"It's good to know yourself like that."

Avra watched Julian work for a few minutes. "What word sounds like Kantu?"

"Is this a game or a real question?"

"Both, I guess. Kapono called the Puppeteer that."

"Oh. Their title, probably. I spoke to Master Red after the meeting with the fences the other day. We had some interesting discussions."

"I'm cuter than him," Avra lied, instantly jealous. "You could have been having interesting discussions with me."

"You were busy doing unspeakable things with the captain."

"I could have been doing that and having interesting conversations with you at the same time. I'm very talented, Julian, I keep a lot of space open in my brain so I can pay attention to multiple things at once. What were all these interesting conversations you were having with other people who were not me?"

Julian was quiet for a moment. In a light voice, he said, "Small talk. At least from their perspective. 'How do you come to know Black Garda?' And 'So, how long have you been in the Isles?' And 'What brings you here?' And 'Are you planning to be here long?'"

"And?"

"They hadn't been here long. They didn't know how long they were planning on staying. They came here because they said they thought there were stories here worth telling. And then they explained—they're like monks of a sort." Julian shrugged one shoulder. "Perhaps I'm projecting my own interpretation. The Vintish faith would consider them very pious people, pursuing their own kind of knowledge and understanding."

"What are they trying to understand? I thought they were just tourists here for the cake competition."

"They said that the people of Scuttle Cove are not the sort whose lives and stories get recorded and remembered. They said that the lore of the common folk is all well and good, but they themselves are concerned with the lore of the *uncommon* folk."

"Huh. How do they know Black Garda, then?"

"She knew Master Red's mother, apparently. And his great-grandmother sailed on that famous ship—the one our mainsail is from."

Avra squawked and nearly fell off the barrels. "The *Nightingale*? Xing Fe Hua's *Nightingale*?"

"That's the one, yes."

Avra noticed his jaw was hanging open, but it took several moments for him to manage to close it. "*HOLY FUCK.*"

Julian only flinched slightly at the volume.

"You all right in there, Avra?" Anxhela called from somewhere on deck. "Or did you finally get to touch Julian's dick?"

"ANXHELA, I CANNOT DEAL WITH YOU RIGHT NOW," Avra screamed.

"Attaboy. Go get it, my lad."

"You're hyperventilating," Julian said, frowning.

"Kantu. Kantu. Kant—*Chant,* his grandmother was *Chant.*" Avra scrambled off the barrels and slammed open the door of the rope locker. "Teveri! That rude ginger man with the red boots and the weird friend is *Chant's great-grandson.*"

"WHAT," Teveri screamed, whipping around to look back at the harbor disappearing behind them.

"Who is whose great-grandson?" someone shouted from far above. Avra looked up. Skully—the man who had devoted his life's work to carving a giant skull in the side of the cliff—was hard at work on his project as they passed beneath, hanging by a rope in front of one of the eye sockets with a chisel, a hammer, and a dream.

Avra put his hands to his mouth. "There's an irritating man with red hair and red boots and he's staying at Black Garda's house and *he's the great-grandson of Chant who sailed with her apprentice on the* Nightingale*!*"

"Oh shit," said Skully, and zipped back up the rope at an astonishing pace for a man of his age, and that wasn't even considering the two peg legs, one ear, and seven fingers.

"WHAT," Teveri screamed again.

"I know!" Avra screamed back, and crumpled to his knees on the deck. "Julian's known for *months* and he didn't tell us!"

"I will point out," Julian called mildly from the rope locker, "that I haven't been on the ship for months. I will also point out that I met Red the same time you did. I will *also* point out that I don't know the significance of Xing Fe Hua, the *Nightingale,* or the silver sails."

"Fucking mother of—Avra! Pull yourself together and explain!"

By this point, Avra was openly weeping. "Do you know who else probably knows? Kapono! And the others! *And* Black Garda! And probably the Mainmast and Papa Kavo and *certainly* Madam mes Rakan—all of them! They all know and nobody told us! We could have asked the irritating ginger man to autograph our tits and gone down to Poky Pearl's tattoo shop!"

13

14. The Sea Serpent

The road ahead is currently extremely risky. You may be able to progress, but it could come at a great cost. High stakes. Unexpected disasters or sudden negative changes. Things are out of your control.

(Reversed: You may have narrowly avoided disaster this time, but the danger is not yet over. Learn your lesson or else face the danger again.)

"And *then,*" Avra said, "after all that fucking badass shit, sailing the Straits of Kel-Badur and everything, Xing Fe Hua decided that he'd gotten bored of the Sea of Serpents. He was too well-known, you see, and everybody recognized the silver-sailed *Nightingale,* as the songs called it, so as soon as his mainmast so much as peeked over the horizon, people would run in the other direction. Not fun to chase one ship for days, you know? And the Araşti ships were getting faster every year, and they'd sent the first ambassador to Scuttle Cove to try to negotiate what would become the Pact—so Xing Fe Hua left with his crew to find waters where nobody knew him or his ship. Five years later, the ship returned without him. The crew said they'd been over in the Sea of Storms and they'd captured a second ship with the intent of starting a whole fleet, and that Xing Fe Hua had found someone to outfit it with glittering silver sails of its own. They said he took half the crew and the new ship and went north, leaving his first mate Faurette in command of the *Nightin-*

gale. Supposedly they were going to rendezvous in Iza Farask, but the crew waited and waited for months and he never showed up or sent word. After everybody in Scuttle Cove was done mourning, the *Nightingale* was torn apart into splinters for relics and sold off. Pretty much only the sails and the flag were left intact, because the captains got there first and took those for themselves."

"The other ship sank?" Julian asked.

"Maybe," said Avra.

"Seems unlikely," said Markefa. Once they'd gotten properly underway, with less to do in the moment except to be ready to spring into action, a few of the sailors had gathered round. "Sinking, with a full complement of enchanted sails? He had enough money for other enchantments on the ship too, and he would have sailed straight past Cascavey on his way north—lots of magic bullshit in Cascavey. They drink wine made out of starlight there."

"Some folks say he had so many enchantments put on the ship that he sailed into the heavens, or right out of time itself, and that he'll come back one day without knowing any time has passed," said Beng Choon.

"It's an insult to his legacy to think that a ship he was captaining could have sunk," said Teveri, their voice tight. "And in any case—"

"Serpents!" bellowed the lookout in the crow's nest, and then very suddenly everything was chaos. Avra hurtled into the rope locker like a cat hiding under a bed.

Julian was close behind him. "You'll have to tell us how they use the serpent juice," he said breathlessly, shouldering past Avra. "That wasn't in the notes—you're the only one who has seen it done, yes?"

"Yes," Avra squeaked. "They usually use four of this size—poured off the prow."

"Good," said Julian. He and Bald Baric heaved a barrel out by the thick rope net that had been tied around as handles. "Three more," Julian called, and another pair of sailors shouldered their way in. Avra slithered out after them and swung up to the fo'c'sle, where Julian and Bald Baric were cracking open the lid of the barrel. "At the same time, or any order?"

"Uh, uh, uh, same time I think—I don't know if that's important, it might just be ritual—they say prayers, make it look like an offering to the sea."

Julian shot him a blinding smile. "Why don't you start that part, then?"

"*Me?* Fuck, fuck, um—" Something broke the surface a stone's throw from the port side of the ship—a great scaled back, the width of one of the barrels, covered in lime-green scales and spiky red dorsal fins, with a thin streak of shimmering, shifting color flashing along the midline. The spikes of the dorsal fins were the only thing that gave any indication that it was moving, and there were *dozens* of those spines breaching one after another—and then the back vanished even before the tail broke the surface. The long column of the serpent arced below them, a pale ghostly shape beneath the water, forcing a sudden and terrifying sense of depth.

"Other side," said Julian tightly.

Avra turned.

The water on the port side of the ship was blue; to starboard and just ahead it was shallow-water turquoise, because a thousand more *shapes* thrashed beneath the surface. They were growing more violent even as he watched, rising slowly from the deep until the surface frothed and roiled. There were glimpses here and there of a head: the squarish skull, the jut of snout opening into a great maw.

"Wow," said Avra. "That's a lot of teeth."

The two sailors carrying the second barrel heaved it up onto the deck. "On the rail," Julian said.

"No rush or anything," Teveri shouted from the helm. "Absolutely keep taking your sweet goddamn time."

"That was sarcasm," Avra said helpfully, trying not to gibber.

Julian and Bald Baric heaved their barrel onto the railing. "We pour it, don't we? We don't push it in?"

"Definitely pour," said Avra.

"The *prayer,* Avra."

"Right! Right, uh, uh—hello, Usmim, Lord of Trials, it's me, Avra. You know what would be nice? Not having any trials sent to me or my friends that involve teeth. This includes but is not limited to: toothaches, cavities, being bitten by blue dogs later today, or being, uh, torn to shreds and devoured by horny sea serpents. Uh, I know this is a little unconventional, especially because we don't talk that much, but I've always thought statues of you looked kind of hot, so as long as you make sure that I die *not at sea* so my body gets buried and my soul can, um um um, mosey—saunter—wiggle—traipse my way down to your domain, we can definitely have a glass of wine or whatever it is you drink down there and sorta see where the night takes us—but that would require me not dying at sea of just so many teeth. Or drowning. Or being crushed to death by big fish who don't have any call being that long."

They'd poured the barrels in by the time he'd finished, and Julian was leaning over the side. "Nothing yet. Where are the other two?" he shouted—sailors were already bringing the other two laboriously up the stairs.

Something thumped heavily against the ship, hard enough that they all felt the jolt. "Reeeeee," said Avra in quiet distress as Julian and the others cracked the second pair of barrels.

"Do you believe in Usmim?" said Julian breathlessly.

"Uh, uh, I mean, does it matter if I believe in him? I don't know that that would make him any more or less real—"

"I would suggest," Julian said, strained as they lifted the barrels and prepared to pour, "petitioning a god of luck. Your choice."

"Oh. Uh. Um. Lady of Fortune. Hello. Hi there. It's me, Avra."

"Get on with it," Oskar snapped as they tipped the barrels.

"I don't know if you remember me, we probably met that time that I was in the Bendran capital and I played that game of cards against one of your priests and won so hard that I cleaned him *out*? And took all his money and that ring he had? Kind of spooky in hindsight, maybe. The ring was pretty, though, and he said it was made of a piece of a heaven-stone. Anyway, it's been, um, a nice relationship we've had, where good things happen to me and then

I express skepticism about whether you exist, or whether luck exists, or whether I have any blessing from you that might incline me to be more fortunate than average, ahaha. I hope you have found that to be a funny little inside joke just between you and me. And you know, ha ha, we've been having a really good run, so why stop now, you know what I'm saying? We could just keep going with our very fun little banter that we've got! But that would necessitate me getting very lucky and not fucking dying today, and you know, as I think about it, if I have to watch all my friends die by being gruesomely chomped into gore by *just so many teeth, holy shit,* I can't see how I would be in the mood to have those good fun jokes between us for a long time. I think that might be a very sad experience that I would be pretty upset about, so um, yes, anyway, sorry for taking up your time, don't let us get dead." He sucked in a huge breath. "Is it working?"

Julian had both hands on the rail, leaning out to look down into the water. "Wait," he said.

Another hard thump against the ship; it juddered. Then a second.

From behind them, there was a great splash, and a hideous *screech* ripped through Avra's nerves like lightning and almost dropped him to his knees before he whipped around. A serpent had launched twenty or thirty feet of itself straight up in the air, holding ten feet of another serpent's severed tail in its jaws. It fell parallel to the ship, and part of Avra's brain said, *Ah, that was awfully close to the side, wasn't it?* just before the column of horny noodle hit the water and the enormous splash rained down onto the whole deck.

"Maybe don't lean out over the water that far," Avra said, grabbing Julian's arm. He tugged with a grip that felt *distinctly* watery and weak, but it was enough for Julian to feel it and turn toward him, his face pale and drawn—

Another serpent erupted from the water and snapped its jaws closed on the *exact* spot of empty air that had contained Julian's head a moment before.

"Hm," said Avra, digging his nails into Julian's arm. "Hm, I don't think I am enjoying this."

Julian wrenched his arm free. "Out of my way!" he shouted at the paralyzed sailors around them. He dove down the steps to the main deck and into the rope locker.

Avra cleared his throat, tossed the hair out of his face, and attempted a casual lean on the rail—the one over the rope locker door, *not* the one along the side of the ship. "Julian has a thing," he told Oskar, who was staring at him with an almost childlike terror. "It'll be fine. It's fine." He looked studiously away from the serpents. "Oh look, there's our friends."

The Ammat ship was fairly well flying across the waves half a mile or so off their port side. Avra waved to them—the ones who were not actively involved in sailing were watching their ship with their hands on their hips or their arms crossed, with long harpoons leaning against their shoulders.

Three more sharp thumps hit the ship, hard enough to jolt them, and the same serpent with the tail in its jaws erupted from the water with another horrifying screech—and this time it fell onto the deck.

The rail on the starboard side splintered under its weight. The serpent screeched again, thrashing its head side to side, trying to free itself from the tail it had bitten off. The tail, *horrifyingly,* appeared to have some kind of lingering death instinct and had wrapped itself tightly around the serpent's head.

Julian slammed out of the rope locker with his bag of alchemical witchcraft and hurled one of his spooky science nuts as hard as he could toward the swarm. Avra watched it arc through the air and hit the water—

There was a shockingly loud explosion and a huge fountain, reaching nearly the height of the masts; blood bloomed in the water, serpents thrashed and screeched. From the depths, an even bigger back surfaced: four times the width of the one on the deck, and who knew how long.

"Hm," said Avra, his heart pounding in his throat. That was probably a female, then. They were usually bigger. He wondered wildly how many teeth *she* had, and gripped the rail to anchor himself into his casual lean so he wouldn't melt into a terrified gibbering paste.

Oskar hurled himself at the one on deck with an axe and a bloodcurdling war cry.

"That's probably good for him," Avra commented to nobody. "Good for Oskar to vent some of his frustrations. Healthsome. Does the body good to get it all out like that."

Julian's spooky science nuts didn't disperse the serpents—the ship slammed into a dozen more of them before they got past the swarm—but it did seem to disorient them, and the blood in the water was enough of a distraction that many of them turned on each other and tore their dying brethren to shreds.

"Well," said Avra, when the swarm was comfortably in the distance. Oskar, panting and covered in blood, was standing over the serpent and its mauled body and decapitated head. "I feel like this is why humans decided to build cities. Wanted to get away from all the beauty of the natural world."

Julian was trembling from adrenaline and panting for breath, but then they all were. "I don't know why that didn't work."

"Julian, no, you mustn't blame yourself," said Avra, pitching his voice just a little louder so it would carry across the ship. He'd never had someone to *share* blame with before. Very appealing thought, the idea that he would only qualify for perhaps half of Teveri's grouchiness. That might not even peak above their frustration threshold, after which they got truly bitchy and needed to be whined at about possums and orphan gruel in order to snap out of it.

"I'm not blaming myself," said Julian, frowning at the barrels.

"Oh," said Avra. "Well, good! That's good. Neither am I. Blaming myself, I mean. I'm also not blaming you. Neither of us carries any blame whatsoever for what just happened."

"I know I translated it correctly. I *know* I did." Julian shook his head. "There must be something else I'm missing."

"How about," said Teveri loudly, "we focus on making it to the fucking island with those fucking blue dogs and not dying."

"Aye, Captain!" Oskar bellowed.

"Oskar, go wash yourself off, I can smell you from here."

"Aye, Captain!" He stopped and looked down at the serpent. "Can we keep it, Captain?"

"Oh, we're absolutely fucking keeping it," snarled Tev. "Drag it on board so the end of it doesn't get eaten. We're having that thing fucking *taxidermied* and we're going to ask Eel-face Yusin if we can loan it to him and hang it in his bar for everyone to look at. We're going to have a little plaque on it that says, 'This is a sea serpent killed single-handedly by First Mate Oskar Wertscraft of *The Running Sun*, on the occasion of their *glorious and magnificent voyage to Blue Dog Island in the middle of fuck season.*'"

"Aye, Captain," Oskar bellowed tearfully. "Thank you, Captain."

"No, no, no," said Teveri.

"Ah," murmured Avra. "They're getting manic."

"No, *no,* Oskar, thank *you.* This was an inspiring sight and I certainly will not forget that it happened or pass up any opportunity to make sure that absolutely everyone knows the best part of this *bullshit day.*"

Avra scrunched down behind the railings of the fo'c'sle and meeped. Julian looked over at him. "This Tev mood is called 'I'm not mad, I'm just disappointed, and now everyone has to hear about it.'"

"Oh," said Julian.

"Maybe we should have taken some blame," Avra whispered.

Julian considered this. "Are we both taking blame?"

"We can throw ourselves at Tev's feet and rend our garments and tear our hair and cast ashes upon our heads and wail most piteously, and they'll be so annoyed at our display of sincere penitence that they'll forget they were annoyed about us fucking up and nearly getting the ship sunk and everyone mauled to death in a salty noodle orgy—me by not stealing the right secret or the whole secret, you by not saving me from myself."

Julian glanced around. "Deal."

"Yay," said Avra.

"Ahoy!" shouted someone. Avra looked up and saw the strangely textured sails of the Ammatu catamaran just beside them, perfectly keeping pace. They were decorated with fascinatingly stylized birds and fish and glyphs that meant nothing to Avra but pinged the part of his brain that recognized codes, which meant they were probably meaningful. He scrambled to the side and leaned over the rail alluringly.

"Hi, Kapono," he said in his most sultry voice.

Kapono, who was sitting at the tiller, exchanged a glance with the others, who laughed raucously and shoved at him in a way that was universally recognizable as teasing. Kapono sighed and rolled his eyes at them.

The one who had called up to him was the woman Avra's rattled brain remembered as the captain. She was as casually topless as the rest of her crew, with a beautifully patterned orange-red sarong around her waist, a belt made of long drapes of tiny shells, and a broad collar of shells over her shoulders and collarbones. She had intricate tattoos around her wrists and ankles, and a tiny one just under the center of her mouth, which was twisted up in a concerned expression.

"Ah," said Avra. "You're . . . Heirani? Yes? Heirani?"

She looked surprised and smiled. "Arra, e sa'o?"

"Av-ra," Avra said, pointing to himself. "Hello."

"Hello," she echoed. She gestured to the ship. "Ship good?"

"Ship good," he said, nodding enthusiastically. "My friend Julian—Julian! Come here, come meet Heirani, she's my other new best friend—Heirani, this is Julian." He grabbed Julian's arm and dragged him close to the rail and pointed at him. "Julian."

"Kuliani," she agreed. "Hello. Good?"

"Good, yes, thank you," Julian said, bowing.

"Heirani," said Avra. "I'm sure you are wondering what the big fucking explosions were." Heirani blinked at him politely. "Ah, uh, hm, the *boom!*" Avra mimed it, throwing his arms in the air and mimicking the sound. "Foosh! Water," he said, pointing at the water, "and then *boom*!" He held up three fingers, and then just to be safe counted them out loud. They'd said in the language classes at the academy that people counted on their fingers in different ways in different places, and then they'd reiterated that point when he'd joined Intelligence and they'd informed him that this was an important thing to remember if he ever ended up going undercover as a local. "One, two, three. Three times. Boom! Foosh!"

Heirani lit up and nodded. "Boom, e sa'o!"

"Julian did it." He pointed to Julian.

Heirani blinked. "Kuliani? Boom-foosh?" She mimicked Avra's gesture.

"Yes. Boom-foosh is *explosion*. Julian made explosion."

One of the other women touched Heirani's arm and murmured something to her, nodding up at Julian. Heirani replied under her breath and repeated the boom-foosh gesture.

"Explosion," Avra repeated. "Haukea, e sa'o?"

Haukea, the younger woman, looked up in surprise and smiled brightly at him. "E sa'o!"

"Julian made explosion because he's very handsome. Killed lots of serpents, more serpents than Oskar killed, probably. Head full of brains, this one." He leaned both hands on the rail and wriggled alluringly a little, exaggeratedly batting his eyes at Julian. Haukea and Heirani laughed.

"Ship good, though, e sa'o," Avra said, patting the side of the hull. "Uh, you?" He gestured to their ship. "Ship good?"

"Ship good," Heirani agreed, and then said something else very fast, and mimed with hand gestures to indicate distance, then boredom, then a ferocious fish, then the crew.

Avra watched intently and nodded. "Serpents aren't interested in you."

"How did you get that?" Julian murmured.

"I'm very good with people, Julian." A few minutes' more conversation established the words *shallow* and *fast* as explanations for why the serpents weren't so aggressive toward the Ammatu ship; a few minutes after that, Avra managed to communicate the request for a favor: Would the Ammatu be willing to take their fast, shallow-drafted, safe ship and nip ahead a ways to scout the path ahead for any more incipient breeding swarms in the area? The Ammatu agreed easily, which Avra thought was probably out of concern for the idiots taking this huge, fuck-off carrack into blue water for *boring errands*. Haukea spent the entirety of this time eyeing Julian appreciatively. When Heirani and Avra had finished their negotiations, Haukea leaned in, grinning, and whispered something to her. Heirani gasped and whapped her in the arm; Haukea giggled, dancing a step or two off, and made a go-on-then gesture. Heirani rolled her eyes and sighed heavily. "Say Haukea, Kuliani good," she said with some exasperation.

Avra burst out laughing. "Julian *very* good. Good good good. Good good."

"Shall I wink at her?" said Julian with a grin, leaning his elbows on the rail beside Avra. He was *all wet* from the splashes of the serpents and the bombs, and his linen robes were sticking to his body in a very distracting way. "Will it help our diplomatic efforts?"

"No, no, she seems a bit young for winks. If she swoons at the sight of your—stop making your biceps do that—at the sight of your flexing biceps and glorious tits, she might fall off the side of her boat and then we'll feel terrible. Also, it is *so rude* to lead people on like you do, going around and flirting and looking handsome and blowing things up and then refusing to pound anyone into dust. You can pull that shit with me because I'm used to being bullied by absolutely everyone I've ever met, but you ought to be nicer to Haukea."

"A reasonable point," said Julian.

Heirani rolled her eyes at Avra, by which he understood that

Haukea was some young relative of hers—perhaps a little sister, as they did have similar features—who caused her uncountable trials and suffering every day.

Blue Dog Island had significantly more vegetation than Three Tits Island, but also had the marked downside of lacking any good harbor. The only shelter from the ocean swells and the serpents were some rocks that would have been underwater and potentially deadly had they arrived at a higher tide. There was just enough of a draft left for them to scrape up as close to the shore as they could and drop anchor. The ship would be tilting sideways within an hour or so when the tide fell enough that the keel hit the bottom.

The Ammatu sailors, of course, just dragged *their* boat right up onto the beach and started unpacking all the snacks and other elements of civilization that they'd brought along.

"That could be us," Avra said, gazing at them in the distance. "We could have a boat like that and then we wouldn't have to do all this bullshit with it when the serpents are up."

"We'd probably have to do different bullshit at other times," Julian said. "And we can fit more cargo. Benefits and downsides," and Avra had to admit that was true.

By the time the ship had been secured and the crew came ashore, the sky was a blaze of orange and pink and streaks of purple-blue. The Ammatu sailors had already set up a campfire and a couple shelters, collected a pile of coconuts and shucked them of their fibrous outer husks, killed and butchered a wild pig, and were roasting it on a spit with a few fat fish.

"Sooooo," said Avra. "Do we want to catch a couple dogs *before* we eat dinner, when our energy is low, or after we eat, when our morale is low because dinner was hardtack and stale water?"

"It'll be dark soon," said Markefa, who was wearily lighting a fire with the dried palm fronds that she'd sent Ellat to gather as soon as they'd landed. "Might be best to wait until morning. Don't know about the rest of you, but *my* nerves are shot to hell."

Teveri was standing on the white sand, just at the edge of the receding waterline, looking out to the now markedly listing ship with their hands clenched into fists at their sides. Avra peered out at the ship as well—the hull had once been painted with striking geometric patterns in the Araşti style, but over the course of the years, it had all but worn away—chipped off when the hull was cleaned of barnacles, or covered up by tar to seal the leaks.

There were now several fresh gouges on the hull, and huge swathes of barnacles had been scraped off.

Teveri abruptly turned away from the ship and stormed up the beach. They paused only long enough to seize one of the lanterns, light it, and snarl, "Don't follow me if you value your lives," before stomping away into the island's scraggly attempts at a jungle.

That further dampened an already moist ambiance, and it took several minutes for anyone to speak again. Finally, Markefa nudged Ellat, who had been clinging to her arm at every opportunity since the Incident earlier that day. "Hand out the hardtack, boy, do something useful."

Avra leaned close to Julian and whispered, "Do you value your life?"

Julian smiled and gave this due consideration. "Leaving the monastery and going to sea, joining a pirate crew because I liked them as soon as I saw them, getting involved in the greatest crime anyone will ever commit, and then producing an entirely experimental alchemical admixture on the hopes that it would blow up some sea serpents? You know, Monsieur Helvaçi, I don't think I do value my life all that much." He regarded Avra with a warm, wry sort of expression. "And you?"

"I once wrote a song about Tev's sexual proclivities and sang it in front of people."

"So no," Julian said, his eyes all bright with laughter in that way that he had sometimes. "Shall we go after the captain?"

"Better that it's us than anyone else. Tev's going to be in a mood."

14

48. The Candle

To keep the shadows at bay, speak quiet truths. When all seems lost, hold on to optimism, faith, and determination. If you head forth into darkness, bring hope with you.

(Reversed: The candle gutters or has gone out entirely. Hope has been drowned by despair, truths have been overtaken by uncertainty, faith has been lost.)

Teveri was easy enough to find, even in the thickening dark—the lantern glimmered brightly somewhere ahead and all they had to do was keep walking toward it.

"Should we be wary of snakes, do you think?" Julian asked as it became harder and harder to see their own feet.

"You think *I'd* have the bad luck to get bitten by a snake?"

"Let me rephrase: Should *I* be wary of snakes, do you think?"

"You could if you wanted to." Avra shrugged. "Or you could hold hands with me, and then you wouldn't have to worry about snakes any more than I do."

"Is that how it works?" Julian said, amused.

Avra turned and winked at him. "Maybe, who's to say?" After a moment, he added, "I winked, just so you know. I can't see your face that well anymore, so you probably didn't see the wink."

"I appreciate that. I did, however, sense a general air of winks."

"Holding hands so you don't get bitten by snakes probably

doesn't count as breaking your vow of celibacy," Avra said with a little hair toss that Julian probably also couldn't see very well. "Just pointing that out."

"That's a reasonable argument," said Julian, which wasn't true at *all*, but then his hand slipped into Avra's.

"Hrkg," said Avra. After a long moment, silent but for the crunch of the forest floor under his feet, he giggled in a delirious little panic.

"It starts counting more if you do that," Julian said solemnly.

They found Teveri by a small waterfall, throwing rocks angrily into the pool. They'd taken off their fancy purple coat, and their hair was wet, as if they'd dunked their entire head into the water.

Julian stopped just out of earshot and whispered, "Do we have a plan of—"

"Tev!" Avra whined, dropping his hand and stepping forward. "Tev, why are you throwing rocks at a nice pond that never did anything to you when you could be throwing rocks at me instead?"

"Go away, Avra," Teveri said in a low voice.

He flung himself on the ground a couple yards off. "But you're *soooo* incandescent when you're throwing rocks, Tev, and you choose to do so all by yourself instead of indulging me in one of my most beloved sexual fantasies? I feel very neglected, Tev, I feel very sad and lonely. I might as well go back to the alley with the possums and let them mob me for every moldy piece of bread I scrounge out of a rubbish heap. How can you throw rocks at things that are not me when *I* am the one who has fucked up so much? Well, me and also Julian. I don't know if Julian wants you to throw rocks at him."

"I said go away."

"Julian!" Avra screeched. "Do you want Teveri to throw rocks at you?"

"Ah, I don't know," said Julian, stepping more slowly up into the circle of the lantern light. "You'd recommend it?"

"For magnificent fuckups like us? Absolutely."

"Hmm," said Julian, settling himself on the ground near Avra. "Do the rocks hit you, or are they only thrown *toward* you?"

"Oh, only toward. Tev hardly ever hits. It's the eye, you know. One eye, poor depth perception."

"Is it possible that they aren't trying to aim very accurately, because they don't truly wish to stone you?"

Avra laughed nervously and glanced at Teveri, who was facing away from them and trembling with rage. "What? No. Haha, what? Don't be silly, Julian, Teveri throws rocks at me and doesn't hit me with them because they know that I like it when they do that and they don't usually think that I've behaved well enough to have earned it."

"Ah. Well, we have both earned it today, I think. Shall we gather up some rocks for the captain? It seems impolite for us to hurl ourselves on their mercy and make them collect their own rocks."

"That's a great idea," Avra said, rolling onto his knees and patting around on the ground. "Then we can select rocks that are small and don't have too many sharp edges."

Teveri whirled around and screamed, "*I said go the fuck away.*"

Avra froze, his hand floating an inch above the ground, and carefully did not look up at Tev. "Maybe we should go away," he mumbled to Julian. "This was a bad plan. Maybe we should just go right now immediately, this is not the time for—"

"Captain?" Julian said softly. "Are you all right?"

"Of course they're not all right," Avra muttered, scuttling over to Julian's side and tugging him ineffectually by the arm. "Come away, come away, don't make eye contact, let's go back to the beach and tell everyone we were having sex and that we definitely didn't see Tev and we don't know where they are, but one thing we do know is that they're definitely not crying by themselves and throwing rocks into a pond that definitely did something fucking awful and deserves everything it's got coming to it." Avra scrabbled in the dirt for a rock and hurled it in the direction of the pond. "Stupid fucking pond, fuck that pond, I don't even need to know what it did, all ponds are layabouts and ne'er-do-wells and should have rocks thrown at them. Let's go, Julian, we can go find some other rocks and throw them at each other, save Tev even more of the work."

Julian pulled his arm out of Avra's grip and stood. "Captain?"

Teveri didn't answer. The lantern was behind them, silhouetting them so their face was in shadow.

"I'm sorry," Julian said, his voice so soft, so *sincere* that it made Avra's insides twist up uncomfortably. "Teveri, I'm sorry."

"For what," they snarled.

"Failing you. Endangering your ship and your—your family."

"*I* put them in danger. *I* made the decision to do this—this stupid fucking *test.*"

"We should go," Avra hissed up at Julian, scrambling to his feet and tugging his arm again. "They wouldn't like to be seen like this, which is just so lucky because we definitely haven't seen them since they left the camp. We were just off for a walk. We were looking for dogs."

Julian gently pulled his arm free of Avra's grip again. Avra watched, wide-eyed with incredulous panic as the bravest man in the world reached out to lightly touch Teveri on the arm.

"I'm sorry," said Julian again, even quieter. "Be angry at me if that's easier."

Teveri made a horrible little gurgling sound. Avra instinctively skittered a couple steps back. Julian squeezed their upper arm, then—then *rubbed* it.

"Julian," Avra hissed. "Julian, they will bite that hand right off."

Julian ignored him. "I'm sorry it didn't work," he said, still in that appallingly sincere tone, and Teveri burst into tears, half turned away, and dropped to the ground with their face in their hands. Julian followed, kneeling gracefully just beside them, still rubbing their arm and shoulder.

Some people could cry beautifully. Teveri az-Ḥaffār was not remotely one of them. Their voice went thick and odd, and they made horrible choking noises like a cat coughing up a hairball, and now that there was lamplight on at least part of their face, Avra could see in the glimpses when they lowered their hands to wipe tears off with their palms or wipe snot away with the back of their hand that their face was all scrunched up and their mouth twisted gruesomely.

Maybe it was lucky that Julian had taken a vow of celibacy, Avra thought to himself through the thick haze of panic. He was really far too pretty for either of them.

Julian just kept rubbing Teveri's arm, and eventually reached into his belt pouch and offered a handkerchief. "I'm sorry," he kept whispering every so often. "I'm sorry, Teveri."

"I'm so fucking *tired*," Teveri choked out, as if they were physically wrestling the words from their throat and throwing them out of their mouth like they so often threw Avra out of their cabin. Or rocks into ponds that definitely deserved it. "I'm *tired*, I'm so tired, fuck this, fuck all of this, *fuck it*, what's even the fucking point—"

"Shh, shh, come here," Julian said, and to Avra's astonishment Teveri toppled sideways into his arms at the barest tug and didn't even pull steel on him or anything, as if Julian was some kind of spooky wizard who had hypnotized them.

Avra stood frozen in horrified amazement as Julian tucked Teveri right under his chin and put his arms around them and—and *stroked their back*, and said *shh*.

Avra shifted nervously from foot to foot and wished urgently that he were back with the serpents.

Julian was murmuring something into Teveri's hair. Once again, Avra's indefatigable curiosity got the better of his self-preservation. He inched forward.

"It's all right. There, it's all right," Julian was saying.

What was all right? Very little of the situation was what could be described as *all right* in the present circumstances. For one thing, Teveri was crying, which probably meant that the world was coming to an end.

Avra's mouth also got the better of his self-preservation instinct. "Tev," he said in a small voice. "Do you want to throw some rocks at me?"

Julian laughed silently, shutting his eyes tight and biting his lips again, shaking almost as hard as Teveri was. Teveri hurled the disgusting snotty handkerchief at Avra, who screeched, "EW," and batted it out of the air before it could hit him in the face.

"So civilized," Julian crooned, rocking Teveri a little. "Everyone around here is so civilized." He rubbed Teveri's back. "No wonder you're so tired, having to be so civilized all the time."

"They're going to get your robes all snotty," Avra said.

"They're grey, it'll blend in," Julian said, opening his eyes and giving Avra a look of frank reproof over the top of Teveri's head.

Avra felt something in him quail and shrink back a little. He shut his mouth.

Julian's expression softened again. "Maybe you could say sorry as well."

Avra picked at a stray thread on his trousers. "I said they could throw rocks at me."

"That's not the same."

Teveri gripped a fistful of the front of Julian's robes. Avra tensed up and wondered wildly if this was the moment that Julian got shoved away and thrown into the pond, or—or marooned alone at sea, or taxidermied.

Julian didn't react at all, just kept rubbing Tev's back and letting them drip snot all over his robes.

"Don't waste your energy on him," Teveri said, voice rough with tears and furious resignation. "There's no point."

"I have energy to spare." He smiled and tipped his face so the front of his chin rested on Teveri's hair, so that he was almost, almost kissing the top of their head. "I'm a bit keyed up from throwing alchemical explosives at sea monsters." He glanced up at Avra. "Try it?"

"Try what?" Avra said, mouth dry. "I don't have good upper body strength, I wouldn't be good at throwing your spooky science nuts at anything. Blow my own dick off, probably."

Teveri muttered an oath under their breath and started to pull away, but Julian tugged them back in. "No, no," he said. "Leave it, I have it."

Avra started to open his mouth to say—something infuriating, something outrageous and irritating and—

"Avra," Julian said gently. "Say sorry."

"Sorry," Avra mumbled. "Sorry, Tev."

"For?" Julian prompted.

"Being an appalling little flibbertigibbet. Not—being a good and sweet little Avra henceforth like I said I was going to."

"Fuck off, Avra," said Teveri. "Just fuck off."

Julian rubbed their back. "I have a feeling that wasn't the right thing to be sorry about. I don't think being good and sweet is really your wheelhouse, for one thing." He looked down at Tev. "Hm? Not his wheelhouse, is it?" Tev shook their head. "Can you imagine if he stopped being a flibbertigibbet?"

Tev made a noise that was either a scoff or a snort. Or possibly they were choking on their snot. "The sun would burn out first."

"And it's a funny performance, isn't it? People like it. I like it." He nudged Tev. "You like it a little bit, hm? Sometimes."

"You don't have to do this," Tev snuffled. "It's not worth it."

Julian just kept rubbing and rubbing Tev's back and looked up at Avra again. "Do you want to try again?"

"You heard them, it's not worth it," Avra snapped. "Maybe I should just go. Maybe I should just—they said fuck off, I'm fucking off." He sprang to his feet.

"Avra," said Julian, in *that voice,* the voice he'd used in the cabin they used as a pantry when he'd pulled Avra's hair and made him spill everything. "Stop." Then, "Sit down."

Avra found himself sitting and vaguely turned on.

"Your friend had a hard day," Julian said, still using that voice. "Your friend has had a hard couple of months, it sounds like. Maybe a hard few years. Maybe a hard *life.*" His blue eyes looked tawny in the lamplight, burning into Avra's. "What do you think of that?"

Avra swallowed hard. "I'm sorry, Tev."

It already sounded different, but Julian pressed, implacable. "More."

"I'm sorry that everything sucks."

Teveri seemed to slump, like a sail when the wind suddenly died. Julian smiled brilliantly at him.

"I'm sorry," Avra said again. He inched a little closer. "Tev? I—I had a hard day too."

Teveri stiffened. Julian said quickly, "To me that sounded as if he was trying to say, 'I know how you feel.'"

"He doesn't."

"But he's trying to." Julian glanced at Avra again. "You're not looking at him right now, but I am. He looks like he's trying. He looks like a man who is screwing up all his courage to try."

Teveri scoffed—and it certainly *was* a scoff this time. "He's never needed to do that except for show. Stupid fucking *act*, playing pitiful like he does."

Julian raised his eyebrows. "Never needed to—you surely don't believe in the fictional Avra Helvaçi from my future memoir, do you? The dashing and debonair one with the rippling muscles and the dick piercing?"

"THE WHAT."

"Mrhgk," said Avra, delighted.

"And the way he's fearless and undaunted? You don't think that part's true, do you?"

"Ugh, he just *acts* all the time, how am I supposed to know anything?" Teveri shoved their face back into Julian's chest.

"He's scared out of his wits right at this very moment," Julian said. "Or out of his wit, at least—he can't come up with a single clever thing to say, because it might make you worse. He doesn't want to make you worse, so he tries to do the only thing he thinks you want: Running away. Leaving you alone." Julian added delicately, "Possibly because you throw rocks at him and tell him to fuck off."

"Or because you stomp off shouting about how nobody should follow you if they value their life," Avra muttered.

"We had a whole conversation about it," Julian said. "'Do we value our lives?' we asked each other. And then we both said, 'Eh, not that much.'" He looked at Avra. "Why did we do that, Avra? Tell the truth."

"Worried about you," said Avra. His heart was pounding in his throat. "Wanted to make sure you were all right. Knew you probably weren't all right. Wanted to . . . to make you feel better."

Teveri said nothing.

"He was afraid earlier today too," Julian said. "With the serpents."

"He wasn't," they said tightly. "You saw him. Practically yawning. Nothing *matters* to him."

"You were at the helm. All the way aft. He was on the forecastle."

"Fo'c'sle," Tev and Avra corrected in unison.

"And you were busy sailing the ship and getting us out of there. Avra was white as a sheet." Julian's voice was low and soothing—not *the voice,* but something nearly as effective. "He dug his little claws into me every time I was within arm's reach, like a frightened cat." Julian freed one arm and pushed up his sleeve. He angled his arm to the lamplight, and Teveri lifted their head to peer closely.

"Here?" they said, touching something—Avra was too far away to see it clearly.

"Mhm. Battle scars from my exhilarating fight with the sea serpents."

Teveri grumbled, pushing their face against Julian's chest again.

It occurred to Avra in a start that Teveri wasn't even crying anymore. They were *nuzzling* Julian's tits like that just because they could! Pure self-indulgence! Conniving fox!

On the other hand, he too had had a hard day, which apparently qualified a person for snuggling into Julian's tits, and that was the kind of incentive that got things done.

Avra scooted closer. "I'm sorry, Tev."

Julian said nothing, but his hands stopped moving up and down Tev's back. After a moment, he tapped his finger on their shoulder blade.

"Thanks," Tev mumbled.

In an even smaller voice, Avra said, "Is it okay if I hug you too?"

"No, there's no room here, sorry," Tev said quickly.

Avra made a peevish noise. "So you just get to hog Julian's tits all to yourself? Poor Tev had a hard day and gets to rub their face in tits, and poor Avra just has to eat worms and mud and shiver to death in the cold and *starve* without even a bowl of orphan gruel—not even a spoonful—not even a crust of bread the possums have already gnawed on?"

"I feel as if I'm missing a great deal of necessary context here," Julian mused. "And there was a time in my life when I would not have minded having people bicker over my, ah, tits. But in the present circumstances, perhaps someone in this conversation might like to make some personal choices based on motives other than whether it gets them access to parts of my body." He paused and added, "In the interest of full disclosure, Teveri, he did get at least a spoonful of orphan gruel. I held his hand while we walked up here to find you, on the logic that it might allow me to share his luck and thereby avoid getting bitten by venomous snakes."

"His idea, was it?" Teveri muttered into his chest. "Sounds like trollop logic."

Julian laughed quietly. "Well, perhaps." Then, wryly, "One isn't required to take an oath of celibacy if one doesn't have a troublesome amount of trollop tendencies oneself."

"Julian," Avra said, sharply reproachful. "Tev had *such* a hard day, and now you're dangling reminders at them of your past as a slutty revolutionary? That's not fair."

"Don't listen to him," said Teveri. "You can talk about your slutty revolutionary past if you want. Feel free to be wistful and nostalgic. Homesick for it, maybe."

"Motives *other* than getting access to parts of my body," Julian said, laughing again. "Motives like whether you'd like to let Avra hug you." Teveri grumbled something under their breath, and Julian said, "Yes, I know you don't really feel like letting him bumble around trying to figure out what the right thing to do is, but may I point out that if you don't let him try, he won't ever get it right."

"At least then there's something to be certain of," Teveri said, devoid of all emotion but resignation.

Avra felt that like a slap in the face and would have tried to flounce off again, but Julian smiled gently at him as he said, "Now, I admit I haven't known him as long as you have, but I would have said that my own certainty about Avra is that he'll *always* keep trying, as long as there's something worth trying for. Case in point: He's still sitting here waiting for you to answer his question."

"Fine," said Teveri, and Avra scooted forward and cautiously touched the hand that Tev had clenched in the front of Julian's robes. Then, when Tev didn't bite it right off, he tugged their hand free and laced his fingers with theirs, scootched even closer, wrapped his other arm around Tev's waist, and tucked his face against their shoulder.

"Spooky that he's not fucking saying anything," Tev muttered. "I don't like it."

"You don't like that he's not saying anything?" Julian said, amused. "After all the times you've told him to shut the fuck up?"

"You yell at me when I talk," Avra whispered.

"Maybe if you didn't say such annoying things, I wouldn't yell."

"Well, I don't know when you're going to yell or when you're going to laugh or when you'll think it's the sexy kind of pitiful and summon me to your cabin like a trembling harem boy."

"He just wants attention," Julian said warmly. "Anyone's will do, but yours in particular, it seems like. He tries *far* harder to annoy you than he tries with me or Markefa."

"It's because Tev is incandescent when they're mad at me," said Avra.

Julian sighed heavily and spared one hand to pat Avra's hair. "However have the two of you gotten along for this many years without killing each other?"

"I'm very lucky," said Avra, at the same moment Teveri said, "I used to have more patience for his bullshit."

Julian snorted. "You're both perfectly marvelous, do you know?"

"*I* knew that," Avra said.

Teveri snuffled and moved their head a little away from Avra. "There's room on this other tit if you want it, I guess."

"Ooh," said Avra, and squished his face against it immediately.

Julian burst out laughing—the loudest and brightest Avra had yet heard from him. It rumbled against his face. "All right, all right, everyone seems to have gotten through the worst of it." He gently levered the two of them off; Avra made a piteous noise and wound himself around Teveri.

"No," said Teveri. "No, I'm still very incredibly sad."

"Tev is so sad, Julian."

"We nearly died today, and the thing didn't work like it was supposed to, and—and we won't get paid, and all I've got to sell if I want to keep from going bankrupt is some nice furniture and a hold full of straw and some jewelry. And my clothes. And—and the mainsail of the *Nightingale*."

"Please. You'd sooner sell your eye," said Avra.

"It's only gold leaf."

"Gold leaf is gold leaf, though." Avra burrowed in closer. "You could get Skully to carve you a new eye. He only knows how to carve skulls, but that'd be wicked neat, wouldn't it? A skull in your skull? And inside one of the eyes of *that* skull, there could be another, smaller skull."

"And," said Teveri, their voice quavering a little, "if I lose the crew and have to sell everything, I don't think I could bear the humiliation of failure. So I'd just have to . . . *go somewhere.* Be a real person. Work in a bar or something."

"A *day job*," Avra whispered in horror. "Tev, *no.* Tev, you mustn't! Julian, bring your tits back here, Teveri still needs moral support."

Julian leveled an amused look at the both of them.

"Try pouting," Avra whispered to Tev. "Always works for me." Tev stuck out their lower lip. "Hm. Make your eyes wider. Can you wobble the lip a little—no, not like that, you look like a fish. Okay, maybe that's not a good look on you." Avra put a fingertip to their lip and pushed it back in. "Julian, have you no pity, can't you see that Tev doesn't even have any practice at pouting?"

"Let's compromise," said Julian, an eminently reasonable man. "I'll go wash the snot off my robe in the pond."

"That seems fair," said Teveri casually, digging their nails into Avra's arm. He dug his nails into their arm back as Julian got up and walked the few yards down the slope of the bank.

Avra seized Teveri and whispered, "*How does a person have tits like that.*"

"Rock hard," Teveri mumbled, "yet pillowy."

"So warm."

"Smells nice."

Julian stripped off his robe and squatted by the edge of the water in his trousers, so of course they both had to stop talking and pay close attention.

"Would it be against his vows if he let us lick his shoulders?" muttered Avra.

"I thought about licking his tits when I had my face squished between them," Teveri muttered back.

"Noooo, why'd you only think about it?"

"Manners." They watched Julian's back muscles move in the lamplight as he submerged the fabric and sloshed it around. "My nose was stuffy for most of it, though, so I had to breathe through my mouth and sort of tasted him that way."

"Like a snake."

"Yes. I licked the air right next to his tits."

"I'm very politely ignoring the furious muttering happening behind me," said Julian. "I can't make out what you're saying, but I can hear Avra hyperventilating, so I assume I'm being objectified."

"No, we're only being so brave and strong and ethical," Avra said aloud. "I'm actually so proud of us."

"Ah," said Julian, his shoulders shaking with silent laughter again.

"I think breathing through your mouth when your face is between his tits counts as licking him," Avra whispered. "Because you get stuff in your mouth. Like lint. You didn't just lick the air, you also licked his lint. That's basically the same as licking him."

"No it's not," whispered Teveri. Their voice was strange—Avra tore his eyes away from Julian's perfect shoulder-to-waist ratio and looked at them. Their expression was tight, closed off; their back was hunched; they were leaning against Avra just a little bit. Angry? Hurt? Sad?

"What is it?"

Teveri shrugged, their mouth twisting bitterly. "Lucky he's a monk," they said, even softer than a whisper. "He's too pretty for either of us."

"Oh." Avra looked back at Julian, who was now wringing out his robe, and squeezed tighter to Teveri. "Yeah," he said quietly. "I had that thought too."

Teveri took Avra's hand and squeezed hard. He squeezed back.

Julian hung his robe over a bush near the water and returned to them, sitting on the ground and leaning back against the rock where Teveri had placed the lantern. "Well. I wasn't expecting to come back to such sad little faces. Are we quarreling again?"

"No," said Teveri.

"Noooo," said Avra.

Julian crossed his arms so his biceps did things that were frankly unfair. "Good. Are we going to sulk out here all night, or go back to camp and eat dinner? Or sulk here a little while longer and take inventory of what we've got so that Teveri doesn't have to go bankrupt or sell their eye and replace it with one shaped like a skull with another, smaller skull in *its* eye?"

Avra rattled off: "One ship, slightly dented. One mainsail of the *Nightingale,* currently our only point of pride. Hold full of fancy straw. A crew that knows they're not getting paid. A dozen or so new friends who don't speak our language but who definitely did see that we couldn't do anything about the serpents except throw spooky science nuts at them, and who therefore now know that they are also not getting paid any cut of the profits. Two Chants who *do* speak our new friends' language, one of whom is basically an honorary nephew of Black Garda. Ambassador Baltakan being nosy. Uh, uh, uh, Oskar's giant dead noodle fish. A day's sail back to Scuttle Cove through the noodle orgies. Uh, Teveri's ability to look sensational in a fancy coat. Me, a known trollop. My ability to win any game of chance whether I mean to or not. Julian's tits and brain. Uh. A distinct lack of any blue dogs so far."

"Oh gods," Teveri said. "What if there aren't any fucking dogs here?" They buried their face in their hands and continued, muffled: "Distinct lack of dogs. Distinct lack of one million altınlar to buy the *Nightingale*'s flag and mizzen royal from Captain Ueleari. Probably the crew's outstanding bar tabs, which they won't be able to pay, so I'll have to pay it . . ."

"Look," Avra said. "Look, if all else fails, I'll go out gambling and bring home all my winnings."

"No one in Scuttle Cove will play with you anymore."

Avra paused. "There are tourists in for the festival, maybe no one has warned them about me. Too late to enter the cake competition. The lower categories go tomorrow and they'll all be finished by the time we get back. And none of us know how to make cakes, anyway." He eyed Julian. "Do you know how to make cakes?"

"Not the kind that would win a festival competition."

"What kind, then?"

"Monastery food."

"Eurgh," said Avra.

"No sex, bad food, what's even the goddamn point?" Teveri demanded. "I ran away from *Tash* for barely more than that."

"*Weeeell,*" said Avra. "I mean . . . It was a bit more than that. Weren't they horrible to you?"

"No sex, bad food, and they were horrible to me," Teveri said flatly. "That's what I said. Barely more."

Avra eyed Julian. "Don't suppose the monastery was also horrible to you, were they?"

Julian's smile was sad and wry. "My first abbot saved my life at the cost of sacrificing my favorite thing in all the world because he thought it was distracting me from holy pursuits. My second abbot . . ." Julian shrugged one shoulder. "I remain too much of a radical to tolerate being ruled by that kind of tyrant for long."

"Interesting. So so so so interesting," said Avra. "I'm going to tuck away everything you just said and think about it later, by myself, specifically the part about your favorite thing in the world."

"Inventory," said Teveri.

"Uh, uh, my deck of Heralds, if they're in a good mood and not being too bitchy about my general life choices. Right. So. Idea number one! We use the straw in the hold to weave a dog costume. I will volunteer to dress in it and attempt to keep Black Garda from discovering the truth as long as possible while Tev walks around the last day of the cake competition in their best coat to show off how absolutely fine we are doing and, um, Julian invents a secret worth millions in any currency. Just comes up with one out of thin air with his giant brain and the backup brains he keeps in his enormous biceps. I would like to clarify right up front that the dog costume is not a sex thing in any way."

"Thank you for the clarification," Julian said. "However, we do not yet know what the blue dogs look like, which would probably be helpful in making a costume."

"Fuck," said Avra. "Okay, new plan."

"One step at a time," Julian said firmly. "The recipe from the Shipbuilder's Guild doesn't work—and not only that, we don't even know what it's *supposed* to do to fend off the serpents. I cannot come up with something that valuable out of thin air." He looked hard at both of them. "I am more than happy to keep working on it, but unless the Emperor of Felicity sends me some huge epiphany, it would take *years* to develop. Decades, perhaps. It's rather difficult to test your theories when you only have six weeks out of the year to do so and you risk your life every time you try."

"That's not the first step," Teveri said dully. "The first step is how do we get off this island?"

"In the ship," said Julian.

"Through the serpents?"

Avra made a dismayed little *reeeeee.*

"Yes," said Julian, as if it were that simple. "We can't ride back with the Ammatu—leaving the ship here is a very easy way to lose it entirely, and I would imagine it wouldn't make us look good back in Scuttle Cove. We'll just keep a closer lookout for the swarms and hope for the best."

"The *swarms*, yes," said Teveri. "But that won't help with the roving bachelors *in between* the swarms with nothing to do but vent their sexual frustration on passing ships."

Julian shrugged. "So we put Avra in the hold."

"Why?" squeaked Avra.

"Love this idea, tell me more," said Teveri.

Julian gave them a reproachful look. "We trust his luck to keep him alive. If he's tied up in the hold—"

"*Tied up?*" said Avra, appalled.

"Hush, Julian wants to tie you up," Teveri said, resting their chin on their fist and gazing fixedly at Julian. "Go on."

"If he's tied up in the hold," Julian dutifully went on, "then the serpents can't breach the hull, because Avra would be the first to drown, and his luck won't let him drown."

"Genius."

Avra wriggled in dismay. "Ooh, I don't like that one bit. I don't trust my luck that far. You can't test it, you know, there's no way to know if it's real or not. Maybe it's not real. Maybe it's a limited resource and this would burn through the rest of my lifetime supply. Maybe it's a daily ration that gets topped up every day and this would just gulp it all down in one go, much like the serpents will do to me if they get me."

"That fixes the immediate problem of whether we will have to camp here for six weeks," said Teveri.

"Or, you know," said Avra urgently, "we could just camp here for six weeks instead of tying up poor Avra and throwing him in the hold."

"We don't have food to last us that long."

"There are coconuts. Fish. Pigs, apparently. Fresh water with only a little bit of Tev's snot in it."

"It was a rather shocking amount of snot, actually," said Julian.

"And what if we are forced to resort to cannibalism?" Teveri demanded. "Who do you think will be the first to be eaten?"

Avra glanced at Julian's tits. "Point taken, he does look tasty."

"Thank you," Julian said solemnly. "Setting aside the issue of whether Avra will be tied up in the hold, the next issue is . . . money? Selling the straw has to be worth *something*."

"No, I have a better idea for the straw," said Avra. "This is idea number two: We dunk it in salt water until it turns the same shade of silver as our sails, and then we bundle it onto the yardarms and tell everyone that when we were on this island we found a secret supply cache belonging to Xing Fe Hua that had some spare sails in it. Then *I* go into the bars, pretend to get really drunk, and say that I want to gamble and that my wager will be all the silver on the foremast. Even knowing what I am like, they will be unable to resist the temptation to give it a shot. And then I will have their money.

"Now," he continued. "I know what you're about to say. 'Avra, everyone's going to figure out that we don't have any sails at all and we just conned them out of their money, and they will not be at all pleased with us.' Yes, you're right, but hear me out: Maybe after we run this heist, we can do a good deed with some of the money so that we're still seen as lovable rapscallions rather than the sort of rapscallions who need to be beaten up in alleys. Maybe we give part of our ill-gotten gains to some orphans who have been wronged. Or the heir to a fortune, who has been wronged out of it. Or someone who was wrongfully injured by negligent conditions in their workplace and lost a leg or a hand or an ear—"

"That's half the crew," said Teveri.

"Ah! Which means we can just keep the money for ourselves and still maintain our lovable rapscallion personas that everyone can sympathize with and whom nobody will be allowed to criticize." A beat of silence, and then Avra added, "It's about *society*."

"What is?" said Julian.

"The poignant and very wrongful things that happened to all of us. The wrongs that drove us to piracy in the first place. For example, I was driven to piracy by accidentally committing treason, but when you think about it, I wouldn't have done the treason if Araşt didn't have a weird fetish for six-to-eight-week trade monopolies—"

But Teveri and Julian had frozen, staring behind Avra with strange expressions.

"Hm," said Avra. "Let me guess. Undead sea serpent that's grown legs or maybe just slithered its way up here and is about to chomp us all to shreds with its objectionable number of teeth. Wild boar that is going to stab us with its tusks and stomp us into paste. A blue dog, but actually as it turns out the dog is the size of a pony and it's got fangs the length of, um . . . Longer than my hand, shorter than my cubit, so . . . uh. Fangs the length of Julian's dick. Very teeth-themed guesses, you may have noticed."

Avra turned around.

"Ah," he said.

And then: "Ah."

And after that, "Hm."

And finally, "I was not expecting that. Uh. Good news about the teeth situation, at least. Um. Unless they're retractable."

There was a blue dog standing a little ways off, looking at them with apparently as much surprise as they were looking at it.

"I didn't think it was going to be blue," said Julian, clearly floored.

"What other color was a *blue dog* supposed to be?" hissed Teveri under their breath.

"Sort of a silvery grey. Like cats. Or horses."

"Nope. It is extremely blue," said Avra. "One of the top five bluest things I have seen in my life. In fact, I am going to float the theory that's a ghost dog. Never seen ghost dogs before, never seen a ghost on *land* before, never seen a ghost anywhere except in the Turtles, actually, but here is the thing—I don't know about you two, but I do not expect a blue dog to be *glowing*."

"Yes," said Julian emphatically.

"It can glow if it wants to, I don't care," Teveri said. "Julian, where's your belt?"

Julian silently handed them his rope belt. Without taking their eyes off the dog, Teveri threw one piece of the rope at another piece of the rope and suddenly had a loop tied in it. Avra vaguely recognized that as the same spooky rope trick Markefa had once shown him.

"Catch it," Avra whispered. "Catch it, Tev. Unless it's a ghost dog. If it is a ghost dog, there's nothing to be done."

"It looks solid," Julian said.

"Tev. Imagine how much Black Garda would *love us* if we brought her not just a blue dog, but a *glowing blue dog.*"

"Trust me, I'm imagining it," Teveri hissed, moving slowly to a crouch.

The dog watched Teveri creep forward. It really was astonishingly blue. It was a little more than knee height at the shoulder, the size and configuration of a N'gakan lion-hunting dog—pointy snout, long legs, a deep chest, and fairly short fur everywhere but for the soft feathering on its ears and markedly curved tail. Its nose was black and wet and twitching; its eyes were bright and intelligent. And blue.

"I guess it's a pretty good dog, if you like dogs," said Avra. "Do you like dogs, Julian?"

"*Shh,*" said Teveri, inching toward the dog in a crouch, the rope clutched in one hand.

The dog put its head on one side and watched.

It yawned hugely with a *rrrrow* sound, gave Teveri a very wide berth as it loped around and past them, and bent to lap water from the pool.

"Okay, so it's fresh water with Tev's snot *and* dog drool in it," said Avra.

The dog looked up.

"Shh!" said Teveri. Avra shushed. "Don't move."

Teveri turned around and inched back across the clearing, still crouching. The dog turned back to drink. Teveri inched closer.

The dog finished drinking, raised its head to sniff around in the air, went to Julian's wet robe hanging on the shrub, and sniffed.

Teveri inched closer.

"Catch it, catch it," Avra whispered. "Tev, catch it."

The dog sniffed the ground intently and came right up to Julian and Avra.

"Don't move," Teveri growled.

The dog stuck its wet nose in Avra's ear, snuffled thoroughly, and huffed as it turned away. Avra endured this with tensed muscles and a very nearly subvocal *reeeee* of discomfort. Not a ghost dog, then.

The dog turned to Julian, snuffled his tits, the inside of his ear, and his crotch. Julian twitched and grimaced.

"Don't move," said Teveri, coming just level with Avra. "Be strong, man, don't fucking move."

The dog turned its head sharply to Teveri.

Teveri froze.

The dog, clearly thinking it through, gave one slow wag.

"It's a vicious wild animal," Teveri whispered. "If you move, it might attack."

They crept a foot closer. The dog sniffed in their direction and rolled onto its back, its long tail wagging in the little twitches that in Avra's experience usually signaled barely restrained glee.

"A vicious wild animal," said Julian, absolutely straight-faced. "Could attack at any moment."

Teveri shot him a glare. "It's a ploy. It's trying to lull us into a false sense of security. Be on your guard."

"Well, now I don't know what to think," said Avra.

"Have you ever *met* a dog before, Teveri?" Julian asked, incredulously.

"Shh! You can see how much cunning and guile it has in its eyes."

Julian reached out without flinching and rubbed the dog's belly vigorously. "Ooh, good girl, who's a good girl," he said. The dog writhed in ecstasy. "A *puppy,* that's what you are. Are you a puppy? Are you a good, good girl? Give me the rope, Teveri."

While Julian was engaged in telling the dog what a good girl she was and slipping the makeshift collar over her head, Avra turned to Tev, who was looking mulish. "I think it is just that every living creature wants to roll on its back and let Julian rub its tummy," Avra said. "It probably would have been terrifyingly vicious if he weren't here. Don't grind your teeth like that, Tev, remember what the spooky dentist said."

"I've met dogs," Teveri objected loudly over Julian's apostrophe. "I've been introduced to Black Garda's dogs."

The dog had jumped to her feet and was enthusiastically licking Julian's face. He was, with all evidence of equal enthusiasm, holding his hands on either side of her head and rubbing in such a way that her ears flapped up and down. "That's all of them, just Black Garda's dogs in passing?"

"What of it?" Teveri snapped.

"Nothing, nothing," Julian said. To the dog, he said, "It just explains a lot, doesn't it? Gasp! Doesn't it! Yes, yes, it does! But it doesn't explain how you are such a good girl!"

Teveri got the lantern. Julian had the dog. Avra had been put in charge of carrying Julian's still very wet robe, which was dripping coldly down the front of his trousers.

"In your memoir, will you say that this island was full of extremely tame blue dogs or vicious wild creatures?" Teveri demanded.

"I will say that it was a very clever dog who led the intrepid Captain az-Ḥaffār on a sprightly chase before the captain finally outwitted her with superior cunning and vastly more refined wiles."

"And I was protecting your helpless vulnerable body," said Avra. "I was prepared to throw all six muscular feet of myself in front of you and hold the beast's mouth closed with my bare hands to keep it from mauling you. You were sprawled on the ground with your torn clothes, baring your heaving bosom, and I was gallantly standing over you while Teveri vanquished the dog and won its loyalty."

"Just so," Julian said seriously. "That is precisely what I will write."

Teveri grumbled under their breath and stomped off with the

lantern. The dog cast enough light that the clearing was far from pitch dark.

The dog was extremely interested in Oskar when they got back to camp—she dragged Julian over immediately and spent several minutes sniffing every inch of Oskar's body and several more minutes enthusiastically licking his boots. Her tongue was even bluer than the rest of her.

Oskar clearly had no idea what to do about it.

While they had been gone, the Ammatu had apparently noticed the general lack of civilization happening for *The Running Sun*'s crew and had absorbed them into their own camp. "There's fish and roast pork," Markefa said, patting the sand next to her, which Avra immediately flung himself onto. "And we've invented some games."

"Games," said Avra, sitting up very straight. "Tell me of games."

"Well, there's 'throw a piece of coconut shell into a circle on the sand, and whoever can do it from farthest off is the winner.' That is fairly self-explanatory."

"That's pretty good. Uh. Do they play any games of chance?"

Markefa groaned. "Boy, don't be like that. We just made friends. They gave us *roast pork for dinner*."

"I'm not trying to clean them out!" Avra said, holding up his hands. "I wouldn't do that to my very best friends Kapono and Heirani, come on."

"We also played kiss games while you were gone," said Markefa calmly. She was eating steaming bits of pork with her fingers off of a broad piece of green palm frond, the ends of which had been woven into a braid so it was roughly circular.

"You did not."

"No, we didn't. I thought about suggesting it, though, just because I knew it'd make you wail, but then I thought you might be off playing kiss games of your own."

"No such luck, but I appreciate your faith in me." Avra stole a bite of pork from her frond-plate and glanced around. "Really, though, who's been up for games?"

"Your best friends Kapono and Captain Heirani," Markefa murmured. "Couple of the others, but the two of them were the most involved and outgoing."

"Great. Great. Love those two, they're great. Good, good." He looked around and found Heirani squatting in front of the blue dog, squishing its face between her hands and baby-talking to it in a high singsong voice, probably with much the same content as Julian's oratorical debate about who the goodest girl was. Several of the other Ammatu were gathered around as well, though Haukea was ignoring the dog in favor of smiling at Julian and playing with her hair. "Hrm," said Avra. "Heirani!"

Heirani looked up and blinked inquisitively at him.

First, Avra tattled. He pointed to Haukea. "Say Haukea, Julian good." Heirani whipped around instantly and whapped at her presumably sister's knee; Haukea jumped back with a squeak. Heirani said something scathing and pointed imperiously to the fire, where the pig on the spit, neglected, was beginning to char on one side. Haukea stalked off with a scowl.

Heirani turned back to Avra with a smile and bowed politely.

Avra bowed back. "Uh, game?" To Markefa, he whispered, "Have we exchanged any more vocabulary?"

"Coconut is *popo,* and we've mostly been miming for *throw*. Like this."

As soon as Markefa demonstrated, Heirani lit up. "Good! You and me?"

"Yes," said Avra, standing and brushing sand off the seat of his pants.

Heirani gave a final smacking kiss to the dog's forehead, which made it dance and wag like it was losing its mind from joy. She looked around on the ground for a moment, frowning, and asked a question that was almost certainly *Hey, has anyone seen the bits of coconut shell we were using for that game?* because all the others in earshot started looking around as well.

After a few moments, someone noticed Haukea's deeply smug expression as she sat by the campfire and turned the spit. Upon being questioned, she answered primly and gestured to the fire. There was a brief tangent for familial shouting and squabbling.

"I'm ninety-nine percent sure they're sisters," Avra said to Markefa, who grinned.

Heirani sighed hugely and turned to Avra, spreading her hands apologetically to indicate that there were no coconut shells left to play with.

"That's all right!" said Avra. "Good! It is good! Uh—popo throwing? Is *game. Game.*"

Heirani was clearly too exasperated with her sister to be in top form for language exchange. Avra bounced forward and took her elbow, pulling her away from the fire a little ways. "Haukea," he said, rolling his eyes theatrically. Heirani snorted ruefully. "Never mind her," he said, with a dismissive wave in her direction. "You and me, game, yes? Avra game! Game good." Two friendly people making an effort to understand one another could get there rather easily, in Avra's experience, regardless of whether or not they spoke the same language.

There was rope aplenty, especially with the Ammatu ship pulled up onto the beach, so Avra demonstrated the concept of jumping rope. He hadn't played since he was a young student in the civil service academy. It was more difficult on the sand than it had been on the smooth cobblestones of the dormitory courtyard.

"Oi," called Markefa. "Are you just taking turns, or do you want me to swing the rope for you?"

"Oh, *would* you?" Avra said, delighted. Markefa got up and ambled over. "Where's Julian?"

"Went for a walk with the dog and, uh, Heirani's sister. Yes, I'm avoiding saying her name on purpose. The rest of Heirani's crew told us not to draw her attention to it." She took the long rope from Avra and secured one end of it to an anchor point near the beautifully carved upward-pointed prow of one of the two hulls.

"Ah," said Avra. "A walk, is it. A romantic walk in the starlight. And the doglight."

"She brought him a plate of pork," Markefa said. "Which is the kind of rock-solid seduction tactic you have to respect. Think he'll go for that?"

"Nope," said Avra cheerfully, but he felt a knot of uncertainty. Haukea was prettier than both him and Tev put together. He took a breath. "Jump rope. How did you establish the linguistic concept of 'winning' in the coconut-throwing?"

"Mostly by excited yelling every time someone got it in the circle," Markefa said.

"Right, that will do. Heirani, come here." He gestured for her to stand by the rope with him, pulled her onto the same side, and pointed to Markefa. "Markefa turns the rope. You and me jump."

"Ooh," said Heirani. "Good, yes."

Re-establishing the concept of how to *win* was effortless. The very first time Avra tripped, Heirani laughed and clapped, and her crew cheered.

"Heirani good," Avra said, beaming as he got back to his feet. "Markefa, did you happen to establish the linguistic concept of betting?"

Markefa groaned. "Avra."

"I know what I'm about!"

"The woman's had a tough day! She's been stuck on a boat for who knows how long with her annoying little sister! They had *harpoons* earlier in case they got attacked by the serpents. Avra," Markefa groaned again. "Don't make her day worse."

"I'm *not*. This is important!"

"For *what?*"

"Saving Tev's reputation."

While Markefa stood thunderstruck and tried to work out the logic, Avra turned to Heirani, who was listening with apparently great intrigue to Markefa's reproach. "You win jump rope!" he said enthusiastically, clapping a little. "You win! Heirani good good good. Very good!"

She smiled and gestured to the rope. "You win?"

"I *play*. You play. Then maybe I win, or maybe you win, who knows."

They played again; after a few jumps, Heirani intentionally stopped and let the rope hit her legs as Avra jumped it. "You win?"

"Yes, I win!"

"You good," she said politely, smiling.

"Thank you! Again?" he said, gesturing to the rope, and she nodded. "First, before we do that . . . Hm." He looked around on the sand and collected a double handful of shells, divided them into two equal piles, and put them on the ground. "These? Mine. Avra's shells. These? Yours. Heirani's shells."

She nodded and pointed to each pile in turn. "Atigi a Avara. Atigi a Heirani. Yes, good."

"Good!" Avra picked out one shell from his pile and held it up. "I wager this." He gestured to her and her pile. She copied him. He handed his shell to Markefa; she did the same. Markefa grumbled. "Now we play."

Avra won. Markefa handed him both shells with a roll of her eyes. Heirani narrowed her eyes, watched Avra theatrically adding both shells to his pile, and glanced at her own pile. "Hm."

Avra took one shell from his pile. "I wager this!"

Heirani selected one shell, then deliberately added a second and turned to him with a light of challenge in her eyes. Avra grinned and squirmed with delight. "Raising the stakes, I see! Good." He added a second shell to his own pile; they handed them to Markefa.

"Hm!" said Heirani, and gestured Avra imperiously to the ropes.

Avra deliberately lost that round, and Heirani collected the shells from Markefa smugly and added them to her pile. "Heirani good," Avra crooned. "Very good. Wager again?"

"Good," she said, and began to pick through her shells.

"Actually . . ." Avra cleared his throat and sat on the sand, gesturing for Heirani to join him.

Markefa sighed heavily. "Avra."

"It's for Tev," he said firmly. "I'm trying to *help*. Let me work."

"This is going to take a bit, isn't it?"

"Probably. Lots of complicated concepts. You can go get a snack if you want."

"Call me when you're ready," she said.

Avra smiled at Heirani, who smiled back and put her head on one side.

Somehow, through a great deal of cooperation and careful clarification, Avra managed to communicate just what it was that he actually wanted to wager. When he called Markefa back over, she eyed him suspiciously. "And what are the stakes in this round?"

"If I win, Heirani won't tell anyone that we got attacked by sea serpents even though we poured stuff in the water. And if she wins, she gets my entire stake in the profits we earn from selling the secret."

Markefa stared at him. "But there aren't going to be any profits, Avra."

"Well, not right *now*. Julian will figure it out. I can feel it. I can *feel* it, Markefa. And if we earn any other money in the next little bit, I'll still give her my whole stake of that. Look—" He pulled his little rucksack into his lap and rummaged in it for one of his cards. "Look, it's—" He squinted closely at it. "*The fucking Bower again.*" He scowled at it. "What do you mean by that, hm? Julian's off getting laid right now? Or Heirani is going to demand that I pay her with my body? Because that would be *fine with me,* I'll have you know." He stuffed the card back in his bag and smiled up at Markefa. "The Bower does technically mean happy secrets and joyful futures in addition to all the overtones of 'congratulations on your upcoming sex,' you know. Could definitely mean that Julian will figure it out eventually and all will end well."

Markefa squatted in front of him, her elbows on her knees, and looked intently into his eyes. "Avra. Are you fucking sure about this?"

"Definitely. Never been more sure in my life."

"Supposing that we do ever see a single copper from this secret you brought us. You're staking *a king's ransom* on a game of jump rope."

"Only my part of the king's ransom."

"On a game of *jump rope.* After you've already lost a couple rounds."

"I lose games all the time, Markefa," he said reasonably. "But only when they're not important." He gave her his best, twinkliest smile. "Best way to make sure my luck kicks in is to make it *matter,* right?"

Markefa sucked in a breath through her teeth. "A king's ransom."

"Yes."

"*A king's ransom, Avra.* And I should *know* what a king's ransom is, because I was the Royal Exchequer of Lapaladi!"

"Yes, Madam Former Exchequer, a king's ransom on the line against Heirani keeping her mouth shut and making sure that all her friends do too. You know what they say! Two can keep a secret if one of them is dead, and one hundred and thirty can keep a secret if there's a lot of money in it for one hundred and twenty-nine of them."

"And you're sure you've communicated clearly to Heirani about what the expectations are if she loses."

"Heirani is my *friend,*" Avra said, aghast. He took Heirani's hand in both of his. "My good good friend!"

"Aww," said Heirani, visibly charmed.

Avra whipped to her. "You know the word *friend*?" he screeched. "Friend? Yes?"

She laughed. "Yes. Friend. Good, yes?"

"See?" he demanded to Markefa. "Heirani and me, friends, friends good."

"Friend good," Heirani agreed.

"So it's fine! It's fine, Markefa!"

"I'm really not sure that it's fine, my boy."

"Markefa," he said, and he must have sounded unhabitually serious, because she jerked back a little in shock. "Markefa, if they tell everyone that we don't have the secret and that we got attacked, you and the crew are going to look like a bunch of crazy daredevils for sailing out in the middle of fuck season, but *Teveri* is going to look like an idiot in one of two ways." He dropped his voice. "Either a gullible idiot for believing me and trusting Julian, *or* an idiot who was so vainglorious that they were willing to risk the lives of their entire crew. If we come back in six months and Julian's got it figured out, are the fences more likely to give us a second chance or to laugh hysterically and slam the doors in our faces? And more important—how's it going to look to the other captains, Markefa? What's going to happen the first time Tev walks into a bar and everyone bursts out laughing?"

Markefa breathed hard through her nose. "Teveri az-Ḥaffār survived years of being called Captain Undertaker and hearing people say they desecrated the dead just to get a ship."

"Teveri az-Ḥaffār," Avra said sharply, "had a truth to cling to then, which was that even though they ran away from home and renounced their religion and disowned their family, they were still enough of a gravekeeper's child that when push came to shove, they said their family's blessings over every single one of those bodies, commended their souls to whatever gods watched over them, and gave them the most respectful burial at sea that could be humanly managed under the circumstances." Markefa stared at him like he was some new kind of slightly horrifying creature she'd never seen before. "Teveri survived being called Captain Undertaker because they knew they'd done something *honorable*, for whatever that's fucking worth in this world."

"Not much, in my experience," Markefa murmured.

Avra let out his breath. "So how's it going to fucking go? How will it go, when one of the other captains throws a drink in Tev's face and says they're a disgrace to their *Nightingale* sail for putting their own idiocy and selfishness and *greed* before the lives of their crew?"

Markefa stood and dropped her face into her hands before running them up and over her hair—iron grey and so close-shorn that you could see every curve and angle of her skull. She turned toward the sea, looking out into the black abyss broken only by the stars, the sound of the waves lapping against the shore, and the occasional flash of something out in the water glowing with its own light.

Heirani leaned close, concerned, and whispered, "You good? Marakefa good?"

"Nothing's really good right now," Avra whispered back. "But thank you for asking." At the expectant quirk of her eyebrows, he sighed and shook his head. "No. No good."

"Ah," she said, and patted his hand in sympathy.

Markefa turned back. "Avra."

"Yeah?"

"You're being very spooky right now, and I would like to ask you, as a friend, if you've been possessed by any ghosts, bitten by any rabid glowing dogs, or experimenting with any new drugs."

"I have not been bitten by any rabid glowing dogs. I don't know what being possessed feels like, but it sounds like it might be kind of sexy, so I'd be interested in trying it out. If I had experimented with any new drugs, I would have offered to share with the crew."

Markefa lowered her hands from her head to her hips. "That's a bit better."

"I'm a complex person, Markefa. I have *facets.*"

She sighed and looked bitterly at the jump rope. "And we don't think that Heirani and her friends will keep the secret just because we ask nice, do we?"

"Black Garda hired 'em to be witnesses. Nothing to do with witnesses but try to buy their silence, eh?"

"Fuck," Markefa whispered, running her hands over her head again.

"I don't know why you're being like this," Avra said, gesturing to all of her. "It's only *my* share. What do you care what I do with my share? I can gamble with it if I want. I could have just offered to pay her outright, but I *do actually prefer to keep my king's ransom,* Markefa, which is why I made it a gamble. I'll win because I'm lucky, and then she'll be honor-bound—"

"For whatever that's fucking worth," Markefa groaned.

"Yes, well! Do you have any better ideas? Do you want to sit here making friends and playing jump rope and cajoling them into not fucking up everything for us so that we have a fish's chance in a sandstorm of getting out of this with, at *minimum,* Tev's dignity intact?"

"And if, by some fucked-up twist of fate, you lose?"

"I'm not going to *lose.* Where's all the grumbling about my witchy luck now, eh?"

"I'd feel happier if this were a game of cards," she groaned, picking up the end of the jump rope. "I have one condition," she said, holding up a finger as Avra and Heirani scrambled up. "Best of three."

Avra turned to Heirani. "Three games," he said, holding up three fingers. "One, two, three. You win two—one, two—you win. I win two, I win."

"Good," Heirani said emphatically.

"I don't like her expression," Markefa said.

"It's just a healthy spirit of competition, Markefa, don't worry about it."

Captain's Log

Day 16, 6th month, 199th yr Mah. Dyn.

Anchored at Blue Dog Island. Survived serpent attack; nerves extremely frayed.

FUCK THE SEA. IT SHOULD HAVE FEWER CREATURES IN IT. Briefly considered adopting a philosophy of "You know what, some Araşti lunatic presumably went out in that bullshit MULTIPLE TIMES to figure out what they were trying to do. Frankly, they earned it and can fucking keep it. Absolutely no thank you."

~~Julian~~

~~Julian saw~~

~~Julian witnessed~~

~~May have to kill Julian~~

~~Have decided to leave Julian behind with these weird blue dogs~~

~~Aura clearly a poor influence on Julian, leading him astray.~~

~~Have been blackmailed with things unfit to be written down, nearly unspeakable. Expecting a list of Julian's demands at any time.~~

~~Circumstances beyond my control are forcing me to~~

~~Julian exists and it's fine for him to do that~~

Inventory acquired:

1½ dead sea serpents, to be taxidermied

1 glowing blue dog

Addendum forthcoming.

15

27. The Beggar

Poverty, need, hunger, lackingness. Possibly a supplicant with a great need, someone who requires help. An absence, a dearth, empty pockets.

(Reversed: Powerlessness, solitude, misfortune. Feeling invisible, abandoned, forgotten. The world is turning its back.)

On the very first jump of the first round, Avra landed a little bit wrong on the sand, twisted his ankle, and fell over.

"I'm all right!" he said, popping back up. "Ow. I'm all right."

"Are you?"

"You good?" Heirani asked, supporting him by the elbow as he rolled the ache out of his ankle.

"Thank you, friend, yes, good. Ow. Small ow. Good." He tested his weight on it. A little sore, but nothing he couldn't walk off. "Good. One win for Heirani! Let's go again."

On the first jump of the second round, Avra landed on a small rock hidden in the sand, screeched, flailed for balance, hit himself in the face with the rope, and fell over.

"Hm," he said, staring up at the stars. "Hm. Hm."

"Two win!" Heirani said triumphantly. She shouted this to her crew, who cheered raucously.

"Hm," said Avra.

"Fuck," said Markefa, who had dropped the rope.

"I think this is probably fine, actually," Avra said, gazing up at the stars. Heirani leaned into his field of view.

"Avara? You good?"

"Yes," he said, sitting up. "Yes. Foot ow, but y'know." He shrugged.

"Foot two ow," Heirani said, grinning.

"Yes, that's true. Congratulations! You win!"

"I win," she said with deep satisfaction. She looked back to the crew. "Hmm. Haukea?" She squinted. "Avara, sorry, no Haukea . . ." She made some gestures indicating that she needed to attend to this mystery immediately, and Avra nodded and waved her off. She clapped him companionably on the shoulder and jogged back to the campfire.

Markefa squatted next to him. "Fuck," she said again, more emphatically.

"I think this is probably a good thing."

"How?"

"Great question." He rolled across the sand to his little rucksack and got out his cards—the whole deck—and gave them a proper, thorough shuffle, which he hardly ever did. "Want to cut these for me?"

Markefa muttered under her breath, snatched the cards from him, cut them seven times, and shuffled them again.

Avra delicately drew the top card with two careful fingers. "The Beggar."

"Apt. Draw another."

He drew another. "The Cove, reversed."

"What's that?"

"Um," he said, squinting at it. "Hm. Upright, it's about security, shelter from the storms and serpents. But reversed . . ." He tipped his head from side to side.

"Danger?"

"Nooooo," Avra said, frowning. "No, not quite, not that. It could be a suggestion to tread cautiously. Sometimes it's about secrets. A *false* sense of security. Things happening under your nose or behind your back. Things under the surface of the water, where you can't see them."

"This doesn't sound very promising to me," Markefa growled. Avra tucked the cards away, and Markefa pulled him up just enough that she could haul him over her shoulder as she stood.

"Reeeeeee," said Avra in alarm. "Where are you taking me?"

"To the captain."

"No," said Avra. "No, let's not go see the captain."

Markefa carted him over to the fire and dumped him next to Teveri, who was eating hardtack soaked in pork drippings with a stormy expression. "Our favorite idiot just lost his entire stake in the entirely theoretical profits, Captain. We need to check whether he's run out of luck."

Teveri narrowed their eyes at Avra, sprawled on the ground at their feet. "We certainly do."

"Markefa is exaggerating, incandescent one," said Avra, rolling himself up. "I think it's probably fine, actually."

Teveri wiped their hands on their pants and said aloud, "Who's got playing cards?" Beng Choon produced a deck, and Teveri shuffled it several times. "I don't have time for an entire game," they said, their voice low and tight. "But if you win this round, I'll let you come with me."

"What are we playing? And where are we going?"

Teveri dealt them each a hand of ten cards. "We're pretending that we're halfway through a game of four-fox." They flashed a hard look at him and added under their breath, "Julian's been gone a long time. Went off with what's-her-name. The girl."

"Haukea. Heirani's sister." Avra sighed mournfully and looked at his hand. "I drew The Bower a bit ago."

Teveri swore colorfully and snatched up their own cards.

"So they're probably making tender love somewhere down the beach," Avra continued, sighing again as he rearranged his cards. "Even as we speak, they might be falling in love and gazing into each other's eyes in the starlight. And the doglight. Four-fox, you said? I'm assuming it's whoever can get the most points, but am I supposed to do that with just a single story-set? Or can I make more than one?"

"The latter," Teveri said through gritted teeth.

"Great. I've got *turtledoves,*" he said, laying down a pair of twos. "Also *bite-the-moon.*" And that was the rest of his cards. He folded his hands in his lap and looked expectantly at Tev. "Did you want to show me yours, or . . . ?"

Teveri let out a long breath and threw their cards on the sand. "He's fine, Markefa."

"I told her I was fine, you know." He gathered up the cards and stacked them all together neatly before handing the deck back to Beng Choon.

"You're going after Julian?" Markefa said to Teveri.

"Avra drew The Bower, so . . ." Teveri spread their hands. "What do you expect me to do?"

"Let him live his own life?"

"Why?" said Avra.

"Don't be silly, Markefa," said Teveri. "He's not allowed to go on romantic walks in the doglight. That's a very valuable dog specially requested by Black Garda, and it might get lost if he's distracted."

"Right," said Markefa. "It's only about the dog."

"Definitely only about the dog," Avra said, nodding energetically. "Teveri is right about everything as per usual."

"Oh," said Markefa, taking a second look at them. "Wait, are you actually going after him, or is this an excuse for the two of *you* to sneak off and fuck?"

Teveri rolled their eyes, made a disgusted noise, grabbed the lantern, and stomped off down the beach.

"Such a great question, Markefa. I'm as interested in the answer as you are," Avra said as he scrambled to his feet and went to follow.

"Draw a card," Teveri hissed at him as he caught up. "What is Julian up to? What is he doing?"

Avra dug in his little rucksack, then took Tev's wrist and raised the lantern enough that he could see which card he pulled. He gave a little whine of dismay. "Oh no, The *Alchemist.* He's pounding her into dust as we speak."

"That's not what it means," Teveri snapped. "It's secrets and knowledge, isn't it?"

"Yes, or discovery—they could be discovering each other's *bodies,* Tev."

Teveri sniffed. "Well, he's welcome to do that with whoever he likes, but he shouldn't have taken the dog with him."

"We do definitely have to go after the dog," Avra agreed breathlessly. Teveri was walking so fast he had to trot to keep up with them. "We are certainly not intruding on his personal life, and even if we were, he deserves it for intruding on your personal life earlier."

"And for taking the dog."

"No dogs allowed in Julian's personal life, absolutely. Tev, hang on, slow down. I've just been playing jump rope with Heirani, I can't go running up and down the beach like this."

"What did she wager before you lost your stake?" Teveri demanded, stopping in their tracks while Avra caught up, dragging his feet through the sand.

Avra leaned on his knees and coughed. "Why are all captains like this?"

He straightened with a wheeze. "I was trying to get her to agree that she and her crew wouldn't tell anyone what happened earlier. My stake against their silence. Should have just paid her off outright, honestly." He shook one finger. "My schoolmasters always said that sometimes the cheapest thing to do is to pay up front! That's a very important part of my culture, Teveri, please respect it."

"You've made that joke already."

"Well, there's more than one important part of my culture, isn't there!"

Teveri started walking again, still quite fast—their legs were longer than Avra's—but not so difficult to keep up with. "Why did you make this wager?"

"I don't know, to keep our options open! To keep everyone from laughing at you! To keep the fences from writing us off entirely!"

"Hm," said Teveri. "You seem *chipper*, considering that you just lost an unconscionable amount of imaginary money."

"Still got my luck, though." He patted his little rucksack. "Well, maybe. Can't actually prove luck exists, can you? Except with Julian's fun little joke about tying me up and tossing me in the hold to keep the serpents from destroying the ship. I don't think we need to go to such lengths as all that, do you? Anyway, I don't know why I should be upset. Don't gamble with money unless you're prepared to lose it."

"And you were prepared to lose your entire stake in *one game of jump rope*?"

"Well, *no*. I thought I was going to win, because of my luck. But then I lost—and maybe that's also because of my luck. You see what I mean? No way to prove anything. Either things happen for a reason and someday I'll look back on this and say, 'You know what, I'm awfully glad I didn't get a truly silly amount of money. Imagine how much of a flibbertigibbet I would have been then!' *or* . . ."

"Or things don't happen for a reason and everything is random and there's no point to any of it," Teveri said flatly.

"Uh, I guess. I was going to say, 'Or things still happen for reasons, such as the consequences of my actions.' I feel like I'm growing as a person either way. Isn't that so sexy of me? Don't you want to push me against that rock and do unspeakable things to my helpless body, Tev?"

Tev did not answer. Avra got the sense that they wished to be left in silence to think about how alluring all his heroics were and work themselves up about it a little.

After twenty minutes, they staggered up a sand dune and saw a new curving stretch of beach.

This in and of itself was interesting, as it was pitch black except for the dizzying multitude of stars above, and they shouldn't have been able to see the beach in the dark at all . . . Except that perhaps two hundred yards off, there was an entire swarm of glowing blue dogs leaping and frolicking and dashing about madly, and even more of them clustered in a long double line around something on the sand.

There was also another source of light, much closer.

"Ah," said Avra, grabbing Teveri's arm. "Found them."

About halfway between them and the swarm was the wagging and unspeakably blue glow of *their* dog, who was rapturously being petted. Haukea and Julian (still without his wet robe, though he'd fetched out his mantle to keep off the chill) were sitting on a log at the edge of the tree line. Haukea was gesturing emphatically in between pets of the dog, and both of them were looking off down the beach at the other dogs.

"Julian," Avra yelled.

"*Shh,*" hissed Teveri, too late. "We could have *eavesdropped on them.*"

"Why do you need to eavesdrop on anyone? You're the captain. You can just have them marooned on a rowboat at sea. *Yoohoo, Julian.*" Avra moseyed across the sand toward them.

Julian had looked back. "Avra? Is everything all right?"

"Tev's mad that you went off with the dog," Avra said, gesturing back to Teveri, who was following behind at a more dignified pace. "You're in trouble. We definitely only came for the dog, not because we were nosy about your personal life. It's just that you were gone for *ages.*"

"Has it even been an hour?" Julian asked, bemused. "Sorry, Captain. I thought it would be best to tire her out before bed."

Avra gasped. "I'm telling Heirani."

"I meant the *dog.*" Julian tsked at them. "We've only been talking and watching the pack," he added. "They've got a beached sea serpent, I think."

"*Ew,* are they *eating* it?"

"Nice to know that something eats them, isn't it?" Julian said wryly. "Must be why this one was so interested in licking Oskar's boots. He was covered in serpent blood earlier."

"We should go back to camp," said Teveri. "Heirani is concerned."

Haukea made a scathing noise and crossed her arms.

"I gather she's upset with her sister," said Julian apologetically. "She's been venting. At . . . great and eloquent length."

"Speak much of the language, do you?" Teveri said.

"None whatsoever." Julian shrugged. "But sometimes you just want someone to listen."

"Aw," said Avra. "That's very sweet."

The dog got up and strained at the leash toward the pack, whining sadly. Avra took notes.

"Avara, go," Haukea said, pointing imperiously back the way they came. "Avara ma . . . Teveri? Teveri, ia. Go!" Enunciating crisply, she said, "*Goodbye.*"

The dog whined piteously again, yelped even more piteously, strained at the leash, and leapt around in frustration, biting at the rope. Julian stood and clucked his tongue at her. "Sit," he said in *that voice.* Avra sat promptly on the sand, as did the dog.

Avra looked up at Tev, who was glaring accusingly at him, and cleared his throat. "My legs were tired."

"Trollop," they hissed.

Julian bent down to rub the dog's ears. "I already gave you all the hardtack," he crooned. "Sorry, puppy." The dog stared up at him with mournfully limpid cerulean orbs, then looked down the beach to the other dogs and whined again.

"Right," Teveri said. "You can stay here in the dark with Haukea if you like, but I'm taking the dog back to camp."

"Certainly," Julian said, and handed them the leash. "Ah . . . Do you know how to walk a dog on a leash, Captain?"

"How hard can it be?" Teveri scoffed. "Good night, Julian." In slightly more sarcastic tones: "And *goodbye,* Haukea."

"*Goodbye,* Teveri," Haukea replied in exactly the same tone.

"Come along, dog," Teveri said, pulling steadily on the leash. The dog whined and braced against it. "I said *come along.*"

The dog wriggled and made a grouchy *hrmff* noise.

Teveri kept pulling. The dog wriggled again, tugging back until, with one cunning, decided *squirm,* it slipped free of the leash and bolted off down the beach toward the others.

Haukea burst out laughing.

Julian watched the dog run off. "Ah."

"Fuck," said Avra. "Okay."

Teveri said nothing and stormed off after the dog. Julian followed; Avra squeaked and scurried to catch up. Haukea stayed back, still gripped in a fit of giggles.

"Are you all right?" Julian said, keeping pace effortlessly with the captain as Avra struggled behind.

"Don't patronize me," Tev snapped.

"I'm not. It's one more thing in a long list of things, isn't it? So I'm asking if you're all right."

"Fuck today."

Julian gripped their shoulder, tugging them to a stop. "I've known dozens of dogs who could pull that trick. Could have happened to anyone."

"Can you *not*?" Tev snarled, pushing his hand off their shoulder and charging ahead. "I have to catch this *fucking dog,* Julian."

Julian glanced back at Avra, who mewled woefully as they jogged to keep up with Teveri. "My legs are so tired. Carry me. Or catch the dog for Tev first, and then carry me back."

"Why are Avra's legs tired, Captain?"

"He played jump rope with Heirani and lost his entire stake of the prize."

"Fuck."

"Yeah, agreed, stupid move."

"I was *meant* to not have that money," Avra declared. "It's going to be a good thing in the end, you'll see. Builds character. Maybe my destiny is to build a community of cooperation and mutual support amongst the possums of the alley where I live in a small rotting crate. Maybe I need to ally myself with the possums and rise up against the systems of oppression that are keeping us impoverished in alleys and fighting for every scrap of stale bread that Teveri wraps around a rock and kicks at me."

Julian looked back at him for a long, long moment, but without the doglight Avra couldn't see his expression at all.

~

Avra was expecting the sea serpent carcass to smell worse than it did when they reached it. It must have been relatively fresh, perhaps beached as the previous high tide fell, because it only smelled like fish.

Well, fish with a strange note underneath that was more of a sensation than an odor—a *fizzling* in Avra's nose, like the sharp ammoniac tang of a tannery packaged up in thousands of tiny champagne bubbles.

The dogs were going absolutely *wild* over the carcass, gnawing and licking at it and then sneezing, barking at it, and zooming off all the way up to the tree line and all the way down to the waterline, rolling ecstatically, snapping and wrestling like puppies, and then dashing back over to the carcass again.

"Theory," Avra said, as the three of them stopped to regroup at the very edge of this bacchanal. "The sea serpents are drugs."

"It does look that way at first glance, doesn't it," Julian murmured. Without taking his eyes off the dogs, he added, "Does that dog by the head look . . . slightly less glowing to you?"

After a beat of silence, Teveri said, "Maybe. I don't know. If it is, I don't want it. I'm not bringing Black Garda some shitty dog that can't even glow properly."

"There's one down there that isn't glowing at all." Avra pointed. "Right there. By the tail."

"Well, I definitely don't want that one," Teveri said. "I want two glowing dogs. Ones that are putting in some effort."

"Actually there's four or five dogs down that way that aren't glowing," said Avra, squinting into the dark. "Tough to see non-glowing blue dogs at night, isn't it?"

"I wonder if they'd let me get close enough to take some anatomical sketches of the carcass so I can compare it against the one on the ship," said Julian, drifting a little closer. "Has anyone been able to study them?"

"I've never seen much of anything about them, even in Araşt," said Avra. "Just a few sketches in books. First time I saw one properly was when I was brand-new to Intelligence, and they sent me on a training mission with a field agent. Some scholar at the University of Thorikou had gotten his hands on one." He added brightly, "That was when I learned how to commit untraceable arson."

"Arson?" Julian turned to him.

"We set the scholar's whole studio on fire. Not while he was there—we just burned up all his papers and stole the dead serpent. It was only a little one. My size. A baby."

"What did you do with it?"

"Replaced it with a different one and dumped it at sea. Dunno why. It was above my pay grade."

Julian's eyes sharpened. He stepped toward Avra, put his hand on Avra's shoulder. In *that voice*, all sultry and low, he said, "Avra, would you like to be a good boy?"

"Yes," said Avra blankly.

"Were there any differences between the two serpents?"

Julian's voice hijacked Avra's entire consciousness. He watched his own brain flash through the memory like lightning and answer automatically, "The one we stole had been dissected."

"And the one you left hadn't been?"

"It had different cuts."

"Different in what way?"

"Uh, they were all along the sides. Like somebody started to fillet it and got bored."

"What is this about?" Teveri growled.

"I told you," Julian said. "He's my research material." Avra made an interested noise, and Julian's hand grew heavier on his shoulder until Avra broke off and his brain went blank again. "How deep were the cuts?"

"Don't know. Didn't look close. Long time ago."

"When you say that it was like someone started to fillet it—the cuts were neat? Were they symmetrical? Both sides?" Julian's hand on his shoulder got weightier still. "Think carefully, Avra."

"Don't remember," Avra squeaked. "I just helped Lieutenant Behiye drag it out of the sack and lay it on the scholar's table."

"Interesting," said Julian. His voice *rumbled.* Avra wobbled, but Julian's heavy hand didn't let him fall. "Was there anything about those two that was different from the ones we saw today? Other than size."

"Um, uh, coloring? They were more silvery, like a minnow. Shorter whiskers, almost no neck frill." Avra wobbled again. "Are you going to kiss me this time?"

"Fuck's sake," Teveri muttered. "Julian, stop wasting time torturing Avra and get me some of these dogs."

"Oh," said Avra suddenly. "Oh, the one we left didn't have the stripes."

Julian's attention snapped back to him. "The stripes?"

"The big ones today had flashing stripes down the side. The one we took from the university workshop had them too, but not lit up."

"Only the one you left behind *didn't* have the stripe, then?"

Avra nodded energetically. "The cuts, the stripe was cut out. All the way down."

"On the one you *left behind.*"

"Yes."

"How sure are you?"

"Swear it on my own dick."

Julian exhaled long and slow. He squeezed Avra's shoulder, ran his hand up to cup the back of Avra's neck, rubbed his thumb across Avra's cheekbone. "*Good boy,* Avra."

"Mreeeeeeee," said Avra, wobbling on his feet.

Julian's voice was low and velvety. "Why don't you sit down, and the captain and I will go catch one of these dogs."

"Two," said Teveri. They'd crossed their arms. "Two dogs."

"Okay," said Avra, and crumpled to the sand. "I will sit here. I will be so good. I will be incredibly good. Julian. Watch me. Do you see? I am being good right now as we speak."

"What was the point of all that?" Teveri said to Julian.

"He said the stripes were *flashing,* and the dead one wasn't *lit up.*" Julian pointed to the carcass, the dogs. "Some of the dogs *aren't* giving off light, but all of them are chewing at the body. I want us to catch one of the dogs that isn't glowing, and I want to let it keep gnawing on this serpent, or possibly the one back on the ship—"

"Not that one. We're getting that taxidermied."

"Did we keep the tail of the other one? The chunk it had in its mouth?"

"It's also going to be taxidermied. Going to have it chomped in the mouth of the first one."

"Dramatic effect," Avra said, scooting toward their legs. "Such a good idea. Speaking of good things: Me. I'm being so good."

Julian reached down and stopped Avra from moving with a hand on his hair. "Will letting a dog gnaw on it spoil the effect?"

"I guess not," Teveri grumbled. "What are you hoping for? That the dog will just *start* glowing?"

Avra looked up just in time to see Julian smile. "Very possibly."

Captain's Log

Day 16 (addendum)

Have beseeched Markefa to prevent me from fucking Avra again at all costs. Received the distinct impression M thought this was incredibly funny. Explained that this was a serious matter and that as her captain I require her compliance/cooperation. M refused, cited that it was "not her job." Be that as it may, if M does not prevent me from fucking A again, then it is ultimately her fault when I do. A engaged in a behavior that seemed at first glance to be "consideration for my feelings" but I know he was doing it on purpose to entice me. Nearly kissed him in the starlight.

who does that???????????

what have I become

(J insists on having his stupid oath of stupid celibacy, but also goes around using a sex voice at A to compel obedience via ?hypnotism??????? Def some kind of spooky fucking

witchcraft. V inconsiderate behavior. Wish he would refrain from this where I have to see it and be horny about it for the rest of eternity. Do not care if he's doing it to A elsewhere; actually deeply vindicated that A is likewise having to be horny about it for eternity.)

Lost Inventory:

1 dog (glowing)

Added Inventory:

1 dog (glowing),
1 dog (not glowing)

Day 16 (addendum #2)

Inventory update:

1 dog (glowing),
1 dog (also glowing)
WHAT THE FUCK JULIAN.

Considering forbidding him from being smart and scholarly in front of me. Far too handsome when he's pleased w/ himself & gripped by thrill of scientific inquiry or whatever. Am going to be forced by circumstances outside my control to fuck Avra again just to work off some steam, can already tell.

Ugh I want to lick J's brain

16

7. The Compass

Seeking direction, being purposeful, following goals, searching and finding. This is a time to make good plans. Know what your ultimate destination is, and then take the paths that lead toward it.

(Reversed: Being lost, wandering, purposeless, confusion, plans falling to nothing. Your compass needle is spinning; you have lost track of true north. Survive the tumult of the current tempest, then take stock when the winds calm. There are other ways of finding out where you are.)

By dawn the next day, the tide had risen to its halfway point. The dogs were loaded carefully onto the boat, and with single-minded focus they set to enthusiastically licking the deck where the sea serpent had been killed.

Avra had been *so extremely good* the night before and, once his brain had cleared of the haze of witchcraft Julian had put him under, he reflected that he had gotten *no* rewards of note besides a pat on the head and being called a good boy. He decided to make a nuisance of himself until justice was served.

He snuck into Teveri's cabin during the commotion of boarding, raising the anchor, and setting the sails, and he installed himself on the top of the wardrobe with a pair of scissors, needle and thread, and his spare trousers.

Avra fashioned the trousers into something that was barely decent, wriggled into them with some difficulty, and was affecting his best alluring lounge when Teveri finally opened the door.

"Fuck's sake," Teveri said flatly. "What are you wearing?"

"Beg pardon?" said Julian, apparently standing just behind them. "Oh—did you find Avra?"

Teveri angled the door mostly closed so the gap was barely a handspan wide. Without breaking eye contact with Avra, they grunted, "Three guesses what he's up to."

"He's on the wardrobe," said Julian promptly. "Doing something absurd."

"Too vague."

"He's having a tea party with a kitten he's been secretly carrying in his rucksack for the last two weeks."

Teveri made a face. "No."

"I don't have a kitten," said Avra, pitching his voice so Julian could hear it. "But I do have something eminently pettable right here." He gestured grandly to his crotch. "And I will remind everyone that I have been extremely well-behaved. Julian said so. I demand that someone do something about it."

Tev made a worse face.

Julian cleared his throat in that way that meant he was trying not to laugh. "What about 'doing something absurd and marvelous'? Is that specific enough?"

"Don't be disgusting," Tev muttered at him. "Guess properly."

"He's fellating a comically sized piece of fruit, either astonishingly large or hilariously small—I refuse to specify which, but it would certainly be at one of the far ends of the spectrum. Oh, but you said something about what he was wearing . . . Perhaps he has somehow sourced a costume to match his fruit?"

"No."

"Good idea, though," said Avra. "I like that one."

"Then he's not wearing anything. He's stripped naked and painted himself to look like a sea serpent, and as soon as I walk in, he's going to offer me the opportunity to do scientific experiments on his body."

"I like that one even more."

Teveri closed their eyes. "Also no, but at least you were heading in the right direction."

"Was I?" Julian gripped the door over Tev's head, pulled it open, and promptly burst into splutters of laughter. Teveri grimaced again and stalked inside.

Avra wriggled enticingly. "I have an idea. What if you don't tie me up and put me in the hold?"

"Get down," Teveri said.

"What *are* you wearing, you strange creature?" Julian said through laughter as he shut the door.

"I decided my pants were wrong, so I cut them short," Avra informed them. "I thought everyone would enjoy seeing my legs." He stuck one of them out. "Because I'm so generous, you see."

Tev glared up at him. "So you have decided to go about in essentially *a loincloth with buttons.*"

Julian put his hand over his mouth, shaking silently. He had tears in his eyes.

Avra grinned and batted his eyes at Tev. "Do you like it?"

"Do I *like* seeing your scrawny legs and your horrible weird knees? Absolutely not. Get off my wardrobe."

"Julian likes it."

"Julian is laughing at you."

Avra squinted at Julian, who had taken one of the chairs at the desk and still had a hand over his mouth. "I get the sense he is more laughing at the sheer delight of being in my presence. Don't you agree that he's right? I am a delight. He thinks I am delightful. He called me a *strange creature.*"

"You are a strange creature."

"The way he said it made it sound like an endearment, though. A pet name."

"GET OFF MY WARDROBE," Tev screamed.

"Wow," said Avra. "I invent a new kind of pants and this is the reception I get?"

Tev went to their liquor cabinet.

Avra wriggled down from the wardrobe onto the sea chest and jumped to the floor with a little *hrk.* "Do you like the new pants I have invented, Julian?"

Julian cleared his throat again and said, not at all neutrally, "They're the shortest pants I've ever seen."

"Very tight too, aren't they? I was inspired by that Vintish fashion where your young men all go around in wool leggings, showing off their well-turned calves."

"Helps to have a well-turned calf in the first place," snapped Tev, turning back from the liquor cabinet with a glass and throwing themself onto their throne.

"I think it would look weird to have good calves when my butt is this flat, don't you?" Avra eyed their drink. "Where's mine? Do I not get one?"

"Absolutely not. Neither of you do."

"I didn't do anything," Julian said, mildly protesting. His eyes were still very bright, and Avra was *almost* sure he caught Julian flicking a glance at his thighs.

"You laughed," Teveri said into their glass. "You encouraged him. You called him a good boy last night and without any follow-through."

"And we all reap the, ah . . . rewards," Julian said, nearly straight-faced. "Such as they are." Teveri growled outright; Julian bit his lip on a laugh. "You seemed like you had some question, out on deck?"

Teveri's expression darkened further. "Not a question," they said in a low voice that betokened very clearly that further antics did not have a hope of being received well. Avra perched on the sea chest and kicked his heels a little. "Avra tried and failed to buy off Heirani and her crew." They set the glass on the edge of their desk, jaw clenched. Fist clenched. "I wanted to ask. If you had any further ideas. To keep us from being laughingstocks."

"Me?"

"You're clever," Teveri said without raising their eyes. "As clever as Avra, and twice as competent, and infinitely more reliable."

Julian took a breath. Let it out slowly. "Only twice as competent?" he said in a low, gentle voice. "You wound me, my dear captain."

Teveri slammed back the rest of their drink. They shoved themself out of the chair and fetched out a couple of belts and sashes from hooks on the inside of the wardrobe doors.

They gestured sharply for Avra to hold out his wrists, which he did with a mournful expression. They wrapped one of the belts around his wrists and bundled one of the sashes around his hands so he wouldn't be able to fiddle with anything.

"Setting aside the issue of money, the minimum goal is preserving your reputation, correct? Maintaining some of the respect of your peers?" Julian mused, watching Tev work. "May I ask what your *greatest* goal is? Whatever is at the other end of the spectrum—your heart's desire, as they say in the stories."

Teveri stopped, their hands shaking. Avra looked up and met their eyes—the gold-leafed one as hot and distant as the sun; the black one stony, angry, bleak. They clenched their hands, swallowed hard, but could not seem to bring themself to answer.

"Legacy," Avra said, still looking up at them. The bindings around his wrists were firm but not tight; the silk around his hands was warm and slippery. The belt around his upper arms was as snug as a fierce embrace. "Tev wants to be like Xing Fe Hua."

"Ah," said Julian, very softly.

Teveri threaded another belt through the bindings on his wrists and buckled it around Avra's waist with brisk, rough movements.

"First time we fucked, Tev told me about how they were going to be the next Xing Fe Hua, and I said it was silly."

"Did you? What for?"

"Because it was," said Tev, rough as raw stone. "Because he was right, and he likes rubbing it in my face."

Avra huffed in annoyance, squirming and fidgeting until it was impossible for them to get the buckle closed.

"Cut it out," Teveri growled.

"I haven't rubbed anything in your face," Avra snapped. "I just said, 'Why waste so much effort trying to be a shitty Xing Fe Hua wannabe like everyone else, why not just be Tev—'"

"*Stop moving,*" Teveri screamed.

"Avra," said Julian immediately, in *the voice.* "Stop moving."

Avra froze.

Julian got up, set his hand on Teveri's shoulder, turning them around to look frankly into their eyes.

"We're going to break up again, I guess," Avra said, aiming for careless and missing by a mile.

"Avra, hush," Julian said in *the voice.* Then, in an entirely different register, far more light and conversational, he added, "Captain, I have not yet known Avra to be *mean.* It sounded like what he was trying to say was that he doesn't understand why someone would aspire to be Xing Fe Hua when instead they could aspire to be Teveri az-Ḥaffār. What I heard was an attempt to express his admiration with the sentiment that he thinks *you* are marvelous. He is correct."

"That doesn't sound like him."

Julian hummed thoughtfully. "Well, what would Avra say, then? But *Tev,*" he said, pitching his voice a little higher and whinier and adopting a quite reasonable Araşti accent, "was Xing Fe Hua's butt as good as yours? Probably not! What if that's the cost of immortality and eternal glory, Tev? What if you have to make sacrifices like that?" Tev snorted; Julian glanced at Avra over the top of their head, his eyes twinkling.

"And I'd be right," said Avra. "Tev's butt is way better than Xing Fe Hua's."

"Oh, undoubtedly," Julian said—and it could have sounded like normal, friendly teasing. It could have. It could have sounded less low and rich and warm and . . . *appreciative.*

"Reeeeeeee," said Avra, very quietly.

Teveri cleared their throat. "I don't have time for idiot nonsense."

"Certainly not, Captain," said Julian, all professional again.

Teveri went back to tying Avra up. "I've got two more belts for his legs, but we might as well get him to walk himself down to the hold."

Avra gave them both his most mournful expression. "I don't want to go down to the hold. It's dark and full of straw and there are sea serpents on the outside."

"There's a sea serpent on the inside as well, I believe," said Julian. "We had to put the carcass somewhere the dogs couldn't get at it."

The hold did not smell great on a normal day—wet wood and pitch and dank, damp, stagnant air, and age, and the sourness of unwashed bodies, and the sea.

The dead sea serpent had been laid out on some of the straw, covered in wet rags to keep it cool until they got back to town, where there might be someone who knew how to taxidermy things. That method had worked well enough, but after twenty-four hours, a dead fish was a dead fish, and this one was a particularly *large* dead fish—sixty feet if it was an inch.

It smelled nearly the same as the carcass they'd found on the beach with the dogs, which Julian's quick inspection had shown to be too mauled to be worth anything but fishing bait. The difference was that one had been out in the open air, and this one was in an enclosed space.

"Smells like ass," Avra announced as Teveri dragged him down the companionway into the hold. "Smells like that *really* old pee that dyers collect and store in barrels."

Julian, following behind them, sniffed. "Huh. So it does."

Teveri shoved Avra onto the bales of straw and knelt over him to buckle the last of the belts around his legs—one around his thighs, then one looped through that and buckled around his ankles. When they stood up, he was *extremely* secure and could barely roll back and forth. Teveri pushed the hair out of their face and grimaced. "Right. Don't drown."

Something about the way they said that made the entire room reel. "Wait a second. *Wait a second, hang on—*"

"No."

"But I have just realized something crucial! Tev!"

"I don't have time for your bullshit."

"Teveri, *weren't we just mad at each other a few minutes ago?*"

Teveri froze and turned back, squinting suspiciously. "Yes," they said slowly.

"Were you?" said Julian easily. "I thought we'd all kissed and made up. Just a little misunderstanding about intentions, compounded with everyone's general crankiness from the late night and poor sleep, no?"

"*He* did this," Avra said, aghast. "*He* said those—those—those *levelheaded things* and made us not fight!"

"Hm," said Teveri, turning their squint on Julian, who held his hands up innocently.

"He's some kind of *witch*, maybe. A *feelings witch*."

There wasn't much light, but it was still enough for Julian to blink politely, all innocence, and say, "Should I have stayed out of it and let the conversation spiral out of control? When there are far more important things to be giving our time and attention to?"

"Hm," said Teveri again, then shrugged. "Well, it's true that I don't have time—"

"Teveri az-Ḥaffār, he agreed you have a good ass."

Teveri froze again.

"Which you do," Avra said. "I said so myself."

"*He* said so, in your voice. Like that stranger with the puppet."

"Yes," said Avra urgently. "Exactly like that. Could be even more like that if he'd put his fingers in me. *But he said, Teveri. He said it.*"

"I don't have time to be paranoid about whatever is going on with Julian and where his attention is being directed," Teveri announced loudly. "I am going to be on deck hoping that we don't get eaten by sea serpents."

"And leaving me all alone here in the dark to think about how Julian likes your ass, Tev?" Avra shrieked.

Teveri, who had nearly reached the steps by that point, waved dismissively over their shoulder. "You've got witchy luck. You probably won't die of suffocation or a blood clot any more than you'll die of drowning or being torn apart by sea monsters."

"Captain," said Julian delicately. Teveri sighed hugely and turned around on the steps. "I don't feel right about tying someone up and walking out of the room, particularly not for an indefinite amount of time."

Teveri twitched. "As you please, then. *If you will excuse me.*"

"*Tev.* Tev, one more thing!"

"What, Avra."

"We're going to be soooo bored down here in the dark all day, can I tell him stories? Can I tell him about your spooky dildo collection?"

"If you really feel you must," Teveri said witheringly.

Julian sat down on the straw. "Please leave the hatch open," he called. "I don't know whether the miasma is harmful." Teveri did not reply, but the hatch remained open as their footsteps became indistinct against the background noises of everyone else on the ship and the sea outside it.

"So, Tev's spooky dildo collection," Avra said with great enthusiasm. "Do you want to hear about it? I wrote a song about it once."

"I would love to hear your song. You may sing it to me as a reward."

Avra rolled onto his side. The straw crackled under him. It was oddly hard, packed into bales like this. "Reward?"

"We'll brainstorm ideas for what we can do to be helpful to the captain once we get back to port, and if you do a very good job, you may tell me all about their spooky dildo collection. Doesn't that sound nice? It will be a reward for both of us."

"You're so good at manipulating me," Avra said happily. "Wait, why is it a reward for both of us? Do you *like* spooky dildos?"

"I don't know what counts as spooky in this context, but I'm sure you will explain that later, and I am intrigued to learn."

"Are you being pious again? Is this piety or horniness?"

"Piety, of course," Julian said, but he was laughing, so perhaps that was not entirely true. "Think of something brilliant for the captain, Avra, go on. Impress me."

"Oh," said Avra blankly, and began to unpack the mental version of his little rucksack.

~

In the end, the best they could come up with was to tell everyone that they had discovered one of Xing Fe Hua's old supply caches, which contained a few scraps of shining silver plant fiber which must have been used to weave the *Nightingale*'s legendary sails—and moreover, that Teveri had ordered the crew to collect every scrap that they could find and braid them into fancy collars for Black Garda's two new blue dogs, as a gesture of the *deep respect* the captain had for her.

Black Garda wouldn't question it—why would she? She would be getting flattery and two glowing blue dogs, which, as a free perk, came with collars allegedly made of *Nightingale* sails. The bragging value was incalculable, and she *would* brag, and the other fences would be envious . . . and, of course, the other captains would hear about it, and they'd know that while Teveri az-Ḥaffār might be a lunatic, at least they were a lunatic with *style*, and that was the important part.

As soon as Julian agreed that this was a potentially viable strategy to take, Avra insisted on his reward of performing his song, the one about Teveri that everyone said was either "unexpectedly sexual" or "surprisingly sexy," depending on how you interpreted their facial expressions.

Avra warbled it with extra feeling, just for Julian. When he finished all twenty-five verses, he fell silent and nodded graciously. "Did you like it?"

"Ah . . . yes," said Julian. He cleared his throat. "It's very inventive. Some very inventive . . . rhymes."

"Oh, *strap-on* and *denouement*? I was particularly proud of that one."

"Yes. Yes, you should be." Julian cleared his throat again. "Thank you for sharing all of that. It's good to know."

Avra whipped to look at him. "Is it?" he demanded. "Is it good to know? Why is it good to know, Julian? Julian? Why is it good to know that?" Julian cleared his throat a *third* time, which was just hugely suspicious. "Julian, are you experiencing some piety right now? Are you learning something? Maybe about yourself? A new sexual interest?"

Julian burst out laughing, full and rich and gorgeous. "Oh, Avra," he said, brimming with fondness as if Avra had said something very endearing. "No, you sweet thing, it's not a new interest. At best, it is an additional flourish."

"Hrngk," said Avra. "Right. Because of your slutty past. So, hrghk, how slutty are we talking, anyway? I am feeling so pious all of a sudden, actually. I am thinking about converting to your religion. What if I try it out by very piously listening and learning as you, also just so pious right now, very piously share the knowledge of how slutty you used to be? So, so, so slutty, I know this. If you weren't an intensely horny person then you wouldn't have had to swear that oath of celibacy."

"Yes, that's true."

"Sooooo, scale of one to ten?"

"Mmm." Julian's voice was low and warm. "On a scale of one to ten, I was averaging somewhere around a sixteen, trending up to twenty-three."

"Aaaaaaa," said Avra in a tiny voice. "*Aaaaaaa.*"

"Hence the oath, you see," said Julian, smiling down at him.

"Mhm," Avra said, very high-pitched. "*Wow.* Hm! You'd, um. You'd have to be pretty non-picky to hit a twenty-three. Unpicky. Anti-picky. Pickiless. Pick-free. Sans picky. A total absence of pickiness."

"Oh, absolutely. You cannot hope to get above a thirteen or fourteen if you're picky."

"An unpicky slut," Avra said, suddenly choked up. "That's one of the most beautiful things a person can be."

Julian smiled down at him again, very gently and as soft as a kitten's tummy. "I'm touched that you'd think so."

"Was it really the only option? For your oath? You couldn't have picked something else?"

"I didn't pick it. The abbot picked it for me. It was one of the terms he set in exchange for protecting me. He wanted proof I was serious about taking the cloth, not some layabout taking advantage of his generosity to escape consequences."

"He knew you were that slutty just by looking at you?"

Julian laughed. "No. I tumbled into the monastery on a cold, rainy night, soaked to the bone and begging for sanctuary, and he sat me down in front of the fire and told me sanctuary would require me to commit myself to holiness. I said I'd do anything if he kept me from the gallows, so he asked me what most consumed and distracted my thoughts during my studies at university. I told him a few different things, and he decided what I'd have to give up when I took my vows."

"Fucking," Avra said in a tiny plaintive voice. "Swiving. Banging. Knocking boots. Shaking the sheets. Making the beast with two backs."

"Sometimes more than two," Julian said wryly.

"*Julian*. What is the most amount of backs the beast you've made has ever had?"

Julian tipped his head from side to side. "All at once, or in sequence?"

"I don't understand the question. Please explain it in as much detail as possible."

"The most people that have ever been in bed with me at one time for the purposes of sexual activities? Or the most people I have gotten off in one evening?"

"Both," Avra said instantly.

"Six and fifty-two, respectively."

Avra had to sit with that for . . . a *long* time. "That's. That's so many. Julian, that is so many."

"Mm," Julian agreed. His smile had grown wistful and distant.

"With a scale of one to ten, you don't make it past twenty unless it's the thing you love most in all the world."

Avra had to sit with that for some time as well. Finally he said, quavering, "I can't believe they took that away from you."

Julian looked down at him in surprise. "Are you crying?"

"I am a *poet, Julian,* of course I am crying!" Avra wailed. "A poet's whole *job* is to celebrate sluts and cry about beautiful things coming to tragic, untimely ends!"

"Ah," said Julian solemnly. "Of course."

17

72. The Sunken Crown

Tragedy, a great loss, heartbreak. Something important has been taken from the world. Give yourself the time to grieve, but remember—sometimes the memory of a beautiful thing can bind us closer together than the thing itself.

(Reversed: Treasure washing ashore with the tide, a windfall, unexpected discoveries, tearful reunions. Something seemed lost to you forever, but look again—the water is not that deep, and there is a glimmer of gold at the bottom. You may not be able to fetch it up in a single dive, but do not stop striving.)

Avra had worked himself up into wracking sobs by the time Teveri came to let him out. Julian had levered him up so that he wouldn't drown in his own snot. Instead, it poured down his face. He couldn't wipe his nose with his hands tied up, and Julian had gently refused to do it for him.

Teveri opened the hatch and stared down at them in consternation. "*Julian.* What have you *done* to him?"

"He used to be an unpicky slut, Teveri!" Avra wailed. "And the abbot made him stop! *Made* him! Forced him to stop! Told him to take his sluttiness out behind the woodshed and butcher it like a pet chicken that the whole family named!"

"He didn't make me," Julian said reasonably. "He offered me a choice."

"Between *dying* and eating your family's pet chicken!" Avra screeched.

Teveri scowled. "Fuck's sake, Julian, he's not even making cock jokes. At least let him nuzzle your tits. Look at him, he's distraught."

"We tried that," Julian said. He'd been rubbing Avra's back consolingly for nearly twenty minutes now. "His nose got too stuffy and he couldn't breathe."

"Tev!" Avra wailed as they rolled their eyes and descended the steps into the hold. "You don't understand! He used to be an *artist.* He used to be a *maestro!* He fucked *fifty-two people in one evening!*"

"He's lying to you," Teveri said, kneeling to undo the belt binding Avra's ankles to his thighs. "He's exaggerating to tease you."

"Julian, tell them!" Avra sobbed.

Julian put a hand on his heart. "By the path to Felicity and the Celestial Emperor, I swear it."

"Mother of *fuck.*"

"See!" Avra said. "*See!* He could've been one of the great lovers of history, Teveri! And he was *cut down in his prime*!"

Teveri had gone still and wide-eyed in either horror or, more likely, tragic horniness. After a half dozen heartbeats, they shook it off and continued untying Avra. "I'm sorry for your loss," they said awkwardly to Julian. "I'm sure Avra's going to write a song about it now, though, so that's. Something."

"An *elegy,*" Avra said, wiping his face on his shoulder and sniffling. "A lament. A *fugue.*"

"All three, maybe, yeah," said Tev, distracted and clearly rattled by the tragedy of this revelation.

"He said," Avra snuffled, holding out his wrists so Teveri could unwrap the sash, "he said it was mostly with his mouth. And hands."

"Yes, I would imagine it would have to be," Teveri said, blinking rapidly as they worked. "Or you'd chafe your dick off." They shot

Julian one more wild look and undid the belt around Avra's wrists. "*Anyway.* We're well into the turtles, so you might as well come up."

Avra snuffled again and wiped the tears off his face with his palms. Thickly, he said, "What time is it? Turtle astrology can't have changed much since yesterday."

"We're due in port around midnight," Teveri said, pulling Avra to his feet by his arm. "Not yet sunset now." They still had a strange look on their face, but Avra was too inconsolable to parse it. "Julian, we're moving your barrels of failed serpent juice out of the rope locker. No reason to have it in the way."

"Of course, Captain," Julian said, getting to his feet. "Ah, you may be pleased to hear that we did not spend all our time in mourning. Avra was *very* clever and came up with something that might be useful." Avra sniffled, winding himself around Teveri's arm and burying his face in their shoulder.

"What sort of useful?" said Teveri. They must have been *very* distracted, because they barely sounded suspicious at all and didn't pry Avra off.

"I'm going to make fancy braided collars for the dogs with the straw," Avra mumbled into the fabric of their coat. They smelled like . . . Well, actually he couldn't tell what they smelled like. The miasma of slowly rotting serpent carcass had burned out his sinuses a few hours ago. He could *imagine* what they usually smelled like, though: Salty sea air and sweat, and a musty-woody smell that soaked into all the clothes that they kept in their sea chest, and a different musty-woody smell from the stale air on the inside of the ship, which clung to their hair. "Do you think tears are enough like seawater to turn the straw silver?"

"I think that would be a very interesting experiment for another day," Julian said. "Since we're on something of a time limit."

After Julian had sketched out the rough plan to Teveri, Avra said plaintively, "Do you like it? It was the last good idea I had before my heart was pounded into dust, just like the six people Julian fucked all at once."

"Hm," said Teveri, but they still weren't prying Avra off their arm. There was a time when Avra would have taken this as a sign to creep farther over them, like a cat that believed it could sneak into your lap for a cuddle if it moved slowly enough that you didn't notice until it was too late, but . . . historically, that had eventually ended with Teveri reaching their limit and shaking him off with a snappish comment.

Avra *did* feel unpleasant in the center of his chest—not just the lungful-of-icy-air sensation of breathlessly poignant poetic tragedy, nor the queasiness of smelling dead sea serpent for hours, but an unfamiliar sore and achy feeling, like the tenderness of poking at a yellowing bruise. He badly wanted to keep clinging to Teveri's arm and sniffling. He wanted to cling until they sighed and patted his hair and said, "There, there," in that flat voice that they used when they felt like they had to be nice to him. Avra liked that voice a great deal.

"Hm," Teveri said again. "What is this supposed to achieve?"

"I just think everyone should see that you're a suave and dashing lunatic," Avra mumbled. "Even more of a batshit sonofabitch than Xing Fe Hua. And just a dash of total fucking maniac for flavor. I tried to explain these terms to Julian. He doesn't get it. He thinks I'm making it up."

Julian added with a nearly straight face, "Yes, I've been *assured* that in the taxonomy of Scuttle Cove captains, there is a, quote, 'subtle but very real difference,' unquote, between an idiot, a lunatic, a crackpot, a crank, a nut, and an eccentric."

"Yes," said Teveri. "There is a subtle but very real difference."

"*See,*" said Avra.

"Despite a great deal of practice at absorbing information, I confess I did not retain much of this, except that an eccentric has money and a particularly fancy hat," Julian said, all amused and gorgeous, which just made the sore feeling in Avra's chest twist and twinge, as if he were being stabbed with his own tiny knife. "And that a lunatic is a goal to aspire toward and involves an element of theatricality."

"Well, Avra is not very good at explaining things." Teveri turned and led them toward the steps up to the main deck. "Crackpots are very old captains who get drunk and loudly insist that Xing Fe Hua or his ghost once kissed them full on the mouth and said their ship looked nice, or similar tall tales. Cranks are late-middle-aged captains who might be imbibing intoxicants or who might just be high on their own imaginations, which lean sharply in the direction of conspiracy theories, such as how the Araşti government trains the serpents to attack. A crucial aspect of a crank is that they think that *anyone else* who expresses skepticism is the one who is willfully refusing to see reality."

Avra continued clinging to their arm as they strode toward the steps. "I told him all that. That's what I said."

"It's not what he said," Julian said from behind them. "He did confusing impressions of the facial expressions people would make, were you to be regarded as one thing or another."

Teveri sighed. "A nut is a captain of any age who has been staring at the horizon for too long or saw one weird thing at sea that they can't explain and are just barely showing the first signs of going strange." They firmly removed Avra from their arm—the steps up to the orlop deck were far too narrow and steep for more than one person abreast, so Avra allowed this with only a small pathetic whine of objection, which Teveri ignored. "An eccentric, in addition to wealth and a particularly fancy hat, also has a motive of some sort for staying in piracy instead of retiring to a villa somewhere," they continued, going up the steps; Avra scuttled along in their wake. On the orlop deck, Teveri reached overhead and banged on the closed hatch to the main deck, which someone helpfully opened. Tev jumped to grab the edge and hauled themself up. "This is often a grudge of some sort, or an oath of vengeance." They leaned down to take Avra's arms when he reached up and helped drag him up. Avra re-barnacled himself to their side immediately. Teveri sighed again but did not shake him off. "An idiot is the worst thing to be, even worse than an amateur. An amateur does stupid shit because they don't know any better; an idiot does stupid shit because they are under the impression that rules don't apply to them. Sometimes these are the laws of foreign nations, such as the Pact with Araşt. Sometimes these are the unspoken rules of pirating, like making sure to send letters home to the family when one of your crew dies. Sometimes these are the basic laws of sailing which prevent your ship from tearing itself apart or getting wrecked on the first reef you come across."

"Coming through," Oskar grunted, just as Julian hoisted himself up onto the deck. The loading platform had been set up next to the hatch, and there were already several barrels on it. He and Nonso were just arriving with another—Julian danced back, out of the way.

"Explaining all the types of captain, Captain?" Nonso said, groaning with strain as they set the barrel on the platform. "You done psychopath yet?"

"Oh, I forgot psychopath," Avra said, lifting his head from Teveri's shoulder. "Julian, there are also psychopaths."

"Psychopaths like killing," Nonso said, rocking and wiggling the barrel until it fit tight against the others. "Blood, murder, spookiness. Fucking sadistic shit like keelhauling—dragging folks down one side of the ship, across the underneath, and up the other side over and over until the barnacles shred them to death, like grating a block of cheese. Most of the time, someone like that already killed a few people back wherever home was and got run out of town. Got a taste for it, so they took up piracy. They don't last long."

"Hm," said Teveri. "That's a subcategory of idiot, I'd say. They still think rules don't apply to them."

"Sure, but all of us do that to some degree," said Nonso, draping a net over the top of the barrels and kneeling to tie it down. "Or we did at one point in our lives. Markefa thought she could get away with embezzlement." He smirked and jerked his chin toward Julian. "This one thought he could get away with *discussing* whether he and his friends might like to assassinate a king."

"These are both extremely good arguments," Avra said. "But I think Tev's right. Tev has subcategories."

"One more, Nonso!" called Oskar, tipping a barrel onto its side at the door of the rope locker. "Careful, coming through!"

"Look, I'd agree about captain subcategories if the impact of a psychopath's disregard was substantially the same as your garden-variety idiot, but it ain't, because the garden-variety idiots just make stupid decisions that break their ships or get their friends killed by accident—"

"No, no, those are *amateurs.*"

"—but psychopaths go out and murder an entire ship full of people *on purpose,* crew and passengers both, just for the fun of it—"

Just off the portside bow, something enormous breached the water. Someone in the rigging bellowed, "*Turtle!*" a split second before two massive nostrils opened and released a geyser of mist and fetid breath.

Avra certainly smelled *that.* He fell to the deck, choking and gagging—most of the rest of the crew on deck did as well. In the same moment, there were several alarming snaps and creaks from above as the gust of the breath hit the sails. The wave of displaced water slammed the hull *hard,* pushing the ship sickeningly sideways, blasting up the side and washing over the deck and everyone who had fallen. They tumbled and slid across the deck, only to be caught in a pile of bodies against the other rail. Avra, still gagging from the horrible stench of the inside of a giant turtle's lungs, felt at least three pairs of hands grab him and hold him tight as the spray from the wave—what had been cast into the air rather than directly onto the deck—fell onto them like heavy rain.

The turtle lowered its head, displacing another huge amount of water now and pulling them again in the other direction, somewhat more gently as the opposing forces evened out. By that point everyone had grabbed onto something solid—and really, what was a little more spray when they were already drenched?

It was over as quickly as it began.

The wind brought fresh air, the water poured off the deck, and Avra spluttered and coughed and wheezed until he could right himself and open his eyes.

The force of the water against the keel had turned their prow into the sunset, which meant the sails were at entirely the wrong angle for the wind and were luffing instead of bellied out full and round. Avra was clamped to the rail by no fewer than four people. Teveri was behind him, holding him with both arms and a death grip; Julian was crouched beside him with one arm around Avra's chest and the other locked around one of the giant cleats for the rigging; Nonso had grabbed a fistful of Avra's shirt; Anxhela had an ankle.

"Aw," rasped Avra as soon as he had a whisper of breath in his lungs with which to speak. "Aw, you *guys*."

Julian was the first to let go, looking around the deck urgently. He leapt to his feet and leaned over the side. A moment later, he relaxed. "No one overboard, thank Felicity. Or Avra's luck, anyway."

The others struggled to their feet, shaky and absolutely drenched. "Get the pumps!" Oskar shouted.

"Maybe we should check for injuries first," Nonso said, rubbing at his ribs. "I took Avra's knee to the ribs."

"I took *all of Avra* to *all of me,*" Teveri groaned. "Fucking pointy bastard."

"I think I'm all right besides being wet," Avra said, blinking owlishly. "Lucky I was wearing my short pants for this so the long ones are dry. Ooh, did all the barrels get knocked into the hold? Yuck. Julian, that stuff won't eat a hole in the hull, will it?"

"Not right away, no," said Julian, who was looking rather magnificent with his wet robe sticking to his skin. The ruckus had pulled loose the wrapping around his queue, and it was slowly unraveling. "I wouldn't recommend leaving it in there for days on end, but the water will have diluted it." He grimaced. "Though we can probably write off at least the bottom layer of straw, and it might make your hold smell like sour wine for a while, Captain."

Teveri shrugged hugely in a this-might-as-well-have-happened sort of way and stomped off to the ship's bell to ring the all-hands call.

"Julian, are you able?" Oskar bellowed.

"Aye, sir!"

"On the pump with us, then."

Avra gasped suddenly. "Oh no, our taxidermy!"

Oskar went white. "No. No, no, no no no no—"

Avra scrambled across the wet deck to the hatch and looked down into the hold for the dead serpent; Oskar followed in a panic.

They both stared.

"Julian," Avra sang, uncertain. "Julian, weren't you saying that stuff would dissolve my lungs?"

"That was the explosive, and only if you inhaled it. Why?"

"*Vampire serpent,*" Oskar screeched, scrambling back from the hatch. "Get me my axe! Where's my fucking axe!"

"It's not a vampire serpent, Oskar," said Avra over the sudden commotion on deck as Julian rushed over. Avra looked up at him. "I'm almost positive it's still dead. He decapitated it."

Julian was staring down into the hold, wide-eyed. He breathed, "Oh."

The serpent—specifically those stripes down its side, which had shown bright, shifting colors when it was alive—was rippling with light.

"What's that, please?" Avra said. "Why's it doing that, Julian? Please explain in small words."

"I don't know," Julian whispered, kneeling and leaning over the hatch. Half his waist-length queue had unraveled, leaving only the ends bound. It was marvelously golden, even wet. "The barrels," he said, pointing—the barrels had all fallen straight down and split open. There was no way that their contents had not washed onto the carcass with the water.

Avra tilted his head to one side, then to the other. "The stuff makes the serpents light up?"

"It does seem that way, doesn't it—a chemical reaction—the acidity of the mixture reacting with some compound contained in those stripes—oh. *Oh.* And the one you were sent to sabotage had the stripes cut out!"

"Oh. Oh! *Oooh, Julian!*" Avra said, sitting back on his heels with a marveling gasp. "Wow, Julian! Please exposit all about this to me, I want to know every detail. Yes, you may use the big words.

Unrelated, you're so so so pretty when you're figuring things out. What are you figuring out, Julian? You have a figuring-things-out look and it's *very* sexy."

Julian looked up at him, his face all open and shining with laughter and delight and wonder, his hair falling around his face in wet, raggedy strands, his eyes dancing. "I don't know yet," he said. "I haven't a clue."

"But we do have a clue! A single clue!" Avra cried, pointing downward. "It glows! It wasn't glowing, and then the stuff fell on it, and now it glows! That's such a clue, Julian! That's a huge, smelly, flashing-lights clue! The dogs glow when they eat it!"

"Stomach acids, maybe," Julian murmured, looking back down at the serpent.

"I can try throwing up on it, if you want. Julian! What does it *mean*?"

"*Something*," Julian said, shaking his head in wonder. The lights from the serpent were just bright enough to reflect in his eyes. "Something, absolutely *something*. No question whatsoever that it means something."

"Is it alive?" said someone. Avra looked around—the crew on deck had crammed themselves against the rails, leaving a large swathe of empty deck around Avra and Julian. Most of them were armed, and none of them looked happy to be dealing with further serpent bullshit.

"No, it's not *alive*," said Avra. "Come on. How can you disrespect Oskar's hard work like that? You think he chops off something's head and it just goes around *coming back to life*?"

"Vampire serpent!" Oskar yelled.

"It's only doing some of Julian's spooky science," Avra said, waving dismissively. "Calm down." To Julian, he said, "Hey, it would be extremely good for me if you could figure out the secret by the time we get back to port. Do you think that can happen? Do you think you can make that happen for me? Teveri will be very horny if you figure out the secret, and they'll take it out on me. I would invite you to come watch, but I don't think I'd be able to keep my dick up if I'm bursting into tears of grief every time I look over at you. Well, maybe if they blindfold me—anyway. Can you make this happen in the next six or seven hours?"

"No," Julian said confidently. "I definitely cannot."

"That's not what I would call good teamwork, Julian." Avra sniffed.

By the time they got the pump set up, the serpent's light had faded and the Ammatu ship had looped back around. Avra leaned over the rail to exchange a few quick words with Heirani, who was *very* concerned and asked several times whether their ship was good.

"Ship good, ship *good*," Avra insisted after twenty minutes of back and forth while Heirani and the others expressed their consternation in increasingly worried tones. Avra got the sense that they thought he might be lying to save face and were trying to reassure him that this was not necessary. "Look, Heirani, ship good, I love you all very much for being so nice and coming back to check on us, but *ship good I swear.* I don't have a lot of time to talk right now! We have to pump out the hold because it's about knee-deep in water right now, and I have to get to work on these fancy collars for the dogs, and sing a song for all these very muscular men and women while they do physical labor. I'm going to be starting with one about a very wet cat, because all of us up here right now are also currently very wet cats. Avra good, ship good, Heirani and friends good. And Julian. Julian is about to be very good, and I don't want to miss it." He blew a kiss to Heirani and waved. "Go, go, go, all is good!"

He turned away from the rail and jumped out of his skin—there was another ship passing by them, a great dark silhouette against the purple-blue of the fading sunset. It was roughly their size, and he had been so occupied with talking to Heirani that he had not heard at all whether anyone had called a hail to it. Then, the details came into focus. Specifically, the flag: On a blue field, a white ship with full-bellied sails and an arch of stars above.

"Reeeeeeeee," Avra said quietly. *Ship not good,* he would have said to Heirani. *Ship in fact very, very bad.*

He dove out of sight behind the rail, scuttled swiftly and silently into the rope locker, and peered out through the slats.

Araşt. A ship of the Royal Navy traveling on government business, according to the flag—three masts and ten stars.

He tried not to panic. It was probably business for Ambassador Baltakan. Hadn't he said that he had signaled to one of the courier ships a few days ago with some requests? If it were merely a *message* they were bringing him, they would have signaled by semaphore from out in blue water—they wouldn't have come this far into the Turtle Shallows unless they were planning on going straight through to Scuttle Cove . . .

More than a message, then. A delivery of some kind.

"Reeeeee," said Avra under his breath.

"Ahoy the ship!" someone called from the Araşti vessel. "And good evening! Though a better evening for us, it seems! We saw you get caught in the wake of that turtle breaching—are you all well?"

Ship good? Avra muffled panicked giggling in his hands.

"Just fine, thanks for asking," Teveri yelled.

"Anything you need help with? We thought we saw your flag earlier—*The Running Sun,* under Captain az-Ḥaffār according to our records, is that right?"

"Aye, that's right," said Oskar. "No help needed, thanks. Just took a dousing and got knocked about."

"Glad to hear it! It is a lucky day when the Lord of Trials sends only minor disruptions."

There was a tense, odd silence over the whole deck. "Yep," said Oskar. "Very lucky." Avra was still luck agnostic, personally.

"Out of curiosity, may we ask what you're doing out of the shelter of port? The serpents have been up for days now—we were astonished to see anyone else on the water."

"Just out to prove a point," Teveri called. "Look, we all know what you're going to ask, so go ahead and fucking say it."

"Ah—you must be the captain, then? Our records did suggest that Captain az-Ḥaffār is known to be forthright," said the spokesperson of the Araşti ship. "Well! Since the request is already expected—may we come aboard and search your ship, as delineated in the Pact between the Araşti crown and the captains of the Isles of Lost Souls?"

Avra could almost hear Teveri grinding their teeth all the way from the other end of the boat. "Of course," they called back. "Please feel free."

18

64. The Troupe of Players

Playing a part, following your cue. All people perform a version of themselves that varies with their audience—look for the version of you that will best serve the situation. Remember that a performance is not the same as a lie.

(Reversed: Parables may reveal fundamental truths. If you feel resentment toward your role or that you're just going through the motions, look for ways to make it your own again. Remain true to yourself—you are more than the part you play.)

The ship came in close; a few sailors threw over ropes to secure them together, just as if *they* were the pirates attacking a merchant ship, and they lifted a pretty little wooden bridge with pulleys to span the gap. Nobody else had a pretty little bridge. They made do with a few planks shoved over, or they rode over on a cargo platform if they were too ill or otherwise physically incapable of managing the planks. Or, if they were very dashing, they swung across on ropes hanging from the yardarms. Teveri did that sometimes, and it was *incandescent*. Made Avra swoon off his feet every time.

But a *pretty little bridge!* Avra cringed with secondhand embarrassment. Teveri would not have been caught dead with a pretty little bridge for their boarding parties, nor any of the other captains in Scuttle Cove. It was nicely painted in bright colors to match the patterns on the hull of the Araşti ship, though it was accented with touches of gold leaf here and there that sparkled in the lamplight. The Araşti had lit *dozens* of lamps, far more than they needed, so their deck was as bright as anything and their night vision probably shot to hell.

Two Araşti representatives came aboard across the pretty little bridge and introduced themselves as Secretary Selim and Secretary Rabia—Ministry of *Diplomacy,* of course they fucking were, they had that typical smarm to them that Diplomacy always had. Both were neatly clothed in the civil service secretarial uniform, including their hats of office and tasseled sashes in bright blue and white stripes, worn diagonally across their chests. One of them had something small flashing on their shoulder, a pin of some kind, probably a reward for excellence in service.

Of course they discovered the dead sea serpent almost immediately.

"Oh, eugh," said Rabia, clapping her handkerchief to her nose as she and her colleague peered down through the open hatch. "Foul!"

"Where did you come by that?" cried Selim—an oryasi, Araşt's third gender. Avra had almost asked Teveri once if they thought of themself as an oryasi, but upon reflection he had come to the conclusion that it was a distinctly *Araşti* kind of thing, and Tev was neither Araşti nor inclined toward modeling themself to be in compliance with Araşti culture.

"What do you mean, *where did we come by it*?" Teveri said. They gestured sharply to the shattered rail on the starboard side of the ship, where the serpent had crashed down and Oskar had hacked it to death with his axe. "*It* came by *us,* and we barely escaped with our lives. Obviously we're taking it to the taxidermist and having it stuffed. It's going to go in Eel-face Yusin's bar."

"Maybe just the head," Julian said suddenly. "The rest of it seems to be decomposing at an alarming rate. I'm not sure the taxidermist will be able to do anything with it at this point—I think we'd be better off dumping the body overboard before we have to deal with this stink for any longer."

"Really?" Teveri demanded. "You said it'd be fine!"

"I'm having second thoughts," Julian said firmly. "It's stinking up the ship, and besides that, getting the entire thing taxidermied is going to be absurdly expensive. Hardly worth it, I'd say—and we'd still have the head to show off. I do think we should dump it."

"Probably a good idea," said Rabia, backing away and coughing lightly. "Secretary Selim, shall we continue?"

"Yes, we can be quick about this. Let's not cause these fine people any more trouble than we absolutely need to."

Rabia peered once more down the hatch. "What are those smashed barrels down there?"

"Some of our supplies," Teveri said. "They broke when we got thrown around by that fucking turtle." It was too dim for Avra to see Teveri's face, but that was their just-barely-polite voice, and he could just picture the not-quite-polite smile. "Please, feel free to search the ship. Take all the time you'd like. We'll just be here pumping out the hold and looking for any other damage to our ship."

"If we can get this fucking pump to work!" Oskar snarled at it. "Can't get a godsdamned drop out of this thing. There's a leak somewhere."

"Or a cracked seal, maybe," said Nonso, sitting on the deck and examining the pipe's connections. "Fucking inexplicable. Worked fine last time!"

"We'll just be here," Teveri amended, their voice too-cheery with tension. "Taking our pump to bits. All over the deck. In the dead of night. So there's definitely no rush. We don't have anywhere to be."

"Ah," said Rabia. "Would you like to borrow ours? Since we are delaying you from continuing as swiftly as possible to port, it seems only fair."

"No," said Teveri firmly. "I'm sure we'll be able to fix ours just fine."

The two secretaries went below for about twenty minutes, presumably poking around under Markefa's watchful eye. The rest of the Araşti crew paid no attention whatsoever and were busily attending to matters on their own ship.

The pump was still not fixed when Selim and Rabia returned to the deck. "That turtle really did a number on you, eh?" said Selim.

"I haven't had a chance to go below and check the damage yet," Teveri said flatly.

"Your quartermaster is doing a fine job of getting all your stores back in order," said Rabia. "Such thorough records! Any captain of the Royal Navy would envy you for having such a talent on your ship."

"Yep," said Teveri. "She's great. Don't know what I would do without her. Probably would've gone broke years ago. She's the only thing keeping us going."

There was a brief commotion as the first ghost of the night shimmered into view, standing on the rail of the other ship. The Araşti captain, almost bored, called out, "Ahoy, sailor, would you like some gold in exchange for lighting our path and guiding us through the reefs as far as you can?"

"Oh," said the ghost, nonplussed. "Gold?"

"Real gold," said the captain. "Two altınlar. That'll keep you and your comrades in beer for *ages*."

"Yes. Yes, we'll take gold," said the ghost.

The entire crew of *The Running Sun* watched in absolute silence as the Araşti captain took two gold coins from his pocket and, without further ceremony, threw them overboard. The ghost vanished, and a moment later an eerie phosphorescence trailed through the water for some distance.

Rabia cleared her throat awkwardly. "Ah, I also had some questions about your . . . strange glowing dogs."

"They're dogs and they glow," Teveri said briskly. "We're bringing them to Black Garda. I'm sure she can tell you absolutely everything you could possibly want to know. She knows a lot more about dogs than any of us."

"Why are you bringing them to her?"

"She had one years ago, she wanted two more. What else do you want to know? Their names? We haven't named them." The scanty politeness of Teveri's tone had almost vanished and was drifting dangerously into sarcasm. "Apparently they are very good dogs. I have overheard many of my crew saying so in absurd voices. I would not know. I don't really get along with animals."

"Fascinating. Do they glow naturally, or . . . ?"

"Do I look like a fucking *naturalist*? Do we look like any of us know why things glow? Sometimes things just *glow*. The *moons* glow. Maybe they're magic moon dogs or some shit."

"Jellyfish glow," added Nonso.

"And some mushrooms," said Oskar, wrestling with the pipe of the pump.

"Saw a teeny bottle of liquor from Cascavey once. That was glowing," said Anxhela. "Captain's right, things just glow sometimes and that's their business."

The secretaries glanced at each other and relented. "Thank you. We're nearly finished—Secretary Selim, if you could go check their rope locker? And, ah, Captain az-Ḥaffār, if I could glance at your logbook?"

"I don't think inspecting the ship's logbook has *ever* been listed in the Pact," said Teveri, just as icy as what was happening to the blood in Avra's veins. "In fact, I know it isn't. *In fact,* I happen to know that there is language in the Pact that explicitly excludes the ship's logs from being searched. In *fact,* I started out my career at sea under Captain Safiya Merovech, the daughter of Captain *Valentine* Merovech, who had once been a lawyer in his previous life before taking up piracy. I'm sure you must have heard of him—he rather famously tore the original draft of the Pact to shreds, threw it in the ambassador's face, and demanded that the captains of the Isles of Lost Souls be included in a *joint* negotiation of terms if Araşt was so eager to strike a bargain. 'Fuck your fait accompli,' he famously said, which is why every child raised in Scuttle Cove knows what a fait accompli is. He was the one who fought for the logbooks to be excluded from your little *inspections*. Which is why it is not in the Pact, and has never been in the Pact, and will never be in the Pact."

"Of course you aren't *required* to comply," said Secretary Rabia. "But—"

"It's not in the Pact," Teveri snapped.

"You have to admit that it's unusual to find an unprotected ship out on the water at this time of year," said Secretary Selim. "Captain, please consider this from our perspective—"

"Why should I?"

"We're only doing our jobs, Captain. Our superiors appreciate thoroughness, that's all."

"I'm sure they do. It's not in the Pact."

"I understand that you're concerned. Please be assured that all of your records will remain private and confidential—"

"They will, yes, because I am not required to allow you to search them. It's not in the Pact."

Rabia sighed. "We won't look through all of them—I'm sure that would be pointless and waste our time and yours. But it would be a gesture of good faith to allow us to look at the most recent records, perhaps just the last five days or so?"

"It is not in the Pact."

"You seem awfully resistant, Captain," said Secretary Selim. "Perhaps you have something to hide?"

"Looking through my logbooks is not in the Pact," Teveri snarled. "Period. You will not be looking at them. I recognize your little rhetorical trick just there, and I think it is amateurish and clumsy. Does that work on most people? I would have thought that the Araşti Ministry of Diplomacy would give its civil servants more training in subtlety and elegance."

The two secretaries exchanged another look. Secretary Rabia sighed. "We'll have to put this in our official report, Captain."

"Oh, please feel free! Perhaps I should make a report of my own about how I was persistently pressured to allow an illegal search of *my vessel's* records, despite the fact that I have *repeatedly* invoked my right to deny access to them. I do not need a reason. I can deny access out of *pure fucking whimsy*. And yet, we continue to go back and forth about this?"

"Come now, Captain—"

"For you? Absolutely not."

A snicker ran through the crew, and someone whispered, "Get 'em, Captain." Avra would have swooned if he hadn't been so frozen with a flavor of alarm that did not blend as well with horniness as it usually did.

Teveri smiled their very meanest smile. "I'm sure that you have a great many dossiers on the currently active ships of the Isles. You've read mine, so you'll be aware that I've had a contact in the Ministry of Intelligence for, oh, thirteen or fourteen years now? He's just taken partial retirement and moved to Scuttle Cove, and I hear he is on *social terms* with the ambassador. Gets invited to his table for dinner, goes up for little chats with him . . . I'm sure that my contact would be happy to carry a message directly to him if I were to ask, and I'm equally sure the ambassador would be very interested in any matter that might cause strained diplomatic relations with the council of captains, particularly if it endangers the Pact."

The two secretaries said nothing.

"Now, you said you needed to look in the rope locker, didn't you? I don't believe there's anything in there at all besides the ropes, but be my fucking guest." Teveri strode across the deck.

Avra flattened himself against the bulkhead in the tiny space behind the door. Teveri opened it, stepped around just far enough to glance at Avra, maintained a perfect expression of boredom, and gestured the secretaries in grandly. "Our rope locker. It's got rope in it. You can put that in your report as well, if you'd like."

Avra could *smell* the two secretaries as they stepped in. They smelled . . . clean. Like soap, and fancy oils, and clean clothes, as if they owned more than two outfits. The part of Avra's brain that was not frozen in panic reflected on the amount of cloth he'd cut off of his second pair of trousers. It might be enough for a third outfit, if it were an exceptionally scanty one.

The rest of his brain continued squeaking in terror.

"Hm," said Selim. There were a few clunking noises. "What's all this?"

"We briefly had an alchemist," Teveri said, bored. "This is all his stuff. I don't know what it is. He said he could explode the sea serpents for us."

"Oh dear," said Rabia. "How did that go for you?"

"One jumped up and ate him."

"I'm very sorry for your loss."

"Fortunately he was not with us long enough for anyone to grow particularly attached. You can take that stuff away if you want, I don't care."

"Were the explosions effective, at least? Is that how you killed the one in the hold?"

"The one in the hold was killed by my first mate Oskar having a mental breakdown and going berserk on it with an axe. The fucking explosions didn't do shit except make a big splash and get those fuckers even more pissed off."

"What a shame," said Rabia. "Well, thank you for your time, Captain az-Ḥaffār. And, ah . . . Apologies about earlier."

"Which part?" Teveri said flatly.

"The matter about your logbooks."

"That's big of you. I'll be sure to take those apologies right to the bank so I can send some money home to our ex-alchemist's family."

"We'll ask our captain to phrase his requests to the ghosts to, ah, accommodate your ship along with ours, if you'd like to follow us into port. It sounds as though you've had rather poor luck the past few days."

"Ah," said Teveri, dripping with cheer as they gestured the two secretaries to precede them out of the rope locker. "A small bribe so I don't tattle to the ambassador? You could just say so outright. I'm quite amenable to being bribed."

Avra didn't release his breath until the pretty little bridge had been hauled away, the ropes untied, and the other ship at least a hundred yards off—he judged this by the reactions of the rest of the crew, who were all tensely watching the other ship sail off if they weren't occupied with scrambling around to get the sails set properly.

As soon as the crew relaxed and turned away from the rails, Avra slammed out of the rope locker, flew down the length of the ship, and threw himself at Teveri's feet. "Oh, *incandescent* one!"

"Shh!" Teveri hissed. "Sound *carries* on the water."

"Captain!" Avra said in a delighted stage whisper. "Tev! Tev, no one has ever been as hot as you!"

"That was *very* good, Captain," Nonso said.

"Fuck off," said Teveri.

"A round of applause for the captain!" Avra whisper-shouted. "Very very quietly! Captain! Yay! Yay for Captain Tev!" He batted his hands together in the tiniest possible claps, but no less enthusiastic for all that, and he was gratified to see that all the crew on the deck that were in earshot did the same—and then was further gratified when the ones who were out of earshot noticed what was happening, deduced what it was about, and joined in.

"A work of art, Captain," said Oskar, wiping away a tear with the back of his hand. "Captain Safiya would be proud as fuck if she were still with us."

Teveri huffed, crossed their arms, and pursed their lips. "Get to work, idiots."

"On the count of three, raise your hand if you're horny for the captain right now," said Avra. "Emotionally horny and intellectually horny also count, for those of you who for some mystifying reason do not think that Tev is your type. Ready?"

"Fuck's sake, Avra."

"One, two, three, go!" Avra raised both hands and a foot. Overtaken by the general mischievous spirit of having so magnificently gotten away with something, the crew as one put up their hands (or in a few cases, their hooks, if their sole remaining hand was already occupied). Avra glanced around, grinning. Through the crowd of legs around him, he spotted Julian sitting by the hatch putting the pump back together, but he'd paused to raise a hand with everyone else. Avra gaped accusingly at him. Julian shrugged, smiling as if to say, *Well, can you blame me?*

"So fucking tragic," Avra muttered to himself, looking back up at Teveri standing above him.

Teveri was, as expected, rolling their eyes a little, but at least now they looked like they were trying not to laugh. "Put your fucking limbs down."

"Take the compliment, Teveri," Julian said, fitting the last piece of the pump back together. "It really was exceptional."

"Hmph," said Teveri. They glanced around at the crew—everyone was grinning, and a few of them were pretending to swoon or blowing kisses almost as ostentatiously as Avra would have—and finally sniffed and tossed their hair and said in a low but deeply pleased voice, "I suppose it was pretty good, wasn't it."

"Fuck your fait accompli, my goodness," said Julian. "Not to interrupt your moment of well-deserved glory, Captain, but I really cannot find anything wrong with this pump."

"Get Avra to kick it," said Nonso.

"It's a *pump,* Nonso, how is my witchy luck supposed to help with a *pump*—"

Julian had lowered the pipe into the hold and fit it into its socket. He gave an experimental heave on one of the levers—there was an immediate and very promising gurgle. He looked up, blinking, as everyone stared at the pump. "Well. Pump's working, I think."

"Even though you couldn't find *anything* wrong with it?" Teveri demanded. "My. What a *coincidence.*" They glared at Avra.

Avra rolled his eyes. "Tev. Incandescent one. It's a *pump.* How does my luck have anything to do with a *pump*? A pump is not a stack of cards. A pump is not a roll of the dice. A pump is not relevant to my life in any way. I have never touched a pump. I barely know what a pump is. Maybe it's a machine for sex, I don't know, is that why it's used as a sexy verb? I probably couldn't even spell *pump,* Tev, why would you glare at me as if I have anything to do with the pump working or not?"

"You know what a verb is, and yet you cannot spell the word *pump*?" Teveri said, one eyebrow raised.

"Yes, I'm a flibbertigibbet, Tev. Don't be mean about it. It's my only redeeming quality."

By this point, several of the crew had leaped to the pump and were hauling at the seesaw levers, and within moments water gushed from the outlet pipe hanging over the side of the ship. Julian leaned over the side near it, then turned back to the captain, frowning. "It really was diluted," he said, coming over. "I can't even smell it."

Teveri's mouth twisted. "*Lucky* that it all fell into the hold next to a rotting serpent foul enough to cover up the smell, wasn't it? *Lucky* that we got the chance to acquire a dead serpent to begin with."

"This is not in the spirit of scientific inquiry, Teveri," Avra sighed. "We can't prove anything."

"No," said Julian, looking off into the dark at the lights of the other ship in the distance. "No, we can't prove it was your luck. But it was lucky, even so." He took a breath as if to speak again, paused, and then looked at Teveri. "There wasn't anything wrong with the pump. It's not a very complicated machine. There was *nothing* wrong with it."

"Except that it didn't work," said Avra. "Sometimes you have to take a thing apart and then put it back together, and it suddenly works, and nobody knows why. Maybe it was a loose screw."

"It didn't work while the ship was right next to us," said Julian. "And then as soon as they left, it worked."

"Coincidence," said Avra, scootching closer to Teveri's legs and wrapping his arms around one of them. "It wasn't going to be working while you had it all taken apart either. You only finished once they were away."

"We have established that your luck is a factor, though."

"I don't think we have done that, not really. I am luck agnostic."

"You talk to your cards like they're people."

"That's different, the Heralds bitch at me, so I bitch at them. This is normal."

"But if your luck broke the pump—just as a thought experiment," Julian insisted. "Just for the sake of scientific inquiry. If it *was* your luck, then . . ."

Teveri spoke slowly. "Then I'm suddenly fucking curious about *why* it was lucky that it happened the way it just did."

Julian tapped his nose and pointed at them. "Captain's on it."

"Oh," said Avra, dubiously. "That seems like a scientifically questionable thought experiment."

"Can't be smelled—certainly can't be seen in the dark like this," said Julian. "The compound is *supposed* to go in the water, as we know. *Just not right then,* if we're following the luck theory. Because . . ."

"Don't just go ominously implying 'because they would have found out,' Julian," said Avra peevishly, rubbing his face against Tev's thigh. "You don't know that that's why. You just *think* that's why. Hey. Listen to me—Julian. Julian, look at me. Hey. Yes, hello, thank you, Julian, nice to be included as a part of the conversation. Do you want to know the thing that I know about luck?"

Julian crouched down, resting his elbows on his thighs. "Yes, I do."

"No, that's not fair, don't do that. Whose trousers are those? They're too tight for you, don't do that. I can't look at you if you're doing that. I can see your dick in those, Julian. Stop attacking me with your thighs like that." Teveri sighed and put their hand over Avra's eyes. "Thank you, Tev. Listen! The thing I know about luck is that *maybe* it happens, but you don't know *why.* Supposing that the Bendran goddess of luck did actually appear to me in a dream that time and kiss me with tongue. Supposing that wasn't just me being horny because I saw a pretty statue of her earlier that day—supposing I did get weird witchy luck—why was it good for me to *lose* my stake of the prize, eh? We don't know! We might never know!" Avra gesticulated wildly. "What if we'd been pumping out the hold and the pump sprayed fish guts all over Secretary Rabia? What if we'd been pumping out the hold and a shark smelled the serpent gunk and leaped out of the water and chomped off somebody's hand? What if it attracted a lot of fish and things and then a giant turtle lifted its head to slurp 'em up and chomped our hull in half? You can definitely have the fun little theory that it was my luck what did it, but 'it was bad to happen right then' does *not* imply 'because the Araşti would have caught us,' and it is *bad science* to assume that's the reason. And you *know* that, Julian. You're just getting all excited about it because it's going to sound really fun in your memoir and you won't even have to make anything up about it."

Julian was silent. Avra heard the rustle of his far-too-tight trousers as he stood. "Those are sound objections."

"You see now?" Tev muttered. "You see why he's an infuriating little twit? It's this bullshit."

"And! This is why you can't prove anything!" Avra said, pushing Teveri's hand up so that it rested on top of his head instead of over his eyes. "You can't prove my luck exists because you can't prove that something *wouldn't* have happened that way regardless! And you can't set up scientifically rigorous conditions in which to test it. You put me in a room with some dice and have me roll them a hundred times, and the numbers that come up are on a fucking *normal* statistical spread. There aren't any stakes, so you can't force luck to happen, so I might as well be sitting there jerking off."

Julian was smiling down at him in an odd way, his hands on his hips. "And how do you know about scientifically rigorous testing conditions and statistical spreads, Avra?"

"I've fucked a lot of scholar types," Avra retorted, peering up at him. "I'm so good at fucking scholars, Julian, did you know that? I sprawl out on the sheets and I tell them, *Experiment with my body, darling.* They go *nuts* for that. They get all hot and bothered, and they start breathing heavily, and then they say, 'First we need to set up scientifically rigorous testing conditions.' And I say, 'Ooh, yes, we do, you're so right, better make 'em as rigorous as possible, I'm very squirmy.' That's how I know about it. Listen—you want to know what other problems there are? If you can't know what *isn't* my luck, then you can't know what *is* my luck."

"Except that usually it's things that directly benefit you," Teveri said. They hadn't taken their hand off Avra's head, which was nice.

"Well, yes. But was it my luck that made Julian arrive in the Sea of Serpents at a really convenient time? Was it my luck that got him nearly caught and killed fifteen years ago so that he had to run away to the monastery and learn scholar stuff so that when he came here, he'd have all the things in his head that we need to blow up sea serpents and gnaw our way through the most expensive secret in the world so that we can all retire from our shitty day jobs? Hm? Was that my luck, Tev? Can you prove whether it was or not? Him being here hasn't directly benefited me yet! Well, except for earlier today when he tricked us into not fighting. And what counts as a benefit to me, anyway? Just money? I haven't gotten any money because of Julian. Sex? I'm very much not getting any sex because of Julian. Maybe the real benefit is just the *beautiful friendship* we get to share, wherein sometimes I look at his crotch and burst into tears. But you can't prove it either way! Here, I'll come up with a much more worthwhile line of scientific inquiry: If you were a jam, what jam would you be? Wait, no, let's do each other's instead. That's more fun. If *I* were a jam, what jam would I be?"

"Toe jam," Teveri replied without missing a beat.

Avra gestured up to them. "You see, Julian? Now *that's* what we call science."

It was well past midnight when they reached port—not that that meant much in Scuttle Cove, particularly not during the festival. The town was bright with lights glittering on the waters, silhouetting the thicket of masts and yardarms in the harbor.

At last, they dropped anchor and reefed the sails. Avra sat on the capstan and braided saltwater-silvered straw into fashionable neckpieces for the dogs—fortunately (haha) the straw had been stacked high enough that even with all the tumbling about from the Turtle Incident, there had been more than enough that was still dry and not reeking of sea serpent.

As an additional piece of good fortune, Julian had mentioned the difficulty in estimating a color match with the sail, since the straw was darker when wet than when it was dry, and Avra had remembered the garland of braided straw he'd made days earlier, the whole length fading from gold in the section where he'd started to a pale pearly color, then all shades of silver, then deepening to iron. Once he'd fetched it from where he'd hidden it in the spooky dentist cabin (since no one went in there except to fuck), he was able to find an *exact* match to the color of the *Nightingale* sail, dip that section of straw into a cup of fresh water until it was soaked, and use it to measure the color of the slowly silvering straw in the bucket of seawater.

Sitting there on the capstan and braiding contentedly, he was *fully* expecting the weary, worn-out crew to call on him for a song to make the work go quick. When they inevitably did, Avra set his bundle of fancy braid in his lap, cleared his throat ostentatiously, and said, "I have a new song for you. It is about a polite, standoffish, elderly chicken and the travails he endures as he seeks for some remedy that will ease his arthritis and aching muscles. Before you ask: Yes, it is a sequel to my last song. Would anyone like to guess what it's called?"

"'The Stiffest Cock in the World,'" called Julian, who had been sent aloft by Oskar to learn how to furl the sails and tie them off.

"How did you know?" said Avra merrily as the crew laughed. "The chorus is very similar to the sad little wet cat song. I'm sure you'll pick it up very quickly."

"Avra," said Teveri.

Avra pouted and looked back over his shoulder. "What?"

They were standing at the door of their cabin with a forbidding expression. "Come here."

"But I'm going to sing my new song."

"Someone else can sing," they said.

"But who will supervise Ellat so he doesn't sneak off to shore for some inadvisable kissing?"

"Markefa," Teveri yelled. "You watching your nephew?"

"Like a seagull at the cake competition, Captain," Markefa replied, as Ellat spluttered in indignation and denial.

"Great. Come *here,* Avra." Avra slid off the capstan and trundled sulkily aft. Teveri pulled him inside and slammed the door. "Take off your stupid fucking pants."

"What? What? Why?" A thought crashed into his mind. "Are we having sex? Holy shit, Tev, are we having some sex right now?"

Teveri violently flung their swoopy coat off their shoulders, which made their hair fly around them magnificently, and followed it with their belt. Avra squeaked with shock and delight and wrestled with the buttons of his very short pants. "This is about Julian's six and fifty-two, isn't it," he said breathlessly. "Be honest. That's what I'm going to be thinking about, and I won't mind if you are also thinking about that—"

"Shut up, Avra." They stormed toward him, marching him backward, and shoved him onto their bed.

"Should I be loud?" Avra said as Teveri tore his shirt off over his head and flung it across the cabin. "Should I be just so unbelievably loud, Tev? He said he was horny for you, did you see? He raised his hand when I called the vote, and he shrugged at me when I noticed—he could be more horny for you, I could be so so *so* loud, Tev, should I be really *really* loud—"

"You're already being really fucking loud," Teveri said, and then they grabbed him by the hair and kissed him.

Captain's Log

Day 17 (maybe 18? is it past midnight?), 6th month, 199th yr

Mah. Dyn.

Anchored in Scuttle Cove safely.

Inventory lost:

Probably some of the straw, from having a dead sea serpent on it + being drenched in Turtle Incident.

Self-respect, from fucking Avra.

Latter item was due to circumstances beyond my control, as predicted (to wit: Julian walking around in wet robes &

borrowing dry ones from someone whose shoulders are not so broad). Markefa didn't even try to dissuade me. Deep betrayal.

Not likely to acquire any new inventory before end of serpent season; no further log entries required until then, thank fuck. Happy Midsummer to me.

PART THREE

19

30. The Bower

Love, passion, happiness, affection. This is a time of happy secrets and the anticipation of a joyful future. Strive to nurture relationships of all kinds into the most beautiful aspect possible for them. To feel truly valued and cherished, love requires you to be vulnerable. Seek intimacy—that is, the sharing of something private and precious with another person. Whatever you love, do so with your whole heart.

(Reversed: Feeling stuck in a tiresome emotional situation, a perversion of what is supposed to be pure and happy, neglect. Vulnerability is currently a daunting prospect. If someone cannot offer all of themself, they cannot be loved in their entirety. Think about what is being held back and why.)

The sex had been all right. He and Tev had never managed to have sex that was really *good*. Generally speaking, it started strong, usually with Tev shoving him up against a wall or into bed or onto a desk, and that was very exciting, even thrilling . . . for approximately ten minutes.

This was something that had long mystified Avra, and he had concluded that it was to do with professional expertise. After all, physicians got paid for knowing what herbs probably wouldn't kill you, or where to stick the leeches, or where to prod just right to get a tweaked muscle to go loose, or how to take a leg off before it went gangrenous—and so maybe courtesans, likewise, were the only people who had the skill to administer the *really nice* kind of sparkling, earth-shattering orgasm, and everyone else had to make do as an enthusiastic amateur. Or . . . an amateur.

Or perhaps it was just that he and Tev knew each other too well. Or not well enough. One of those two. Maybe both.

Or maybe it was that Tev seemed to like *parts* of sex quite a lot, specifically the second and fourth acts of the sex opera, as it were—the part where they finally just snapped and *had* him (which was fairly fantastic as a concept, in Avra's opinion, yet inexplicably kind of *meh* in execution) and the part where they finished each other off. Avra himself felt that while *all* of sex was very nice to have, his personal strengths were solidly within the first and fifth acts—that is, the flirtation and foreplay, and then the afterglow. But Tev got annoyed when he tried to flirt, and the afterglow always had a distinctly begrudging ambiance, as if they were suddenly disconcerted to have discovered something slimy and sticky in their bed (i.e., Avra) and were obligated by courtesy not only to let it stay there and catch its breath and babble incoherently for fifteen minutes or so, but *also to cuddle it*. Or at minimum, allow it to cuddle them.

Neither of them was good at that third act, right in the middle. Avra wasn't even really sure what would *go* in the third act of the sex opera starring himself and Teveri, and he was fairly sure Tev wasn't sure either. The two of them usually rushed through that bit as quickly as possible—the mood was too precarious to risk lingering in it long enough for one or both of them to embarrass themselves, and even a leg cramp or a stiffening joint might throw off the delicate balance.

He wondered which act Julian liked best. Probably all of them. Probably he'd know what sort of things the sex opera's third act was supposed to have.

This was what Avra was wondering when he shuffled out of Teveri's cabin at dawn the next morning and found Julian standing at the railing with a steaming cup of coffee and looking out over the crowded harbor to the town with the shadowed slopes of the Tits behind it and the soft pinks and blues just brightening the sky above.

Julian's hair hung loose to his *knees,* unbound other than a bit of string tying it back out of his face. He was still wearing the objectionably tight clothes he'd borrowed from someone yesterday after the Turtle Incident, and he had a piece of plaid-woven cloth draped around his shoulders like a shawl to keep off the chill and the damp. A very damp morning it was too, with dew beading thickly on absolutely every surface and dripping now and then off the yardarms.

"Good shoulders," Avra said. "I mean morning. Shoulders morning. I mean hello."

Julian hid his smile in his cup. "Good morning, Avra. Did you sleep well?" He took an innocent sip. "When you did eventually sleep, that is."

"Yes, thank you." He added proudly, "I got to sleep on the floor."

"*Got* to? Sleeping on the floor is your preference?"

"Tev's floor is better than anywhere else," Avra said. "Can I have some coffee?"

Julian shrugged and held it out; Avra bent to sip from it without actually taking it in his own hands, which seemed to be vaguely amusing for Julian. "I am growing accustomed to the hammocks, but I prefer a bed, myself."

"Oh, I don't get to sleep in the bed." Avra laughed, waving this off. "Out of the question. I don't even bother wheedling to be allowed to sleep in the bed. I don't think I've *ever* bothered wheedling for the bed. It's between the floor in their cabin or anywhere else on the ship. They don't like cuddling when I'm slimy, you see. I'm 'too hot and sticky' and 'very gross.' Also I get soppy and then they're embarrassed to know me."

"Ah," said Julian.

"Hey, what goes in the third act of sex?"

"I beg your pardon?"

"In the sex opera. What's in the third act? You have probably already achieved holy understanding about sex things right? I feel like you will be able to tell me this. Or is it secret? Is it a secret known only to courtesans and sex scholars? I'm prepared to believe that there are trade secrets about sex that enthusiastic amateurs haven't achieved enough mastery to know about. But I am ever so pious this morning, so please assist me in seeking this knowledge."

Julian contemplated the town and the Tits and sipped his coffee. "In operatic terms, the third act would suggest a change or a turn, whether through a shift in perspective, an abrupt but inevitable twist, the introduction of a new factor of significant impact, or the increase of tension."

Avra nodded sagely. "I hear what you're saying. Change positions, confess a long-held secret fetish, go on a brief spanking detour, and if it feels like you're going to come, don't. Got it. Thank you, Julian, that's so helpful."

"You're welcome," said Julian solemnly. His eyes were dancing with the laugh-light again. He offered Avra another sip of his coffee, which Avra accepted with a pleased little noise. Julian watched him carefully in a way that sort of made Avra feel strange and squirmy and rather laissez-faire with his impulse control, which was dangerous at six o'clock in the morning.

Avra smacked his lips and said, "Well! That's enough coffee to wake me up! Ha ha! Shouldn't have any more or I'll be impossible to live with! I need to go finish those collars for the dogs, actually! Can't stand around here talking!"

"I finished them for you," Julian said. "Last night, after you were . . . summoned."

"What, really? You didn't have to do that, haha, I would have finished them this morning."

"It was no trouble," Julian said, his eyes glittering over the edge of the coffee cup. "I couldn't sleep in all the ruckus, and I needed something to do with my hands."

Avra's thoughts screeched to a halt with the noise of something going very wrong with the ship's pump, but his mouth continued on its own. "The ruckus was me."

"It was, yes."

"Because I was having such a good time."

"That was the impression I was getting."

Avra winked to cover how inexplicably flustered he suddenly felt. "Plenty of things to do with your hands in that kind of situation, I would have thought. If you know what I mean. I mean touching yourself. Unless that counts as breaking your oath of celibacy. Don't tell me if it does, I'm already in mourning over you losing the best and horniest years of your life. Does it count, though? No, don't tell me. But does it? I don't want to know, actually."

"What mixed signals," Julian said serenely. "I'll err on the side of not telling you, then."

"Hrgnhk," said Avra. "It is too early for this. I'm going back to bed—floor. I'm going back to floor."

"I made an extra," Julian said, nodding over to the capstan where the collars had indeed been hung to dry. "Just in case one of them went wrong."

"Okay?" said Avra. "Okay? That's good? Thank you?"

Julian leaned on the railing and smiled like he wasn't the worst person alive. "You could take them to the captain and ask if they have any use for the extra one."

Avra spluttered through several responses, and landed finally on a screechy and discomposed "Show them yourself!" as he tottered away at speed.

He tottered right into Teveri's cabin, right up to the side of their bed, and dropped to his knees. "Tev," he hissed, scrunching down so only his eyes peeked over the edge, in case they were mad about being woken up and needed to be mollified by endearing faces, or guilt-tripped into perceiving him as small and harmless and ethically unacceptable to kick bread-wrapped rocks at. "*Tev.*"

Teveri's eyes opened immediately, in a deeply spooky way that Avra had always been terribly fond of. "What."

"Julian finished the collars for the dogs, and he made an extra one and he *smirked* at me and—" Avra jammed some quilt against his mouth and screeched softly.

Teveri squinted at him. "And what."

"He basically suggested *out loud* that you might like to put the extra one *on me. Out loud, he said this.* Essentially. That was the implication. He implied it right over his coffee cup with a normal expression like that was a normal sort of thing that two good pals might say to each other. *Teveri.* This is why I have woken you up. This is an emergency."

Teveri sat up, hair wildly tousled. They twitched their facial muscles on the side with the golden prosthetic and rubbed a bit of gunk out of the corner of their eye. "Hand me my stuff."

Avra dove half under the bed, dragged out the small box wherein Teveri kept their so-called stuff, and placed it next to them. "Tev. Tev, he said it out *loud.*"

"Wait." From the box, they uncorked a blue-glass bottle and poured a few drops into a little spoon, then tipped their head back and dabbed it onto their gold eye with the tip of their finger.

"What's in that stuff, anyway?" Avra whispered.

"That one's just special salt water."

"What's it do?"

"Makes it wet," Teveri said, as if that should have been obvious. A little excess had overflowed the outer corner of their eye; it ran down their cheek like a single perfect tear. Tev wiped it away with the back of their hand and corked the bottle.

Avra peered into the box. "What's the red one?"

"Special salt water, but with stuff in it. For when it's itching." Teveri packed away the bottle and spoon and closed the box. "All right. Start over."

"Juuuuuuuuulian said," Avra said, carefully putting the box back under the bed and then clutching at the quilt, "that I. Should show you the collars. And ask you. Whether you wanted the extra one. For something. That's what he said, Tev. Out loud."

"Out loud."

"With an innocent look, like a person who knows they're talking about sex but there's plausible deniability so that the Avra they are addressing will be flustered and surprised at six o'clock in the morning. It was *definitely* a sex thing."

Teveri gazed into the middle distance.

"Tev," Avra whispered.

"Tev," Avra whispered again.

"Tev," Avra whispered, more urgently. "What does it *mean*? It was definitely a sex thing, Tev. *He made a collar and suggested you might want to put it on me.* Teveri. Why would he do that? Why would he do such a thing? That's such an unpicky-slut kind of thing to do, but he left his slut ways behind him long ago, *tragically. So what does it meaannnn.*"

"He is toying with us," Teveri said darkly.

"Hrgnk," said Avra. "I don't think that should be allowed."

"It shouldn't be allowed, no." Teveri narrowed their eyes. "At the same time, I respect him for this."

"Yes," Avra agreed vehemently. "Yes. It should not be allowed, but also I respect him for it, and I would like him to keep toying with me. He touched himself about us last night. You know, when I was being loud."

Teveri drew a sharp breath. "Did he."

"Well—well, actually, I don't know, because I told him not to tell me whether touching himself counted as breaking his oath. And then I asked if it did and then I said not to answer that, and—look, there was an *implication*. There were some things he was implying with that smirky mouth and those long eyelashes. Implying it. Out loud. In front of me. At six in the morning. When I've only had two sips of coffee out of his mug."

"So he is toying with *you*, and through you, also toying with me."

"Yes. And I don't know what he is doing or why he is doing it," Avra enunciated, smacking his hands on the quilt with each phrase. "It was a very horny moment, *but* he took an oath and he has laughed at me every time I attempted to seduce or beguile him. So what other motive could he possibly have? My brain is not big enough to come up with whatever other answers it could be. Please do my thinking for me."

Teveri released their breath. "I am not going to waste my time on a man who is not going to do anything but toy with me," they said firmly. "And neither should you, for that matter. He can toy all he wants, and we will ignore it. We will not even condescend to acknowledge it."

"Teveri, that is impossible. You are asking me to do the impossible. You've seen his shoulders."

Teveri flung off the covers, hauled themself out of bed, and crossed over to their wardrobe with great dignity for a person wearing nothing but yesterday's shirt. "It sounds as if he, a known slut, is prodding around at the boundaries of his oath. That is his business. There is no reason why I should spend any of my time thinking about it."

"But *Tev,*" Avra wailed, throwing himself sideways on the rug.

"Which of these coats should I wear to visit Black Garda?" Teveri said loudly, examining their collection. "This is the only question I will deign to give my attention to."

Avra managed to argue Teveri out of wearing the dark grey coat with the green couched embellishments, as it *was* Midsummer on the equator and they would be grouchy if they were sweeping around the festival in heavy wool, even if they did look severe and terrifying and untouchable.

Teveri had disdained Avra's suggestion of the blue coat, as they apparently did *not* want to match with the dogs.

They compromised (if one could call it a compromise when Teveri got bored of bickering and made a decision by fiat) on the long eleven-gore coat, a beautiful cream color accented with red brocade for the signature gores and the wide cuffs. It made them look distinctly blood-drenched, which was possibly the whole point.

Avra's scandalously shortened pants were still damp and clammy to the touch from the day before, so he couldn't even retaliate about the coat business by refusing to wear his intact ones.

Those of the crew who were heading to shore piled into the dinghies—everyone but Nagasani, who did not care for festivals or crowds and was, moreover, very happy to have the ship nearly to herself.

The crew avoided eye contact with Avra, which he supposed was fair. He had been *really* loud, squealing and begging and carrying on and narrating nearly the entire time, because Teveri was incandescent and deserved the best propaganda he could invent for them.

The dogs did not seem to mind riding in the dinghy at all except for the oars, which had the audacity to *exist* and were apparently dreadful sea monsters, which the dogs lunged and barked at in a frenzy every time they rose from the water until they dipped back down again.

It was a very noisy trip to shore.

It became even noisier when they threaded their way around the last ship and came to the shallow section of the bay that nothing but the dinghies or the wonderful shallow-drafted Ammatu catamaran could traverse. The blue dogs caught wind and then sight of Black Garda's pack of hounds on the shore and immediately went into transports of joy. This was uncomfortable for everyone—the dinghy was rather full, and the dogs did not notice or care who they stepped on as they scrambled to the prow, nor who they whacked in the face with their furiously wagging tails as they yelped and whined like they were being reunited with long-lost family members who had been presumed dead.

It took three people per dog to keep them from leaping out of the boat until it had been beached and dragged up to dry sand for the sake of Teveri's boots and long coat, by which point the dogs were having such hysterics that even Julian, holding the leashes, was dragged nearly off his feet when they were allowed to jump down and scramble over to Black Garda's rather more well-behaved pack.

"Good morning, madam," Teveri said stiffly, coming up in Julian's wake as the blue dogs tried to sniff absolutely everything and lost their tiny minds with delight. "We have brought you two blue dogs."

"So you have," said Black Garda. "And one of them's a bitch, right?"

"Yes, of course."

"Also," added Avra. "You cannot really see it in broad daylight like this, but they glow."

"They do glow," said Teveri. "They are blue dogs that glow."

"What do you mean they glow?" demanded Black Garda.

"Means you don't need a lamp when you go on walkies at night," said Avra. "A major feature of these extremely good, extremely blue dogs. I'm sure you will agree."

Black Garda frowned, then snapped her fingers at some young assistant who was standing nearby. "Umbrella."

The assistant rushed to open a parasol, which Black Garda positioned to shade one of the dogs.

"Hard to see in the daylight," Avra said nervously. "But they do in fact glow."

"No, yeah, I can see it," said Black Garda slowly. "Well, fuck me in a nettle patch."

"They might stop glowing at some point," said Julian. "They began glowing after consuming part of a dead sea serpent that had washed up on shore. I'm not sure how long the effect lasts."

Black Garda had crouched to fondle and croon to one of the dogs, who clearly thought this was the most marvelous thing that had ever happened. "But I'll be able to make 'em glow again if they stop, that's what you're saying. If I can get somebody to bring me a sea serpent."

"In essence, yes."

"We went to some trouble to make sure we brought you two *glowing* dogs," Avra said. "We could have caught any dogs, you know, but we said to each other, 'You know what Black Garda would like? Glowing blue dogs.'"

"You weren't wrong," Black Garda said, administering the same fondles and croons to the other dog, which had rushed over to see what this new wonderful thing was. "Not bad. Not damn bad."

"So you don't have to be mad at me anymore, for one thing," said Avra with his most winning smile.

She peered at him. "Do I know you?"

"Oh. Nope!"

Teveri cleared their throat. "We have something else for you as well, madam."

Black Garda looked up with an eager smile. "A third glowing blue dog?"

"Nearly as good as that," said Julian.

"When we were on the island—" Teveri looked around for eavesdroppers. "Do you mind sending your assistant a little ways off?"

Black Garda waved her hand and the assistant duly retreated a dozen yards or so.

"When we were on the island," Teveri continued in a low voice.

"Speak up, Captain, I'm going a bit deaf," Black Garda said. "Comes of getting old around all the barking."

"Apologies. Of course." Teveri flicked back the skirts of their coat and crouched. The cream of the coat was the same blinding color as the sand; the red gores stood out like spilled blood. "When we were on the island, we found a secret supply cache belonging to Xing Fe Hua."

Black Garda's eyebrows went back up, but she did not stop petting the dogs, one of whom had rolled ecstatically onto its back for belly rubs. "Did you now?"

"It was mostly rotted old crates and barrels, nothing of any use—nothing we could even carry back as relics. It all crumbled as soon as we touched it."

"Damn shame. Would have been a good haul for you, eh?"

"There was one thing, though," Teveri said. "In amongst some of the moldering crates, we found stalks of a fibrous plant. As soon as we saw these stalks, we knew that it had to be what was used to weave the *Nightingale*'s silver sails."

"Oh shit," said Black Garda—her hands *did* pause now, and she looked searchingly at Teveri. "How much was there?"

"Not much. Not enough that we felt it could be sold—and it was the *stalks* of the plant, not the spun threads or the fabric. But we thought that it would be a gesture of respect to gather them up, and a few of our crew fashioned them into something for your dogs." Teveri withdrew the collars from their pockets. "They are a gift for you," Teveri said solemnly.

Black Garda slowly took one of the collars. "*Well*."

"We have not had a prosperous season," Teveri said in a low voice, watching Black Garda intently. "But when *The Running Sun* is gone from these seas, no one will be able to say we were so money-grubbing that we forgot our dignity."

"Ah, yes, money-grubbing. On that subject, Captain Heirani already reported the whole story to me, of course. A real shame—I do sympathize. I was looking forward to the chance of a fat payout myself." Black Garda buckled the collar onto one of the blue dogs and smiled at the effect, rising to her feet. Teveri did as well. "Very gracious to bring me such a gift, though. I suppose you'll be angling for some kind of favor in turn."

"Are you offering?" Tev said bluntly.

Black Garda threw her head back and guffawed, one hand resting high on her chest and the other on her thick belly. "Forthright as ever, Captain! But you know I don't do loans. Not good for business, what with people dying or crashing their ships into rocks or changing their names and running off into the sunset. No loans."

"I'm aware."

"But you need money. At least enough to restock for another voyage, eh? Or two, or three—or however many it takes until you hit on a ship carrying a prize that's worth something." She shook her head. "A real shame about the Shipbuilder's Guild thing. You were so awfully convincing. No, no, don't get your feathers ruffled," she said, holding up one hand to forestall Teveri's objection. "I know that you thought you had something. Hell, maybe you did have a little *piece* of something—logically, it's got to be something complicated with a lot of little pieces, otherwise somebody else would have figured it out by now."

"Indeed," said Teveri through gritted teeth.

Black Garda pursed her lips and seemed to assess them. "You need a boost to your reputation too, don't you," she said shrewdly. "Too much dignity to be money-grubbing, my ass. If any other captain had found bits of Xing Fe Hua's sails or what they were made of, they would have cut them down into thumb-sized sections and auctioned them off as relics. But you? Oh no, nothing could be so important but the gallantry of making a *gift* of them to one of the most well-connected fences in Scuttle Cove, eh? And with no benefit to yourself! Dignity over money! Pretty words, but that does suggest to me that at minimum you're looking for something to be able to brag about." She put her head a little on one side. "Can't have felt good, to come back empty-handed after a stupid jaunt like what we sent you on."

"High hopes have farther to fall," Teveri said with a tiny shrug of one shoulder. They'd clasped their hands behind their back and straightened their spine.

"Yes, and unfortunately you can't even brag about what you *thought* you had, can you? Not with the ambassador breathing down all our necks—he's been poking around, by the way. Asking questions. It's very possible that the theft has already been noticed and his superiors passed him instructions."

"No. That is not possible." They jerked their thumb at Avra. "He was the thief."

Black Garda squinted at Avra again. "And who is he?"

"Avra Helvaçi," Teveri said.

"Yes, like the poet," said Avra casually. "Maybe you've read my work."

Teveri closed their eyes for a moment. "He was until recently a spy with the Araşti Ministry of Intelligence."

Black Garda narrowed her eyes. "Oh yes, I begin to remember you. You're the appalling little twit that cheats at cards so well nobody can figure out how you're doing it, right? And we're supposed to trust you?" Her thick black eyebrows rose steadily. "Seems much more likely that he's conning you, doesn't it, Captain az-Ḥaffār?"

Teveri snorted. "That would require him to have an attention span longer than a gnat's."

"That's true," said Avra. "That's very true and a great point."

"Are you *sure*? What if he's been sent as a test, to see whether we're loyal to the Pact, or to find leverage for negotiating new, worse terms?"

"He's not," Teveri said.

"You could be wrong."

"If I'm wrong, I swear on my *Nightingale* sail that I'll give up my captaincy and my ship, and you all can performatively run me out of town to prove I was an individual, isolated idiot who went rogue."

Black Garda studied the two of them. "All right. All right, yeah, I'll buy that. Back to the matter of your reputation, then—I think the collars were a clever plan. Clever, because it makes a *statement,* and because it butters me up right where I live—fancy dog collars, my goodness, whoever thought that up for you is a genius."

"Me," said Avra. "It was me. It was my idea. Also Julian helped me workshop it. This is Julian." Black Garda barely spared Julian a glance, but Avra supposed that he was the precise opposite of her type—Black Garda's wife was petite, dark-skinned, and wore her hair in perfectly coiffed arrangements like a fine lady. Really the only quality her looks shared with Julian's was that they were both exceptionally pretty, but Mistress Navya's prettiness was that of a delicate spring blossom, and Julian ought to have been cast in bronze holding a discus and put on a plinth.

"A clever plan," Black Garda continued. "Clever enough to patch the hole in your hull long enough for you to figuratively bring your ship into port, at least. But I think you know as well as I do that the water is coming in, Captain, and the ship is going down."

"My first mate killed a serpent single-handedly," said Teveri, and gave a strained smile. "We were thinking of having it stuffed and hung in Eel-face Yusin's bar."

"Another good patch," Black Garda agreed. "It might buy you some time. Do you have the money to have it stuffed?"

"We have a few assets that we can sell if need be."

"So no." Black Garda sighed. "Captain, I do like you. Do you know that? I don't like all the captains—no one amongst my colleagues likes *all* the captains, we all have our preferences—but I do like you. You've lasted fifteen years. A respectable thing, for one who started so young. Had you possessed a different nature, you might have gotten further than you have. If you were easier to work with, for example, and if you were less stubborn and forthright and quick to anger . . ."

"If I had a different nature," Teveri said in a low, hard voice, "I would not be here at all."

"That's also true," Black Garda allowed with a nod. "You would have quit years ago, I would imagine."

"Or never left Tash in the first place."

That gave Black Garda pause. "Indeed," she said, matching Teveri's low, serious tone. "And I believe that Scuttle Cove would have been the poorer for it. You have not brought in much money, nor any particularly good tales of adventure, nor won yourself success in any other way . . . But there is an *energy* when your ship comes into port. People notice you. You are *exceptional* at making a spectacle of yourself—and I do mean that as a compliment."

"I thank you kindly for it," Teveri said, clearly holding on to their temper with both hands. "If I am so valuable, perhaps you would like to do literally *anything* to help me keep my fucking crew."

Black Garda smiled. "Perhaps indeed. I will have to consider how much material influence I am willing to allocate to such an endeavor—and I will have to ask my wife her thoughts as well. But for the moment, I will give you a gift in return for the one you have so kindly brought to me with *no thought* for your own benefit but dignity."

"Yes?"

"My colleagues and I occasionally gather to discuss matters that we find important to this place," she said, with a wave of her hand.

"And so the gift that I give you is the knowledge that we have been watching you very closely since you became a captain, and that we do have some respect for the fact that you have lasted fifteen years. You have always showed such *promise,* Captain az-Ḥaffār. In fact, after you departed on my errand, my colleagues had one of our little gatherings. After some conversation amongst ourselves, we were all rather astonished to discover that you have somehow *maintained* that sense of promise. We cannot figure out how you've done it. Fifteen years, and we're still saying, 'You know, I feel like Teveri az-Ḥaffār might make something of themself one day.'" She looked out over the beach and the harbor, looked back to the town. "We are also of the opinion that things around here have become rather civilized—no bad thing for us fences, because I do damn well prefer it when my warehouses don't burn down—but we find that the captains these days are just a little too *comfortable.* Not so motivated. Not so *hungry.*"

"I've always been hungry," Teveri snapped.

"So you have," said Black Garda, smiling. "That's the energy that comes into port with your ship. A hunger. A little wildness. Like a dog that ran into a tree as a puppy and keeps getting weirder and crazier every year." Her smile broadened. "This is also a compliment, of course."

"Of course."

"It's good for the town, you know. Reminds people of the bad old days."

"I doubt that."

"Ah, but it does. You walk down the street in your fancy clothes, looking like a pretentious upstart with aspirations of being Xing Fe Hua when you grow up, and all those decrepit old captains snort and scoff and roll their eyes as you walk by—and then they turn to each other and say, 'Do you remember when *we* were that obnoxious? Do you remember when Captain Coriavi poached Captain Jiu's purser and Captain Jiu got revenge by fucking Captain Coriavi's first mate so good he was walking bowlegged for a week? Do you remember when Captain Mitsuri's ship came in with a hold so full that she damn near *waddled* into port like she was eight months pregnant? Remember that?' This doesn't happen to anyone else, you know."

Teveri said nothing for a long moment. "I see."

"A gift for you, in thanks for these fancy collars and these glowing dogs. Really, Captain az-Ḥaffār, let it never be said that you did anything without style."

"And that's what's important," said Avra cheerfully.

Black Garda paused, tilting her head thoughtfully, eyebrows raised. "So it is, isn't it," she murmured. Then, more briskly, "Come by my house this afternoon. I will have either a business offer for you or, failing that, tea and some of my wife's pastries—and you'll be wanting to freshen up, I would imagine. I have a pair of suites set aside at the Green Hotel. You may tell the proprietress that I'm lending it to you for . . . let's say until the day after tomorrow. That should sleep at least twenty of your crew—more if you pack them in like sardines. Then you may enjoy the festival and the finale of the cake competition in convenience. That's another little gift for you. Glowing dogs and *Nightingale* collars will get you a *long* way, apparently. I am mildly surprised with myself for how far this is getting you, but—well, the dogs *do* glow. But as for this afternoon, perhaps three o'clock?"

"All right," said Teveri warily. "Thank you."

"Bring Markefa too, would you? And whoever else you'd like." She eyed Avra. "Not that one."

"Wouldn't dream of bringing that one to tea anywhere, to be honest," Teveri said. "I'd rather pull my own teeth out."

"You know what, I get that," said Avra.

Teveri strode down the streets to the Green Hotel with such *intent* that Avra overheard a few people muttering speculations about who they were heading to kill. Julian kept pace easily; Avra's legs and attention span were much shorter, so he had to keep scuttling to keep up every time he fell behind. About half the crew had already rowed ashore the night before, and those that had made the trip this morning peeled off one by one, dispersing into the festival.

Scuttle Cove didn't put up as many decorations as Avra had seen bedecking other cities during their important holidays, but there was the scent of food everywhere, and there was music and proper carousing, and everyone was wearing their absolute finest—lush, gorgeous, vibrant, luxurious fabrics: silks from Genzhu and Imakami, delicate cotton muslins from Arjuneh, the eye-bendingly bold geometric prints of Kholekhole, damasks of Araşt and N'gaka, velvet and intricate lacework from Vinte and . . . Avra even spotted some of the Ammatu sailors wearing *entire sarongs* of a glistering ivory-gold that could only be seawich, one of the most expensive fibers in the world—apparently markedly less expensive for them, as they hailed from the only place it was produced. There were hats and headdresses and turbans and veils and fountains of feathers—even coronets, though their jewels had likely long since been replaced with glass.

Much of this finery was sun-faded and threadbare. Those that weren't were obviously remade from other garments that had been taken apart and adapted, or paired with items that had never been intended to go together.

The whole display was, in a word, tawdry, and in Avra's opinion it was the second-most-beautiful thing in the world after an unpicky slut: *Here we are—for now, for at least today,* it said. *Here we are, as splendid as we can manage, because we might not be here tomorrow, because we won the right to do what we are doing on the tip of a blade—and because they should* know, *all those people out there in the world, that we were here and proud and free and that they couldn't and can't do a thing to stop us.*

The captains were the most splendidly tawdry of all, of course, but that was because most captains were egomaniacs without a scrap of taste. Teveri was of course also an egomaniac, but at least they knew how to dress.

They needed a hat, though. They'd had a hat once.

He was just jogging to catch up with Teveri and ask what had happened to their hat, while simultaneously trying not to get distracted with the street performances, or the *tourists,* or the pretty boys and girls on the balconies calling out and blowing kisses to the passersby, or with seeing which of the crew had abandoned them for any of these marvels—and so he almost missed Julian angling himself a little closer to Teveri and saying softly, "How generous of you to give all three collars to Black Garda."

"Supposed to be a monk," Avra muttered to himself. "Actually a very rude man."

Teveri put their nose in the air. "My priority is my ship and crew, Brother Julian. What I could have possibly done with a third, I haven't the faintest idea. I don't have any pets except Avra, and I *very much* do not want to ensure he is within earshot of me. In fact, I would greatly prefer that he was well out of it."

"Ah," said Julian, half laughing, and glanced back over his shoulder at Avra.

"He's a very rude man," Avra said mournfully, sitting in the middle of the floor. The suite in the Green Hotel was nicer than the rooms they usually took in the High Tide Hotel—taller ceilings, slightly less battered furniture of slightly more extravagant original quality, *wallpaper* that was only peeling a little bit . . .

Teveri had shucked off their coat and shirt, scrubbed down with a washcloth, and was rinsing the sweat and salt out of their hair in a basin. "He is one of the ruder men I have ever encountered, yes. Absolutely appalling behavior on his part."

"I was appalled," said Avra. "I have never been so appalled in my life."

"I will not stand to be *flirted* with."

"You have started knife fights for less," Avra agreed. "I could stand to be flirted with."

"He does not flirt with you, he *toys* with you. Like a cat with a little dead mouse. Half of a mouse. A partial vole."

Avra tipped over on his back and groaned at the ceiling. "Don't get me horny right now, Tev."

"Discussion of eviscerated vermin gets you horny now?"

"The idea of Julian toying with me like a cat with a small helpless creature."

Teveri scrunched the water out of their hair with a towel, crossed over to Avra, and thoughtfully put their foot in the center of his chest.

Avra screeched immediately and flailed every limb. "Teveri az-Ḥaffār, that is not fair, you can't do that to me! Tev! I know you're not going to stop to fuck me in the middle of the day in Black Garda's hotel suite, so this is *very rude to do,* no better than Julian with his cat-toying—"

Teveri removed their foot. "I was proving a point."

"What point! What point could you possibly need to prove? That you can also toy with me just as good as he can? I know it, Tev, I know that, do you think that I do not know this about myself or you? You toy with me always—"

"At least I am polite enough to touch your dick after I toy with you, though."

Avra pointed emphatically at them. "Yes, you are. Sometimes. Not always. Sometimes you stop at toying with me."

"No, sometimes I just *bully* you. That's a different thing."

"It feels like the same thing to me," Avra said, dropping his head back to the floor and staring at the ceiling. "Julian is making me crazy. I am going crazy. What is he doing? What is happening in his head? What is going on in there? Is it because I reminded him about his six and fifty-two? I keep having sexy thoughts of him snapping and making out with me, and then I break away and gasp, 'But Julian! Your vows!' and he says something like, 'I don't care about my vows, your short pants have tormented me long enough,' or sometimes he just growls and kisses me again and—"

"Mngh," said Teveri, who had paused halfway through putting their shirt back on.

"What are yours? What does he do in yours?"

"We make extremely charged eye contact during a tense public moment, but say nothing. Later, he comes to my cabin and takes all his clothes off while I drink a glass of rum and look at him. We still say nothing."

"Oh, that's *very* good." Avra paused. "I am not in this vision, am I?"

"If you were, you would be on top of the wardrobe making weird mouth noises," Teveri said, shaking themselves and pulling their shirt the rest of the way on. "So no, you're not."

"What if I'm squirreled away in your sea chest with the lid propped open just a crack so that I don't suffocate and can watch the goings-on? I'd have to be extremely quiet."

"Then how do you expect me to know whether or not you're in this vision?" They regarded Avra. "You aren't coming to Black Garda's for tea. Will you be here?"

Avra sighed. "I should go see the ambassador, probably. I had to tell him some things to keep him from getting too suspicious about why we were going out on the water—I should let him know that we're back and that you're a lunatic."

"Hm," said Teveri. "I would say good luck, but I don't think you need it."

"It's the thought that counts."

20

22. The Cove

Shelter from the storm and serpents, a rest, a pause. You have reached safe harbor, and there is time to catch your breath and restock your supplies. Inspect everything closely and make any necessary repairs or adjustments to what you're doing—something that was sound when you set out may have been damaged during the journey, and it is better to know about it now.

(Reversed: Secrets, things happening below the surface, sneaking around under someone's nose. Someone is hiding something from you—be wary. The waters may seem calm, but you do not know what lurks beneath.)

Avra attempted to traipse up to the ambassadorial villa, but all that he could manage was a trudge. His feet dragged—the walk seemed three times as long as it had ever been, but that was what came of getting very little sleep two nights in a row, having wild mediocre sex with Teveri, and then being forced to jog through half of Scuttle Cove.

"I'm tired," he whined to the rocks, the sandy path, the scrubby trees, and one very unimpressed goat that had gotten loose from someone's pen. "I want to nap."

He should have eaten before coming up—he should have stopped for a drink of water, at least. Breakfast would've been plain black coffee, a bit of hardtack, and some leftover dried squid, but Avra had failed to fend off the blue dogs from swarming upon him and scarfing the dried squid right out of his mouth, just the same as had always happened metaphorically with the alley possums and the bread-wrapped rocks that Teveri kicked at him.

He sat on the ground to catch his breath and reflected that the one quantifiable benefit he had gotten from knowing Julian so far was to be united with Teveri against him and his toying. Or at least verbally agreeing with Teveri that the toying was intolerable, and then pretending to be casual around Julian while, on the inside, being absolutely transfixed about what new sadistic form of toying the dreadful man was going to spring on them next.

The goat ambled up and mouthed at his sleeve.

"Not you too," said Avra, pushing its head away. "I am beset. I am beset by possums and dogs and Julian's dick continuing to exist in front of me." The goat stared accusingly at him. "Only kind of half-assed in front of me, though. It could be more in front of me. Like right here." Avra waved directly in front of his face.

The goat yelled at him again—hurtful—so Avra heaved himself to his feet and continued trudging up the path.

Just as he reached the villa's front door and raised his hand to knock, someone called out from behind. He turned to find Lieutenant Viyan coming on a perpendicular path to his own along the slope of the North Tit, which presumably led to that lookout point opposite Skully's magnum-opus-in-progress.

Avra waved and wearily pulled on his professional persona as Lieutenant Viyan jogged up with a smile. "Good morning, Helvaçi! You're back already? Or did Captain az-Ḥaffār think better of it after all?"

"No. I mean yes, we did leave, and we came back. Short trip. Just a wager, really."

"Did they win? Oh, come inside, let's get out of this sun." Viyan led him inside. She was clearly off duty, wearing civilian clothes rather than her uniform, and she looked *dreadfully* Araşti—squeaky clean, her clothes nicely laundered and pressed and new enough that they weren't showing wear. They'd been made for her too, which stood out more here than it would anywhere else Avra had been. There was something about the clothes in Scuttle Cove that looked wrong if they were too well tailored. It made people look like . . . well, foreigners. *Tourists.* Locals made do with whatever the pirate captains brought back from their voyages.

"Didn't sink the ship, at least. That's a win in my books."

Viyan laughed and led him through into the central courtyard garden. It was *markedly* cooler than outside. "You look parched, would you like anything to drink?"

"Please," he said. "And snacks, if the cook won't mind me begging."

"I don't think we'll be seeing the cook for the next few days," Viyan said, scrunching up her nose. "She's a local, you know, and she's doing something with her family for the festival. Ambassador Baltakan tried to explain that we couldn't spare her, but she just looked at him as if he had two heads and said that she wasn't sure what that had to do with anything. We went back and forth for a while, and the ambassador and I *thought* we'd come to an understanding with her, but she must have left sometime in the night. She hasn't come back yet."

"Oh no," said Avra dutifully.

"I know!" Viyan said. "If you come to the kitchen, I'll get us something to drink, and you can scrounge for food. The cook left us a loaf of bread, and there's things in the larder. But nothing *cooked,* you know, and I didn't do at all well in my cookery classes at the academy. All I can manage is eggs and toast, otherwise it's just cheese and things in jars. And some Pezian prosciutto, but that's reserved for the ambassador, of course."

Viyan led him into the kitchen, filled a beautiful ceramic ewer with water from a barrel, and fetched a few lemons and a sugar bowl from the larder. "Go ahead and poke around in there. Help yourself to anything you like."

Avra duly poked around in the dark, cool larder. There was a great quantity of jarred things—olives, pickled pearl onions, preserved eggplant in olive oil, grape leaves, at least twenty different kinds of jam, a bag of rice big enough that if it had been empty Avra could have crawled into it and knotted it over his head . . .

"Wow," he said. He was so tired he felt like one of those Vintish automatons, moving and speaking according to the scripted demands of his internal mechanisms rather than under any of his own intention. "So many options."

"Oh—yes," Viyan said from out in the kitchen. "Ambassador Baltakan was very concerned that there wouldn't be any nice things available, so he brought a few favorites with him—but the old ambassador did that too. Three shipments a year with little necessities and luxuries, you know, because there's no guarantee that you can get *anything* in the market in this place. They don't grow much of anything here, can you believe that?"

"Bad soil," Avra said, dazedly tucking three jars of jam and a jar of olives into his little rucksack.

"Well, yes, but they've had a town here for *ages,* haven't they? Hundreds of years! I'm just surprised that they haven't done anything to amend the soil and improve things, you know? People have little kitchen gardens, but they don't want to *sell* anything! They keep telling us that it all goes to feed their own families, and then we end up paying an extraordinary amount of money—but I suppose it's a matter of supply and demand, isn't it?"

Avra gazed in deep contemplation at the giant leg of prosciutto. He got out his tiny knife, sawed off a very generous wedge, and put that in his little rucksack as well. He did the same to the wheel of cheese next to it. He contemplated the butter, but it was quite soft from the warmth of the day. He had the feeling that if he put it into his bag, it would melt all over everything, including his Heralds.

"Wow," said Avra again, absently. "That sounds really hard."

The townsfolk *did* sell or trade produce to each other, but there wasn't anything like a proper *market* for vegetables, only for imported things. For everything else, people just knew someone (or knew someone who knew someone) who was growing eggplant or tomatoes and showed up at their house to ask if they had any to spare, and people who were growing zucchini snuck around in the dead of night and left unsolicited bags of them on people's doorsteps.

Everyone would know the ambassador and his staff by sight, of course. Avra was not at all surprised that they were excluded from the vegetable network, and only mildly surprised that they were excluded even from the guerilla zucchini delivery list.

Avra took a jar of cherries in syrup, a packet of candied almonds, and a small salami for his bag as well. And a large, round-bellied bottle of wine, because as soon as his eyes landed on it, he recollected that he still owed one to Cat and his colleagues. This filled his bag to bursting, but with any luck (haha), no one would notice.

Then he took a second jar of cherries, a second salami, the cheese, and the butter out to Viyan, who was just finishing the lemonade. "I'm wittering on, aren't I!" Viyan said with an apologetic smile. "What about you? Did anything of note happen on your . . . trip?"

"We were attacked by a sea serpent." Avra set everything on the kitchen table and set to sawing off a large chunk from the loaf of bread. "The first mate killed it single-handed. With an axe."

"Holy shit." Viyan pushed a glass of lemonade across the table to him, wide-eyed. "Holy shit. Thank the Lord of Trials that you're all right!"

"Yes," said Avra, slathering as much of the butter as possible on his wedge of bread and then stacking it with cheese. "It was the scariest fucking thing I've seen in my life, I don't mind telling you."

"Gods. It sounds like you need a break—do you have a place to stay? I have no idea how many spare rooms there are down in the city, but I'd imagine any of them would be loud with all the festival commotion . . . All our guest rooms are full up as of last night, otherwise I'd offer you one of those. The weather is beautiful right now, though, and I sometimes sleep on the divan in the garden on fine nights, so if you just wanted to get away from the noise . . ."

"No, no, no," said Avra around a mouthful of primarily butter and cheese with a little bread for texture. He waved this off as he chewed and swallowed. "Very kind of you. I have accommodations down in one of the hotels."

"Probably better that you're there, then. We can't even supply you a bath this weekend."

"The help didn't show up either, eh?"

"It's shocking! With the last ambassador, we always had a cook and at least one servant, even during festivals!" She laughed and leaned against the kitchen counter with her own glass of lemonade. "The other kahya is down with a cold, so it's all falling on me, you know. I'm going around playing pretend that I'm one of the core guard attending the royal family, which at least makes the chores a bit fun, but today was supposed to be my day off! Ambassador Baltakan really is a gentleman, though. He caught me flying about and wringing my hands about what we're going to do for all the guests, and he insisted that I take at least part of the day to go on my walk and have some time to myself. Awfully kind of him. *And* he helped sweep out the arcades around the courtyard so they'd be presentable."

"Who, uh, who are the guests?"

"Oh, a couple minor clerks from the Ministry of Diplomacy. The captain, first and second mates, bosun, purser, and quartermaster of the ship that brought them—you probably saw it in the harbor. And . . ." Viyan leaned in. "*A satyota.*"

Avra paused in the middle of taking a huge bite from his slab of bread. It took a moment for his brain to process the word. Satyota. Truthwitch.

Wariness formed a knot in his stomach. He was not sure what kind of knot it was. Markefa would have known. Markefa could do this trick where she just *threw* one bit of rope at another bit of rope and then it was somehow knotted. That was probably what this knot was. That was how fast it had . . . beknotted itself.

The only truthwitch Avra had met was the one who had interrogated him and concluded that his head was as empty as a new bucket and that it would be a waste of time to accuse him of anything. He therefore only knew three things about truthwitches:

First, that they were very mean to him.

Second, that they came from Inacha and that they were as loyal to their crown as any of the Araşti civil service (other than Avra), due to the fact they were all recruited as young children and brought to the temples to receive intense training and refinement of their gifts.

Third, that they could be hired out the way that you might hire an architect, a physician, or a courtesan. This was useful when, instead of a problem with a building, a mysterious ailment, or an embarrassing sexual fetish that you wanted to indulge without anyone laughing at you or throwing you out of their cabin (*Teveri*), you had a problem with needing to know whether people were lying to you, *and* you were willing to pay absolutely eye-watering, stomach-churning, bloodcurdling amounts of money to make it happen.

It was such a vast expense that, much like with a building that was still mostly fine, a weird mole that hadn't yet become sentient, or a *particularly* embarrassing sexual fetish, no one went to the expense of hiring a truthwitch unless things were getting really fucking serious.

That meant that *either* someone back in Araşt had noticed that something had been disturbed in the Shipbuilder's Guild after the initial investigation, panicked, and hired a truthwitch to be on standby in Scuttle Cove, or—*or*—if Avra was very lucky—which he was—the ambassador had merely *convinced* someone in his chain of command that he had reason to believe that things were getting really fucking serious and that a truthwitch would be a good thing to have around for a bit.

Avra blinked at Viyan to cover his sheer panic. "Wow. A satyota. So many questions! Sorry, perhaps I shouldn't pry . . . I wouldn't want to put you in an awkward position. It's just that . . . Well, Diplomacy and Intelligence are so closely aligned! Like siblings. Brother and sister. Just like the Mother of All and the Lord of Trials." Viyan beamed at him. "I'm terribly curious to get a briefing about what's been going on, but if you are at all concerned that the ambassador wouldn't be pleased for me to have that information, then of course that's far more important than my mere intrigue."

"Gracious of you to say so, but I don't know all that much more than that."

"Well, what a curious situation!" Avra said jovially. "I shall be most interested to see what develops in the next few weeks. Do you know how long the satyota and your other guests are staying?"

"No idea. They got in quite late last night. Ambassador Baltakan was planning to be in a meeting with them until lunchtime—which I suppose is about now! I ought to run over to his offices and ask if they'd like anything brought in. Would you like me to ask whether you can sit in on the end of the meeting?"

"Will he mind if I bring my bread and lemonade?"

"I can't imagine he would. He's a very reasonable man—I really like working with him so far. The previous ambassador had been here long enough that she'd started to go native, if you know what I mean."

"Mm," said Avra around a huge bite of bread and cheese.

Viyan tapped on the ambassador's door and peeked in when he answered. "Hello, sir, I'm back from my walk—do any of you want something to eat? We have bread and cheese and things from the larder, or I could attempt eggs . . ."

"Oh, don't worry about food, Lieutenant, the captain informed me this morning that he'd summon up the cook from his ship to help! We're to expect them quite soon, I would imagine."

"Excellent," Viyan said with audible relief. "Also, Avra Helvaçi is here."

"Send him in, Lieutenant, by all means!"

Avra fixed his professional mask firmly into place, tossed his hair, squashed his panic into his boots, and sauntered in.

The ambassador's private office was even more egregiously Araşti than the rest of the house. It even had one of the little decorative fountains that Avra had seen in a few audience chambers of the palace. Supposedly, they were intended to provide enough soft, persistent noise to deter eavesdroppers. Avra, as a former member of the Ministry of Intelligence, had more professional opinions on them than most people. Specifically, he knew that they did have to either be of a certain size *or* be placed strategically near doors or windows in order to be really effective. Also, you had to be whispering.

The ambassador was looking dignified and rich as fuck, as per usual. The two clerks were, indeed, Secretary Rabia and Secretary Selim. Without the veil of darkness and Avra's blood-freezing terror of imminent discovery, they looked . . . normal. Exceedingly normal. In fact, they looked like nearly every other mid-to-low-rank clerk in the Ministry of Diplomacy, which was to say a couple of eggheads.

The truthwitch was one of those people about whom things were said along the lines of "She could not be called beautiful, but she was nevertheless *striking*." She certainly was nevertheless striking. She was remarkably tall and shaven bald, and her eyes were the shape of willow leaves. She had a mild ochre cast to her complexion, utterly *perfect* eyebrows, an aura of absolute and unassailable poise, and just so many bones in her face. Just *so many bones* in that face. Avra found himself a little entranced by how many bones she had in her face. At least fifteen more cheekbones than the average person had per side. Fascinatingly beautiful (or at least nevertheless striking) planes on her skull. A jawline that Skully could have used to carve out the cliffside. In fact . . .

"Wow," said Avra. "I know someone who would love to look at your bones. Can I introduce you?"

"I beg your pardon?" intoned the satyota, which was so *weighty* with untouchable poise and dignity that Avra instantly developed a ferocious crush.

He coughed. "Sorry, that was an odd thing to say, wasn't it? There's a sculptor I know. He's very ambitious. He likes . . . heads. You have a very nice head, and I couldn't help but think of him and how he would probably . . . admire . . . your head." He coughed again. "Apologies, everyone, I didn't get much sleep last night. Or the night before. I'm a little bit punchy." He glanced down at the bread and cheese. "I also didn't really get breakfast this morning. Or very much dinner last night. Or a proper lunch yesterday. Or—anyway. Hello. So good to meet all of you, I'm Avra Helvaçi."

"My new acquaintance, formerly of the Ministry of Intelligence," said Baltakan. "He has a great deal of experience with the local community—in fact, he went out on some mad wager with one of the captains two days ago."

"We got attacked by a sea serpent," Avra said blankly. "As you might expect. Glad to be alive."

He stuffed a bite of bread in his mouth, a lucky split second before Secretary Rabia sat straight up and said, "Wait, that wasn't Captain az-Ḥaffār's ship, was it?"

"Indeed," said Baltakan.

"But we searched every inch of it!" cried Secretary Selim. "We didn't see you at all—whyever didn't you step out to greet us and save us the trouble?"

Fortunately, the bite of bread had been quite large. Avra held up one apologetic finger while he politely finished chewing, swallowed, and took a very poised and collected sip of his lemonade to help it down. As he did, he frantically scanned through and discarded several responses. The problem was, the truthwitch was *right fucking there,* so whatever statements he made had to be absolutely honest.

By the time he lowered the lemonade glass, he was able to offer Selim a saucy wink and a grin. "Secretary Selim, isn't it? And Secretary Rabia? Well, of course I was hiding! What else do you think Intelligence agents do for fun once they're on partial retirement?" This got a great laugh from Selim and Rabia. "I do apologize for putting you to the trouble, though. Please don't take it personally—I'll buy you a drink to make up for it if you like."

"Very kind, thank you," said Rabia.

"I don't think you will have met our other guest," Baltakan said, gesturing to the truthwitch. "This is Witness Amita, of the Fourth Temple of Truth."

"Charmed," said Avra. "I cannot express how charmed. Also

very sorry and embarrassed about opening my mouth and mentioning your bones like that. Sometimes when I'm tired, I just say whatever silly things pop into my head. I've been told many times that I should shut up."

Witness Amita inclined her magnificent head. "I have received compliments before," she intoned. "But rarely ones so openly sincere as yours."

"Ha ha," said Avra nervously. "And you'd be able to tell, wouldn't you."

"I would, yes." Avra wondered wildly whether she ever spoke in a way that *wasn't* intoning. She smiled very faintly. "We consider the speaking of the purest and most perfect truths to be a holy thing, much akin to the shining white light of the sun. So I thank you for the purity of the truth you spoke in admiration—and for the graciousness of the apology."

"Very good," said Baltakan briskly. "Now, while I would very much like to hear all about this *fascinating* adventure that you went on, Helvaçi, there is a matter to address first. I do apologize, and I hope *you* won't take this personally either, but I'm sure you'll agree that the current situation calls for utmost care."

"Mm," said Avra, *painfully* aware of the nevertheless-striking truthwitch, and took another bite of bread. He made it look like a larger one, but the bread was a resource in this conversation and he wanted to ration it. He had an idea of where this was going.

"It is not that I don't trust you, Helvaçi," said Baltakan. "But I have only known you a few days, and it would greatly help to put my mind at rest if you would consent to being questioned by Witness Amita."

Shining white truth, she'd said. She'd liked that.

If there was one thing that Avra Helvaçi knew how to do besides traipsing, it was charm. He smiled easily, called up the thought of his powerful crush on Witness Amita, and said, "I would love for Witness Amita to question me. However . . . Ah, this is awkward. Yes, I'm on partial retirement, but there are still things I *can't* talk about."

"If a question regards something that Intelligence would object to you divulging, you may tell us and Witness Amita will rephrase her inquiry," said Baltakan with an impatient wave. "Selim and Rabia, I'll ask you to wait out in the garden, if you don't mind." They nodded and quietly departed. "There. Will that do?"

"Thank you for your understanding." He took Selim's chair, set his bread and lemonade on Baltakan's desk, folded his hands, and looked attentively at Witness Amita.

She nodded. "Very well. Ambassador, will two minutes do?"

"Probably. We can add more time on if need be."

"Of course." From some hidden pocket in her voluminous, exquisitely draped robes, flowing down from her shoulders and arms like billows of wind or dunes of sand, Witness Amita took a tiny golden hourglass, set it on the table, and fixed her eyes on Avra. "What are your feelings toward Araşt and its royal family?"

"I have never once wished to harm the sultan or her family," said Avra. "My own family were quiet villagers out in the backcountry, and I entered the civil service academy at the age of seven—it provided me with an education and, eventually, the opportunity to serve something greater than myself. I gave Araşt twenty-eight years of loyal service. I was unhappy when I realized I would have to take partial retirement, but it was necessary for the sake of my health."

"True," said the satyota. "Are you aware of anyone who might have removed items of value from the Shipbuilder's Guild in Kasaba City?"

Avra had not *removed* anything but a few pieces of paper, which were not valuable. What was written on them was, but he'd *copied* that. "No, not at all."

"True. Are you aware of anyone currently researching the technique that Araşti ships use to pass by the sea serpents at this time of year?"

The knot in his stomach tightened. "Pretty sure everyone with a coast is trying to research that."

"I will rephrase. Are you in *personal* contact with anyone currently attempting to research it?"

He shrugged. "Captain az-Ḥaffār has a Vintish monk aboard the ship who knows a bit about alchemy, but that's far from his primary area of expertise." Fifty-two people in one night. Now *there* was an expertise.

"Are you aware of anyone who might attempt to sell such knowledge, were they to acquire it?"

Avra raised his eyebrow in the way that Teveri always did and kept a firm hold on his gibbering nerves. "You may want to rephrase the question—I feel like *anyone* who got their hands on that might attempt to sell it, no?"

"Objectively hyperbole, but he does believe that is true," said Witness Amita. "Are you aware of anyone in Scuttle Cove who is planning to sell illicit information from the Shipbuilder's Guild?"

"No," he said, because all those plans had fallen through.

"True. If illicit information from the Shipbuilder's Guild were to be sold, would you stand to profit from it?"

Avra burst out laughing so hard he nearly fell face-first into his bread and cheese. He covered his face with his hands and slumped back in the chair, giggling helplessly.

His fucking luck.

"No," he gasped as soon as he could get a breath. "*Fuck* no, even. No, I wouldn't get a penny of profit from that. What a question!"

"True," said the truthwitch, and it *was* true, because he had lost his *entire stake* to Heirani a little more than twenty-four hours before.

The timer had long since run out by the time Avra managed to compose himself from his minor fit of hysterics. "Thank you, Helvaçi, for your willingness and good humor," Baltakan said as Avra wiped tears of mirth and badly frayed nerves from his eyes.

"Not at all, not at all!" Avra said, still faintly gurgling into his lemonade. He felt *distinctly* drunk on adrenaline and the success of escaping a gruesome death, and his nerves were entirely frayed. He kept up the performance of lighthearted chatter. "Important to know who you can trust, and you must be stressed out of your mind! Have you been getting enough sleep? Any fresh air? Exercise?"

"Probably not as much as I should," Baltakan allowed.

"True," said Witness Amita with a faint sidelong smile, tucking away her little hourglass.

He sighed and tapped his fingers on the arm of his chair. "No time for rest yet. There are a few more avenues that I would like to pursue—"

No! Avra wanted to screech. *No more avenues! No more pursuit!* "Ambassador. May I be just astonishingly frank with you for a moment?"

"Certainly."

"You heard about the break-in at the Shipbuilder's Guild—*everyone did.* Well, all right, that's hyperbole, isn't it," he said, glancing at Witness Amita, who quirked a smile. "A lot of people did. Of *course* rumors are going to spring up. That's just human nature." Avra tapped his temple. "Ministry of Intelligence. I know all about these kinds of things. But here's the thing, Baltakan—you're very new to your position, and you're understandably worried because you're not used to how things are done here. Don't you think it is *possible* that you're being a little overly vigilant about all this?"

Baltakan considered this, gazing at the edge of his desk, then met Avra's eyes with a rueful look. "The possibility exists, I will admit that. But I would not be able to rest easily if I did not fulfill my obligations to give my best work and exhaust every avenue of possibility."

"You could do better work if you were rested."

Baltakan shook his head, smiling, then leaned forward and set his palms on the desk as if he were about to push himself up. "I shall have Witness Amita question the fences, I think. And—that alchemist on Captain az-Ḥaffār's crew—"

"He's not an alchemist," Avra said quickly. "He's a monk who knows some things about alchemy. The same way that you're an ambassador who knows some things about being a courier with the Ministry of Intelligence. Alchemy is not his primary field of study."

"Do you know what that is?"

Avra was once again painfully aware of Witness Amita sitting right there, regarding him steadily. He tipped his head back and forth as if thinking, which . . . well, gave him time to think for real. "He seems to know a bit about a lot of things. He came to Scuttle Cove to pursue personal research. He was doing a translation of a holy text—some kind of travel diary about the Vintish religion's founding prophet, if I recall correctly, so I'd assume that besides languages, he'd also know history and geography. My impression is that his true passion was something related to human anatomy, but he was discouraged away from that quite early on. He is a hobbyist alchemist at best. At *best.*"

Baltakan hummed and nodded. "You mentioned that everyone with a coast is trying to research the secret technique . . . Does he have any theories?"

"When we were attacked by sea serpents, he tried to blow them up with some sort of alchemical bomb. Didn't seem to deter the fuckers very much. One of them leapt right onto the deck and broke the rail. You can go down to the harbor and see it yourself. The first mate hacked it to death with an axe." He paused. "Have you ever been so fucking afraid that all your bones turned to water? That's what that was like. Didn't piss myself, but it was a close thing."

Baltakan and Witness Amita were both looking rather pale. "Alchemical bombs, you said," the ambassador said, clearing his throat and visibly pulling himself together.

"Yes. I'm not sure that he managed to actually kill any of the serpents, though. *Maybe* he could have gotten lucky if he'd hit one directly, but . . . Look, where there's one serpent, there's usually a lot more than one, right? You'd have to have hundreds of those things, and *perfect* aim, and incredible luck—and even then, you risk blowing up yourself or your ship, because just one drop of water makes them go off. You'd be better off just giving everyone on board a cutlass and a strong drink to steady their nerves. And I think that if the technique involved explosives, people would have heard about it. Hard to keep that secret."

"Was that the only theory he was pursuing?"

Avra shrugged and took a bite of his bread and cheese as cover. *When* could he escape from this situation? He was so tired. He was going to burst into tears soon if he couldn't get out of this. "When we first saw the breeding swarm, he tried pouring some stuff in barrels into the water, but that's not particularly notable. I've met more than one person who suspects that has something to do with it."

Baltakan looked puzzled. "Poured something—like the offerings to the sea, you mean?"

"Like that, yes."

"How strange. I suppose I can see where such a theory might come from, but . . . I find it difficult to believe. If the technique is held by the Shipbuilder's Guild, then clearly it must be something to do with the ships themselves."

Avra nodded. "You know, Ambassador, your capacity for logic is a rare trait."

"Thank you. Do you think you could arrange a meeting for me with this monk?"

"Eh? Why?"

"Of anyone I have heard about so far in my inquiries, he seems like the most likely person to know something."

Through the haze of exhaustion and adrenaline high, Avra lightly panicked. "Does he?"

"Compared to all the other crackpots on this island?"

"Ah. There you go being logical again!"

Baltakan laughed and spread his hands. "I am a thorough sort of man by nature, Helvaçi, I cannot help it. And besides that, it would seem wasteful to invite Witness Amita all this way and not make use of her prodigious talents."

Witness Amita once again inclined her head with breathtaking dignity.

"Ha," said Avra. "Yes, I can see why you would say that. Wasteful, and also disrespectful."

"Indeed. So, the meeting? Can you arrange it?"

"If I may," Witness Amita intoned. "In many cases, it is best for the questioning to happen without the subject's knowledge. An unguarded heart is easier to look within."

"But I knew I was being questioned," Avra said. At least, this time he had. That first truthwitch, back in the palace . . . They had tricked him then, hadn't they?

Witness Amita nodded once. "You did. We recommend different tactics with those who are likely to be allies. A friend may withdraw their friendship if they discover that subterfuge and cunning have been used against them, but friendship may be strengthened when the situation is set before them frankly and there is a clear assumption of good faith."

Baltakan had brightened visibly. "But subterfuge *can* be used with a potential suspect! What a perfect opportunity!"

"I'm not following," Avra said weakly.

Baltakan stood up and came around the desk. "Here's what we'll do—I keep hearing all this fuss about some kind of important festival event that's happening in the next few days."

He was far too animated and enthusiastic; Avra already wasn't sure he liked where this was going. "Uh, do you mean the finale of the cake competition tomorrow?"

"Yes. What if Witness Amita and I disguise ourselves as locals, and you meet us there with that Vint? You can introduce us as acquaintances of yours, and we'll find out everything we need to know through casual conversation."

"Ah," said Avra. "There are a lot of people at the cake competition."

Baltakan looked to Witness Amita. "Will that be any trouble, madam?"

"In busy or noisy situations, I am still able to divine a spoken lie if I can hear it with precision. That is little use if the precise words are drowned out in chaos."

"I'm sure we can find a quieter moment. Perhaps we'll pretend to invite them to dinner."

"Eel-face Yusin's place is very good," said Avra weakly. "Best yellow curry in town."

"Oh, I quite like curry," said Witness Amita, in the first moment of actual humanity that Avra had yet witnessed from her. She hadn't even *intoned* that one.

21

17. The Matchmaker

Sensible partnerships, relationships growing quietly from mutual respect. It's time to open your heart. A new friend, lover, partnership, or idea is coming; if you are having trouble finding it, ask for help. Someone may offer an introduction that will become vital.

(Reversed: Divorce, broken promises, disappointed hopes. A possibility that looked good on paper is not viable in practice. However, even reversed, The Matchmaker reminds us that there's plenty of fish in the sea. There will be other opportunities; she will try again to find you the thing that is right for you.)

Avra walked—yes, *walked,* may all the gods have mercy on him—back down the North Tit.

"Reeeee," he said to the goat as he passed. The goat lifted its head from a tuft of saw grass and yelled at him.

He continued walking—of all things—back down to the town, giving off as much of an air of *everything is fine and normal and nobody should pay any attention to me* as he could, making his way to the Street of Flowers.

Of course he was recognized nearly immediately. "Hi, Avra!" someone called from one of the balconies, and several other people waved.

"Hi," Avra said, clutching his little rucksack and looking up piteously at all the beauties.

"Aw, what's wrong?" said Opal, a lady who was no longer what you could call young and nubile, but who still had the most masterfully applied eyeliner in the entire archipelago. Avra liked her. He liked nearly everyone on this street. "What's such a sad look for, baby boy?"

"I had a hard day yesterday," he said. "And so far this one isn't going that great either. Is Cat around?"

"He just stepped inside for lunch, dear," called Maya, one of the beautiful flowers adorning Cat's balcony. "Did you bring that bottle of wine you owe us?"

"Yes, ma'am."

"Good boy! Go right in—oh, but we have a new receptionist, love, I don't think you've met him. Hang on a moment, I'll come down and tell him you're a friend. I'm sure Cat would be happy to entertain you after he's finished eating."

Avra skittered nervously inside. The airy front room was tiled with terra-cotta and hung with marvelous tapestries and beautiful paintings, and in the center was a desk and the new receptionist. He was a burly man with a pair of spectacles and one of the more magnificent coats Avra had ever seen on someone who wasn't a captain—gold-and-red-striped brocade with fantastically slashed sleeves. Eye-catching, but too floofy and fussy for Teveri's taste. The man was perhaps fifty years old, with iron-colored hair shaved almost to the scalp and a row of gold earrings up each ear that tinkled as he looked up and nodded. "Good day, sir. Do you have an appointment?"

Before Avra could answer, Maya burst in through one of the side doors in a fluttering-butterflies cloud of golden and orange silks and flung her arms around Avra. "Ooh, it's good to see you! I heard you were spotted the other day, and *then* I heard that that captain of yours went on some mad jaunt just to prove a point and run an errand for Black Garda! *Blue dogs,* we heard? Of course it would be dogs with her, but *blue*? And I heard they're *really really blue.*"

"So well-informed as always," Avra said.

Maya turned to the man at the desk. "Avra, this is Zoris! He's our new doorman and he is marvelous. Zoris, this is Avra Helvaçi—he pays all his bills on time and he has the prettiest manners you've ever seen."

Zoris dropped his professional chilliness right away and grinned—he had two gold teeth, one of which was fashioned into a little skull. "That's what we like to hear. Welcome, Master Helvaçi."

"Ah, please, call me Avra—do I see that you know Skully?"

"Ah!" Zoris tapped his skull tooth. "My cousin."

"A good man. Very inspiring."

"Avra's a friend of the house," Maya said.

"If he has manners pretty enough for you, Miss Maya, then I would say so."

"Much to my shame and devastation, I did leave an open tab the last time. Bottle of wine. I've brought a replacement," Avra said, patting his little rucksack. "And an apology for it being so delayed, which comes in the form of it being quite a large bottle of wine. I stole it from the ambassador's house."

Zoris raised his eyebrows by several feet.

"Ooooh!" said Maya. "Oh, I wish I could see Cat's face when you tell him that, but I ought to go back up to the balcony."

"Seeing Cat today, is he?" Zoris said, flipping through his ledger.

"Just dropping off the wine," Avra said weakly. "Maybe a chat and a bit of a cry. Actually, no, I don't have any money, so I suppose it will just be dropping off the wine."

"Hard day?" Zoris said, with a sympathetic glance up at him.

"In all manner of ways, including a very gorgeous monk sexually toying with me even though he has taken a vow of celibacy."

"That's rough, my friend."

"Thank you!" Avra said loudly. "Yes, thank you, it is rough!" To Maya, he said, "I like it here. People are nice to me here."

She laughed and patted his cheek. "It's those pretty manners of yours, dear. Also the fact that you have no dignity to lose in admitting that what you really want is for all of us to like you. Anyway,

Zoris will take care of you, I must go back up and flirt with the crowd."

Zoris went into the back to talk to Cat, and returned a few moments later. "He's in the kitchen. You know the way?"

"Yes, thank you. Very nice to meet you, Mister Zoris. I like your earrings and your spooky tooth."

Cat was sitting at the kitchen table with a book and a sandwich. "Hi, Avra," he said around a mouthful, slipping a scrap of paper into the book to mark his place.

"Hallo, Cat. Sorry for interrupting your lunch. I brought you that bottle of wine."

He set it on the table, and Cat blinked at it. "That's at least three bottles of wine, Avra."

"Call it compound interest. I really didn't mean to leave an open tab like that."

Cat smiled. "Charmer. Are we visiting today?" He took another bite of his sandwich. "You seem a bit . . . delicate. Like you could use a medicinal cuddle."

"You have no fucking idea." Avra sat heavily on the stool and put his head on the table. "But I don't have any money, just jam and olives and things. So it depends whether you're interested in a barter economy."

"Hm, what kind of jam?"

Avra rolled his head to one side on the table so he could see Cat and valiantly fluttered his eyelashes. "It's stolen-from-the-ambassador's-house jam. So is the wine."

"Oh, you never! Did you really? *Charming* man. What a delight. Wine stolen from the *ambassador*!" Cat grinned and pretended to swoon with one hand over his heart. "You know what, just for that, I *will* have a barter economy today, thank you. Trade me the entire story and you can keep me company while I finish lunch, and perhaps I'll walk you back to your hotel. I heard you were staying in Black Garda's suite at the Green?"

"Wow. That happened *this morning*, Cat." Cat smirked at him around a bite of sandwich. Avra pushed himself heroically upright and peered at him. "What else do you know?"

"Story, Avra," he said, reproachful and muffled by sandwich.

So Avra told him the story—everything since he had parted ways with Teveri and the others at the inn. Cat was good to tell stories to. He made all the right astonished and delighted noises at all the right moments, which Avra supposed had substantial overlap with the skill set of his day job. "And then I came here," Avra finished. "Because Tev won't go back to the hotel until they've finished their business, and my nerves are frayed to shreds. This is why people take partial retirement, you know."

"Business with Black Garda, I'm guessing, since you're staying in her suites," Cat said shrewdly, licking the last crumbs from his fingers.

"Tev was invited to tea," Avra said proudly. "I was not, on account of the fact that I cannot be taken anywhere and no one wants to be seen in public with me."

There was one particular thing that Cat did—that all the beauties on this street did, in fact—that Avra did not like at all: Sometimes they looked at him and their eyes went right fucking through him. Like that truthwitch. Like they were noticing something about him and conspicuously not saying anything about it.

"Don't be spooky at me, Cat. You're making spooky eyes."

"I don't know what you're talking about, Avra," said Cat. "Shall we walk, then? I wouldn't mind stretching my legs, and I don't have another appointment booked until three." Cat got up and swept out of the room without waiting for an answer. Avra scuttled along after him. "You know, the impression I get from everyone else is that you are absolutely appalling, completely intolerable to know, and the most exasperating person that anyone has ever met." Cat stopped at a coat closet in the hall for a parasol and a gossamer scarf, which he draped over his scarlet hair. "And yet, you set one toe onto this street and everyone's happy to see you. Why is that, do you think?"

"I'm unbelievably invested in not getting banned," Avra said seriously.

Cat led him out to the foyer and waved at Zoris. "Just out for a walk, back in a bit." He took Avra's elbow in a proprietary sort of way and opened the parasol over both of them. It was in the Imakami style, delicate bamboo and silk dyed deep blue and painted in a pattern of carp and flowers around the edges. "You *are* unbelievably invested in not getting banned. When did I meet you, seven or eight years ago? And for all that time, you have been unfailingly polite. You remember practically everyone's name, you make yourself amusing, and you've never assumed that any of us wish to be friends with you outside of professional engagements. Comparing it against what the rest of the town says about you, I find it mystifying." Cat shot him a look out of the corner of his eye. "Would you like to be friends, Avra?"

Avra's poor frayed nerves jangled in alarm. "Ah. Uh. With you? Or . . . ?"

Cat laughed brightly. It was gorgeous, and several people turned their heads to look. "Like a teenage boy getting asked out on his first date, I swear. Avra! It's just *friends.*"

He gave a small *reeeee* of distress, which made Cat smile inquisitively. Avra squirmed and blurted, "I'm not sure what friends would entail and I'm scared to guess in case I get it wrong."

"Just the usual sorts of things friends do. Going to bars to help each other flirt with cute strangers, getting drunk and going down to the beach to throw rocks in the water and talk about things that matter to us . . ." Cat glanced at him, frowned, and drew him into the next alley, away from the crowd. "Perhaps this isn't a good topic to discuss today—you did mention your nerves were already frayed."

Avra clawed for a jovial, lighthearted tone, though he'd crammed himself back against the wall like Cat was some kind of spooky dentist trying to steal his teeth. "Wow, what a nice alley this is! Feel right at home in an alley. With the possums. Waiting for someone to kick rocks at me."

Cat gave him another of those terrifying looks. "You're hyperventilating." Avra gave another piteous *reeeeee* and looked around for a rubbish heap or a pile of rotting crates he could hide in. "Right, I'm going to count that as a watchword. Would it put you at ease if this were a business engagement instead?" Avra nodded vigorously. "Good. I'll trade you a kiss and my professional time for one of those jars of *deliciously* stolen jam in your bag, then."

Avra scrambled for his little rucksack. "I have rose-petal jam, pine jam, apricot jam, spiced apple jam, and cherries in syrup—which would you like?"

"The rose-petal jam sounds nice." Avra handed him one. Cat leaned forward and kissed him, very gently, on the cheek, then again on the corner of his mouth. "There. Better?"

"Ever considered a career in the Ministry of Intelligence?" he said with a weak laugh. "You'd be a good spy. Sharp eyes. Adaptable. Quick on your feet."

"They couldn't pay me what I'm worth," Cat said, grinning.

Avra laughed, somewhat less weakly. "That's true. Stolen wine and stolen jam."

"Lavish riches. I shall be the envy of the entire street. I might not even eat it—I might just keep it in my room and invite people round to admire it. 'Stolen from the ambassador, you know. Avra Helvaçi is an *investment* of a client,' I'll say."

Avra stopped trying to fuse with the wall and rallied the remaining tatters of his nerves. "I have a stolen salami in my bag too."

"*Stolen meat,*" Cat said rapturously. "Stolen meat that I could make dick jokes about to all my colleagues!"

Avra relaxed further and slowly scraped himself off the wall. Good old Cat. "You can have it instead of the jam, if you want."

"Oh, but I think I'd have to *earn* that one. It would be worth far more than just a kiss and a chat," Cat said with a silky, meaningful smile. "And I like my jam. It's pretty." He cocked his head and *looked* at Avra again. "Feeling better?"

"Always makes me feel better when you flirt with me, Cat."

"Good." But Cat kept his head tilted, kept *looking*.

Avra kicked the ground. "Oh, just say it. Stop being *spooky.*"

"I think you are an interesting person, Avra. I enjoy talking to you. I think you're very funny. I have books I want to recommend to you. I have never once felt, even for a split second, that you saw me as anything less than a real person with my own inner life. Those are the reasons I would like to do things with you as friends. And," Cat added firmly, "after *eight years* of knowing you and every so often having the honor of being entrusted quite profoundly with caring for you for an hour or two, I feel confident in saying that I would not simply withdraw my friendship on a whim."

Avra rubbed his face with his hands. "To be fair, you haven't seen how irritating I can be."

"Friends irritate each other from time to time." Cat darted in and gave him another peck on the cheek with a grin. "That's your tip. I've purchased your services as a jam thief, so I'm allowed to give you tips if I feel like it."

Avra squinted at him. "So this is still a professional transaction, right?"

"Yes, of course!" Cat said, making his eyes very big and innocent as he took Avra's elbow and led him out of the alley. "I haven't the foggiest idea what else this would be. How are things with your captain? Or the gorgeous monk who I hear is tormenting you?"

"Okay, *spooky,* how do you know that? How do you just know those things? Fuck's sake."

"Zoris mentioned it when he came in." Cat smiled smugly to himself and waved at someone across the street as they continued down to the Green Hotel.

"My captain is fine. Other than not having any money. The gorgeous monk is appalling. He insists on having shoulders right in front of me, and one time he pulled my hair and whispered in my ear, and then refused to let me swallow his dick like a python. Teveri says he is toying with us."

"Oh, *us,* is it? He must be a canny one, knowing the two of you have to be adopted as a pair."

"Teveri says," Avra said loudly, choosing to ignore this comment, "that they are not going to waste their time on a man who will do nothing but toy with them, and neither should I."

"Fascinating. Do keep me up to date on the gossip as things develop—or fail to develop."

"Nothing is going to develop. He has an oath of celibacy. He reminds me about this every five minutes, and then he contrives some reason to take his shirt off, or wear very snug pants, or draw my attention to his shoulders. It's unfair and ungentlemanly behavior, Cat."

"Is it," said Cat, laughing.

"I'll introduce you at the cake competition," Avra muttered. "You should ask him what 'six and fifty-two' means. Ask him this immediately. I will say, 'Cat, this is Brother Julian, the worst person in the world,' and you'll say—"

"'Such a pleasure to meet you, Brother Julian. I've heard ever so much about you. I'm supposed to ask about six and fifty-two?'—Oh. *Oh.* My goodness, who in the world is *that*?"

They had just rounded the corner onto the avenue dominated by the Green Hotel. Julian was standing near the front door with his back to them, talking to those two Chants—Red and his spooky friend with the puppet-Red on their hand.

"That's Brother Julian." Avra sighed. "You see now the source of my trials and woes. And tribulations. And sufferings. And torments."

"My *goodness.* So I do. Oh, Avra, you poor thing."

That was a very *friends* sort of thing to say. Avra was undecided between squeezing Cat's arm or climbing into the nearest drainpipe and wailing for the rest of the night. But where there were two options, there was almost always a third, so he yelled, "*Julian.*"

Julian glanced over his shoulder, smiling, and gestured: *One moment.* He turned back to the Chants, obviously excusing himself from conversation.

Cat gripped Avra's arm reflexively, then leaned toward him and half laughed. "Oh, he could get it for free *whenever* he wants." Then, three-quarters laughing, he added, "As long as 'whenever' is on my day off or after I finish work."

Red clapped Julian on the shoulder with a friendly grin, and he and the Puppeteer went inside. Julian waited by the door as Cat and Avra approached—he looked like a sun god, standing there in the light like that with his long, *long* hair braided and shining like a coronet of glory, bare of that grey wrapping he'd kept the queue bound into. He had the sort of blond complexion that went gold, rather than burning easily, but he must have spent a great deal of the day walking outside—even with his resistance to sunburn, his nose and cheeks were a little pink.

A very rude man, Avra decided as they came up to him. "You should wear a paper bag over your head. Julian, this is my—my friend Cat." Cat squeezed his arm again and gave him a brilliant smile. "Cat is the worst person alive besides you." Cat's brilliant smile shattered into an equally brilliant laugh. "He has no sympathy for what a hard day I am having, and what a hard day I had yesterday, and the day before."

"None whatsoever," said Cat, turning his brilliant smile on Julian and extending his hand. "Hello, Julian. I've heard *ever so much* about you. I'm supposed to ask you the significance of 'six and fifty-two'?"

Julian shook Cat's hand, still smiling easily. "I'd explain, but I think most people would find it shocking without fair warning—it's about sex, you see."

"Cat works on the Street of Flowers. You cannot shock him."

"This is true," Cat said, twinkling at Julian and twirling a lock of scarlet hair around his finger.

Julian absolutely noticed the hair-twirling, and Avra noticed that he noticed. He briefly considered twirling his own hair around his finger to see if it would get him any further than alluring lounging had. He decided against it, firstly because Teveri would be *so proud of him* (theoretically—or at least they wouldn't sigh and roll their eyes, which was substantially the same thing), and secondly because if anyone could lure Julian back into his slutty phase, it was probably Cat. He was a lot prettier than Avra and Teveri, for one thing. Nicer hair. Less knobbly joints. Bathed regularly.

Smelled like perfume. Owned a parasol, which he was now also twirling. Possessed the poise and elegant restraint to make both hair-twirling and parasol-twirling look casually whimsical rather than performative.

Julian just smiled and smiled and smiled, as if he were perfectly happy to be standing there with his oath of celibacy while someone as pretty as Cat twirled their hair and parasol at him. "The Street of Flowers is where the pleasure-houses are, I've gathered?"

"That's right," said Cat sunnily. "Avra's very popular there, you know. So, six and fifty-two?"

"It regards an anecdote from, to use Avra's own phrasing, my slutty past. Six is the number of people I have had in bed at once; fifty-two is the number of people I've gotten off in one night."

"And then he took an oath of *celibacy*," Avra hissed to Cat, who had entirely paused his hair-and-parasol-twirling. "I cry every time I think about it."

"That takes some dedication, good sir." Cat had dropped the slightly flirtatious inflection in his voice. "If you don't mind my professional curiosity . . . Were you able to speak or grip a pen afterward?"

Julian grinned. "Oh, only whispering for two days, and my handwriting was atrocious for a week."

Cat laughed. "Well, all glory has a cost." He glanced up at the sky. "Goodness, it's hot even in the shade, isn't it? I'm sweating like a pig already—I should get back to the house and freshen up before my client." He gave Julian a friendly smile and a nod. "Pleasure to meet you, Julian, I hope to see you at the cake competition tomorrow." He squeezed Avra's arm and gave him a much more sultry look from under his soot-blackened lashes. "Could I have a moment alone to say goodbye to my *darling friend*?"

"Of course—I was just headed upstairs," Julian said. "A pleasure to meet you as well, Master Cat."

Julian went inside; Cat pulled Avra a few steps down the street and leaned in close. "I speak first as a friend: That man has a *crush* on you."

Avra screeched under his breath and flailed every limb except the one Cat was holding. "No, he doesn't."

"He absolutely does. He is a *breath* away from shoving his tongue down your throat. He thinks Avra Helvaçi is a gift of the gods. He doesn't just want to fuck you through the mattress, he wants to *hold your hand in the moonlight.*"

Avra chose not to mention the fact that Julian *had already* held his hand in the moonlight. Well, the starlight. Actually, there hadn't been much light of any kind when they were tromping through the jungle to find Tev. "Don't be silly, Cat, he's a walking tragedy sent to break my heart with the thought of a slutty past cut down in its prime and forced to take an oath of celibacy."

Cat put a hand to his chest as if to steady his heart, his eyes closed in agony. "Write a song about that, Avra. Fifty-two is the kind of number that should be sung about for a hundred years."

"I'm a poet, Cat, I know my job."

"Good boy. He definitely has a crush on you, though, I saw the way he smiled when he turned around. *Secondly,*" Cat said before Avra could object. "Now I'm speaking partly as a friend and partly as a professional. I don't hold with this hesitating nonsense that he's doing."

"Pussyfooting," Avra said. "You see, because your name is Cat and also it's a sex joke."

"Not your best work, but I'll take it. Listen, I agree with that captain of yours—he shouldn't be toying with you. He should stop doing that, make a fucking decision about whether or not he's going to keep his oath or not, *tell you* what his decision is, and then either back off and stop visiting torments and suffering upon you, or recommence with *flirting.* Please note that I am drawing a fine distinction between flirting and toying. The difference is consent."

"I have definitely been consenting to the toying, though. I am very enthusiastic about the toying. But also, *what does it mean*?"

"Quite," Cat said crisply. "What *does* it mean? A very incisive question, Avra, and one that you are absolutely correct in asking. I too am deeply curious. What does it mean that he is doing this, and why is he making it your problem? Speaking as one man to another: *Ugh. Men.*"

"You're so right. Yes. Correct."

"Thirdly, I am now speaking purely as a professional." He leaned in closer. "I have a business proposal for you. I really want that stolen salami in your bag. I want to have a little museum of things stolen from the ambassador's house, and I want to charge people money to come in and look at them. Are you by any chance interested in bartering for it?"

Avra opened the flap of his little rucksack and rummaged through it, clinking jars of jam and olives and cherries. "Sure, but it's quite a small salami."

"That's fine. My museum guests can use it as a prop to make mean jokes about how small the ambassador's cock is. Here is what I am offering in return—oh my, that is a small salami, isn't it, wonderful—if you can contrive to bring Julian to the Street of Flowers, then I'll contrive to let everyone know that they should absolutely *gush* over you in front of him. We'll all fawn over you and treat you even more like our special pet, but I will tell everyone that *he* should be ignored as much as possible. We'll take you into one of the parlors for drinks, and I will drape myself on you and flirt with you like you're some fancy Araşti tourist with bottomless pockets, and then I will get on my knees and look up at you through my eyelashes, and I will suck on you slowly and luxuriously and right in front of him. I will of course signal my intentions quite openly so that he has time to excuse himself and leave the room if he doesn't want to watch, but I have a hunch that he will stay to see you be a very good boy for me. By the time I'm done with you, he will be terribly jealous and horny, and then he will be yours."

"Hmgknnn," said Avra.

"This will be your delicious revenge for all the toying and torments he has visited upon you. Does that sound like a fair trade for the stolen salami from the ambassador's house?"

"What if. What if he doesn't want to come?"

"Oh, he'll want to come," Cat said in ominous tones.

"*Hmghkgn.* I meant what if he doesn't want to go to the Street of Flowers with me?"

"Then I'll return the salami or we can renegotiate for something else." Cat paused. "Actually, if you'd like to continue supplying me with things stolen from the ambassador's house for my museum—"

"Where did this museum idea come from?"

"Always wise to invest for the future, don't you think? I'm turning thirty next year, you know, and these knees aren't always going to be so good as they are now. And while I do like my job, it makes navigating my personal relationships and sex life a bit tedious. I would imagine it is the same for many other professions—I deal with dicks all day, and then on my days off, I often want to put my feet up and not deal with any more dicks, even if they're attached to people I love. Which is a shame, because those are the dicks I like best."

"Ah," said Avra sagely, handing the remarkably small salami to Cat. "The dangers of making one's hobby into a career."

"Indeed," Cat said, with that lovely, brilliant smile and a laugh twinkling in his eyes. "Now, taking my professional mask off again—you see the absurd things I have to do?—would you like a hug before I go, as a friend?"

22

38. The Broken Quill

Obstacles, inconveniences, impatience, recklessness. Lines of communication have been broken or are endangered. Frustration will ruin delicate things. If you feel that you have broken several quills in a row, take a step back and recenter yourself.

(Reversed: Necessary information is confessed or revealed, to great relief. This is a time to strive for particular clarity in your dealings—say what you mean, and ensure that you fully understand what is being said to you, even if it seems perfectly clear at first glance.)

Avra detoured to the hotel's kitchen to beg for a tray or a large plate and trudged upstairs. The two suites Black Garda had lent them took up half of the top floor of the hotel. On the door of one, the crew had hung a sign that read QUIET PLEASE! THIS ROOM IS FOR SLEEPING ONLY (with a doodle of a bed and an angry shushing face for those of the crew who could not read), so Avra let himself into the other suite.

Julian was being long and stunning on the divan between the two tall windows, his feet propped up on the windowsill of one with light from the other falling on his miles of golden hair and the pages of the book he was reading.

Avra valiantly attempted to ignore this, set the tray on the table, and began unpacking things from his little rucksack. "Everyone still at Black Garda's?"

"As far as I know," Julian said, turning the page. "She deemed me too new to trust with whatever they were discussing, so I went for a walk and got to know the town. Found all sorts of interesting things, including a *local newspaper.*"

"Town full of outlaws and rebels. Of course we have a newspaper." *We.* Avra paused over that word and felt a chill up his spine. It had always been *they* before.

Oh, he really wasn't going back to Araşt, was he? That made it official. *We.*

"They need a proofreader, frankly. Or a better typesetter," Julian was saying. "Though I was pleasantly surprised at the quality of some of the philosophical rants. I would have bought one, but I spent all my money at the used bookshop."

"You could have offered to stand in the shop for an hour and be decorative to lure in custom, and they would have given you a paper in payment." Julian smiled at this and turned another page. "What are you reading?"

"Pornography."

Avra glared at him and began viciously chopping the chunk of stolen ambassadorial prosciutto into smaller chunks with his tiny knife.

Julian apparently did not notice. Avra glared harder and contemplated the lack of wardrobes in the room that he could climb on and cause problems.

"You know," he said loudly, in lieu of wardrobes. "Cat says—you remember Cat? My *very dear friend* Cat, with the pretty red hair? Cat is the nicest person I've ever met in my life. Cat gave me a *hug,* you know. Mhm! Just down there. After you left." This did not seem to strike jealousy into Julian's heart. "Cat said," Avra said again, louder, "that you ought to stop toying with me."

Julian looked over in surprise.

Avra hacked cubes from the prosciutto as ostentatiously as possible. Possibly he should have wiped off his tiny knife before he'd started, since he used it for trimming his finger- and toenails. Too late now. "He says even if I am consenting to the things you do as part of the torments, I am not consenting to the—the *torment* of the torments." He waved his tiny knife vaguely toward Julian and kept his attention fixed on the chopping. "You know what I mean. So you should not make that my problem. Teveri also thinks so. Teveri is being toyed with vicariously through *me* being toyed with, and they don't like it and they said they will not waste their time on a man who is toying with them, and Teveri's very smart and—and good at personal boundaries. Maybe too good at personal boundaries. Maybe sometimes a little unhealthily fixated on their personal boundaries to the point that their boundaries and their *guard* kind of become the same thing, and then they don't let their guard down so that anybody can come in. Tev knows all about personal boundaries. Also Cat, because Cat's a professional expert in personal boundaries. So!"

Julian didn't speak for several moments. "I'm sorry," he said. "I'll stop. I didn't know that you . . . No, that's the wrong phrasing—I appreciate that you said something. Thank you for letting me know."

"Okay," said Avra, stabbing off the wax seal from one of the olive jars. He fished out most of the olives onto the tray with his fingers, set the jar aside with an angry thump, and did the same with his other assorted spoils of theft.

Julian sat up, resting his elbows on his knees and turning the book over in his hands. "It's not actually pornography," he said. "I intended to invite you to joke with me, because I like joking with you, but I misread—"

"I said okay," said Avra.

"You still seem upset. Would you like to talk about it, or about something else? You could tell me about your friend Cat. Or . . . I'm sorry, I should have asked how your visit to the ambassador went. That was rude of me."

Avra squinted suspiciously at him over the jar of cherries in syrup, but Julian didn't seem offended at all, nor like he was about to throw Avra out of the suite, which meant this was some new type of reaction that Avra was unfamiliar with. "Bad," he said. "It went bad."

"Do you want to talk about that?"

Avra opened his mouth to reply, and froze.

Baltakan had a truthwitch. Baltakan wanted the truthwitch to question Julian. Baltakan might ask Avra, possibly in front of the truthwitch, some tricky question like, "And you didn't tell Julian anything about this, right?"

"I can't say anything about it until Teveri or someone gets back," Avra said. He contemplated the wedge of cheese. "Is cheese supposed to be sliced into bits? I'm making a charcuterie board for Tev."

"I don't know enough about cheese to say."

Avra shrugged and hacked at the cheese.

"Cat seemed like a lovely sort of person. How long have you been friends?"

"Half an hour. Also eight years." Avra shot another glance at Julian. "Cat said I should bring you to the Street of Flowers so you could watch everyone petting and doting on me and him sucking me off."

Julian visibly ran through several responses, then frowned. "I'm confused. This is the sort of conversational topic that led me to believe that teasing you back was part of the game."

"*I'm* not teasing," Avra said. "*I'm* telling you sincerely that you're invited to come watch Cat suck me off. *I'm* not holding it above your head and then smirking like 'Tee hee, but actually I didn't mean it, I was just saying it to get under your skin.' And when I offer you sincere invitations, *you* don't go away feeling like you are going insane because you don't know what I think or what my angle is, do you!"

"No, I don't." Julian dropped his eyes to the book in his hands.

"Cat thinks you are going to break your oath," Avra said airily, arranging some of the almonds in an intricate scalloped row along the edge of the charcuterie board to keep the loose jam he'd fingered out of the jar from spilling off the edge. "I told him that was silly. Cat says you should stop toying with me until you figure out whether you're going to or not. He said you should tell me clearly what you decide so that I am not wracked with trials and suffering and woe and torments. Also Teveri. Teveri is wracked with so many trials and sufferings. And torments. And suchlike. More than me, probably."

"Cat is a very wise man," Julian said quietly.

"*Are* you going to break your oath?"

There was a beat of silence. Avra froze.

"I don't know," said Julian.

Avra threw his tiny knife on the floor. "This is not my problem!" he said loudly. "I am not dealing with this! I am not going to even begin coping with this! I am not devoting any of my time and energy to this! Tev is going to be so proud of me. Don't let anyone touch the charcuterie, I stole it from the ambassador." Avra snatched his little rucksack off the floor and stormed over to one of the doors to the other rooms of the suite and flung it open. "Dammit," he announced, then went to another door to another room. "Where are the fucking wardrobes in this place!" He went to a third door, which was the larger bedroom of the suite. He already knew that it didn't contain any wardrobes, but it did have a massive four-poster bed draped with white curtains.

He attempted to slam the door behind him, but the latch was shoddy like everything else on this island, and the door bounced partway back open. He stuffed himself beneath the bed, pulled his little rucksack in after him, and yelled out, "Tell Teveri where I am when they get back."

"Do you want me to finish arranging your charcuterie board?" Julian called tentatively.

"*I said don't touch it,*" Avra snarled.

The front door opened. There was another conspicuous silence.

"I heard yelling," said Teveri. "And you look guilty as hell, Julian. What have you done to Avra?"

"Other than apologizing for toying with him, I'm not precisely sure," said Julian. "He's under the bed."

"TEVERI," Avra screeched. "*Teveri, he's doing it again.*"

Teveri's boots came into view through the open door. They paused by the table. "What's all this?"

"I made you a charcuterie board," Avra said. "With things I stole from the ambassador."

Teveri pushed the door open, paused again. "Why is the doorknob sticky?"

"Avra didn't wipe the jam off his hands," Julian said. Teveri tsked, strode into the bedroom, knelt beside the bed, flung up the end of the quilt, and peered beneath.

Avra had scrunched himself into the far back corner against the wall. "Hello. I missed you. I had a bad day. I hope your day was all right. Do you like charcuterie? It's cheese and fancy meat and olives and loose jam. Extra delicious on account of being stolen from the ambassador."

"Why are you hiding under the bed?"

"Because Julian is visiting torments and woe upon me. I saw Cat today. I owed him a bottle of wine, so I gave him one that I—"

"Stole from the ambassador's house. I'm sure he liked that."

"He did like it. We bartered a jar of stolen jam for a little bit of kissing in the alley, also. No possums in the alley, just sadness and bittersweet tragedy. Also, stolen salami in exchange for Cat possibly sucking me off in front of Julian, but I'm mad at Julian, so Cat will have to think of something else. He's starting a museum of objects and foodstuffs stolen from the ambassador's house, you see."

Teveri scowled. "Julian's toying with you again?"

"You were right, Tev," Avra said, scrunching farther into the corner. "I will not stand to be flirted with either. I am following your good example. I am growing as a person. I am becoming pious, a little bit. Not Julian's kind of pious. Araşti pious, about the Lord of Trials sending us tests because it builds character. I am building so much character. I am developing a sense of personal dignity, Tev."

"You are hiding under the bed and chattering."

"It's a work in progress. I told Julian to stop personally victimizing me, and he said sorry, but then he said that he *doesn't know* whether he's going to break his oath. So I collected my dignity and climbed entirely under the bed and yelled at him not to let anyone touch the charcuterie. That was the yelling you heard."

"I see."

"Are you proud of me? I did a personal boundary. I said that it was none of my business and that I wanted no part in it. I extremely want a part in it, but I have decided that I am having not even one part in it anymore. I am too old to be having any part in it. Cat is the smartest person in the whole world. Do you want to come to the Street of Flowers and watch Cat suck me off? I think you deserve it more than Julian does."

"I'll consider it," said Teveri.

"Wait, what, really?"

"I will give it consideration."

"Wow," said Avra and sat with that for several marveling seconds. "You must have had a really good tea party with Black Garda."

"I did. Would you like to come out and explain your char-whatsits?"

"Oh. You . . . want to eat it?"

"I'm interested in whether being stolen from the Araşti ambassador does in fact make things more delicious."

"I think it probably does."

"I think so too. Come on, get out."

Avra beamed, unscrunched himself from the corner, and rolled out. "Tell him not to make eye contact with me. Tell him not to look at me or breathe in my direction."

"Julian," Teveri shouted. "Avra doesn't want you to look at him or breathe in his direction."

"Thank you, Teveri," Avra whispered adoringly. "You should never leave me alone with him. He is a rake. He is a cad. Cat was going to try to make him jealous as a favor to me so that he would snap and make a decision, but I have decided I don't care for that. I have decided that I am too dignified for that. You and I can go play with Cat together instead. You like Cat, don't you?"

"Yes, I do."

"Cat is going to have a museum of things stolen from the ambassador's house."

"So you said."

"Did I? What do you think of that?"

"It's genius." Teveri pulled him to his feet and led him out to the main room. "Do I do anything with the char-whatsits besides eat it?"

"Nope," said Avra, showily pulling out Teveri's chair for them. He sat beside them and dragged the board closer. "This is fancy ham. This is fancy cheese. This is some loose jam. These are fancy almonds and olives."

"Is Julian allowed to have charcuterie or is it just for me?"

"It is a gift for you. You can do with it whatever you like. You can eat it all yourself or you can share it with nearby rakes."

Teveri delicately picked up an olive and regarded it as if it were a murderer on trial for killing seventeen people. "Julian."

"Yes, Captain?"

Avra put his hands over his ears. "I don't want to hear him speak. I can't go through this right now. I have dealt with enough things today."

Teveri and Julian must have exchanged a few words, because Julian came to the table, took three cubes of prosciutto, two olives, and a slice of cheese, and retreated to the couch. Teveri tapped Avra's shoulder.

He lowered his hands. "Done?"

"Yes." Teveri ate the olive. "Hm."

"Is it more delicious because it's stolen?"

Teveri chewed in contemplation. "My tongue only tastes olive. But there is more *spiritual* flavor to it." They took a piece of cheese.

"Good flavor?" Avra asked breathlessly. "You like the flavor?"

Teveri nodded casually, as if that wasn't the nicest thing they had said to him in fifteen years. Avra puffed up and barely averted the impulse to give Julian a smug, triumphant look. Teveri licked olive oil off their fingers, which immediately arrested Avra's attention. "Ask me what Black Garda offered."

"What did she offer?"

Was Teveri smiling? Teveri was nearly smiling. "She and Captain Stone had a falling-out a few days ago, and she fired him and his crew."

Avra experienced a split second of confusion, then his brain made lightning-fast connections between three to five separate things. He gasped, clutching at the table so violently that several olives rolled off the charcuterie board. *"She's hiring us for the cake competition!"* he screeched.

"Yes." Teveri smugly ate one of the stray olives.

Avra screeched again. "Aaaaa! Aaa! Tev! Aaaaa!"

"She said she thought I was a reckless lunatic with a thirst for blood," Teveri said with great relish. "And on top of the money for our services, she said she'd pay for the taxidermist, as a thank-you present for the dogs and the collars. Oskar has already taken them out to get to work."

"And us! Guarding Mistress Navya's *cake*!" Avra said rapturously. "Tev!! Did she already pay you some?"

"Markefa has it."

"We should get you a hat."

"Only if we can find one that will go with my coat." Teveri sniffed, but they seemed pleased. "How was Ambassador Fuckface?"

"Oh," said Avra. "Ah. Yes. Well. There is a small problem. Tiny, really." Teveri stopped smugly eating olives and narrowed their eyes into the middle distance. "I will whisper it in your ear and then if it happens that you want to repeat it out loud . . . coincidentally within earshot of Julian . . . that would be fine with me. That's not my business either. I can't control you or your actions."

"All right," said Teveri warily.

Avra cupped his hands around their ear and whispered, "Baltakan has a truthwitch. He had her interrogate me."

"Fuck." Teveri slammed a fist on the table. "You got fucking lucky again, didn't you."

Avra nodded vigorously and continued whispering into Tev's

ear. "She asked if I would stand to profit from anyone selling the Shipbuilder's Guild secret."

"And you cheerfully said no, because you lost your fucking stake to Heirani. Fucking *gods. Avra.*"

"We can't prove that was luck," Avra said. "We really can't prove anything."

Teveri dropped their head into one hand. "What else?"

Avra leaned in close again. "Baltakan wants to have the truthwitch interrogate Julian at the cake competition tomorrow."

"*Dammit,*" Teveri snarled, slamming their fist onto the table again. "How are we supposed to keep the fucking cake safe if you're off pretending to be a loyal Araşti citizen instead of standing right next to it and psychically smearing your luck all over it like the jam on every goddamn surface in this room?"

"Tell Julian!" Avra hissed.

Teveri snarled again. "Julian, the ambassador has a *fucking* truthwitch and he's going to *fucking* interrogate you tomorrow."

"Oh," said Julian blankly. "I could just not go? I could hide on the ship."

Avra whispered urgently, "He can't just not go, Baltakan specifically asked me to bring him! He's really paranoid, he wants to 'exhaust every avenue of inquiry.' Direct quote."

"So it's better for Julian to show up and try to outwit the truthwitch so Ambassador Fuckface stops thinking that we're a *potential* to chase."

"Yes," said Avra.

"*Fuck,*" Teveri spat.

Julian cleared his throat. "Captain, will you ask Avra if he's speaking to me so that I can ask a few questions about truthwitches?"

"Absolutely not, he's sitting right there."

"Tev, tell Julian—"

"No." Teveri took a cube of prosciutto.

"Tell Julian that the truthwitch might ask me if I told him anything."

"He can hear you."

"Tell Avra that I don't think it's likely the truthwitch will ask about whether he explained how truthwitches work."

"This is stupid."

"Tell Julian that he can ask you the question, and then I'll tell you the answer, and then you can tell him."

"That seems reasonable," said Julian. "Teveri, would you ask Avra—"

"I'm in hell."

23

67. The Hearth

Warmth and hospitality; *stay and be welcome*; nourishment and good company, a sense of belonging and family. Know who you belong to, and who belongs to you. Huddle close and hold fast.

(Reversed: Being shut out in the cold, rejection, public ridicule, a cast-out. Something or someone does not belong. Fill all the cracks in the walls before the winter wind sucks out the warmth.)

Dawn came early—the day of the cake competition was at hand.

Avra barely slept. He'd meekly dragged in a few pillows from the divan and made a little nest for himself against the wall in the larger bedroom, and was greatly relieved when Teveri didn't offer a word of objection.

"Remember what we talked about," Cat had whispered in his ear just before he drew back from the hug.

"Which part?" Avra had replied.

Cat had booped him on the nose with one fingertip and grinned brilliantly. "Oh, all the things we didn't say out loud."

Before dawn, Teveri dragged themself out of bed and everyone bestirred themselves. Six or seven of the crew had slept on the floor in the main room; another five in the second bedroom; another dozen in the other suite.

The sky outside the windows was deep, predawn blue; the room still thick with shadows as Teveri dressed and unpicked the strips of cloth that they'd used the night before to tie up their damp hair so it would dry into fancy ringlets. They had their very best coat today: This one had a high collar and skirts of a more practical length than the cream-and-red one from the day before, and the armscye was tailored comfortably enough that they had nearly their full range of motion. Most significant of all was the silver embroidery down the front, around the collar and bottom hem, and even up the vents in the back of the skirt that allowed for them to wear a sword.

It would never tarnish or fade, that embroidery.

The *Nightingale* had carried spools of silver thread to repair its sails if ever, somehow, they were torn. The story was that the spools had been more of a symbolic gift than a practical one from whoever had made those sails, because they had *never* torn. Not once in Xing Fe Hua's lifetime, and not once since he had died.

Teveri's first captain, Safiya Merovech, had possessed one of the spools, which she'd left to Tev in her will. She'd died the year after Avra had won the mainsail from Captain Luchenko, he remembered drowsily. Won it, and then wondered what in the *world* he was supposed to do with it, and then turned to the new young captain he'd been having an entanglement with, and asked if they'd mind if he put it on their spooky haunted ship. Gods, but they'd both been young in those days—twenty-one, twenty-two . . . Practically *infants.*

He wondered suddenly, in one of those half-asleep moments of clarity when keeping his brain as tidy and empty as he preferred it to be got tricky to maintain, whether Captain Safiya would have bequeathed her *Nightingale* thread to Tev if they hadn't had the mainsail. People *had* talked about them differently once there was silver on their mast.

"You had that coat made, didn't you?" Avra's sleepy mouth mumbled before his brain could think better of it. "Went to a real tailor, 'stead of stealing it off a boat?"

"Yes."

"Mm. 'S nice. Looks nice on you." Teveri didn't say anything. "You did the embroidery, didn't you? Ages ago." Avra had only seen the coat a few times, and he had not taken much notice of the embroidery before, other than noting that it was expectedly beautiful and unexpectedly skillful.

It was only now in the blue light of predawn that one of those lightning-connections sparked in his brain, and Avra thought, *Huh.*

It looked a little like some of the embroidery on the Puppeteer's sleeves. Tashaz embroidery, then, which made sense. But the Puppeteer's embroidery was repeating patterns, and though Teveri's had elements of repetition here and there—a knife blade of a line, a dot, a curl—Avra couldn't discern any larger-scale patterns in the jumble of dramatic abstract shapes.

He was more awake now, beset by this thought. Some instinct—maybe his own indefatigable curiosity, maybe his training with the Ministry of Intelligence—made him ask softly, "Does your embroidery mean something?"

Tev was brushing their hair out in the small tarnished mirror hung over the ewer and basin. They gave him a sidelong glance, the brush pausing only for a heartbeat. "Yes."

"What is it?"

"A poem. Of a sort."

Avra pushed himself up. "I like poems."

"You like fuck poems."

"Those especially. What's this kind of poem?"

Teveri sighed and sat on the bed to put on their boots. Avra knee-walked over and sat at their feet. Not too close, and he carefully did not touch. Teveri finished their boots and was still for a long minute. "It is a poem that says who I am. That's what people in Tash wear—like the Puppeteer. You can't see anyone's face, so you learn to recognize and read embroidery the way people elsewhere do with features and handwriting." They swallowed. "Usually the patterns are made of symbols that show your alignment to a family, a caste, a profession. Mine is severely atypical. It's mostly calligraphy." They raised their hand to their collar. "This says, 'I am the gravedigger's child, and my body is my own. I name myself runaway.'" They ran their fingertips down the right front panel. "This says, 'I reject Qarat'ash, and moreover I call her a bitch and a' . . . a cruel word, in Tashaz. It usually means someone of approximately Cat's profession, but the cult of Qarat'ash has a *deeply* fraught relationship with the human body. It considers gravediggers, undertakers, physicians, midwives, and tailors to be filthy because they deal with the body by necessity; it considers courtesans filthy because they deal with the body by choice. I used the cruel word because it drags the prophet Qarat'ash down to *my* level, and there is no other word in Tashaz that comes close." They touched their fingers to a collection of swoops and slashing lines of embroidery. "That word, and the word *her.* Recognition and acknowledgment of the prophet's physical sex is heresy, and of anyone else's, deeply immoral. Put together, those two filthy words are sacrilege on a scale that in Tash would get me killed immediately. No one would face trial—all they'd have to do is show the guards my coat. They'd probably desecrate my body after that, as well. Tear it apart, tread it into the dust, trample it with horses and camels. Whatever remained would be left out for the jackals." Avra did not dare say anything. He barely dared to move, or breathe. Tev touched the left side of their coat. "This says, 'I am the runaway of the gravediggers' clan; though I reject the prophet, I do not reject my homeland, for the earth and air and water nourished my body, and my body is my own, and thus Tash is inalienably my own.' In juxtaposition with the opposite side, this is another layer of insult, and the overtones with which it is presented are those of an unassailable form of literary argument. If I am rejecting the cult, they would like me to reject everything. Sever myself entirely from Tash. Then they could wash themselves clean of me." Teveri smiled, a tight, mean thing. Avra repressed a swoon. "But this means I win, because they cannot. Not in any way that matters."

"Fuck yeah, they can't," Avra whispered enthusiastically. "What does the rest say?"

Teveri lifted the hem. "All of this is the litany of my identity. No one gets these but royalty, the highest priests, and Qarat'ash. The more important you are, the longer it is, and I made mine longer than that of the prophet herself." They stood and turned to indicate the vent running up the back of the coat's skirt from the hem. "This just says, 'Priests of Qarat'ash can eat my shit and kiss my ass.'"

Avra nodded solemnly. "Breaking it up with a compliment, I see."

Teveri snorted and rolled their eyes. "I was running out of creative things to say by that point. And since it goes right up to my ass, it felt like that was another good poetic juxtaposition."

Avra looked over it, his eyes tracing the glimmering lines of silver against the deep black of the fabric. "May I touch?"

Teveri gazed at him for a long moment, then warily said, "All right."

Avra brushed his fingertips over part of the hem—the *litany of identity*. The silver threads were as cool to the touch as starlight; the light wool fabric was warm and smooth. It was a poem to spit in the face of people who deserved it, sewn in threads that anyone in Scuttle Cove would recognize with outrage—or at minimum, with hugely taken-aback astonishment at the casual audacity of wearing *Nightingale* relics as personal adornment.

O, *incandescent* Teveri!

He raised the hem to his lips and kissed the litany, and placed it carefully back where it hung rather than letting it drop. "I like this poem," he said.

He glanced up at Teveri and found them looking down at him in profound consternation. They turned away immediately, clearing their throat. "Get up, get dressed."

A few minutes later, Avra had put on real pants—and a clean shirt, *and* combed his hair and tied it back—and was just about to go out into the main room when Teveri caught his arm, then caught his face, then *kissed* him.

On any other day, Avra might have squawked with surprise, or swooned (he still did swoon a bit, frankly), or demanded to know whether Teveri had been possessed by demons.

But it was cake competition day, and the cake competition was a different beast.

Teveri was gripping both his arms very hard. "Look after Julian," they muttered. "If he gets himself stabbed, we'll have to find another scholar. Fucking inconvenient."

"Yeah. Better to just look after the one we've got."

"It's just that he's already partway through cracking the secret."

"Huge headache to find someone else. Let's not do that." Avra found himself gripping their arms just as hard. They stood there in the dawn blue, and it was *so* quiet, even with the rustling and the low noises of people moving about in the main room. "Look after Tev for me too, eh?"

"I will not stand to be flirted with," Avra said to Julian as they all trooped down the stairs in a mass with Teveri at their head. The rest of the crew was in their festival best (except for Julian, who was in his monk's robes, and Avra, who only owned one and a half pairs of pants and three kaftans at the moment), but no one was as glorious as the captain.

"I understand," Julian said. He didn't even have that twinkle of shared laughter in his eyes.

"Are you mad at me?"

"No."

"You look like you're mad at me."

"I'm not mad at you."

"You're not smiling at me."

"I smiled at you when I said good morning five minutes ago, and you made a face and hid behind Teveri."

Avra had done that. "Well, you looked too pretty, and I remembered your tragic past and wanted to cry. Smile less pretty."

"How's this?" said Julian, baring most of his teeth and scrunching up the rest of his face. It was hideous.

"Yes, that's better, do that. Teveri! Tev, Julian's only going to smile like this from now on, look."

Teveri, rounding the next landing just below them, glanced up, looked extremely tired, rolled their eyes, and returned their attention to the stairs. "They like it," Avra said. "That's the face that means they're too busy to deal with my bullshit but they don't actively disapprove of whatever antics I'm applying myself to."

"From them, that's basically the same as liking something," Julian agreed.

Avra felt . . . better. A great deal better. Whatever strange energy had been hanging between them had dissipated—and besides that, it *was* cake competition day, and that meant all minor intra-crew squabbles had to be set aside. "Teveri told me to look after you today, which I would have already done, because you don't know about the cake competition and that's a good way to get physically injured or killed."

Julian raised his eyebrows. "Apparently I know far less about this cake competition than I was assuming."

"Correct," said Avra severely. "Stick close to me and I will explain."

The cake competition had a long and storied history stretching back to the days when even Xing Fe Hua had been but a lowly cabin boy.

It had begun much the same as any cake competition.

"But then," Avra said dramatically as they made their way through town toward Black Garda's house, "then came the year of the Great Seagull War. Those bastards," Avra said, pointing up to a seagull on the roof of a building. He bent, picked up a rock, and hurled it. The rock fell far short, and the seagull gave him a condescending look far meaner than any of Teveri's. "Better to throw rocks while you can. Projectile weapons are banned at the cake competition."

"Can seagulls go to war?" Julian mused.

"*Yes,*" said Avra and everyone in earshot.

"The Great Seagull War was the fourth or fifth year of the cake competition," Avra said. "The seagulls, being creatures of pure evil and insatiable, ravening greed, had learned that cakes were for eating. The previous year, nearly all the cakes had been decimated before the judges were even picked out of the hat. The year of the Great Seagull War, people saw them gathering in unusual numbers *days* in advance, and on the day of the competition, there were thousands of the fuckers swarming all over, more than there had ever been. So one enterprising soul—"

"Anne the Bastard," chorused several people.

"Yes, I *know*." Avra picked up another few rocks. "Anne the Bastard hired Fishfoot Flanners and the crew of the *Princess*. Her entire cake had been plundered and devoured by flying vermin the year before and she had sworn an oath of vengeance on them. Captain Flanners considered her request a *great* honor, swore himself to her service for the day of the cake competition, and joined her oath of vengeance against the seagulls. His crew brought everything they could think of. Nets. Bows and arrows. A slingshot. There was someone with one of those cool throwing sticks that they have in Kholekhole, the kind that fits a rock on the end and then you *hurl* the rock—a seagull will basically explode if you hit it with one of those. Fishfoot Flanners brought a crossbow and two thousand crossbow bolts."

"That's a lot of crossbow bolts," Julian said solemnly.

"It was a day of glory and terror," Avra declared. Several of the crew had slowed to match pace with them now, murmuring agreements and amens. "Fishfoot Flanners and his crew spread out over the competition grounds and started shooting down seagulls at dawn, well before the cakesmiths arrived with their cakes. According to legend, when the winged devils saw the cakes, they multiplied a hundredfold, and the swarm was so thick in the sky that they blacked out the sun. Fishfoot Flanners was shooting three of the fuckers out of the sky with every bolt he fired. But it made no difference—there were too many seagulls. There were more seagulls than crossbow bolts.

"And then, tragedy struck. In the furor of seagull ravening and seagull death, some of the other cakes were destroyed, not by falling seagull corpses but by rocks and crossbow bolts. And thus, instead of uniting together against the threat from the sky . . ."

"Friend turned against friend," Oskar said, choked up. "A tragedy."

"They thought it was intentional sabotage?" said Julian.

"Some people say that it might have been," Avra said. He was not used to this many people quietly listening to him and agreeing with him. It was rather nice. He could be as dramatic as he wanted, because . . . Well, it was the *cake competition.* High drama and huge stakes were inherent and unavoidable. "A couple of the old families, like the Kavos, tell stories about the crew of the *Princess* aiming for the other cakes as often as they were aiming for the birds. It is true that several projectiles were found in some of the cakes afterward, apparently without seagull viscera. But of course Fishfoot Flanners swore up and down, and held to it until the day he died, that he had only been trying to protect his sworn cakesmith's cake and wreak vengeance on the seagulls on her behalf. The following year, there were fewer seagulls—possibly because of the sheer quantity of them that had been killed by Fishfoot Flanners shooting until he ran out of bolts—but the cakesmiths whose cakes had been spoiled by human interference rather than the depredations of the sky rats had sworn their own vengeance and hired honor guards of their own. And that is how the cake competition as we know it today came to be."

"Amen," said Oskar and Beng Choon.

"It is the social event of the year," Nonso added. "It is the crowning event of the entire festival. Tourists come from all over just to witness it."

"More serious than you thought, eh, Julian?" said Oskar. "There's always at least one knock-down-drag-out fight at the cake competition. Not uncommon for people to get stabbed. Sometimes a death or two."

"From all the sabotage," Beng Choon added. "Or attempts at sabotage. People know you're with us, so you won't be allowed within twenty feet of any other cake—*not that you would want to look at any other cake but Mistress Navya's,*" he added loudly enough for any passersby on the street to hear.

"AYE," agreed Oskar at the top of his lungs, which was very, very loud, especially for barely dawn. "MISTRESS NAVYA IS THE SURE WINNER, NO QUESTION. I HEARD THE OTHER CAKES ARE ALREADY MOLDY AND RANCID."

"This is so fucking important," Avra whispered to Julian as the rest of the crew bellowed agreement. "Listen. You *cannot* say anything complimentary about anyone else's cake, or Tev will pull your fingernails out and throw you overboard."

"*If I don't do it myself first,*" Oskar hissed.

"*Don't you dare fuck this up for us,*" said Anxhela, walking backward for a few steps so she could point an accusing finger in Julian's face. "*This is our big fucking break.*"

"I will permanently stop finding you hot if you fuck this up," Avra said, dead serious. "Nobody's going to give a shit if you're new and ignorant. 'Sorry, I didn't know' will not fucking cut it."

"I see," said Julian. "Are there any other . . . rules . . . I should be aware of?"

Avra patted his arm. "Don't worry about other rules, I've been assigned to supervise you." Julian raised his eyebrows and gave Avra an amused, incredulous look—then raised his eyebrows farther when no one batted an eye. "You won't have an opportunity to fuck up except by complimenting a cake that isn't Mistress Navya's. Lukewarm comments count as complimentary. You have to *insult* the others, or people will think you kind of like them, and then we're done for, and Black Garda will not hire us again."

"Someone fucked that up last year," grunted Oskar. "Fucking idiot said one of the other cakes 'looked okay from a distance, but . . .' and it didn't matter that the rest of what she said was about it being ugly up close. That first part was the only bit that mattered."

"Wow. Rookie mistake," said Avra. "Embarrassing for everyone. I'm embarrassed to hear about it. I would like to know who that person is so that I can be sure to never stand next to her in a bar."

"It was a newcomer on Captain Rovag's crew. Word is she changed her name and moved to Pezia," said Beng Choon.

"Well, thank fuck for that." Avra squinted up, trying to remember. "Rovag was sworn to . . . Granny Layla, yeah?"

"Not after that." Anxhela snorted. "Soon as Captain Ueleari heard about it, he grabbed his crew, rushed over to Granny Layla's cake pavilion, and offered to swear to her for the remainder of the day, no compensation required."

"Now that's chivalry," said Avra. "A *good save,* and a great strategic move to break into the cake-guarding business. That's the sort of initiative you want to see."

"Doesn't that count as a compliment?" Julian whispered.

"It's fine to compliment the other *captains,*" said Avra. "As long as it isn't related to the cakes or their cakesmiths."

"I see. Have any of you seen Mistress Navya's cake yet?"

"Oh no," said Oskar.

"No no no," said Beng Choon.

"Hah!" said Anxhela.

"The cakes are made in *absolute secrecy*. Black Garda has had her usual guards on it since Mistress Navya started baking earlier this week," said Oskar.

"But not for the competition?"

"It's about showing off," said Avra. "Reputation. Status. Like flexing your giant muscles at someone. The guards are just normal folks, not lunatics." He pointed to Teveri at the front of the group. "*They're* a lunatic. It's like bringing a rabid mongoose to a dogfight."

"And the sail," said Oskar.

"Oh yes, absolutely. There just wouldn't be a point to hiring a crew who didn't have a *Nightingale* relic. Shows they're not a bunch of come-from-away nobodies."

Black Garda's house was a large and stately building by Scuttle Cove standards. It was perhaps a quarter of the size of the ambassador's palace, painted a sun-faded scarlet with intricate floral patterns in a much fresher-looking black around the doors and windows. Another fifty or so of the *The Running Sun*'s crew already thronged around it, headed by Bald Baric, who Teveri had stopped to talk to.

"They've been here all night," Avra whispered to Julian. "As a *display*."

Black Garda appeared at the door with a cup of coffee and a bleary expression. "Morning, Captain."

"Good morning, madam," said Teveri. "We're ready when Mistress Navya is."

Black Garda squinted at them. "Don't you have a hat?"

"Couldn't find one."

"Need a hat, Teveri."

"None of them went with my outfit."

Black Garda squinted. "That *Nightingale* thread on your coat?"

"Yes, madam."

"Hm. That's pretty fuckin' good. Haven't seen you wearing that."

"I don't wear it often."

"Stupid of you." Black Garda yawned hugely enough that even from twenty feet back, Avra could see she had several missing molars. "What, are you embarrassed? Trying to have the reputation to get away with it first?"

Teveri's shoulders stiffened. "I beg your pardon?"

"Worried that people'll call you uppity and pretentious?" Black Garda sipped her coffee and squinted somehow even more blearily. "They already say that, Captain Undertaker. Might as well lean into it. Who gives a fuck? Need a hat, though." She called over her shoulder, "Flower, what hats have we got?" A pause. "What was that, love?" A very distant, muffled voice replied. Black Garda shook her head. "Got her hands full with the cake. Wait here." She shuffled inside, closed the door, and locked it. Several locks, it sounded like.

Teveri was grinding their teeth, Avra could just tell. He patted Julian on the arm, whispered to him to stay right there, and wormed his way through the crew to Teveri's shoulder. "Tev," he whispered. "Remember what the spooky dentist told you. Tev. Your teeth, Tev."

"Yes, fine," Teveri said tightly. "*Thank you,* Avra, fuck off."

Black Garda flung open one of the upstairs windows and peered down at them, muttered something to herself, and disappeared once more.

A few minutes later, the locks clicked again and the door opened. "Hat," she said, holding out a hat to Teveri. "Fuckin' don't even look like a captain without a hat. Stupid of you."

Teveri took the hat. It was similar to their old hat, black and made of molded wool felt with one side of the wide brim pinned up to the crown. It was unlike their old hat in that instead of a ratty old tiger-striped pheasant feather, such as anyone might have, the plumes in the band were *much* nicer: A full and fluffy white ostrich feather from Ondoro, magnificently curled, overlaid by a pair of beautiful, pearly, grey-white feathers with an iridescent shimmer—two long, streaming banners ending in a teardrop-shaped tip.

Teveri seized the nearly burnt-out lantern Bald Baric held and raised it so the guttering dregs of its light fell on the feathers—the two pearly ones flashed and glittered with sparkling rainbow fire like a pair of diamonds.

"You're giving these to me?" Teveri said, their voice emotionless.

"Mngh," said Black Garda. "Nice try, but I *do* in fact know what they are. No, I'm lending them to you for the day. You can keep the hat, though. Hell, you can even keep the ostrich feather."

"What—" Teveri's voice shook. "What do you call them in this language?"

"Diamond-tailed bird-of-paradise."

Teveri gave a sharp knife of a laugh and put the hat on. The ostrich feather curled under the brim, just brushing the glossy black curls they'd spent so much time arranging this morning. The banner feathers, fluttering and twisting at every slightest breeze, draped to the middle of their back, stark and splendid against the black of their coat and just a shade or two brighter than the *Nightingale*-thread embroidery.

"Looks good on you, Captain," Oskar called. Then, louder, "Almost as good as Mistress Navya's cake." There was a chorus of vehement agreement.

"Speaking of the cake!" A hand appeared on Black Garda's shoulder and pushed her gently out of the way. Mistress Navya opened the door as far as it could go, glancing over her shoulder at three burly men carrying a very large box. "Careful, boys, careful."

"Just tell us where the steps are, milady," said the one at the front, who was being forced to walk backward.

"If you drop that, I'll have you killed," Black Garda said.

Mistress Navya clucked reprovingly at her and offered comments of direction and warning as the men eased their way down the two steps to the level of the street. When it was safe, seventy people breathed a sigh of relief, and Mistress Navya dashed back up the steps and stood on tiptoes to kiss her wife's cheek. "Take your time, darling, there's still an hour or two before things get going."

"Good luck, flower." Black Garda glared around at the crew. "Don't fuck it up." And finally, with a firm nod to Teveri, "Give 'em hell, Captain."

The staging ground for the competition was the wide flattish field just in front of Eel-face Yusin's bar—in other words, the cave mouth at the foot of the South Tit where the founding prophet of Julian's church had either been murdered or ascended into Felicity.

There were hundreds of people on the staging ground already, milling around eight large white pavilions spaced well apart from one another in a wide circle: For every cakesmith, one pavilion, and one pirate crew bristling with weapons and glaring suspiciously at all the others.

Mistress Navya led them straight to the last unoccupied pavilion, put her hands on her hips, and looked around. "Right, let's start with checking the tables *thoroughly*. No scratches, no loose legs, no fucking jiggling. I want to see them solid as stone before anything of ours touches them." She turned to Teveri. "Captain, shall we make it official?"

"At your service, mistress," Teveri said.

Navya took their arm and marched them out into the broad middle space, well within view of the circle of pavilions.

"Swearing to her as admiral," Avra whispered to Julian. "The showing off is important."

"Assume most everything is showing off today," Anxhela said from nearby, grabbing the edge of a table and giving it a violent jostle. "This one's solid."

"They sabotage the tables, I'm guessing?" Julian said.

"Well, it's considered an amateur move these days, but still better to check than to be caught by surprise."

Teveri, out in the middle of the field, swept off their hat magnificently and made a beautiful bow to Mistress Navya, who stood straight and solemn with her hands clasped before her.

At the other pavilions, most of the other captains had come to the edge of the awnings to watch. "Who are we up against? Any surprises?" Oskar muttered.

"Doesn't matter," Avra said loudly. "Who cares? They're working for people with shitty cakes. I can smell them even over here—both the dung cakes and their crews."

A single ray of sunlight speared through the low dip between the South and Middle Tits and fell in a long streak right across the middle of the field. Teveri's feathers fractured the light like a shattering diamond.

"Oh shit, that's pretty," Avra whispered. "*By which I mean Mistress Navya's dress! It's so becoming on her! You can definitely tell that she is the destined champion of the cake competition just by her exquisite taste in fashion.*"

The tables were tested for sabotage, and Navya's tablecloths shaken out and inspected for stains, smudges, and wrinkles. The crew hung banners from the poles of the pavilion in Black Garda's colors of red and black and draped streams of delicate Genzhun paper bunting within.

Finally, the burly men placed the ominous box on the table. One side had hinges like a cabinet; Navya undid the padlock holding it shut, opened it an inch to peek inside, nodded firmly, and relocked it. "Looks well enough. We'll add the finicky bits after the box comes off."

Teveri had posted themself by the front of the pavilion, their chin up and their back stiff. They cast a sidelong look to Avra and Julian. "Get some distance. Better not to be seen too close to us whenever the ambassador shows up. Just walk past for luck now and then. And don't start insulting the other cakes until there's a bigger crowd."

"Don't want to waste all our best material," Avra agreed. He sidled over to the nearest support pole and placed one hand on it. "Hey. Hello, tent. Be lucky, okay? Good. Good tent."

"I thought you were agnostic about your luck," said Julian as Avra led him away.

"Yes, but it's the *cake competition*. Can't take any chances."

Within the hour, throngs of people had poured onto the staging ground.

The first fight broke out around nine o'clock, just as the chair of the cake competition's organizing board stepped up onto the small platform at the center of the field. Avra waved it off before Julian could say anything. "Nothing to worry about. Potential judges squabbling. It's all to keep the cake competition as scrupulously fair and unriggable as possible—*nobody* but the contestants knows what that year's theme is, and no one at all knows who the judges will be, because *they* only get picked on the day of the competition."

"I beg your pardon, they make it *double-blind* until the day of the event?"

Avra gave him an injured look. "It's a very important cake competition, Julian. *Very important*," he added at the top of his lungs, "*because Mistress Navya's cake is a jewel amongst garbage. Actually, can you even call these cakes? I'd call them ugly piles of shit and extremely bad artistic interpretations of the theme.* Ooh, look! Cat's over with the potentials! Cross your fingers for Cat, he's an excellent cake judge. Very impartial and fair. Always brings a good rubric to judge by. Actually—" Avra dove a hand into his little rucksack, pulled a card, cackled to himself, and stuffed it back in his bag.

"What was it?" Julian murmured.

"The Matchmaker. Cat's definitely getting it."

The potential judges' names were added to the hat (witnessed by four randomly selected members of the audience to ensure that each slip bore a single name and that no names were repeated), and five slips were drawn by a child so young they were impossible to bribe.

Cat was called first; nearly everyone on the field applauded. From the pool of other respected luminaries of the town ("They have to apply in advance to be considered as potentials, Julian, and they have to have three letters of reference, plus documentation of five years of service toward the benefit of the community, and they have to be *known,* and they can't have any family connections to the contestants, and—"), four others were summoned: Skully, the sculptor of the skull-in-progress on the cliff face; the owner of the newspaper; one of the ancient retired captains, still tottering about on his own with great dignity, though Avra noticed that he was relying more heavily on his cane than he had in years past; and one of the first bartenders who had ever kicked Avra out of a gaming house for "probably cheating, somehow."

"And now, Julian, the judges will confer with each other and announce the rubrics they will be judging with—"

"Helvaçi," someone hissed. Avra screeched and whirled around, brandishing his tiny knife.

"Oh," he said. "Uh. Good morning, sir. You startled me." Baltakan was wearing a huge cape and hood made out of what appeared to be burlap potato sacks. What good a burlap cape would do at keeping off the rain and wind, Avra couldn't say. Not that there was much rain or wind due at Midsummer, but this seemed to be irrelevant. "Is this your . . . disguise?" Baltakan also had an eyepatch on, and several of his teeth had been messily blackened with soot.

"How is it? Effective? You didn't recognize me at first."

It was a little conspicuous. A lot conspicuous. Everyone was looking at him, in fact. "Uh, it's fine. Julian! This is—the gentleman—the *person,* the *guy,* the *man in question* who I mentioned I wanted to introduce you to. Amb—sssssir, this is Brother Julian."

"Charmed," said Baltakan stiffly, giving Julian a once-over. "You're not much like I had pictured."

"The Emperor of Heaven has blessed me with the strength of body to pursue wisdom and improve the strength of my mind," Julian said. "Master Helvaçi mentioned you were interested in my studies?" Baltakan shot a hard look at Avra, who froze. "Nothing would please me more than to discuss what humble, scanty scraps of wisdom I have gathered. The Emperor commands us to multiply our knowledge by sharing it with one another."

"I'm sure he does," Baltakan said. "Well, shall we go meet my companion? She is waiting just outside this . . . event."

"What, right now?" said Avra. "Can't we wait a few minutes to hear what the rubrics are?"

"The what?"

"The judges. What rubrics they're going to be using to judge. They're supposed to pick really weird ones so that none of the contestants will have been able to make their cakes to cater specifically to one particular rubric. Well, except for Flavor. All the judges have Flavor as one of their six—really, though, this is one of the best bits of the competition, everyone loves this bit—"

"Why do you care?" said Baltakan, baffled.

Avra opened his mouth and paused.

We, he'd said the day before. Not *they.*

But there was Baltakan right in front of him, who had to believe that Avra was a loyal, partially retired agent of the Ministry of Intelligence, at least until Julian had managed to clear himself with the truthwitch and preferably for a great deal more time after that.

All around them were people who were part of Avra's *we,* and they were absolutely listening. Insulting the cake competition, or even being lukewarm about the cake competition, could spell disaster for Teveri's crew just as surely as it would if Avra were to say something even marginally nice about any cake besides Mistress Navya's.

Avra tossed his hair and said primly, "I could not possibly explain to you why the cake competition is so crucially important, sir, but I must insist we wait until we hear the rubrics. *And* the theme of the competition."

Baltakan looked thrown. He lowered his voice. "Is this Intelligence business?"

Avra shrugged one shoulder as a loud gong rang over the staging ground. "I'm not at liberty to say. But if you'll excuse me, we have to shut up and pay attention now."

They were almost directly opposite from Navya's pavilion. Teveri still stood before it with their arms crossed—the sun was coming full over the mountains now, and their two diamond-tailed bird-of-paradise feathers glittered like hoarfrost refracting the light into prisms.

The chair invited each judge up to announce their rubrics. Avra was too jittery to fully internalize what any of the judges announced as their rubrics after Cat (Compassionate Insight, Presentation, Allure, Hospitality, and Celebration of the Body) and Skully (Number of Skulls, Anatomical Accuracy, Sculptural Artistry, Engineering, and Durability).

"Is this a joke?" muttered Baltakan, just a little bit louder than a mutter.

"No," said Avra sharply. "This is so deeply important."

"I cannot imagine how. Why would Intelligence care about this, of all things?"

Avra was jittering with anxiety. "Sir," he hissed. "*No one* would leave during the announcement of the rubrics and theme. It would be very rude. And suspicious."

The gong sounded again. A somber woman of middle age came onto the platform and cleared her throat. "Friends," she said, projecting her voice loud enough to ring through the field. "As you know, the announcement of the theme is traditionally made by the oldest living captain in Scuttle Cove. For the past six years, this has been Captain Kgosi."

A stir ran through the crowd; several people breathed out *oh no.*

"As many of you know, Captain Kgosi has been ill for much of this year. The board received the terrible news last night—"

The crowd, as one, shouted in dismay.

The woman on the platform raised her hands. "Yes. Captain Kgosi passed yesterday evening, surrounded by his five children, twenty-two grandchildren, and three great-grandchildren. While we did contact his successor to the title to arrange for her to take over in case of this tragedy, both we and his successor have concluded that for her to do so this soon after Captain Kgosi's passing would be disrespectful to his memory. Therefore, we will be reading a eulogy in his honor which recounts the story of his life and his deeds in service to the Isles, and his eldest grandchild will read the speech that Captain Kgosi had prepared for today."

Baltakan gave the tiniest and most diplomatic sigh of annoyance.

No one else would have been close enough to hear it—but Avra, powerfully choked up, felt something in his brain snap. He began to contemplate a fate for Baltakan far worse than death. He allocated thirty percent of his mental power to this and turned the rest of it back to the eulogist, who was describing Captain Kgosi's early life in Upper Tayemba, his youth as a hired guard for merchant caravans traversing the grasslands, his thirst for adventure. She recounted an amusing story, apparently provided by one of Kgosi's children, about the first time he had glimpsed the sea and thought it was a monster devouring the land and that they would all soon perish—the crowd, solidly in tears by that point, laughed until they clutched their sides and had to sit down.

The eulogist told of Kgosi's near-escape from the law in the capital of N'gaka, where some unscrupulous sorts had attempted to frame him for smuggling, followed by his escape on a vessel crewed by *actual* smugglers, which had been the beginning of his life of piracy.

Everyone—even Avra—was streaming with tears by that point, broken only now and then by the wittiness of the eulogist's occasional jokes.

"He retired at the age of sixty-eight," the eulogist said, "and has been living quietly here ever since, in the home that welcomed him and gave him all the adventure he had ever hungered for and a view of the sea that he had fallen in love with. On his passing, he was ninety-four years old. He requested that his ashes be scattered in the Turtle Shallows by whichever captain represents today's champion cakesmith."

The crowd inhaled as one—another murmur and stirring passed through them.

Julian and Avra exchanged a glance. Julian leaned very close and whispered, "How is your luck feeling today?"

"Don't say that," Avra hissed.

"How will Teveri feel about being tasked with part of someone's funeral?"

"Don't know. Don't want to think about it."

"Now for Captain Kgosi's final speech," said the eulogist. She gestured to a young man with a baby on his hip. He stepped up to the platform and awkwardly unfolded a few sheets of paper with his free hand.

"'Dear friends, greetings and farewells,'" he began, his voice already cracking.

Baltakan leaned in to whisper, *very* diplomatically, "Do you know how much longer these ceremonies will last?"

"Sir," Julian murmured. "A man has died. Have some respect."

"'I had written a few drafts of this speech already,'" continued the eldest Kgosi grandson. "'And I had considered several times that I could easily reuse one of my old speeches without anyone noticing, except perhaps to think that the battiness of old age was making me repetitive. However.'" The young man had to stop to swallow several times. "'I—I can feel that it is nearly time, and so I would prefer to leave you with a few words of encouragement to get your vim up for this year's competition, which I know will be fiercely contested. I am one of the last alive who remembers the old glory days, and so I will take this opportunity to speak about the most important thing that I'd like you all to remember, namely that Xing Fe Hua once kissed me full on the mouth in front of the gods and everyone.'"

The crowd, which by now had been entirely shattered and was slowly crumpling to the ground, yelled in a mixture of delight and the particular existential dismay unique to hearing one's grandparent imply the existence of a sexual history.

The baby on the young man's hip did *not* approve of the wall of sound, and decided that the thing to do was to add to it, which at least gave the young man an excuse to occupy himself with her and thereby cover a blush powerful enough to be seen for ten miles. A young woman, presumably the baby's mother, stepped forward to take her, further providing the father a few moments to collect his composure as she was gently pried off of him.

The young man cleared his throat and warily returned to the speech. "'I will spare you the details of any further exploits.'" He slumped in relief; so did most of the crowd. "'And I will spare you too much of a laundry list of nonsense that only an old man cares about—at least for today. I have, however, directed my descendants to deliver the full list of my thoughts to the editor of the *Scuttlebutt*, though I still hold that's a stupid name for a newspaper. The other main point I wanted to announce publicly at an event as inestimable as our beloved cake competition is that—'"

The young man choked and put a fist to his mouth in renewed dismay.

"What!" several people shouted. "What is it!" The shouters grew in number. "Say it! Read it, boy! Obi, read it!"

The young man—Obi, presumably—took a moment to collect himself again. "'. . . At an event as inestimable as our beloved cake competition,'" he began again, "'is that Araşt as a whole can eat my death shits, and the new ambassador specifically can go out to the Shallows and get fucked with turtle dick, presuming that turtles have dicks.'"

Avra bit his lip and was very glad that his face was already sopping wet with tears from the eulogy so there was camouflage for any tears that fell from the *massive* effort it took not to shriek with laughter and keel over.

This was not an effort that anyone else in the crowd bothered to make, including Julian, who put both hands to his face and *shook* as everyone else screamed with delight and enthusiasm.

When Avra bothered to glance at Baltakan, he had gone absolutely white, barely maintaining his Diplomacy poker face.

Obi raised his hand; everyone struggled to quiet themselves enough to hear him. "'In conclusion, and following on from that sentiment, I know you will enjoy the theme of this year's competition.

"'To the cakesmiths, make me proud and give 'em hell.

"'To the captains, Scuttle Cove expects that every one of you will do their duty. I salute you.

"'To the rest of you degenerates, you're some of the worst people I know and I love you dearly. Farewell!

"'P.S. There's some bitch on the cake competition board who keeps assuring me that if should I die before the competition, she'll see to it that my death is celebrated, quote, "according to the manner of your people." This is very stupid, and I have attempted to tell her so—my family is more than capable of arranging things without interference. Do not allow her to delay any longer than it has already taken to read this speech. Feed her to the seagulls. My death is *absolutely not* a higher priority than the cake competition, and I will haunt anyone who tries to convince you that it is. *Just get on with it.*'"

The crowd burst into furious applause.

Baltakan cleared his throat. "Well," he said, disguising his cold anger almost perfectly—but Avra heard it. "A very tragic situation, but we seem to be intruding on these people's grief. Shall we excuse ourselves, gentlemen?" Avra didn't move. Baltakan said more briskly, "Helvaçi, *come*."

Avra held up one finger to him without taking his eyes off the speaker's platform. "Don't say that to me when I'm fully clothed and in the middle of the cake competition."

"What? Say again, I can't hear you over this ruckus."

"I said wait just one minute more, sir."

"We are intruding," Baltakan said with a slightly strained smile. "And besides that, I feel a little faint from the sun, don't you? Perhaps a drink in that bar over there until the somber mood passes somewhat. Brother Julian, would you like to join me?"

"Thank you, but I should like to stay and hear the theme. Certainly after that ending note, don't you think?"

The gong rang out. The crowd fell silent instantly, except for Obi's wailing baby, who he was collecting back from her mother and cuddling onto his shoulder.

"With no further ado," said the woman who had read the eulogy, looking rather grim, which suggested she was the lady from the postscript. "As you all know, the theme of the competition is usually in regards to a recent significant event in the news of the world. When the board gathered to discuss the matter, we discovered that for the first time in the board's history we were unanimous in our choice. The contestants, when informed of the theme, were just as unanimous in their delight and eagerness to tackle the subject. We are confident that the political commentary expressed via their cakes will be both insightful and vigorous, given such a juicy subject to dig into."

Avra had started vibrating with glee. "Oh no," he said, vaguely aware that he had his most manic and feral grin on. "This is very bad, isn't it?"

Baltakan had gone very still and pale again.

"The theme we set them is, of course . . . the security breach at the Araşti Shipbuilder's Guild in Kasaba City earlier this spring!"

If the noise of the crowd before had been loud, this was *deafening.*

24

11. The Gallows-man

Consequences for your past deeds are approaching swiftly. There is no more time to earn forgiveness. This card potentially represents someone who is an enemy, but an impersonal one; possibly an authority figure who is working against you, or perhaps merely the system itself (either just or unjust) that seeks retribution.

(Reversed: The possibility of forgiveness is still available. You have brought an ill fate upon yourself, but there is time to avert it or turn it to your advantage. If someone wronged you, they will go free—take what vengeance you can before they slip through your grasp.)

Baltakan was shaking with fury as he led them up to Eel-face Yusin's bar. It wasn't yet lunchtime. "You knew, I take it," he said under his breath.

"What, about the theme? Nope." Avra stuck his thumbs in his waistband. "Well, I probably could have made a good guess if I'd thought about it. I did not. I just had an instinct to stay. Also, I like the cake competition."

"After *that* display? That—that—*disgrace*?"

"What disgrace? You mean a fucking hilarious old man speaking from beyond the grave to tell you that he dislikes you personally? That's not a disgrace, Baltakan, that's just spooky."

Julian spoke up from behind them, "Oh, Master Helvaçi, you didn't mention that your friend is the ambassador."

Baltakan took a deep breath, pasted Diplomacy all over his face, and turned to Julian with a small bow. "I apologize for the subterfuge. I thought it would be fun to show up if no one knew I was here."

Several people nearby had spotted him and were elbowing their neighbors and pointing him out. "Good morning, Ambassador Turtle-fucker!" someone called cheerfully.

Julian's monkly smile didn't waver. "It's very warm today, isn't it? Should we get out of the sun?"

"*Yes, we should.*" Baltakan turned on his heel and stalked with exquisite dignity to the door of Eel-face Yusin's place.

Inside was dark and quite damp, and it smelled like . . . well, like cave, primarily. And cooking fish, and curry, and spilled beer, and stale wine. "Hi, Yusin!" Avra said, waving merrily as he followed in Baltakan's wake.

"Helvaçi," said the man behind the bar, who did have a face remarkably like an eel, particularly in his distinctly snaggly teeth. "Heard you were here. Thought I'd see you earlier than this."

"Well, I've been busy the last few days. Doesn't mean I don't love you, Yusin!"

The truthwitch was sitting at a table toward the back, deeply shadowed except for the single candle on the table before her. She was drinking tea, though gods knew where Eel-face Yusin had found tea. Perhaps she'd brought her own. Baltakan collected his composure once more as he reached the table and bowed to her. He sat, gestured a little imperiously for Avra and Julian to take the seats opposite, and snapped his fingers in the air.

"What's that?" said Avra.

"I'm calling the attendant? I thought I would offer to buy a round of drinks. Brother Julian, would you like anything?"

"Thank you, but I'm fine for now."

Avra added helpfully, "If you want something, you'll have to go up to the bar. He doesn't have table service here."

Baltakan closed his eyes.

Witness Amita glanced over the rim of her mug at him, then at Avra, then at Julian. "Pleasure to meet you," she said to Julian. "You are a monk of the Vintish church, are you not?"

"I am," said Julian, smiling. "For the moment."

Witness Amita raised an impossibly elegant eyebrow. "For the moment?"

"I am reflecting on the direction of my life and asking the Emperor of Heaven to send me some hint that might suggest my course."

Eel-face Yusin came over with two bowls of yellow curry, which he set in front of Avra and Julian. "What's this!" Avra cried. "Yusin! You make a liar of me! I just told them you don't have table service."

"It ain't table service."

"It looks like table service to me!"

Yusin shrugged. "You weren't here for your birthday." He walked off.

Avra surged half out of his chair. "*How do you know when my birthday is, Yusin!* Yusin! Come back here! Why'd you bring *two* bowls!"

"He wasn't here for your birthday either. Man ought to have a friend to celebrate his birthday with, Helvaçi."

"Yusin!" Avra screeched. "What is this kind of luxurious treatment! How dare you! Yusin! You've heard me drunkenly philosophizing about the virtues of half-assing it! I thought we were united in this, Yusin!"

"Birthdays are different. And you always tip well."

"I don't have any money today, though!"

"That's all right. You brought in the ambassador. If he orders anything, I'm going to spit in it and charge him double. Feels like a fair trade to me."

Baltakan really did have marvelous control of his face—he barely pursed his lips.

Witness Amita took a pointed sip of her tea. "You mentioned your new course, Brother Julian?"

"It is one of those spiritual questions—I would imagine you might know about that? You seem to be wearing the robes of an Inachan mystic, unless I miss my guess?"

Witness Amita blinked. "Yes."

"How wonderful! I have studied several religions across the world, and I've heard so many things about your order. We are both seekers after truth in our own way, aren't we? I feel as though we could have a great many fascinating conversations about spirituality and comparative religion."

Witness Amita blinked again. Avra shoveled a spoonful of curry into his mouth and prepared to keep score. That had been a hit without question, and it was probably *deeply* true to boot. "I would imagine so," she said. "But please tell me about the potential new direction of your spiritual path. My own has been straight and steady for three decades now, and I am well content with it."

"I hardly know where to start—what would you like to know?" Julian folded his hands on the table and smiled. "I'm an open book." He glanced down at the curry. "By the way, would anyone else like this? It smells delicious, but I'm not hungry for lunch just yet."

"I'll have it," Witness Amita said quickly, before Baltakan could even open his mouth. "What spurred this reflection upon your path?"

"*Well,*" said Julian, with the air of a man about to launch into an extraordinarily long-winded rant. "First you ought to know the backstory. As a young man, I went to the university in Ancoux, the Vintish capital, and fell in with a group of young revolutionaries . . ."

Julian held forth for nearly twenty minutes *just* on the backstory of how he came to the monastery and the years he spent there. The only exchange of note was when Julian offhandedly mentioned the anecdotes of the legendary six and fifty-two.

"Was that true?" Avra demanded, his mouth full of curry. "Witness Amita, please give me this one, just tell me if that bit was true."

"It was," Witness Amita said.

"I'm going to fucking cry," Avra muttered to his curry, and let Julian continue.

"And finally," Julian said at the end of this long backstory, "I decided that the new abbot was a petty tyrant. Instead of helping to direct me toward the pursuit of Understanding in the areas of skill and interest that the Emperor of Heaven had gifted me with, he was in fact *holding me back* from it. I decided that following the commandments of the Emperor to seek joyfully toward knowledge and sate my simple human curiosity was more important than being meek and obedient to some mortal man who thought that he had authority over me for no other reason than because he had a title in front of his name. So I packed my things, and I left. I wanted to see the world. I wanted to . . . come here." He looked around the cave.

"To the Isles?" said Witness Amita, her eyes sharpening.

"To *this cave.* I'd translated a text—it took me years and years of my studies at the monastery, but when I finally finished, I thought that I had unlocked some great mystery. I made my way here, thinking that I would spend years more seeking the island described in the text and the cave in which the founding prophet of the Vintish church ascended to Felicity. By luck, I met Captain az-Ḥaffār and was quickly disabused of my . . . presumption, I suppose you could call it." He spread his hands. "The holiest site of my religion is a bar that serves excellent yellow curry."

"That must have been a disappointment."

Julian considered this for a long moment. "It was, I suppose. At least for a little time. And then I reflected on how the Emperor of Heaven wishes for us to be curious about the world, to ask questions, to *go and find out.*" He smiled. "As I had recently become acquainted with the crew of a pirate ship, that seemed as good a vehicle as any."

"I see. I imagine that they do not give you free passage, even aboard a pirate ship," said Witness Amita. Baltakan was sitting silently, his hands clasped together tight atop the table—so tight his knuckles were going white.

Julian laughed politely. "Indeed not. They taught me to sail, and they gave me into the keeping of the quartermaster as her assistant. It has been a surprisingly invigorating exercise for the mind."

"Was there anything else they asked you to do?"

"I have some gift with languages, so I assisted with the translation of a few texts. I began teaching Ellat, the youngest member of the crew, to speak Vintish. He thinks it will help him get into the good graces of women he meets in bars."

"Oh, I'm telling Markefa," said Avra.

"Master Helvaçi mentioned that you know something of alchemy."

"The merest dabble. Why?"

"I was intrigued by his tales of the exploding things you utilized to fend off the serpents."

Avra waited for the swoop of alarm to hit him, but—he didn't *care.* More than that, he *wasn't afraid.* Julian had brains in his head, and probably backup brains in his biceps, shoulders, and thighs, which was why they bulged like that. Probably backup-backup brains in his dick, which was why it too—

"Hardly fend them off," Julian said with a regretful shake of his head. "A failed experiment, I'm afraid. But even those can be gifts of the Emperor in their own way. You learn the strangest things from setbacks, I've found."

"What did you learn from this one?"

"That I don't particularly enjoy alchemy," Julian said with a straight face—which he managed to hold for only a moment before he laughed. "And that I'm terrified of sea serpents. And that the most crushing setback is to fail in a way that puts people you care about in danger."

Witness Amita was looking a little—dazed, almost. Or drunk, or dizzy, as if she'd been out in the sun for too long. Avra watched with fascination and wondered whether it was possible to overshare a truthwitch into submission.

"What is the part of your path that you are reconsidering?" Witness Amita said, shaking her head a little bit as if to wake herself up. "I don't think you mentioned that yet."

"Oh," said Julian. "You're right, I didn't. My apologies. I'm reconsidering my vow of celibacy and whether I want to keep it."

Avra's eye twitched a little. He waved a hand at Yusin to catch his attention and, through a series of silent gestures ending with a beseeching expression, indicated to him that he would very much appreciate another bowl of curry, please and thank you.

"Are you—" Witness Amita's voice cracked. "Pardon me." She took a sip of tea. "Does your religion allow that?"

"Do you mean the institution of the church, or the commandments of the Emperor?"

"The—the church, I suppose."

Julian got a rather terrifying light in his eye and straightened his spine. "This is something I feel very strongly about."

And that, of course, was a pure and shining truth.

The following diatribe was a *glorious* disquisition on institutions of power being no better than kings, and how humans by their very nature would mutilate even holy, sacred words if it meant they could gain power and accrue material benefit for themselves, and that while the impulse to *conquer* and *consume* was indeed also a part of human nature, and indeed part of the nature of all living beings, there was a moral obligation for all people to interrogate such impulses within themselves, or else risk consuming and exploiting even their fellow humans—

Avra got a little distracted with thanking Yusin for the second bowl of curry, and by the time he turned his attention back not even ten seconds later, Julian had somehow gotten into a particularly impassioned thread of his argument, concerning organized religion (especially state-sanctioned religion) being not an entity of holiness at all but merely a facade of playacting covering up purely imperialist motives—"We tithe to our church, because the church tells us that we must, but rather than using that money to build schools and libraries in the backcountry, or to otherwise fund learning for the masses, the great majority of it is used for the monks' own benefit! For more books in *their* libraries, for food and shelter for *themselves* while they seek their own knowledge! Barely a trickle of all that tax is passed along to the common people! And then, then! Then they have the breathtaking audacity to complain that the common people are *lazy* and *unpious*.

"How, I ask you, *how* are the common people supposed to devote themselves to the holy pursuit of learning and advancing our collective understanding of the world? How are they supposed to spend any useful time contemplating the mysteries that the Emperor of Heaven gave us so that we would have *something* to strive for and remind us that we are small?" Julian was banging his fist on the table to punctuate every few phrases. "How are they supposed to 'go and find out' if they are *starving*, Witness Amita? How are they to devote themselves to what the church tells them they should be devoted to if all their time and attention and energy is devoted to basic survival? Are the poor excluded from holiness, Witness Amita? Will a mother of twelve children be turned away from the gates of Felicity because she learned nothing but how to love her family until she *died* of overwork?"

Baltakan was also rather dazed now. Avra avoided catching his eye and occupied himself with eating his yellow curry and trying not to get too turned on by Julian's rant.

Julian by this point was standing up and stabbing his finger against the surface of the table to punctuate himself. "And so, Witness Amita, you ask me if it is *allowed* in my religion to break a vow I took fifteen years ago and would not have chosen for myself, and I answer you with all the truth in my heart: No, probably fucking not! Probably it's not allowed at all! I would imagine that it certainly wouldn't be allowed for me—not because I have a soiled past consorting with the people on the losing side—not the *wrong people,* mind you, simply the *people who did not win*—but because, Witness Amita, I am *troublesome.* And troublesome people, as we all know, are not something that institutional power wants to have to deal with. Institutional power wants to *crush* troublesome people and break their spirits—and may the Emperor bless my old Abbot Symon who gave me sanctuary, because until my dying day I will believe that he truly thought that he was doing me a kindness—and perhaps in some ways he was! At the end of the day, the vow I made then brought me *here to this place,* to the cave where the founding prophet of my religion was *murdered,* probably for being troublesome herself! And here we sit, sipping tea and eating curry! It's funny how things work out, isn't it! But while I do not hold a crumb of resentment in my heart for Abbot Symon as a man, he nevertheless was allowing himself to be used as a tool of institutional power, and the vow I made—speaking institutionally—*was intended to break me.*"

He sat down heavily, chest heaving. He had tears in his eyes.

Avra and Witness Amita watched him, wide-eyed—Avra had frozen with the curry spoon in his mouth at some point. Baltakan was wearing his utterly blank Diplomacy face, which in this context looked mildly, politely confused.

Yusin silently brought over a mug of beer, set it in front of Julian, and patted him on the shoulder.

"Thank you," said Julian, and drank. "Did that answer the question truthfully, Witness Amita?"

Amita looked as though . . . as though the ship she'd thought sound had crashed onto a reef carried by some fucking turtle that had moved in an irregular way not recorded by any of her charts.

"How's that straight and steady path going for you?" Avra asked. She looked at him reflexively. Her bone structure really was beyond compare—Avra hoped Skully was not so busy with judging the cakes that he didn't at least catch a glimpse of her fantastic cheekbones—but that tranquility and perfect dignity had . . . shattered.

"But," she said quietly. "But do you just . . . walk away? This is your life's work, Brother Julian. If you break that vow, do you turn your back on everything you've done?"

"In general terms, I think that would depend on who you ask," Julian said. He openly stole Avra's bowl of curry and pulled the spoon right out of Avra's mouth.

"Mrhghgm," said Avra, comprehensively failing not to be horny about it.

"My captain made the choice to walk away," Julian continued. "They abandoned the cult of Qarat'ash. I do not feel that it is the *teachings* of the Emperor of Heaven that stifle me. I feel, in fact, that they have done much to open my eyes to a broader world of possibility. Abbot Symon used to say, 'Alas, I have much yet to learn—and hurrah, I have much yet to learn! The Emperor of Heaven is generous!' I feel no need to turn my back on that. There is nothing in that adage for me but *joy*." He ate some of Avra's yellow curry with Avra's spoon. Which Avra's mouth had been on. "But I do not think I need permission to devote my life to learning in accordance with the Celestial Emperor. I do not think anyone needs permission. The poor *do* learn, just as all people do. For example, I have no doubts that they have a better grasp of how to survive poverty than I do—who's to say that kind of learning isn't worthy of entry into Felicity after death? I think a mother with twelve children *certainly* has a better grasp than I do of household management and balancing accounts, not to mention the everyday virtue of how to love something unreservedly, unconditionally, and without expectation, even when one is tired to one's bones and has vomit in one's hair. Who are we to say *that* learning is not worthy of Felicity? So no, I do not feel that I will be rejecting everything."

Avra noticed, as through a thick fog, the change in verb tense. "Mrrrrr," he said very quietly. Baltakan gave him a look that was slightly more desperate than the perfect Diplomacy face.

"Then what?" said Amita.

Julian shrugged and ate another contemplative bite of curry. "The idea of making a vow to give up the thing that most occupies one's thoughts is nowhere in our original holy text. It was an idea thought up by one monk or a small group from a cloistered order, perhaps five or six hundred years ago. It was, by the most literal definition of the word, a heresy. Heresy, but not apostasy."

"I don't know the difference between those words," Avra managed, barely. He reached slowly for Julian's cup of beer with both hands like a wretched little raccoon—which is rather what he felt like—and even more slowly slid it toward himself. "I know blasphemy. Tev's coat has blasphemy all over it."

"Does it?" Julian asked with interest, pushing his beer toward Avra with somewhat more speed than Avra was using.

"Says, 'My name's Teveri the Incandescent and actually Qarat'ash, both the person and the cult, can go out to the Turtle Shallows and—' Uh. I mean, it says, 'Heck those—those guys.' But fancy."

"That is what blasphemy is, yes," Julian said, with a deeply approving smile. "Well done, Avra. And here I thought you insisted you didn't know any big words."

Avra accidentally made eye contact with Baltakan and laughed nervously. "Ha ha, only ones related to my job. Ha. A fun little joke. Between me and Julian."

"Apostasy is what Teveri did," Julian said, very helpfully in small words that Avra knew about even when he was holding himself together with fish glue and yellow curry and attempting to find the exact spot on the beer mug where Julian had put his mouth. "Heresy, by its common definition, is what I've been doing just now. But heresy has a . . . less fraught meaning, shall we say, in that it is simply a theory or teaching that goes against orthodoxy—that is, it is either an opposition or addition to the established canon of wisdom."

"Thank you," Avra said into the beer mug.

"Certainly." Julian returned his attention to Amita. "Where was I? Oh, yes, I was making the prelude to the thesis statement—your very apt question of 'What then?' seems to be pressing for an answer of practicality rather than spirituality. What does one do, when one faces these things? Speaking personally, I am weighing the decision of whether the heresy of those monks, which was later adopted into or pasted over the orthodoxy, is necessary for me. Do I believe that I need a sacrificial vow in order to make room in my mind for holy pursuits? And if I do need a vow, do I need it to be the same one that I made fifteen years ago?"

Avra valiantly attempted to bury his face deeper into the mug.

"Frankly, Witness Amita," Julian said, just as calm and friendly as ever you please, "the further we go in this conversation and the more things I say out loud about what I believe—and how thankful I am to have had the opportunity for this!—the more inclined I am to say fuck the vow, pun absolutely intended."

Avra snorted beer out of his nose and spluttered so hard he splashed half of the mug onto the table. Julian patted him firmly on the back as he coughed.

"You all right over there, Helvaçi?" Eel-face Yusin called.

"He seems to be inhaling every now and then," Julian said. "Do you have any napkins?"

"Hah. No. Too fancy for the likes of me."

Julian gave Avra his handkerchief.

"Witness Amita," said Baltakan, very polite and not at all as if he were mentally grinding his teeth hard enough to merit a scolding from the spookiest possible dentist. "This is taking a great deal of time."

Amita was distinctly wobbly. She gripped the edge of the table and rasped, "Do you know whether anything was stolen from the Araşti Shipbuilder's Guild?"

"I do not," Julian said. "Monsieur Yusin, could you bring a glass of water for—oh, thank you, monsieur."

"*Monsieur.*" Yusin chuckled to himself, setting the water in front of Avra. "Like I'm *fancy.*"

Julian laughed. "No reason why you can't be fancy if you want to, monsieur."

"Do you know—" Amita steadied herself, looking greener around the gills by the second. "Do you know of anyone planning to sell information related to the Araşti technique of passing safely through the serpents' breeding swarms?"

"Witness Amita," Julian said as Avra finally finished coughing. "You do not look well. I beg you, *please* do not injure yourself for the sake of protecting the monetary profit of what is arguably the world's *greatest* institutional power." He paused, and reached across the table, his palm open. "May I take your hand?" Amita laid her shaking hand in his. "Felicity, you're clammy! Have some tea. Good, that's good. It takes effort to use your power, I assume?"

"Only when I'm . . . opening my eyes wide, as it were," she said, a little hoarsely.

"Then shut your eyes for a moment, *as it were,* and catch your breath. I'll answer you when you're ready to continue. I want you to feel absolutely confident that your insights are accurate—if there is any shred of doubt as to whether you did your job properly, the institutional powers above you will not extend compassion to you the way a person would."

"Brother Julian, this is not necessary," Baltakan said. "She is a satyota, she doesn't believe in your radical ideas. Your consideration is commendable, but inappropriate."

"Compassion for someone who is clearly unwell is commendable but inappropriate?" Julian said with a polite smile.

"It's all right," said Amita, setting down her teacup. "I can go on."

Julian squeezed her hands. "Whenever you're ready," he said in a gentle voice. "I'll make it quick. I apologize for being so long-winded. I didn't realize it would hurt you."

She took a breath, braced herself, met his eyes intensely, and said, "Go."

"I'm not stupid, and I know what you're asking. I do not know of anyone currently planning to sell the technique, but if I did, I would attempt to keep it from you at all costs."

"True."

"I admit that I, as a man of science, am desperately curious about how it works—I imagine most people are—and that I have theories that I have tested and which have failed. I do not know whether anyone will discover the technique in my lifetime—or discover an entirely new one, for that matter—but I will tell you without any prompting that if the secret were within my possession, if I could verify that it was complete, safe, reliable, and *replicable,* and if the decision were entirely up to me, I would not choose to sell it."

"*True.* Why not?" said Amita. There was sweat on her brow.

"Are you sure you can continue?"

She nodded.

"I would not sell it because I would give it away for free to whoever wanted it. I would deliver copies of it to every major university in the world. I would teach it to every fisherman I met. I would make that secret *worthless,* because as things stand now, its worth comes from its exclusivity. After everything I have said about institutional power, how could I make any other choice? To sell the secret on the world's black market—and I admit that if I were going to do that, this island would be the place to start—would only be taking that secret away from Araşt and putting it in the hands of *some other* institutional power. It would do nothing; it would achieve nothing; it would not substantially change the world, except that now there would be two countries that know it rather than one—and Araşt has enough money and allies and debtors that it could, if it wished, go to war with that country, bring a few truthwitches like you along for a little weekend jaunt of an invasion, and systematically root out and murder anyone who knows how it works. And then we would be back to square one." He smiled and squeezed Witness Amita's hand between both of his. "At the end of the day and despite saying 'fuck the vow,' I still believe that some of the teachings of my faith are as true as the foundations of the earth, such as the assertion that underpins our entire religion: Sharing knowledge freely and openly is a great act of piety, perhaps the greatest of them all. All right, that's enough. Please let go now, Witness Amita, you do look *very* sick. I must insist that we stop this interview for today."

Witness Amita drew a sobbing breath and slumped back in her chair, shaking violently.

Julian rubbed her hand, looking at her with great concern. "Would you like more tea? Or some fresh air? I would be happy to walk you outside."

"Fresh air, yes," Witness Amita rasped.

"All right—wait, wait, don't rush it, let me help you up. We'll take it very slowly, all right? And there are plenty of tables between us and the door, so if you need to sit down again, just let me know."

"You can take a couple chairs outside with you," said Eel-face Yusin, polishing glasses with a rag behind the bar in the grand tradition of barkeeps everywhere and throughout history.

Avra dragged the bowl of yellow curry back over and scraped the last few spoonfuls into his mouth. He felt quite *comfy* and loose-limbed, all glowing-satisfied, like after a professionally administered orgasm. Which—Julian was more of a virtuoso amateur but—

He felt as though he'd rolled his shoulders and finally gotten a crick in his neck to pop. He felt as though he'd won a second *Nightingale* sail for Tev, but this time understood the weight of what he'd done. *Something* had clicked into place in the mechanisms of the universe—call it luck if you will, but Avra didn't believe in luck. He was standing with his feet on solid deck and the wind at their backs, and the thing he most believed at this point in time, the thing he *knew* with a certainty down to his bones and beyond, down through all the turtles beneath, was that he was going to swallow Julian's dick like a python. "You seem a bit ill too, Baltakan," he said curryfully.

Baltakan was absolutely still, one hand covering his mouth and a wildly manic look in his eyes. "He. But he was lying."

"I feel like this is the fundamental difference between the Ministries of Diplomacy and Intelligence," Avra said pensively. "You eggheads in Diplomacy always think you know what people are like and that you can predict how they'll behave. On the other hand, Intelligence has seen some shit and knows that it only takes one absolute madman to fuck up your whole day."

"Does he sound mad to you?" Baltakan said, gesturing toward the door. "He sounds *terrifyingly* sane to me, apart from the—the *content*—"

"Intelligence knows," Avra said airily, "that 'sane' doesn't exist. Nobody is sane. Nobody has ever been sane. Sane is fake. Sane is . . ." He waved to his own face. "One of those things you wear to a masked ball."

". . . A mask?"

"Yes, thank you, one of those. Behind everybody's sanity mask is someone who is unalloyed batshit in one way or another. This is the truth of human nature, Baltakan." He polished off the last dregs of beer. "When I say 'one absolute madman,' that's not somebody less sane, because nobody's sane. That's just somebody who's decided that leaving his mask off gets him where he wants to be, which is usually somewhere really weird that nobody expects him to go." He paused. "Like the top of a wardrobe."

"What?"

"I can't possibly explain everything you don't know about, Baltakan, please." Avra got up. "Yusin, if there's anything we didn't pay for, could you send the bill to the ambassador's house? He's legally required to pay all his bills to local merchants or risk disciplinary action."

"Yup," said Eel-face Yusin. "One roast goose, three bottles of wine, roast potatoes, broccoli soup, and four blackberry custards for dessert, wasn't it?"

"It definitely was all of those things. Come along, Baltakan, I'm supposed to keep an eye on Julian."

Baltakan had to run to catch up with him. "Those were your orders?" he said intently. "You're watching *him*?"

"Mmnnn . . . I feel like I told you that before. Were you not listening to me, or is it that you're only just now realizing why my job is important, even if I am technically on partial retirement? Mother of All, Baltakan! Do you *really* think you're the only thing standing between Araşt and ruin? I can't stand you Diplomacy assholes, you know, you're all like this."

"You're a *courier.*"

"*You're a courier,*" Avra mocked in a squeaky falsetto voice. "*My name's Ambassador Baltakan and that means I know everything about everything and I'd be good at any job I decided to fumble my way through!* Didn't you yourself say you were transferred out of Intelligence to Diplomacy after a little while as a courier? Which suggests that the higher-ups, who do go to *just so much trouble* to place people where their natural talents will best aid them, thought that you weren't suited for the job. I really don't know why you keep insisting on trying to do mine, when *I* don't try to do yours—I have never once traipsed around negotiating treaties or spent any time trying to remember whether it's polite to bring my own dinner knife to a fancy party or not." He shouldered the door open and stepped out into the eye-smartingly bright sunlight, made some undignified noises about it, and found his arm caught by a hand he knew was Julian's before he even opened his eyes again. "Hello. Hello, Julian. I'm being so incredibly normal about your oath. Please let go of my arm, I need to scamper over to Teveri and ask if they would like a massively distracting piece of urgent news while they are focused on the most important day of their life and Mistress Navya's gorgeous cake."

"Please repeat what you just said very slowly and listen to what you are saying."

"I hear what I am saying, Julian! I said I'm going to *aaaaasssssssk* if they want massively distracting news. That's just good communication."

"No," said Teveri. "Get away from me."

"Tev. Tev. Tev Tev Tev."

"Get away from me, and also get the fucking ambassador away from me before I rip his balls off with my bare hands."

Baltakan scowled and moved a single step back. He had been impossible to shake off, unlike poor Amita, who was sitting quietly in the shade by Eel-face Yusin's restaurant with a splitting headache—Avra had asked Yusin to check on her from time to time, and she had assured them all that she would be well enough to make her way slowly back to the ambassador's house given a little time to rest and recover from the expenditure of strain.

Teveri spat at Baltakan and threw a dead seagull at him, which he dodged easily—though he needed to turn away and gag into his palm for a few moments. "Why is he here? Why is he wearing a bunch of potato sacks?"

"Because turtles think they're sexy, Tev," Avra said soothingly. "Anyway—"

Baltakan made an outraged noise. "*Helvaçi,* what has gotten into you? I have a mind to write to your superior officers and—"

"*I have a mind to write to your superior officers,*" Avra simpered. "Maybe I should write to *your* superior officers and report to them that I discovered at least four outstanding bills with local merchants who you were refusing to pay, hm? Or maybe I should write directly to the Ministry of Internal Affairs and tell them that Diplomacy is knowingly allowing their ambassadors to skip out on their bills and that I recommend doing a full audit of *every* ambassador's ledgers and maybe Diplomacy as a whole, just in case? Should I do that? *I* can provide proof in the form of unpaid receipts that local merchants will be only too happy to provide to me, and all *you* can say is that I was vaguely rude to you and you're *vewy vewy mad about it*. But who would you be writing to? Oh yes, Ministry of Intelligence. Do you know what they do with whiny letters from Diplomacy? So many mean jokes. Performing dramatic readings at office parties." Teveri whipped out their scimitar and took a wild swing at a seagull who had gotten a little too bold—they missed, but the seagull at least changed its mind about attempting to sneak into Mistress Navya's pavilion. "Not too many of those varmints here today, eh?"

Teveri pushed their hat back and wiped sweat off their forehead with their sleeve. "The board is trying a new thing this year. Black Garda told us last night. Extra opportunity for the crews to posture to each other."

"Oooh?"

"Whoever donates the most dead fish to spread out on the beaches on the other side of the Tits gets praise and glory, blah blah blah. We weren't prepared, so we don't outright *win,* but . . ." Teveri shrugged. "Black Garda arranged for all the serpent's innards to be carried over there after the taxidermist had skinned it. So that's worth bragging about, at least."

"Glad to hear that we're getting some use out of that fucking thing," Avra said loudly, aware that Baltakan was right there. "So are you sure you don't want incredibly distracting news? It's about . . . *Julian.*" Avra gestured to Julian, who was standing back with a rueful expression.

"I want to know *absolutely nothing* until Mistress Navya's *extremely beautiful and breathtaking cake wins the whole competition, as it so richly deserves to do, because every other cake here is embarrassing to even look at.* Get the fuck away from me, Avra, and take Ambassador Turtle-fucker with you. *And* Julian. Go insult some cakes. Go set some of the pavilions on fire. Catch some seagulls and hurl them inside."

"I think that would count as a projectile weapon," Avra said regretfully, clasping his hands under his chin and making his eyes very big. "We might get in trouble for breaking rule number one."

"The board just ruled that *live* seagulls do not count as projectile weapons," Teveri said tightly. "Because someone tried to do that to us half an hour ago."

Avra spluttered in outrage. "What, because it's a live animal? And it can control its own movements? Well, fuck, then what's to stop us from throwing *me* at the other cakes? Let's bring a fucking Avra-sized catapult next year, why not!"

"Good idea," Teveri said flatly. "Do that. Julian, take him and the turtle-fucker away."

25

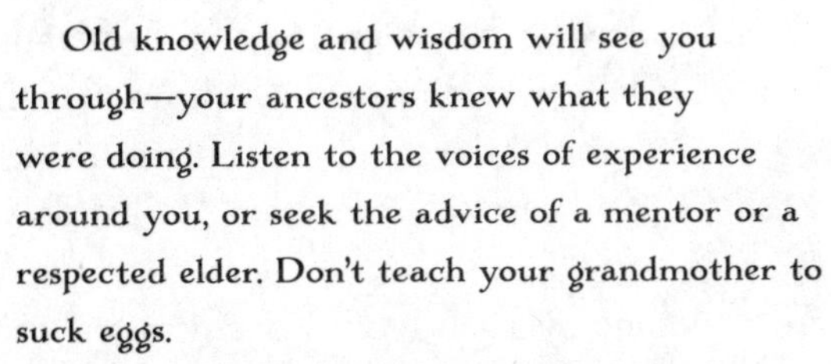

76. The Crone

Old knowledge and wisdom will see you through—your ancestors knew what they were doing. Listen to the voices of experience around you, or seek the advice of a mentor or a respected elder. Don't teach your grandmother to suck eggs.

(Reversed: Old grudges, being stuck in your ways, turning away from new knowledge or information. Change is constant and eternal; therefore, stagnation is a choice. If you keep challenging yourself to learn and grow and improve your skills, you will never *feel* old.)

Avra reflected that it was rather nice of Julian to have been kind to Amita, and that perhaps Avra could follow his good example. It really wasn't Ambassador Baltakan's *fault* that he was an intolerable prig. It was just his own brand of batshitness, concealed behind a sanity mask that he'd developed through a career in Diplomacy. *Everyone* in Diplomacy was an intolerable prig, after all. And an egghead.

"Ambassador," he said loudly as they ambled across the wide gap to the next pavilion. "I've decided it's not your fault that you're an intolerable prig. Though I really don't know why you're still following us."

"I am attempting to understand your methods," said Baltakan, the man wearing some potato sacks and calling it a disguise.

Julian and Avra exchanged a look. Avra was charmed down to his toes (even the little toe on his left foot, which was distinctly weird) and strengthened his resolve to be vaguely polite to Baltakan. "That's the spirit. Good to keep learning things. Julian is very proud of you. Ahoy the pavilion, may we approach? We are representatives from Mistress Navya. Well, not this man following us. We're not associated with him in any way and you don't have to let him in. In fact, I recommend that you don't."

"*Well well well,* look what the mangiest cat in the islands dragged in," said Captain Dallah, sauntering over. She had a magnificent hat edged with gold lace around the brim, and a plume made of a very large dried fish fin of a deep iridescent blue. "What do you want, Helvaçi?"

"We were overcome by a sense of masochism and morbid curiosity, so we have come around to look at objects claiming to be cakes and perhaps offer some unsolicited but richly deserved constructive criticism to your sorry excuse for a cakesmith. We are not armed."

"You can look at the cake from right where you fucking are."

Avra craned his neck. "I can't see it. You've got it surrounded by, what, thirty people? Captain Dallah, be reasonable." He winced sympathetically. "It's that ugly, is it? I expected that, but I didn't expect you to be so defensive about it. Did it come out burnt? What a shame."

"This is one of the stupider sabotage attempts I've seen today. Helvaçi, *you're Araşti.* You work for the Ministry of Intelligence. Why the fuck would we let you anywhere near our cake after you heard the theme? *Please.*"

Avra held up his hands. "Hey, I've got a sense of humor! It's *the cake competition,* Dallah, all bets are off for the cake competition. *I* don't care what your cakesmith is saying about the Shipbuilder's Guild. It's probably stupid and poorly thought out anyway, not to mention insipid in execution."

"No," she said flatly. She eyed Julian. "Who are you?"

"A Vint," he said sunnily.

"You can see the cake. From right where you're standing. Don't fucking move or we'll put you in the seagull bin."

"Describe it for me," Avra said. "I want to hear how ugly it is."

Dallah gestured vaguely behind her and one or two of the thirty people surrounding the cake shifted just far enough aside for Julian—who was much taller than Avra—to be able to see the cake.

"Hm. It is unbelievably ugly," Julian said. "There is a large cube-shaped rock—oh, is that part of the cake? You'll have to forgive me, Captain, but it does look like it's covered in seagull shit."

"That's the Shipbuilder's Guild, sculpted in cake."

"Well, *sculpted* is an awfully strong word for what has been done to that. I mean this sincerely: I would not have known what it was if you had not told me. It is hideous. For some absurd reason, there are wilting flowers messily stuck into it, I haven't the foggiest idea what that's supposed to be—"

"Those are fireworks, and it's a very good and very creative way to artistically represent them," Dallah said.

"At the front of the building is an unsettling gaping maw with a clumsy and childish attempt at representing teeth—"

"That's a splintered and broken-down door."

"And on the other side of this so-called tableau—goodness me, this isn't to scale at all, is it! Did the cakesmith even try?"

"Amateur move," Avra said. "Stupid. Embarrassing."

"On the other side is a group of deeply unrealistic and childish dancing bears—"

"People," said Dallah.

"Are they really? Astonishing. They are made of . . . rancid pâté? No? Cake as well, is that right! I truly cannot tell. Are they participating in some kind of distasteful ritual?"

"Wow, Julian, you can't even tell what they're doing?" said Avra. "The cake is so bad that you can't even tell what part of it is supposed to *be*?"

"They are *the people of the world* joyously celebrating," Dallah said through gritted teeth. "They are dancing around a bonfire."

"Oh, is that why your cake is on fire?" said Julian smoothly. "I thought it was just personal incompetence."

"It's a candle."

"Wow," said Avra. "So your cakesmith decided to use ugly flowers to represent fireworks, but actual fire to represent an actual fire? No internal consistency whatsoever. Your cakesmith passed up an opportunity to utilize repetition and thematic resonance and just left it lying on the table like a sad piece of wet bread. That's what your cake is. It's just wet bread. Gross."

"Helvaçi," said Baltakan tightly. "I cannot help but feel that this is not how your superiors would wish for you to be representing the Ministry—"

"He's not with us," Avra said. "He is not affiliated with Mistress Navya or the crew of *The Running Sun*. Thank you, Captain Dallah. Condolences about your extremely bad and very ugly cake. I hope you personally as an individual enjoy the competition and this fine weather, because your cake is godawful and I am not enjoying even being near it. I haven't even seen the wretched thing and I am not enjoying it."

"Neither am I," said Julian. "In fact, I feel sorry for you that you have to pretend to like this cake. I wish I hadn't looked at it."

"Good day, *Running Sun*," Captain Dallah said, flicking her hand at them. A split second later, she seized the hefty wooden club leaning against her thigh, took a running leap, and smashed a seagull out of the air just as it looped around for an attempt at getting under the edge of the pavilion.

Her crew cheered. Avra politely clapped. At Julian's alarmed look, he whispered, "We are allowed to express appreciation for other crews nailing a seagull in a particularly impressive way. The seagulls are the real enemy of the competition, and we must be united against them. Well done, Captain Dallah!" he said, raising his voice a little. "A fine and elegant move. Your seagull-smashing talents are wasted on this terrible and undeserving cake."

Captain Dallah tweaked the brim of her hat to him in the tiniest of acknowledgments as she picked up the seagull and hove it into a large nearby barrel with its other fallen comrades. "Move along, Helvaçi, and tell Navya that I'd rather die than even look at her cake."

The rest of the pavilions went in much the same way. Baltakan followed with ever-increasing horror, objecting several times to the "diplomatic nightmare" he was causing.

They passed the group of judges making their way around the circle, widdershins to Avra and Julian's clockwise. "Judges!" Avra called. "May I beg a moment of your time? The briefest moment?"

Cat, apparently elected the chief of the judges, greeted the two of them smoothly and glanced down at his scoring ledger as he flipped to an earlier page. "It seems that Mistress Navya's crew has not yet taken advantage of their single allowed attempt to sweet-talk, bribe, threaten, blackmail, or otherwise coerce the judges into favoring their cakesmith. Are you choosing to do so now?"

"Yes, please."

"One moment." Cat made a note in the ledger, then turned it toward Avra. Skully held out a dip pen and bottle. "Sign here, please," Cat said, tapping on the line next to *Mistress Navya / The Running Sun* with one perfectly manicured fingernail. Avra scrawled his name on the line and handed the pen back to Skully. "Thank you, *Running Sun*. You may proceed."

Avra took Cat's hand and said solemnly, "I'm sorry I said you were the worst person I know after Julian. You are actually the nicest person I know. You so incredibly deserve to be cake competition judge every year." He took out the remainder of the packet of stolen ambassadorial almonds from his little rucksack, which he had brought with the intention of having them as a snack later. "This is a gift for you, so that you might favor our cakesmith. Don't ask me where I got them from; I think you know. You should cherish them for always and put them on the shelf next to that salami and jam I brought you." Cat's magisterial composure was fracturing. He took the bag of almonds, glanced at Baltakan, and bit the inside of his cheek, returning his expression to Avra with innocent inquisitiveness. "I also think your hair looks so so so so pretty today, particularly red and magnificent, and that you objectively have the perkiest butt on this whole island. I would rather look at it than any cake in this contest, including Mistress Navya's—though her cake *is* more magnificent than all the others, and I think we both know that is true. I also would like to tell you that Julian—this is Julian, I'm sure you remember Julian—that he just decided to say *fuck the vow*"—Cat's eyes lit up, entirely destroying the rest of his magisterial composure, and he pressed his fingertips to his mouth to hide his expression of mounting glee—"and I definitely credit that to your wisdom and the excellence of your advice. I look forward to doing friendship activities with you, and also possibly professional activities such as regards the salami. Thank you for the excellence of your service to the cake competition and, really, to the entire human race by merely existing and being as marvelously Catty as you are. Julian, as my colleague you are permitted to offer an additional comment to *one* of the other judges."

"I greatly admire your sculpture on the cliff, sir," Julian said to Skully. "It is a work of breathtaking magnificence already and I look forward to seeing future progress—I find your dedication and ingenuity truly inspiring." Skully looked mildly pleased, but only mildly so.

"In conclusion," Avra said, "I hope you will both be favorable to Mistress Navya's cake. Thank you for your time." He nodded. "We are done."

Cat cleared his throat and made another note in the ledger. His cheeks were a little bit pink. "Thank you, *Running Sun*. Your comments will certainly be taken into consideration."

"And my bribe."

"Yes, and your bribe of these . . . delicious almonds, which I will not be eating. They will go on my shelf. Good day."

"Helvaçi." Baltakan sighed. "*Bribing* the judges?"

"Don't pretend like Diplomacy doesn't hold with bribery," Avra said.

"Not out in the open!"

"It's in the rules that we're allowed to try one time. You saw, I had to sign a receipt for it and everything."

"Why did that redheaded man keep looking at me and laughing after you handed him the—"

"Baltakan! I am working right now, I truly do not have time to explain everything to you." He turned to Julian to explain the things he did have time for. "A little bit of an amateur choice on your part, but this is your first cake competition, so at least he knew you were sincere—it's just that everyone says that to Skully whenever he's cake judge. That's all right, you just need to know more people and get some practice. Like right now. *Julian,*" he said loudly as they approached the last pavilion before they completed the circle and came back around to their own tent. "*Which has been your least favorite cake so far?*"

"I don't think I can choose. To say that one was my least favorite is to imply that the others are better, and all of them so far make me feel sad and tired."

"Yes, so true, they are all dreadful in their own uniquely awful way, and I regret the time we have spent on this useless endeavor. Hello, Captain Ueleari, lovely to see you again, condolences about your cake."

"Helvaçi," said Captain Ueleari. "Condolences about your cake as well. I wandered over there during my lunch break out of a sense of morbid curiosity."

"Yes, yes, morbid curiosity, yes indeed, that is also what brings us over here. This is my friend Julian—he is new to the crew. Could we see your cake, please?"

"Sounds like you *want* to see it. Sounds like you're *looking forward* to seeing it."

"Oh, no, no, it's not that, it's just that Julian took his eyes off me for two seconds and I swallowed a handful of pennies, so we're trying to make me throw up and we thought the sight of your cake might help. That's the only reason. That and morbid curiosity."

"Captain Ofia's cake didn't do it for you?" Ueleari said, nodding to the neighboring pavilion, which they had just come from.

"No, unfortunately! I found it the sort of bad that is more likely to give me nightmares for the rest of my life than turn my stomach." It had been, apparently, a representation of the Araşti sultan sitting on her chamber pot and weeping, with gold coins coming out of both ends. (Baltakan had lost his diplomatic composure for a full thirty seconds. He had nearly *fainted*.) Most of the other cakes had been variations on sentiments such as "Isn't it great that this has happened? The entire world should be filled with glee," and "If I had broken into the Shipbuilder's Guild, here is what I would have done."

"That you, Ambassador?" Ueleari said, frowning. "The fuck are you doing here? Are those potato sacks?"

"He's not with us," Avra said loudly. "And as a fellow countryman of his, I apologize for his everything. Just his whole demeanor. And personality. And presence. I would say that I hope him being here doesn't ruin the cake competition for you, but I expect that your cake has already done that. How are you doing emotionally?"

"Granny Layla's cake is a triumph and it brings me incalculable joy and eases my heart's burdens every time I glance upon it," Ueleari said with a perfectly straight face. "So I'd say I'm doing pretty well, thank you for asking."

"Who's that?" quavered the voice of a very elderly lady from somewhere behind Ueleari's wall of crew. "Matty, who's that you're talking to?"

"Some blond man named Julian, and also Avra Helvaçi," Ueleari called back. "Teveri az-Ḥaffār's pet weasel. That's *The Running Sun*, Granny."

"I prefer mongoose," said Avra. "Or raccoon."

"I *know* Captain az-Ḥaffār's ship, Matty," Granny Layla said, annoyed. "Let them in, come along."

Ueleari raised his eyes to the heavens. "Granny. We cannot keep letting people into the tent."

"Are you disrespecting me, boy? I said let them in."

"Do you want me to let Ambassador Turtle-fucker in as well? He is also here."

There was a silence, broken only by a couple of Ueleari's crew leaping into action to destroy a seagull that was edging a little too close for comfort. "Hm, no, you can continue being rude to Ambassador Turtle-fucker," said Granny Layla. "He's not a nice boy. Avra Helvaçi is a nice boy. I would imagine that a blond man named Julian is also a nice boy."

"It's just that I wonder whether they are nice enough as boys to *not fucking sabotage your cake,* Granny," said Captain Ueleari, glaring daggers at the two of them.

"They wouldn't sabotage an old lady's cake," Granny Layla said confidently. "Now stop being rude and let them in, Matty. It's a hot day. You haven't even offered them any lemonade."

"We don't want your shit garbage lemonade," Avra said instantly. "We will not be seen consuming food or drink under the roof of people with a terrible fucking cake they're so ashamed of that they won't even let us inside to peek at it and retch into our hands."

"Attempting to poison us with lemonade?" Julian said. "What a laughably obvious ploy."

"Well, that was worth a shot," said Granny Layla. "We got what's-her-name from Dallah's crew with that one, at least. Let the nice boys in, Matty."

"I will remind you that you're surrounded on all sides and that we are armed to the teeth," Ueleari said calmly. "And that she is an old lady and the matriarch of the cake competition. Show some fucking respect."

"No," said Avra.

"I cannot ethically show respect to a sickeningly bad cake or the person who made it," Julian said. "It would go against my personal values."

Ueleari nodded. "I understand. I would hurl Mistress Navya's cake into a sewer if I could. That's where it belongs."

"Matty, let them in."

Ueleari stepped aside and gestured them in.

Granny Layla was sitting in a beautifully crafted wheelchair next to her display table, knitting industriously. She smiled at them as they came in, and her already wrinkly face creased up with more wrinkles than there were stars in the sky. "Hello, Master Avra. How are you?"

"Very bad," Avra announced. "I wish I were not here. Where's your so-called cake? Oh, is it that strange and unappealing thing on the table? Astonishing. It doesn't look like any cake I have ever seen. I think it is awfully rich of you to call that a cake. I would be embarrassed if I were in your shoes."

Granny Layla kept smiling and knitting. "Matty took me over to see young Navya's cake and I wished I were dead the moment I laid eyes on it."

"Dead of jealousy? I understand."

"Who's your handsome friend?" Granny Layla eyed Julian up and down with open appreciation. "Does he want to turn coat? I can pay triple whatever Navya's paying you, young man."

"I feel physically ill at the very thought of representing you or your terrible cake," Julian said politely.

"Well then!" Avra said, setting his hands on his hips. "It is the cake competition, so I would not dream of extending any courtesies such as a kiss on the hand to you, an incompetent, irrelevant, and obsolete cakesmith—"

"Keep your filthy fucking lips to yourself. They've probably tasted Navya's revolting excuse for a cake, and no amount of scrubbing would get the stench off."

"—so why don't you put us out of our misery and explain this—this—whatever this is."

"Ah, well!" Granny Layla said, setting her knitting down and sitting up eagerly. "I would be most happy to. This is an Araşti ship. Please note that it is not a *representation,* but in fact a replica at one-to-thirty scale."

"Ah . . . To scale, you say?"

"Of course."

"Doesn't look like it."

Granny Layla laughed raucously. "As I was saying, it is executed in four different varieties of cake, as well as coffee-flavored caramel brittle for the wooden effect on . . . well, everywhere you would expect wood to be. The ropes and rigging are made of spun sugar; the sails are edible rice paper; and all the little crew are marzipan, except for the captain, who is a molded chocolate."

"Yuck," said Avra weakly.

"Disgusting," said Julian, equally weakly.

Granny Layla smiled like a shark. "You will notice that it has the classically Araşti decorative patterns painted on the hull. The paint was made of a rice-flour-and-water paste blended with colored spices, such as saffron, powdered pistachios, and the petals of dried roses and violets. There is also a secret."

Avra scoffed. "Stupid secret, probably. I'd rather not hear it. What is it?"

Granny Layla raised a finger to her lips, beckoned them closer, and leaned forward to breathe gently on the hull of the ship.

A shimmer of light rippled across it. Avra went ice cold, every hair on his body standing on end and *staying* there.

"Matty was *such* a dear and managed to acquire a thimbleful of Cascaveyan starwine for me a few years ago," Granny Layla said smugly. "And I knew immediately what cake I wanted to use it for—but I had to wait for the right theme to come around, of course. You can't waste something that precious on just any cake."

"Nrkgh?" said Avra.

Julian took a deep, steady breath. "Sorry, could you show me that again, grandmère?"

"As many times as you like," she said, and did it again.

"He doesn't *enjoy* seeing it," Avra said quickly. "It's sort of like picking at a scab, you know."

Julian exhaled. "Grandmère," he said with deadly seriousness. "I realize this is the cake competition, and I do assure you that this is in the running for the worst cake I've seen in my life and nothing would give me greater vindication than to see it devoured by seagulls which then die en masse. That said, if I swear to you on my honor that I will not touch your horrible cake, may I please come quite . . . *quite* close?"

"By all means."

"Granny," groaned Ueleari from the front of the pavilion.

"Mind your business, Matty! If a handsome young man wants to take a very close look at my cake, I'm not too old to turn him down."

"Granny."

"Don't mind him," Granny Layla said with a saucy wink. "Why don't you kneel down right here by me, so that I can put a hand on those handsome shoulders of yours to support me while I lean forward, and so that if you turn out to be dishonorable you'll be well within reach for me to stab you in the ear with my knitting needle. You said your name was Julian, was it?"

"Yes, grandmère." Julian watched intently as she leaned forward and blew again—the same shimmer of silvery light rippled up and faded away just as quickly. "I see."

"The starwine stops glowing when it's dry," she said. "But a breath has enough moisture to make it shimmer again." Her eyes were as sharp as her knitting needles as she shot a glance at Julian. "Do you know what it is?"

"I . . ." Julian gazed at the ship. "I don't know what you mean. You said it's starwine that does this?" Quickly, he added, "I think that's sickeningly ostentatious and a reprehensible display of wealth, by the way."

"Of course, of course," she said with a sigh. "Well, either you know it or you don't."

"Grandmère," Julian said. A strong chill went up Avra's spine. "I am struck speechless by the failure of this cake to engage with the subject matter in any kind of meaningful way."

"Mm."

"And so I do not know the question I should be asking."

Granny Layla shrugged and picked up her knitting.

"I know what to ask," said Avra loudly. "Your metaphors are entirely obtuse and obscure and—and opaque. This is not good political commentary at all. It is among the worst examples of political commentary I have ever seen in my life. How did you dream up something so pathetically insipid and trite? And also what is that supposed to symbolize?"

"When I was a girl," Granny Layla said, in a whisper so quiet that Avra had to crowd as close as Julian to hear her, "I worked as a cook up at the ambassador's house. Not the last ambassador—the one before her. I liked it because it gave me an excuse to go walking up on the cliffs by myself at night with my spyglass. One fine clear night around this time of year—I remember it was summer and the moons were dark, and all the captains had brought their ships safe into harbor—I was out there to see if I could spot any of the sea serpents coming up. I saw a swarm of 'em out at the edge of the Turtle Shallows, flashing their colors under the water and sometimes thrashing above the surface. And then I saw something." She looked at them both.

"A ship," whispered Avra.

She shrugged. "Maybe. Maybe not."

Julian was trembling faintly and biting his lip, staring at Granny Layla's ship. "May I?" he whispered. "May I try breathing on it?"

"May he try blowing the rancid fumes away with his mouth," Avra corrected. "That's what he means."

"Go ahead," she said, readying one of her knitting needles.

Julian leaned forward and blew, very gently. The ship shimmered. He sat back heavily on his heels, staring at it. Slowly, he said, "What did you see out there, that night?"

"Hm." She studied them both. "Do you know what it is or not?"

Julian looked up at her. His eyes were wide and shining with—with something. "I'm not . . . *sure*," he whispered. "But I think I might."

"What's the rest of the story worth to you? Enough to go tip over Navya's table?"

"Grandmère, it's worth more than this entire absurd competition," Julian breathed. "*Please. Please.*"

She tilted her head and studied him. "What are you going to do with it?"

Julian laughed breathlessly, his eyes as bright as if they had tears in them. He caught Layla's hand and squeezed it. "I'm going to tear down something that the most powerful people in the world very much don't want to have torn down. And I'm going to get away with it."

Goose bumps once again broke out all over Avra's body.

She grinned and touched his cheek, then gave it a little grandmotherly pinch. "Never been able to resist a pretty face. Helvaçi was right—I saw a ship. And then I saw the ship's hull, which I should not have been able to do, as it was beneath the black, black water on the darkest night of summer. I thought it was the serpents at first, but it didn't move like serpents move. It moved like a ship. So then I thought it was a ghost ship, but it was the part *under* the water that shone, and ghost-light is smothered by salt water. I sat there for an hour watching that ship, and then the light faded and the dark swallowed it up."

Avra felt another hard chill.

"And the serpents?" said Julian.

"Took no notice," said Granny Layla. "I thought it was interesting. I went to bed, woke up and made breakfast for the house, went out for a walk, and saw an Araşti supply ship in the harbor. So I thought to myself, 'Layla, perhaps that's actually *too* interesting and you ought to hold on to that just for yourself.'" She smiled and nodded. "You may now tell me it is a very silly fancy and I dreamed the whole thing."

"Very silly," Avra said quickly. "Dreamed it. So silly. Ha ha. Granny Layla being fucking *whimsical* at the cake competition instead of taking it seriously. Insulting, if I'm being honest. I'm insulted by the sheer amount of whimsy I'm hearing right now. The cake competition is not for fucking around, Granny Layla, you ought to know that better than anyone."

"I do," she said with another sharklike smile. "I was informed of the theme of this competition, and I thought to myself, 'Layla, you're an old lady and you've lived a good long life, maybe it doesn't matter as much if you find yourself taking a gamble and sailing closer to the wind than you usually would—maybe you're old enough now to sail that close to the wind on purpose, just to see what happens, and if you forfeit something big in losing that wager, well! It's been a good long life, hasn't it?' Thought to myself that there's never been a security breach at the Araşti Shipbuilder's Guild before. Thought that anyone who was there and took something would keep it awful quiet, maybe as quiet as I've kept my whimsical little story for these seventy years. Thought that there was a chance that this story might be . . . important. Maybe because there's some clue in the telling that even I can't spot because I was only a girl and all I know is what I saw that night. Maybe just because someone who was at the Guild, and who got out with their life, and who made it to the place that anyone would take a secret like that . . . Well, that person or persons might feel as alone as I felt when I thought that I was the only person who was watching. It helps, I find, to remember that there is *always* someone watching. Always." Her sharklike smile turned impish. "And then a couple days ago, my Matty came charging into the house and told me that *The Running Sun* was setting sail and leaving the safety of port, right in the horniest first days of the serpent season. And I thought to myself, 'I wonder if Teveri az-Ḥaffār is an idiot . . . or a lunatic.' And then I thought to myself, 'Avra Helvaçi is on that ship, and Avra Helvaçi is an Araşti spy, and I've seen Avra Helvaçi scuttle up a palm tree like a little rat that's got something badly wrong with it, so he could probably climb into anything he wanted, even a heavily guarded building.' I thought to myself, 'Avra Helvaçi has never seemed particularly beholden to Araşt, and Avra Helvaçi was once so wildly in love with Teveri az-Ḥaffār that he gave them the mainsail of the *Nightingale*—gave it freely, like the hero in a fairy tale, and asked for absolutely nothing in return.' And I thought, 'I wonder what else Avra Helvaçi might do to get Captain az-Ḥaffār's attention . . .'"

"Reeeeeeee," Avra said. "Hhhgnnng. Aiiiiiiee."

"There's *always* someone watching, young man." Granny Layla smirked. "So I kept my mouth shut and I told Matty that he ought to tell me the names of everyone who stopped by to look at the cake today. And whenever *The Running Sun* has come by, I've told Matty to let them in, and I've blown on the cake for them, just to see what they'd do."

"Whhhhhy have you done this," said Avra. "Wh. Why."

"Well, partly because I thought that if my little hunch was right, it would *badly* discompose at least one of you, and possibly several of you, and then you'd be off-balance for the rest of the cake competition, which can only be good for me. Credit where credit's due to Teveri az-Ḥaffār, I was not expecting the *entire crew* to look as disturbed as they have—what a good captain, to trust their crew enough to keep them so well-informed. But the rest of it, well . . . There are things in the world more important than the cake competition."

"*Granny,*" said Captain Ueleari, because this last part had been at normal volume. "Keep your voice down if you're saying things like that!"

"Oh, nobody can fucking touch me anymore, Matty, I'm a fixture of this competition! What are they going to do, throw me out?" She rolled her eyes and leaned forward to pat Julian's cheek again before she picked up her knitting needles. "Try to get yourself sorted out before I die," she said briskly. "All I want is to know what the fuck I saw and how it works so that I can stop thinking about it all the time."

"Deal," said Julian, and rolled up to his feet. He seized Avra's arm and dragged him out of the pavilion. "Distract the ambassador," he hissed. "I have to leave *right now.*"

"Very unfair of you to pull me around like this if it's not followed by pushing me against a wall," Avra said. "Ambassador! Hello! The cake was sickening, in case you were wondering. I can see by your face that you've been standing out here in your potato sacks and thinking some thoughts to yourself, and you've come up with something very important that you probably want to say. I will happily listen to all of that, but as you can see, Julian is dragging me back to our pavilion. He's a very horny man, Baltakan. You'll just have to, yes, follow along with us, and as soon as Julian releases my arm, I will definitely listen with the greatest solemnity to every word you might want to impart to me. Please excuse me for just one moment, though, while I consult with Brother Julian about why he is choosing to be so rough and proprietary with my poor helpless body. *Also, just as a side note, I am truly shocked at the poor quality of this year's cakes. Having inflicted upon myself the unmitigated torture of looking at each and every cake, I can say with absolute confidence that Mistress Navya's cake is the only one worthy of winning the competition, as it is scrumptious in appearance, well-thought-out and nuanced in its political statements and interpretation of the theme, and masterful in its execution.*" Avra dropped his voice to a whisper. "I thought you said you had to leave right now."

"I'm taking you to Teveri first, hush."

"Very rude. Very rude of you. After we had that very deep and serious conversation about how I would not stand to be toyed with or flirted with, and after I have been so incredibly casual and unaffected about you saying that thing about your oath—even after all that, you do this."

Julian stopped in his tracks, turned to face Avra, took his face in both of his hands, and said with deadly seriousness, "Avra, we're in the middle of the fucking cake competition. This is very important to Teveri. I would stop your mouth right now, but we *cannot* distract them. In a very real way, the fate of the world is at stake."

"Mreee," said Avra, slightly squished between Julian's hands. "What does that mean. What does that mean. What does 'stop my mouth' mean?"

"It means I would kiss you to make you shut up."

"Classic," squeaked Avra. "Classic. Classic. A classic."

Julian let him go and kept striding toward their pavilion. "Teveri," he said, as soon as they were in earshot. Teveri looked over just as Julian put a hand in the middle of Avra's back and pushed him toward them. "Watch Avra."

Avra wheeled around with a bright, wide grin for Baltakan. "And here we are at the pavilion. What was it you were going to say? You had something just so important to say."

Baltakan took a deep breath. "Yes, Helvaçi, in fact I did. I have been thinking about what you said so crassly about how I have been attempting to do your job for you, and that my talents lie in areas of more nuance than yours."

"Did I say that?" Avra mused. "We can pretend I did, I suppose. Yes. So much nuance, Baltakan. Balls deep in nuance and turtles, that's you." Baltakan was not paying any attention to Julian, who had bent to whisper something extremely brief to Teveri and continued striding off in the direction of the main part of town.

"I acknowledge that there are skills and expertise about the situation that you might not have—and while your behavior today has been profoundly shocking, you did clear your name with Witness Amita yesterday, and so I have no choice but to accept that perhaps your methods have some kind of reasoning to them that eludes me." He dropped his voice to a crisp murmur. "Perhaps this is some kind of persona you put on for . . . these people's benefit. I cannot say. I acknowledge as well that the Ministry of Intelligence has jurisdiction over a rather different aspect of protecting Araşt's interests than Diplomacy does, and to disparage that, even in the privacy of my own mind—"

"Has it been in private?"

"—is to disparage the work of an entire ministry of our government—a ministry which undoubtedly has as many secret projects and private concerns as Diplomacy does. We may serve the crown in different ways, but as they say, we are all equal in Her Majesty's service."

"Mhm," said Avra. "So true. So incredibly true."

"I think," Baltakan said with magnificent poise, "that perhaps I have offered offense by not behaving in accordance with that adage."

"Wait, are you apologizing? Is this an apology?"

"Doesn't sound much like an apology to me," said Teveri from several feet away. Avra edged backward toward them and reached behind to fumble for their hand. Teveri snatched it away and batted sharply at him. "Get off, Avra."

"Trying, incandescent one!" Avra said over his shoulder. "Trying every day! Trying my very best!"

"Helvaçi, please pay attention," Baltakan said.

"Hmm?" Avra said. "I'm paying attention. You were telling me whether it was an apology?"

"Well, not as such."

"Oh. All right. I would have been surprised if it was, haha."

"It is more an acknowledgment of the fact that there may be some misunderstandings between us, perhaps some friction due to the differences in how we conduct our business, and that—"

The gong sounded.

"Cakesmiths," bellowed one of the competition organizers. "Judging is nearly finished! However, as you have all heard by now, one of your esteemed judges has named a rubric which requires some special considerations in order to execute and quantify it in such a way that is *fair and objective* to all."

Avra whipped around. "Tev, what's this?"

"Skully," Tev said darkly. "One of the rubrics he's judging on is *durability.*"

"Durability of the cakes?" Avra whisper-screamed.

"Shut up." They nodded to the platform, where the speaker was showing an empty hat and carefully and visibly counting out eight scraps of paper into it. "They're having all the cakes moved to one randomly selected pavilion."

"Randomly selected," Avra said faintly. "Hm."

Teveri gave him a pointed, rather feral look.

"So are we hoping it's ours or someone else's?" he said with a nervous little laugh.

Teveri held that pointed, feral stare without moving a muscle until the announcer called, "The cakes will be moved to Mistress Navya's pavilion."

"I cannot stand you," Teveri said.

"Well, I think you're great, so that averages out to both of us being only okay. You know how I feel about half-assing it, Tev."

26

46. The Feast Day

Joyous times spent with loved ones, celebrations, sharing the wealth with those who helped you. Whether you have survived a long winter or just reaped a plentiful harvest, this is a time to enjoy the fruits of your labors. Rejoice, for there is more than enough to eat—fill your belly. Happiness shared is happiness multiplied.

(Reversed: Feeling disconnected from community, walking alone even though you are in a crowd of people, the disappointment of no one showing up to your party. A joyful occasion or moment is interrupted and spoiled.)

The moving of the cakes was a delicate process, between the hypervigilant and paranoid pirate crews watching each other like seagulls for any twitch of a move in the wrong direction, and the hypervigilant and hungry seagulls watching the cakes like seagulls—Avra admitted that the analogy was perhaps running away from him—for any opportunity to swoop and fill their wretched beaks, and the delicacy of the cakes themselves.

Skully, whose fault it was that all this malarkey was happening, was *not* in high favor with anyone. In the grand ancient tradition of the cake competition, the judges could demand that the cakes be put to nearly any fair and measurable test in order to determine a winner for their rubric.

"You could just leave, you know," Avra said to Baltakan. Avra had edged under the pavilion to find a scrap of shade; Baltakan was sticking by his side closely and kept trying to say collegial things to him. "You're not having fun, you're not invested in the cake competition, your potato sacks are clearly getting itchy . . ."

"Helvaçi," said Baltakan, supremely exhausted. "You have told me in no uncertain terms that I should not attempt to do your job for you. I have acknowledged this. It would be gracious of you to return the favor. This is, I assure you, a matter of Diplomacy."

"All right," said Avra dubiously. "Seems like a matter of stubbornly trying to prove a point."

"Sometimes they look very similar."

Avra went over to have a bothering-Tev break. "Tev."

"Not right now." Every muscle in their body was tense.

"Did you go see Granny Layla's cake? It's bad."

"I did not go see any of the cakes, as it would be a massive waste of time and I respect myself too much to inflict pointless existential misery on my soul. I will remind you that I only have a single remaining eye—why would I wish to risk having it struck blind by allowing my gaze to fall on cakes other than Mistress Navya's?" Tev said loudly. *"Imagine if that were the last sight I ever saw. Imagine if the last thing I saw was a pile of wet feces someone claims is a cake. No thank you."*

"Right, yeah, I know, but you should go be miserable at Granny Layla's cake. In private. Before they bring it over. So no one has to see the face you make when you throw up."

"I have less than zero interest in seeing that cake, or any cake. I am actively invested in not looking at any cakes but Mistress Navya's, which is a beautiful and very insightful cake with interesting things to say about the theme."

"Tev," Avra said in a voice that didn't have any whining in it whatsoever. Teveri looked at him as if he'd been replaced by a revolting cake golem. "You should go make retching noises at Granny Layla's cake."

Teveri narrowed their eyes. "Why does everyone keep coming back from Granny Layla's pavilion and telling me that her cake is particularly awful and that my ears will start bleeding if I look at it? I know these things. I already know these things are true."

"Tev," Avra said pointedly. "*Go insult Granny Layla's cake.*"

"I have better things to do with my time."

Avra rummaged for his little rucksack and pulled out a card. "Oh, look at that. The Alchemist. Mysteries and secrets of the world. Want a second one? Let's have a second one. The Sea Serpent. Interesting, interesting. So interesting, don't you think? What could it mean? Will a third card clarify it, do you think? The Loom. Fascinating. A pattern coming into focus out of what was previously disconnected and meaningless things."

He stuffed the cards back into his little rucksack. "The cake was so bad I was *shaken,* Tev. One day, you'll want to tell stories to all the baby captains about how bad this cake was. It is a cake that will go down in history as truly fucking awful. Go look at it."

Teveri stalked out of the pavilion and across the way to Granny Layla's tent.

Avra went and stood by Baltakan again. As he passed the tent pole he had told to be lucky earlier, he gave it another little pat. "You're doing great, keep up the good work."

Teveri returned a few minutes later with the same bright, fierce look as Julian. They were faintly vibrating. "Hm?" Avra said as they came up.

"Mhm," Teveri said tightly.

"A truly awful cake."

"Yes, I threw up in my mouth just looking at it. Did Julian see that?"

"Yes."

"Where did he go off to?" said Baltakan. "I haven't seen him for a while."

"Sick," said Avra.

"Very sick," said Teveri.

"Ran off to be sick. Don't know that he'll ever be able to look at a cake again. Poor lad."

Teveri did not stop vibrating. The next seagull that so much as glanced their way got comprehensively obliterated.

"Sometimes a cake is just so bad you have to hack a seagull into bits to vent your feelings about it," Avra said as he trotted up to help collect pieces of seagull to deposit in their seagull bin.

Teveri continued vibrating until all the cakes had been painstakingly moved across the field and into Mistress Navya's tent, placed in a careful line on a long table. Hundreds of people clustered close around the pavilion.

Teveri turned, grabbed Avra's arm, and dragged him out of the crowd.

"Getting dragged a lot of places today," Avra said. "And hardly anyone is following through on the implicit promise and shoving me up against a wall."

Teveri dragged him under Granny Layla's now-abandoned pavilion and shoved him against one of the tentpoles; the entire tent jostled.

The kiss was something rather more like an attack, but that was what kissing Tev had always been like.

"Mmph!" said Avra appreciatively, and wormed his arms under Tev's coat and around their waist, pulling them snugly against himself. "Wanna know something very distracting now?"

"Fuck off. Fuck off. That fucking cake. Julian *saw it,*" Teveri muttered into his mouth.

"Julian saw the shit out of it. Should have seen his face. No one has seen a cake as much as Julian saw that cake."

"Fuck."

"You were looking the other way when he went off just now, so you didn't see—he *ran.*"

"Does he have it all?" Teveri pulled back just far enough to look him in the eye. *"Avra. Does he have the whole thing?"*

"I don't fucking know—maybe? Maybe. He's *close,* if nothing else."

Teveri growled at that and attacked his mouth again.

"Want to know something else distracting?" Avra said, muffled by Teveri's tongue in his mouth.

Teveri pulled away with a growl. "Is this the thing about Julian?"

"Yes."

They closed their eyes and took a deep breath.

"Judging's all but over," Avra crooned. "Skully's off getting ready to drop each of those cakes from a five-foot height or whatever his plan is. Nothing else for us to do. Job's as good as done. Once the rubrics are filled, doesn't matter what happens to the cake, does it."

"Fuck." Teveri's hands tightened in his hair and Avra gasped and grinned wider. "Fuck, fine, tell me."

"He said, and I quote, '*Fuck the vow*' in front of the truthwitch."

Teveri stared at him.

"Dibs on banging him first," Avra added quickly.

"*Wretch! Harlot. Trollop*—you can just fucking try, you *mongrel*—"

There was a loud crack, a shout of pain and a scattered screech from the crowd, a second crash, someone shouting, "*Grab the tent, grab the tent*—"

A beat of silence.

And then *raucous* laughter, punctuated here and there with cheers.

"*Fuck you,*" Teveri snarled to Avra, and dove out of Granny Layla's pavilion.

"Fuck *me*?" Avra flew after them. "*You* were the one who dragged me over here to make out! It's not *my* fault we missed whatever that was!"

Teveri fought their way through the crowd, stopped at the very edge of the space inside the pavilion, and clapped a hand to their mouth. Avra, a moment later, crashed into their back and goggled.

The crowd was incoherent with mirth. Markefa, a little ways away, had tears streaming down her cheeks. Oskar had crumpled to the ground with both hands over his face, giggling like a twelve-year-old. Captain Dallah and Captain Ueleari were clutching each other for balance and wheezing. Granny Layla had her shark's grin on and was applauding *furiously*.

Time seemed to slow down to the drip of cold molasses as Avra took in the scene.

The long table, formerly bearing all the cakes, had broken two legs at one end; it was sharply sloped down. The cakes, as cakes are wont to do, had found themselves at the mercy of gravity. By some lucky chance (haha), Mistress Navya's cake had been at the opposite end of the broken legs, so by the time it had slid down the slope, it had a lovely cushion of other cakes to break its momentum. It was almost perfectly intact.

There was a flailing pair of legs underneath the mountain of ruined cakes, toes pointing up, suggesting the unfortunate (haha) victim had fallen backward. Underneath the legs was the torn bottom hem of a potato sack cape.

The edge of the tent just above Teveri and Avra was sagging without its support pole—*that* was lying on the ground near the ambassador's wriggling legs.

Teveri turned and *looked* at Avra.

"Not my fault," Avra said immediately. "I wasn't even here. I was necking with you in the other pavilion."

"Sure," said Teveri. "But that's the tentpole you kept patting today."

Avra looked at it. Avra looked up at the pavilion. Rather than a pocket sewn into the edge of the pavilion's fabric or a buttonhole and a metal spike on the end of the pole to keep the two elements in place and firmly married together, every intact support pole was secured with a cord tie running through a hole bored in the wood and two reinforced eyelets in the fabric above. The ties were *supposed* to be pulled tight and knotted snugly so that a gust of wind or a supernaturally clever seagull couldn't lift the pole and fabric apart, fuck up the tension, and knock the whole thing over.

The ties that should have secured this pole were hanging loose from the eyelets.

"You can't prove that was *my* luck, though," Avra said. Baltakan tried to get enough traction to wriggle himself free from the cake mountain, and the crowd burst into new gales of hilarity. "That could have been sabotage. That could have been a seagull. We just can't know for sure—"

But maybe they could know for sure. Maybe they could, because Teveri started laughing, seized Avra by the hand and the waist, and dragged him out into the cleared middle of the pavilion in one of those galloping, whirling Bendran dances that made the skirts of their coat flare out magnificently. The crowd greeted this with cheering and applause that quickly resolved into rhythmic clapping in time with their dancing. Then Captain Ueleari grabbed one of his crew and leaped in to join them, and Captain Dallah followed with her second mate, and—

Markefa and Oskar launched into "The Wettest Pussy in the World," and the other captains were stepping in to fill the gaps in the dance, and Ambassador Baltakan kept slipping on whipped cream and custard, or unluckily catching his foot on the edge of his cape and falling over into the mountain again, somehow miraculously missing Mistress Navya's cake every time—

And the captains of the cake competition danced.

Avra would remember, later and in years after, that in that moment there had been no thoughts at all in his head except terror that he was about to step on Tev's toes . . . and the sudden crystal certainty that just before the champion was announced at the end of each cake competition hereafter, the captains would always dance with one of their crew.

Funny thing, traditions.

When everyone was too breathless to go on dancing and laughing and cheering (and Ambassador Baltakan had finally managed to extricate himself and stalk off, covered head-to-toe in dignity and cake), Skully declared that the unfortunate accident with the table had resulted in unfair testing circumstances, and insisted on moving the table away from the cake mountain and sliding Mistress Navya's cake down it a second time, just to be sure.

Mistress Navya's cake had been encased with a load-bearing framework of gingerbread slabs glued together with melted sugar. It probably could have survived one of Julian's walnut-bombs. Skully was deeply impressed.

The scores were very close—they always were—but no one was *very* surprised when Mistress Navya took the championship (having received an *excellent* score on Cat's rubrics of Allure and Compassionate Insight), followed closely by Granny Layla in second place.

"You got me on that Durability rubric," Granny Layla said, shaking Mistress Navya's hand. "But it was an ugly cake and your construction techniques were ham-handed."

"I hope to be capable of such skill and delicacy as yours one day," Mistress Navya replied. "But I found your interpretation of the theme to be either impossible to understand or perhaps simply lazy."

"Yeah, I would imagine you would find it that way." Granny Layla gave Avra and Teveri, standing just behind their cakesmith, a little wink. "But maybe someday you'll be having a nighttime walk with your wife along the beach and the answer will come to you."

Black Garda, who had arrived just in time for the cake-moving endeavor, pulled Teveri and Avra aside as soon as she could. She was beaming from ear to ear. "I don't know how you did that, and I don't want to know. The sheer elegance of that—that's something that most crews don't have a sense of, Teveri, that *elegance*. But I had a feeling that you'd pull off a marvel for me. The *elegance* of it all! The tentpole! And not just sabotage, but the *obliteration* of all the other cakes! It's a shame it couldn't happen before the rest of the judging—that's not a criticism, just an observation—but as a *symbolic* gesture it was peerless. And the fact that you *and* known cardsharp Avra Helvaçi were yards and yards away at the time—that *no one* from your crew was anywhere near that tentpole so that you couldn't be directly implicated—and that the *ambassador* of all people was the butt of the joke! Oh! I am undone. Captain, my expectations were very high to begin with, and this is beyond even my wildest dreams. You will be compensated most generously, as agreed, for the sabotage and the excellence of your work in guarding Navya's cake, but—oh, ye gods, *the ambassador,* Captain. *The ambassador,* covered in cake. Slipping on custard. Falling back in, over and over, I—gods, I cannot keep thinking about it or I'll start crying with laughter again. How can I possibly reward you for that flourish? This isn't a rhetorical question, Teveri, what would you like?"

"Two diamond-tailed bird-of-paradise feathers," Teveri answered instantly.

"Done. They're yours, and well-earned. Wear them to glory, Captain."

"I will, thank you."

"Ah," said Avra meekly. "If I could just . . . offer a comment. Are we at all concerned about the, um, food stores of the island? What with how we're cut off from the world for another five weeks or so? And, um, the fact that there's supposed to be a couple supply ships from Araşt arriving midway through the serpent season? And we just publicly humiliated the ambassador in front of the entirety of Scuttle Cove *and* a couple hundred tourists from abroad? Are we stocked up in case he retaliates, or are we going to be eating fish and seagull when the rest of the food runs out?"

"Hmgh," said Black Garda, her expression sobering. "I wouldn't put it past him." She brightened. "But you people are lunatics! If he signals by semaphore to dismiss the supply ships from coming into port, you can just sail out to board them and loot them, no? Or trot up to his house and tie the lot of them to a few chairs before he even has a chance to send the ship away."

"I can do you one better," Teveri said. "Making sure the supply deliveries come in is his side of the Pact. If he sends them away, then he's broken his own country's treaty with us without leave from his superiors, which means that Araşti ships are fair game for the next year, or until he convinces the captains to sign again."

"Delicious," said Black Garda.

"How much trouble would he get in with Araşt for doing something that stupid, Avra?"

Avra considered for a moment. "Imagine a snail. Now imagine a volcano. Imagine throwing the snail really hard, and a very stupid seagull swoops in to nab it, and then the volcano explodes." He nodded. "The snail is a metaphor. The snail represents an opportunity for petty vengeance. The seagull is his career. The volcano is—well, you get it, we've been looking at cakes all morning. Maybe I'll learn how to bake and express this concept via the medium of cake. Maybe I'm meant to be a famous cakesmith instead of a poet. Lots of overlap between the two, you know." His attention was caught by a flash of red, and for a moment he had the gleeful thought that he could run over to *his friend Cat* and tell him *all* the gossip about Julian's vow—but then he saw it was a flash of Red, in fact, standing next to the Puppeteer and talking to several of the Ammatu sailors. "Ah," said Avra. "Black Garda, you'll have to divide our fees so that equal shares go to Captain Heirani and her crew—and Heirani gets my full share as well—*what,* Teveri, what's that look for? We made a deal with them, what do you expect me to say? How else are we supposed to settle up in good faith? I *always* pay my tab!"

"Oh, calm down, you two," Black Garda said, rolling her eyes before Teveri could do more than glare at Avra. "My wife was delighted with all of you and she's giving you half her winnings as a tip—and that's on top of all the fees and bonuses and presents I'm already lavishing on you. There's plenty to go around."

27

> *12. The Alchemist*
>
> Mysticism, the secrets of the world, discovery, new understanding, changing lead to gold, pursuing immortality through great deeds or art or scholarship. Potentially represents a scholarly person, or one who seeks knowledge.
>
> (Reversed: Conspiracy theories, paranoia, being ruled by imaginary things, unwillingness to admit to being wrong. Your eyes are clouded, your understanding is lacking. You cannot discover something new if you are using only old methodologies. Trust the process.)

Julian was not to be found at the hotel, though the attendant in the front parlor reported he had dashed out not long before they arrived.

Avra took Teveri's hand and swung it gently between them. "He's probably gone out to be a genius somewhere. Do you want to go carousing with the rest of the crew? Or we could walk around and have dinner somewhere. Can't imagine Cat would be working tonight, so we can't go play with him."

"He'll be carousing as well, yes," Teveri said. "And letting people buy him drinks for doing such a thoughtful job with judging the correct, righteous, and most deserving champion cakesmith."

"We also can't go to any of the gaming houses, on account of I am banned from all of them." He was still swinging Tev's hand,

and Tev was *allowing* it. A thrilling development. "We could go upstairs and have a good hearty squabble about which of us gets to fuck Julian first."

"Oh. Yes, we do need to finish that argument, don't we."

꩜

The thing about bickering with Tev was that it was *good* fun, especially when Tev was in such a fantastic mood as they were today, with bags of money and bags more favor with Black Garda and an entire hold full of all the honor and adulation that came with being hired for the cake competition, and two *deeply* fancy feathers in their hat. They were in such a good mood that when Avra asked what the feathers were all about, they answered almost casually that the diamond-tailed bird-of-paradise was native to the desert oases and lush riverbanks of Tash, and that they'd laughed when they heard the name because those parts *were* paradise beautiful, deep in the backcountry where the cult had less influence and people still kept old holy texts squirreled away in caves, the records of what the prophet Qarat'ash had actually said and done and taught before the hierophants had become dictators and the religion had wobbled into cult.

"Qarat'ash killed a king," Teveri said, pouring themself a glass of wine and sprawling on the couch. "He was a very cruel man and suspected that Qarat'ash, one of his concubines, had been inconstant, so he set them an impossible task to prove their faithfulness: They were to leave the city and climb the mountain—the northernmost peak of the Wall of the World—and fetch back a star that the king said he'd seen fall there. When Qarat'ash left, the king ordered all the lamps and candles in the city to be put out so that they'd die of exposure and cold, lost in the desert and unable to find their way back in the dark. But one child lit a candle in a window, and that was enough to guide Qarat'ash home, where they used powerful magic to slay the king for his cruelty—"

"Julian should take notes."

Teveri snorted. "The king had mistreated his concubines terribly and kept them locked up, so Qarat'ash preached against segregating society by sex, because they thought that would stop what'd happened to them from happening to anyone else. They said that if we are all one under the stars, it is immoral to differentiate ourselves based on our physical forms, and that everyone should simply be a *person,* and thus everyone would be liberated equally. Which sounds nice enough at first, but you see how that can *very* quickly go to shit in the hands of the wrong people."

"Hm, yes," said Avra. He was wary of letting Tev's good mood flag and knew himself to be unequipped to navigate this topic without Julian as a safety net. "Back to the sparkly birds, though. Are they good luck or something?"

"What happened to 'you can't prove luck exists'?" said Teveri, sprawling on the couch with a glass of wine and a smirk. They'd doffed their hat, boots, and coat, and rolled their sleeves up to the elbow. "In the stories, they bear messages to heroes, and only sovereigns are allowed to wear their feathers. That's it. Are you trying to change the subject?"

"Yyyyyyyes. Yes. Badly. Please help."

"Julian's dick."

"DIBS," Avra screamed.

They settled in for a healthy squabble. Teveri picked at the rest of the jar of olives and drawled bitchy comebacks as Avra flung himself on the floor, screeching and wailing and carrying on and weeping real tears. They were both in *fine* form, and somehow they managed to keep the squabble from wandering off onto hurtful tangents about past grudges and mutating into an argument.

"But I called dibs first!" Avra wailed for the thousandth time—this had been the main thrust, as it were, of his argument. He was lying face down on the floor, kicking his legs and beating his fists against the carpet for effect. "I called dibs *ages* ago! I called dibs the first day I met him! I said I would swallow his dick like a python! *You* gave up and stopped trying to seduce him as soon as he mentioned his vow."

Julian slammed through the door, wild-eyed. He was distinctly damp and straggly, as if he had been sopping wet an hour ago and had not yet fully dried, nor bothered to stop and comb his hair. Unfortunately, his clothes were not wet enough to be clinging to his body anymore, which Avra considered a personal insult from the universe. Still—

"*Dibs,*" Avra shrieked. "See! I did it again, Tev! I have called dibs every time! Julian! Tell Tev that I've called dibs first every time!"

"It is not a matter of dibs," Teveri said calmly. "It is a matter of who Julian thinks deserves it more, and there is no question that person is me. Hello, Julian."

"We're arguing about who gets to fuck you first," Avra said, rolling onto his back. "How is your science going? Have you been stymied by some new conundrum? I've heard that getting your dick sucked helps with that."

"Come with me," Julian said, diving across the room and dragging Avra to his feet.

"Well, *with you* might take some practice, but I believe in us," Avra said. "I gather that you would prefer me bent over that table rather than right here on the floor?"

"I meant *follow me,*" Julian said, crossing to the couch and pulling Teveri up as well.

"You see, Avra, that's what you get for being a trollop," said Teveri. "He realizes his mistake and changes his mind."

"That's not fair, I called dibs!"

"Sex is not the most important issue right now!" said Julian. "Please! I have something to show you—I think. I hope. I'm almost certain, I just need to confirm it—*let's go.*"

"Oh, I see, he wants to do science as foreplay," said Avra, allowing himself to be shepherded firmly toward the door. "I suppose it is a very special occasion, losing one's second virginity—"

"I have told you eight times in the past hour that if you keep calling it that, I will roll you in cake and feed you to the seagulls," said Teveri, stopping at the door to put on their boots. "Virginity is made-up."

"Yeah, but so are oaths of celibacy, so the fakeness cancels itself out, and I feel like virginity grows back over time."

"Not after six and fifty-two, it doesn't," said Julian briskly. "No, Captain, leave the coat and hat, we're being inconspicuous." He led them clattering downstairs. "Apologies, I should have begun by saying congratulations on the win—the whole town is afire about it."

"Good," said Teveri, tossing their hair. As they came to the bottom of the stairs and swept through the front parlor, they added loudly, "*But it was really a team effort and of course we could not have done so well without such a marvelous and inspiring cake to protect.*"

Julian took them down to the beach. The sky was the deep velvety purple of dusk, and the sea gates at the mouth of the port had been closed, protecting the harbor from the extremes of the Midsummer tides.

Julian stopped only long enough to rummage through a pile of debris and dead palm fronds, from which he produced a large ceramic bottle, corked and well sealed with wax. "Took me most of the afternoon," he said. "But this should be enough." He handed it to Avra, unburied their dinghy's miniature anchor from the sand, looped up the long painter into a neat coil over his arm, and stowed it all in the boat as Teveri and Avra ambled along in his wake. It was low tide, and the slope of the shore was quite shallow here—Julian had to shove the dinghy across fifteen or twenty feet of hard-packed, damp sand before he got to the water.

"You could at least do us the courtesy of taking your shirt off for this part," Avra said.

Julian laughed breathlessly and steadied the boat with one hand while Teveri leapt in to avoid getting water on their boots. Avra, with no such standards, sloshed in up to his ankles before scrambling in. He sat on the aft thwart next to Tev; Julian pushed the boat farther out into the water, wading up to his thighs before he vaulted in.

"*And* he's going to be rowing now," Avra said, clucking his tongue. "Truly selfish, keeping his tits from us."

Julian was smiling to himself as he got the oars fitted into the locks. "Is it selfish, or am I being considerate? You might find it too distracting." The oars dipped into the water; Julian's muscles bulged under his shirt; the boat *moved.*

"*Eeeee,*" said Avra. "What are we doing, anyway? What science is this?"

"Hush," he whispered. "We're going to the Araşti ship."

"*Oh,*" said Avra.

"Do you have it?" Teveri said, low and intent. "Do you have the whole thing?"

"Don't know yet." Julian grinned. "That's what we're going to find out." With a teasing glance at Avra, he added, "I thought it prudent to bring a good-luck charm for this part."

"This?" Avra asked innocently, holding up the bottle.

"That's serpent juice," Teveri muttered, rolling their eyes.

Julian nodded. "I had a very limited amount left of some of the cheapest components, which was fortunate—"

"Avra."

"I can't help it! That's not proof, Tev!"

"Which was fortunate," Julian continued, "because of course everyone was at the cake competition, and the only shop that was open was one apothecary who managed to scrounge up just enough of the last ingredient I required. I couldn't make much, but I am hopeful that it will at least be enough to . . . test the thing I need to test."

"Are we breaking into an Araşti ship?" Teveri said warily. "Even with Avra's luck, I'm not sure. It would break the Pact, for one thing—though only if they catch us, I suppose."

"They didn't catch me in the Shipbuilder's Guild," Avra said, propping an elbow on the stern and attempting an alluring lounge. "Bet they won't catch me on the ship the Guild built."

"We don't have to break in," Julian said, glancing over his shoulder to check what direction they were going. "We're going to go up to *our* ship, because fortunately—Avra—"

"*I don't have control over it.*"

"—they're anchored quite near to us, two hundred feet off or so. We'll nestle into the shadow on the seaward side of *The Running Sun,* where none of the light of the town will hit us. Then I'll *very quietly* swim over to the Araşti ship . . . and try to light up their hull." Teveri took a sharp breath. Julian smiled at them. "You saw Granny Layla's horrible cake, then?"

"One of the worse cakes I've seen in my life," Tev said. "But what were we *missing*? We *have* an Araşti-made ship!"

"Could be that starwine shit," Avra said. "Throwing absurd and disgusting amounts of money at a problem is a very solemn thing of great reverence where I come from. Please respect my—"

"I'm not going to respect this part of your culture, Avra," Julian said.

"You know what, that's fair. Carry on."

"Captain, any guesses?"

"It wasn't starwine, that was just the edible *representation* of the thing Granny Layla saw." They looked out over the harbor where the Araşti ship and *The Running Sun* were just visible between the other anchored ships. "The paint? That's the only difference between their ship and ours. Their hull is still painted, and ours wore off years ago."

Julian's eyes were bright. "What *kind* of paint?"

"Something that lights up when you pour in the serpent juice—" Teveri slapped the gunwale. "The stripes on the serpents. And that's why the Ministry of Intelligence sent Avra to replace one dead serpent with another that had the stripes cut out."

"Oh shit," Avra said, flailing himself upright. "*Tev. Smart.*"

"*Very* smart, Teveri, well done," Julian said, all warm and approving.

"Don't talk like that, Julian, or I really will have to insist that you take your shirt off," Avra said reprovingly.

Teveri rubbed their hands over their face and looked at Julian, stunned and hungry. "This is it. This is it, isn't it?"

"I'm not absolutely certain yet, but this is the current best theory," Julian said. "And this is what we are testing. But I came out earlier to look at their hull—"

"You came out to the Araşti ship in *broad daylight*?"

"Yes," Julian said cheerfully.

"They have guards!"

"They do! They caught me. I let them catch me, actually. Well, I don't know if it should count as *catching,* because I was not using any subterfuge whatsoever."

"What did you do. *Julian.* Stop smiling like that, *what did you do*?"

"Showed them his tits," Avra said, kicking his feet back up on the gunwale. "That's my guess."

"And Avra wins that round," Julian said. "Good boy, Avra."

Teveri seized Avra by the shirt before he could fall out of the boat and clapped a hand over his mouth before he could do more than draw breath to screech in protest.

"Mmf mm mrr mrmf?"

"He says, 'How much of your tits?'"

"Well, I rowed up, and the guards leaned over and asked what my business was, and I leaned back on the thwart and smiled at them, and I told them that I live here in Scuttle Cove and I'm starting a new business venture, going around to all the ships in the harbor and diving down to chip barnacles off the hull for them, and would they be interested in my services? And by then I had gotten the measure of which one of them was most likely to be . . . susceptible to masculine charms, shall we say, and I gave them a little wink."

"Harlot," said Avra, pulling Teveri's hand off. "Tev, I'm going to cry. He gave away his second wink-virginity to some stranger—" Teveri put their hand back over his mouth.

"Of course they said no thank you," Julian continued. "So I

offered to dive down just to see what kind of shape they were in, whether there were any barnacles to worry about—I said I'd do that for free. And then I bit my lip at them and toyed with the ties of my shirt a little, et cetera and so forth."

Avra keened in dismay behind Teveri's hand.

"The susceptible one said, 'Oh, maybe we should let him dive down once, just to see, he said it was free after all, better to know these things, it'll take him ten seconds.' One of the others was dubious—"

"Not so susceptible to masculine charms, then," Teveri said dryly.

"Alas, not everyone is. But that one was outvoted. So I stripped off my shirt and dove in."

"And?"

"Their hull was clean as a whistle, for one thing, which was already odd. Not a barnacle anywhere on it. Besides that, I couldn't see much of anything notable. Just the complicated geometric patterns, like on every Araşti boat—but all of those are different from ship to ship. Different colors, different patterns. So I ran my fingers over their hull, and I found oddly *regular* irregularities in the texture of the paint. There were all these thin lines, about the width of my thumb, that were raised and *very* smooth—no wood grain that I could feel, as if there were five or six more layers of paint there."

"Fuck. We have it."

"Well, no. Not yet."

"What are you talking about? It's obvious! We've done it!"

"That's not how science works," Julian said, warm but firm. "Even what seems blindingly obvious has to be tested, and we don't have anything until we can prove it for certain. What we *have* is a collection of evidence—what Granny Layla saw, and the dogs glowing after they eat the serpents, and the serpents glowing after we spilled serpent juice on them, and the recipe from the Shipbuilder's Guild, and the fact that they pour barrels of stuff overboard, but it didn't work for us when we did the same . . . We have all that evidence, and we have a hypothesis: *Somehow,* they're making their hulls glow, and there does appear to be *something* on their hulls . . ."

Avra licked Teveri's palm; they snatched it away with a disgusted look and washed it off in the water as Avra said, "And if you hear hoofbeats, don't look for zebras."

"Unless you're in Tayemba or the Kholekhole grasslands," said Julian, nodding.

"That's what I've always said!" Avra said delightedly.

Julian glanced behind himself again to check their course. "Voices very quiet now," he whispered. "I'm going to slow us down and row *very* softly."

"If it works," Teveri said. "Julian, if this works, all that's left is to figure out how to make the paint?"

He shrugged. "That'd be the next step."

"But paint's easy," Avra said. "Everybody makes paint."

"Everybody makes paint for *dry* environments." Julian dipped the oars into the water so gently they barely made a sound. "Araşt is the only country that bothers painting their hulls like that—and how long do those ships go between paint jobs, Avra? Do you know? How long do they last without any barnacles?"

"No clue. That's easy enough to find out, though. Turn me loose in a bar with one of the sailors from that ship, I can get them to tell me how often she goes in for repainting in ten minutes or less."

"The parts that are left are knowing how the paint is made, knowing how often the paint needs to be reapplied . . . Knowing what those patterns I felt actually look like. Knowing whether the shape is important, knowing whether the thickness of the paint affects the strength and duration of the glow or the durability of the paint. Knowing whether the rest of the hull paint has any effect, even if it's just that it helps keep off the barnacles, or if it's a convenience to camouflage the fact that the ships have to come in for *special* servicing every now and then . . . I would wager that the workers themselves don't know what it is that they're applying to the ships or what it's for, otherwise the secret would have gotten out *long* ago."

"I don't think the colored patterns are important," Avra whispered. "Araşt has been painting ships forever—there are old manuscripts that show boats with painted hulls. It's traditional. They say it's for luck at sea."

"And those manuscripts are older than the technique of sailing across the serpents?"

"Oh, yes. Yes. The manuscripts are four, five hundred years old. The technique was, uh, uh, uh, thirty-eighth year of the Shahre Dynasty, which is negative-four Mahisti, and we're in Mahisti 199 now, so just a squinch over two hundred years ago."

Teveri gave him a strange look. "Since when do you know *historical trivia*?"

"Since I found out that Julian will pull my hair and call me a good boy if I remember useful things. I know so many facts. Here, watch: After the Mahisti family finished research and development of the technique, the first official maiden voyage during the fuck season was from Araşt to Amariyan and back. The name of the ship was the *Ocean's Light*—oh, you cheeky motherfuckers."

Julian bit his lip on a laugh. "Quite."

"My reward, if you please."

"Good boy, Avra."

"You could say it sexier than that. You said it flat and boring on purpose."

The sunset had faded entirely from the sky, but there was just enough light from the stars and a lamp on a nearby ship for Avra to see Julian's shoulders shaking with silent mirth. Avra turned to Teveri to beseech them for sympathy and found them staring down at their lap, their hands clasped tight.

"Formula of the paint, patterns of the paint, thickness of application, frequency of application—and then we have it?" Teveri whispered. "That's all that's left?"

"If the test works," said Julian softly. "And if we don't discover any other complications."

"And then we can *sell it*."

Julian was silent.

"Tev," Avra whispered. "Tev, Julian doesn't want to sell it."

He didn't have to see Teveri's face in the dark to practically *hear* the frown. "What, keep it for ourselves? And astonish everyone with our fearless lunacy?"

"He definitely doesn't want us to keep it for ourselves."

"I don't see what other option there *is*! Either sell it or don't sell it, what else is there?"

"Give it away," Julian whispered. "For free, and to everyone. All the other captains. Scholars. Merchants. Fishermen. Pleasure barges. *Everyone*."

All that Avra could hear was the soft dip of the oars, the silky slip of the boat through the water, the distant sounds of raucous human life from the shore . . . the distinct lack of seagull shrieks, now that they'd all nested and gone to sleep.

"Give it away," Teveri whispered, as if they'd never heard the phrase before. "Why?"

"Because something like that should never have been secret in the first place," Julian said softly. "Because it would change the world. Because it's the right thing to do. Because sharing knowledge freely is a great act of piety in my faith." And just as surely as Avra had heard Teveri's frown, he could hear Julian's smile. "Because no one would *ever* stop singing the praises of Captain Teveri az-Ḥaffār, who brought the Araşti economy to its knees and gave the summer sea to the rest of the world. People love a song about a heroic outlaw taking from the rich to give to the poor, don't they?"

"They'd eat it up with a spoon, Tev," Avra said. "Take it from me, a famous poet and cakesmith-to-be."

"But the *money*," Teveri said in a helpless little whisper.

They were approaching *The Running Sun* now. The light of a single lantern on deck glimmered off the water, but all was silent. Someone must have come out to fetch Nagasani when they'd won so she could carouse in triumph with the rest of the crew. It was strange not to hear her singing softly to herself as she often did when she had the ship to herself, and stranger still to be able to *sense* how empty the ship was.

Julian brought them up close to the hull, shipped the oars, and grabbed *The Running Sun*'s anchor chain. Avra pushed against the hull before the dinghy could noisily bump into it. Julian tied off the painter to the chain, then leaned forward and took Teveri's hands. "I know you're worried about the money," he said, no louder than a breath. "But I suspect that if you did this thing, there would be no one in the *world* who wouldn't be willing to give you aid."

"Except Araşt," Avra whispered. "But they already weren't going to aid us for free."

"Yes. But *every other port in the world* would shelter you. The very smallest fishing village would let you stop to refill your water barrels—and I daresay that if you indicated you were in need, they'd give you every scrap of food they could spare, or lumber to repair the ship, or strong thread and deft needleworkers to mend your sails, or physicians to tend to your crew when they're ill."

"As many spooky dentists as you could want, Tev. And they'll all tell you to stop grinding your teeth."

"Maybe you wouldn't have to grind your teeth anymore."

Teveri was silent.

Avra snuggled up against them and put his head on their shoulder. They did not grab him by the neck and throw him over the side.

"Teveri, this is something I believe in," said Julian. "This matters very much to me. But it's your ship, and you're the captain. If you decide to sell the secret, that's your choice. I think it will lead to trouble for Scuttle Cove—Araşt will bring more truthwitches, at the very least. Or they might decide to withhold the supply ships until someone gets desperate enough to point a finger at you."

"But . . . the money."

"You grew up poor, didn't you?" Julian asked gently. Avra felt Teveri nod. "Have you thought of what it would be like to suddenly have that much money? You'd be conspicuous wherever you went. You'd have to keep it secret and live *very* quietly, or Araşt would get wind of you eventually, and . . . they're not just going to wring their hands and say, 'Oh no, I guess they got us fair and square.' No matter where you went, sooner or later consequences would arrive in the middle of the night with knives."

"It'd be Ministry of Intelligence," Avra whispered. "They don't like knives if there's a more elegant and less detectable option. A tragic accident, for preference. Or arson. Or slow poisons, the kind that look like a long wasting illness. Never had to do that myself. Did set a few things on fire, but assassinations were above my pay grade."

"Having no money brings a whole host of problems," Julian said. Avra could just see that he was stroking Teveri's knuckles with his thumbs as he squeezed their hands. "But having *too much* money does too. It sucks your soul dry, eventually. Even a sweet-natured and well-intentioned person starts making decisions based on protecting the money rather than helping other people. It becomes a burden—a god that you're shackled to, one that's even more difficult to abandon than the others you've already turned away from."

Teveri wasn't moving; they were barely breathing. Avra could feel their pulse racing under his cheek.

"There's time," Julian whispered. "Tev. There's *time.* We don't have anything that we need to make a decision about—and as your de facto alchemist, I'm going to strongly advise that even after we think we have the whole thing figured out, we *test it. Exhaustively.* Regardless of what we do with it, the people going into danger trusting us to have gotten it right will be *common sailors.* Not the rich and powerful, but people who are just trying to get by. I will burn my notes before I let you give them away untested." The wry half-laughing note came back into Julian's voice. "I told you it would take years. It probably still will."

"And if I do sell it? If I decide to—to risk it? To take the gamble, to—"

"To never see any of your friends again? To scatter to the four corners of the earth and vanish, and start a new life with a new name, and never become so great that Xing Fe Hua would have *eaten* his sails from envy?"

Teveri huffed the softest, quietest breath of a wretched laugh.

"What if it all goes wrong? What if we give it away and we—we starve, or have to give up the ship?"

Avra nuzzled into Teveri's neck and slipped an arm around their waist. "Then you can come live with me in my little rotting crate in the alley and fend off the possums from every crumb of stale bread that Julian wraps around a rock and kicks at us, because he's too selfish to take his shirt off when he's rowing."

"I see I am being cast as the villain now," said Julian, smiling and smiling and smiling. "Congratulations on your promotion to pathetic and tragic protagonist of a morality fable. But listen—if you decide to sell it, so be it. Your ship, your choice. But I will know the secret too, and I will give it away as often as I fucking can. I will build a printing press on the ship and hand out *boxes* of pamphlets in every port we come to, and hope that we can keep outrunning Araşt long enough to give the news a head start. But there is *time.* There are *years* left for us to go over our plans for *after* with a fine-toothed comb, until we can be sure that we'll be safe, that all our friends will be safe, that Scuttle Cove will be safe, and that the people physically on board those ships will be safe. *There is time.*"

"So much time. We have money enough to get by," said Avra. "Right? You won the cake competition."

"It was a team effort," Teveri said thickly. "Couldn't have done it alone, wouldn't have worked without such a magnificent and insightful cake to inspire all of us."

"Just so," said Julian, smiling. He reached up to touch Teveri's cheek. "Good, not crying. Teveri az-Ḥaffār is too fierce and splendid to be crying over anything."

"Feels like I'm dying when Tev cries," Avra whispered.

"Now you'll make *me* cry," Julian said. "All right, we're counting and recounting our chickens, and we don't even know if we've got any eggs yet." He let go of Teveri's hands, pulled off his boots and socks (placing the boots *quietly* beneath the rowing thwart), and stripped his shirt off.

"Fucking finally," Avra said. "Can't believe how long that took. I expect better from you, Julian."

"You have no idea what kind of *better* you can expect from me, sweetheart."

"Hrkgh?"

"I can't stand him," Teveri murmured.

Julian pulled the boat close to the anchor rope, wrapped his arms and legs around it, and lowered himself slowly and silently into the water. He ducked beneath to wet his hair and surfaced again just next to them. "The bottle, Avra," he breathed.

Avra had gone fully catatonic and was frantically trying to parse the word *sweetheart* and rack his memory as to whether anyone had ever called him that before. Someone on the Street of Flowers, maybe. Teveri sighed and pried the bottle out of his grip and handed it down to Julian. "Good luck," they said wryly.

Avra shook himself sharply. "Kiss. Kiss for. Luck. Kiss for luck. That's a thing. People do it."

"He's already gone, idiot. He went fifteen seconds ago."

"I think I blacked out for a little bit."

"Good for you. I'm definitely going to fuck him first, though."

"I called dibs. So many times."

"He called you a gross soppy name, so I get to fuck him first."

"I think it was probably sarcastic," Avra said desperately. "Yes. Definitely sarcastic. A very sarcastic man, that Julian."

"I don't care. I'm going to lick his ribs."

"But *I* was going to lick his ribs," Avra whispered piteously.

Teveri shushed him.

They sat in silence in the dark.

Julian surfaced several times to breathe in the long swim between them and the Araşti ship. Avra held his own breath whenever Julian was beneath. He couldn't tell if Teveri was doing the same.

Other than the ripples from Julian's occasional surfacing, the water was as still as glass. In daylight, or on the bright nights of the equinoxes when both moons were full, they would have been able to see Julian beneath the surface, making his way steadily toward that immense question. That *immense, immense* question.

Finally, after what felt like hours, Julian came up beside the Araşti ship on the seaward side. Avra held his breath again. His eyes strained in the dark. There were lamps on the Araşti ship, and he could just see the faintest suggestion of Julian there in the shadow of the hull. It seemed to take some effort for Julian to get the cork out of the bottle with wet hands and no knife, or perhaps it was just the air slowly running out of Avra's lungs . . .

And then.

And *then:*

Light.

Teveri seized Avra's hand in a crushing grip. Avra gripped back, goose bumps breaking out over his entire body, chill after chill coursing up his spine—

The hull came alight—a small patch, six feet long and perhaps two feet below the surface, as if Julian had poured the bottle out in a long line. Through the vibrantly turquoise water, the light was greenish, beautiful, *unearthly.* As unearthly as the strangest creatures to rise from the deep, as unearthly as the very stars far above.

The light wavered and blurred; Avra blinked and felt hot tears spill over his cheeks.

They could *see* Julian now, silhouetted against the hull by that eerie aurora. He was lingering—perhaps as enraptured and entranced as Avra himself was; perhaps taking in as much as he could for that giant, gorgeous, analytical brain to pick apart later.

"People will sing of this," Avra whispered. He felt—he felt—*gripped* by something. Like his tongue was not quite his own in this moment, like it moved to the bidding of whatever bullshit higher powers usually sassed him through his deck of Heralds. "Our descendants for a hundred generations will sing of this."

"I don't fucking care," Teveri said, tense with emotion. "I'm going to eat him alive. I am going to wreck him. I am going to make him *beg.*"

"Mhrgk," said Avra, jolting free of whatever had come over him. "Good, good, yes, that's also a thing that will definitely happen and should happen and ought to happen. Tev. Tev, I will remind you that we are right next to our own ship. And your cabin is right up there. With your own bed, and your collection of spooky dildos, and a year's supply of lubricant—I know that word in Vintish, you know. So just in case Julian is too wrecked to remember how to speak Arasük, we will be okay."

The light was just starting to fade when Julian returned, coming up right next to them with his hair slicked back by the water and a smile that shone brighter than the Araşti hull.

Teveri leaned over the side, seized him by the back of the neck, and attacked him. Julian gave a pleased little hum and chuckled into the kiss, sliding his wet hand up to the back of Teveri's head.

"Get in the boat," Avra hissed, leaning hard to the other side of the boat as counterbalance before the two of them capsized it. "Get in the boat. Get in the boat. Tev. Tev, get him in the boat so we can fight over him."

Julian laughed again—apparently giddy as hell, and who wouldn't be—and broke from the kiss. "You'll have to help me in," he said breathlessly, hanging on to the top of the gunwale. "Felicity, I'm *shaking*. I don't think I can row back."

"A likely story," Teveri grunted as they dragged Julian into the boat as quietly as possible. "Oh no, Julian's too tired to row us back, *whatever shall we do*? A convenient excuse from a man very obviously angling to get himself invited for a nightcap. Next he'll be telling us that he's tragically chilled, and we'll be forced by basic fucking etiquette to say some dumb shit like, 'Why don't we get you out of those wet things before you catch your death . . .'"

Avra, still leaning to the opposite side as counterbalance, patted the hull of *The Running Sun*. "Well, fortunately—haha, just a little joke there—fortunately, we're already home."

ACKNOWLEDGMENTS

This book broke so many of my writing habits in the oddest ways. Usually I fly through the beginning, languish in the middle, and claw my way exhaustedly through the end. With this one, however, the beginning languished for four or five years, the middle felt like jogging up a steep hill (with breaks to gnash my teeth and tear my hair), and the end was effortless and exuberant: fifty thousand words written in seven days, and twenty thousand of that in two days. It also changed tone rather dramatically from how it began—I started out thinking it was going to be a serious and gritty book, and it took those four or five years of banging my head against the first couple chapters over and over before I realized that it wasn't going anywhere because in its heart, it really wanted to be a comedy.

I dunno, man. Writing is weird sometimes.

Effusive thanks first of all to Jennifer Mace, who was witness to the very first breath of life for this novel before I ever set a single word to the page, and who helped me come up with the three main characters and engineer a marvelous OT3 during a long road trip to the Nebulas.

A huge thank you to the amazing team at Tor and Tor UK: Ruoxi Chen, Becky Yeager, Caro Perny, Oliver Dougherty, Sophie Robinson, Dakota Griffin, Lauren Hougen, and all the other wonderful and talented people who work so hard to make my books the best they can be.

Enormous thanks to my agent, Britt Siess, for her invaluable insight and guidance, her business savvy, her patience and good humor, and her unfailing support and enthusiasm for my work.

Thank you to Lee, Jenny, Lin, and Celebros for the hand-holding and the cheerleading, and double thanks to Rae for talking out the cake competition with me. Uncountable thanks to my Patreon supporters, the members of my official Discord server, and all my other readers—you have no idea how powerful of a collective force you are, and I am so honored to have your support and enthusiasm. It means so much to me when I see someone recommending my books online, or when someone tells me that their friend introduced them to my work. *THANK YOU!!!* (Also, please keep doing that, because I still live in the same late-stage capitalist hellscape as the rest of you. Insert "yikes" emoji here.)

And finally . . . eternal and undying thanks to Terry Pratchett. I never got to meet him, and that breaks my heart to this day. His books taught me so much about comedy and about how devastatingly, breathtakingly *kind* it is to be able to openly love the messy, beautiful, deeply imperfect, and yet deeply *human* experience of being alive, and trying your best, and sort of just doing an okay job at it along the way. His books taught me even more about anger and justice and the grim necessity of engaging in a scrungly, undignified mud-wrestling match against Entropy just for the sake of wresting from its jaws one single scrap of fairness that's gotten a bit raggedy and smells rank (but take it to a good dry cleaner and maybe they can work a miracle or two for ya). Injustice abounds—the injustice of institutions, of entrenched systems of hegemony, of capitalism itself. Terry Pratchett's works (and mine, I hope) serve as a reminder of the single most important lesson we have in resisting oppression: The best comedy comes from a place of deep, righteous anger—and as long as you can laugh, there's still a part of you that's free.

ABOUT THE AUTHOR

Charles Darrel

ALEXANDRA ROWLAND is the author of eight fantasy books, including *A Taste of Gold and Iron*, *A Conspiracy of Truths*, and *Some by Virtue Fall*, as well as a four-time Hugo Award–nominated podcaster. They have a degree in world literature, mythology, and folklore, and all their work is supervised by their feline quality control manager.

alexandrarowland.net
X: @_alexrowland
Goodreads: Alexandra Rowland
Instagram: @_alexrowland